P9-COP-625

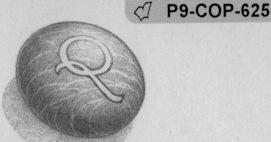

No! *No no no no* no. It couldn't be. It couldn't *possibly* be. Septimus stared at the heavy, oval lapis lazuli stone in his hand, and the golden **Q** inscribed deep into it glinted back at him mockingly. And, when he turned it over, the number 21 began to show and Septimus knew with a horrible certainty what he had—*the* **Questing Stone**.

He stared at the **Stone**, trying to remember what Alther had told him at the **Gathering**. But it was all a blur—only the phrase *Once you Accept the* **Stone**, *your Will is not your Own* came into his head.

Septimus tried to think clearly. But he *hadn't* accepted the **Questing Stone**, had he? He had accepted what he thought was a **SafeCharm**. So surely that was different—wasn't it?

Septimus shoved the **Questing Stone** back into his pocket. He would ignore it, he decided. There was enough for them to think about without worrying about some stupid **Queste**, which he wasn't going on anyway.

ALSO BY ANGIE SAGE

Septimus Heap, Book One: **Magyk**

Septimus Heap, Book Two: **Flyte**

Septimus Heap, Book Three: **Physik**

Araminta Spookie: **My Haunted House**

Araminta Spookie: **The Sword in the Grotto**

Araminta Spookie: **Frognapped**

Araminta Spookie: **Vampire Brat**

Araminta Spookie: **Ghostsitters**

SEPTIMUS HEAP

⊹ BOOK FOUR ⊹

ANGIE SAGE

ILLUSTRATIONS BY MARK ZUG

KATHERINE TEGEN BOOKS

HarperTrophy®
An Imprint of HarperCollinsPublishers

Harper Trophy® is a registered trademark of HarperCollins Publishers.

Septimus Heap is a trademark of HarperCollins Publishers.

Septimus Heap Book Four: Queste

Text copyright © 2008 by Angie Sage

Illustrations copyright © 2008 by Mark Zug

All rights reserved. Printed in the United States of America. No part of this
book may be used or reproduced in any manner whatsoever without written
permission except in the case of brief quotations embodied in critical articles
and reviews. For information address HarperCollins Children's Books, a divi-
sion of HarperCollins Publishers, 10 East 53rd Street, New York, NY 10022.

www.harpercollinschildrens.com

Library of Congress Cataloging-in-Publication Data

Sage, Angie.

   Queste / Angie Sage ; illustrated by Mark Zug. — 1st ed.

     p.   cm. — (Septimus Heap)

   "Book Four."

   Summary: Nicko and Snorri are trapped in Time, and Septimus Heap
goes on a quest to find the House of Foryx, a place where all Time meets.

   ISBN 978-0-06-088209-9

   {1. Magic—Fiction.} I. Zug, Mark, ill. II. Title.

PZ7.S13035 Que 2008   2007049661

[Fic]—dc22   CIP

                                                      AC

Typography by Karin Paprocki

10 11 12 13 CG/BR 10 9 8 7 6 5 4

❖

First Harper Trophy edition, 2009

For Katherine,
my editor—
thank you

✦ CONTENTS ✦

Queste

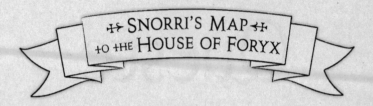

SNORRI'S MAP
TO THE HOUSE OF FORYX

PLAIN

REFUGE

REFUGE

REFUGE

REFUGE

HOUSE OF FORYX

MARSH

STREAM

BOTTOMLESS PIT

BEWARE THE TOLL-MAN

REFUGE

STONE BRIDGE

REFUGE

PLANK BRIDGE

REFUGE

REFUGE

FOREST

REFUGE

for Marcellus, with thanks,
from Nicko & Snorri

PROLOGUE:
NICKO AND SNORRI

It is the *weekly market* on Wizard Way. A girl and a boy have stopped at a pickled herring stall. The boy has fair hair, twisted and braided in the style that sailors will be wearing sometime in the distant future. His green eyes have a serious, almost sad expression, and he is trying to persuade the girl to let him buy her some herring.

The girl, too, has fair hair, but hers is almost white. It is straight and long, held in place with a leather headband, the kind worn by Northern Traders. Her pale blue eyes look at the boy. "No," she tells him. "I cannot eat it. It will remind me too much of home."

"But you love herring," he says.

The stallholder is an elderly woman with pale blue eyes like the girl. She has not sold a single herring all morning and she is determined not to let a chance of a sale go by. "If you love herring, you must try this," she tells the girl. "This is done the proper way. It's how herring should be pickled." She cuts a piece, sticks a small pointy wooden stick into it and hands it to the girl.

"Go on, Snorri," says the boy, almost pleading. "Try it. *Please.*"

Snorri smiles. "All right, Nicko. For you, I will try it."

"It is good?" asks the stallholder.

"It is good, Old Mother," says Snorri. "Very good."

Nicko is thinking. He is thinking that the stallholder speaks like Snorri. She has the same lilting accent and she does not have the Old Speak patterns that he and Snorri have become used to in the few months they have already spent in this Time. "Excuse me," he says. "Where are you from?"

A wistful look comes into the old woman's eyes. "You would not understand," she tells him.

Nicko persists. "But you are not from here," he says. "I can tell by the way you speak. You speak like Snorri here." He puts his arm around Snorri's shoulders and she blushes.

The old woman shrugs. "It is true I am not from here. I am from farther away than you could possibly imagine."

Now Snorri is looking at the old woman too. She begins to speak in her own language, the language of *her* Time.

The old woman's eyes light up at hearing her own tongue spoken as she had spoken it as a child. "Yes," she says in reply to Snorri's tentative question. "I am Ells. Ells Larusdottir."

Snorri speaks again and the old woman replies warily. "Yes, I do—or did—have a sister called Herdis. How do you know? Are you one of those thought-snatchers?"

Snorri shakes her head. "No," she says, still in her own language. "But I am a Spirit-Seer. As was my grandmother Herdis Larusdottir. And my mother, Alfrún, who was not yet born when my great-aunt Ells disappeared through the Glass."

Nicko wonders what Snorri could possibly be saying to make the old woman grip her flimsy stall table with such ferocity that her knuckles go white. Although Snorri has been teaching him her language, she spoke to the old woman much faster than he was used to and the only word he recognized was "mother."

✳ ✳ ✳

And this is how it happens that Great-aunt Ells takes Nicko
and Snorri to her tall, thin house in the Castle walls, throws a
log into her tiled stove and tells them her story. Many hours
later Snorri and Nicko leave Great-aunt Ells's house full of
pickled herring and hope. Most precious of all, they have a
map showing the way to the House of Foryx, the Place Where
All Times Do Meet. That evening Snorri makes two copies of
the map and gives one to Marcellus Pye, the Alchemist in
whose house they are staying. For the next few weeks their
days are full of plans as they prepare for their journey into the
unknown.

It is a gray and rainy day when Marcellus Pye stands on the
Castle Quay and waves their boat farewell. He wonders if he
will ever see them again. He is still wondering.

✢ I ✢

NICKO'S RELEASE

Jannit Maarten, *boatbuilder, was on* her way to the Palace.

Jannit, a lean, spare woman with a long stride and a sailor's pigtail, had never in her strangest dreams thought that she would one day be tying up her rowboat at Snake Slipway and heading for the Palace Gates. But, on a chilly gray spring day, here she was, doing just that— and feeling more than a little apprehensive.

Some minutes later Hildegarde, the sub-Wizard on door
duty at the Palace, looked up from her night-school assign-
ment titled "The Politics, Principles and Practice of **Transformation**." She saw Jannit hesitantly walking over the wide
plank bridge that spanned the ornamental moat and led to the
Palace doors. Happy to have a break, Hildegarde jumped to
her feet with a smile and said, "Good morning, Miss Maarten.
How may I help you?"

"You know my name!" said Jannit, amazed.

Hildegarde did not tell Jannit that she made it her business
to know everyone's name. Instead she said, "Of course I do,
Miss Maarten. Your boatyard repaired my sister's boat last
year. She was very pleased with the work."

Jannit had no idea who this sub-Wizard's sister could possibly be, but she could not help wondering what boat it was.
Jannit remembered boats. She smiled awkwardly and took off
her battered sailor's boater, which she had worn especially for
her visit to the Palace—it was Jannit's equivalent of a party
frock and tiara.

"Ladies are welcome to keep their hats on," said
Hildegarde.

"Oh?" said Jannit, wondering what that had to do with her.

Jannit did not think of herself as a lady.

"Is there someone you wish to see?" Hildegarde prompted, quite used to tongue-tied visitors.

Jannit twisted her boater around in her hands. "Sarah Heap," she said. "Please."

"I will send a messenger. May I tell her what it is you wish to see her about?"

After a long pause Jannit replied. "Nicko Heap," she said, staring at her hat.

"Ah. Please take a seat for a moment, Miss Maarten. I will find someone to take you to her right away."

Ten minutes later Sarah Heap, thinner than she had been but still in possession of the usual quota of Heap straw-colored curls, was at the small table in her sitting room. She gazed at Jannit with worried green eyes.

Jannit was perched on the edge of a large sofa. Although Jannit felt ill at ease, this was not the reason she was on the edge of her seat. It was because that was the only space left on the sofa—the rest was covered with the clutter that always seemed to follow Sarah Heap. With a couple of plant pots digging into her back and a teetering pile of towels settling cozily up against her, Jannit sat up very straight and then almost jumped off the sofa as a soft quacking came from a pile of clothes beside the fire. To Jannit's amazement, a pink-skinned, stubble-covered duck wearing a multicolored crocheted waistcoat emerged from the pile, waddled over and sat beside her feet.

Sarah clicked her fingers. "Come here, Ethel," she said to the duck. The duck got up and went to Sarah, who picked it up and sat it on her lap. "One of Jenna's creatures," Sarah said with a smile. "She never was one for pets and suddenly she has two. Strange. I don't know where she got them from."

Jannit smiled politely, unsure how to begin telling Sarah what she had to say. There was an awkward silence and at last she said, "Um. Well . . . it's a big place you have here."

"Oh, yes. Very big," said Sarah.

"Wonderful for a large family," said Jannit, immediately wishing she hadn't.

"*If* they want to live with you," said Sarah bitterly. "But *not* if four of them have decided to live in the Forest with a coven of witches and they refuse to come home, even for a visit. And then of course there's Simon. I know he's done wrong, but he's still my first baby. I miss him *so* much; I would love to have him living here. It's time he settled down. He could do a lot worse than Lucy Gringe, whatever his father says. There's plenty of room for them all here—and children, too. And then there's my little Septimus. We've been apart all these years and there he is, stuck at the top of that Wizard Tower with Marcia Fusspot Overstrand, who whenever she sees me has the *nerve* to ask if I am enjoying seeing so much of Septimus. I suppose she thinks it's some kind of joke, since I hardly *ever* see him now. In fact ever since Nicko . . ."

"Ah," said Jannit, seizing her chance. "Nicko. That's what—well, I expect you can guess why I'm here."

"No," said Sarah, who could but didn't want to even think about it.

"Oh." Jannit looked down at her boater and then, very purposefully, put it on top of a pile of something behind her. Sarah's heart sank. She knew what was coming.

Jannit cleared her throat and began. "As you know, Nicko has been gone for six months now and as far as I understand, no one knows where he is or when—indeed, *if*—he is ever coming back. In fact—and I am very sorry to say this—I have heard that he will never return."

Sarah caught her breath. No one had dared to say this to her face before.

"I am very sorry to have to come here like this, Madam Heap, but—"

"Oh, it's Sarah. Please, just call me Sarah."

"Sarah. Sarah, I am sorry, but we cannot struggle on without Nicko any longer. The summer season is looming, when even more foolhardy idiots will be putting to sea to try and catch a few herring. They'll all be wanting their boats ready, plus the fact that the Port barge is in for repair *again* after this month's storms—well, we are facing our busiest time. I'm so sorry, but while Nicko is still apprenticed to me, according to the Boatbuilders Association training regulations—which are an absolute minefield, but I do have to abide by them—I cannot engage anyone else. I urgently need a new apprentice, especially as Rupert Gringe is nearing the end of his Articles soon."

Sarah Heap clasped her hands together tightly, and Jannit noticed that her fingernails were bitten down to the quick. Sarah was trembling and did not speak for some seconds. Then, just as Jannit thought she would have to break the silence, Sarah said, "He *will* come back. I don't believe they went back in Time—no one can do that. Jenna and Septimus just thought they did. It was some wicked, *wicked* spell. I keep asking Marcia to figure it out. She could Find Nicko, I know she could, but she's done nothing. *Nothing.* It's all *a complete nightmare!*" Sarah's voice rose in despair.

"I'm so sorry," Jannit murmured. "I really am."

Sarah took a deep breath and tried to calm down. "It's not your fault, Jannit. You were very good to Nicko. He loved working for you. But of course you must find another apprentice, although I would ask you one thing."

"Of course," replied Jannit.

"When Nicko returns, will you renew his apprenticeship?"

"I would be delighted to." Jannit smiled, pleased that Sarah had asked for something she could readily agree to. "Even if I have a new apprentice, Nicko would step straight into Rupert's shoes and become my senior apprentice—or journeyman as we call it down at the yard."

Sarah smiled wistfully. "That would be wonderful," she said.

"And now"—this was the part Jannit had been dreading—"I am afraid I must trouble you to sign the Release." Jannit stood up to pull a roll of parchment from her coat pocket, and the pile of towels, suddenly losing their support, fell down and took her place.

Jannit cleared a space on the table and unrolled the long piece of parchment that formed Nicko's apprentice Indentures. She secured it top and bottom with whatever came to hand—a well-thumbed novel called *Love on the High Seas* and a large bag of biscuits.

"Oh." Sarah caught her breath at the sight of Nicko's spidery signature—along with her own and Jannit's—at the foot of the parchment.

Hastily, Jannit placed the Release—a small slip of parchment—over the signatures and said, "Sarah, as one of the parties who signed the Indentures, I have to ask you to sign the Release. I have a pen if you . . . if you can't find one."

Sarah couldn't find one. She took the pen and ink bottle that Jannit had taken from her other coat pocket, dipped the pen in the ink and—feeling as though she was signing Nicko's life away—she signed the parchment. A tear dripped onto the ink and smudged it; both Jannit and Sarah pretended not to notice.

Jannit signed her own signature next to Sarah's; then she took a needle threaded with thick sail cotton from her bottomless coat pocket and sewed the Release over the original signatures.

Nicko Heap was no longer apprenticed to Jannit Maarten.

Jannit snatched up the hat balanced behind her and fled. It was only when she reached her boat that she realized she had taken Sarah's gardening hat, but she stuffed it on her head regardless and rowed slowly back to her boatyard.

Silas Heap and Maxie the wolfhound found Sarah in her herb garden. Sarah was, for some reason Silas did not understand, wearing a sailor's boater. She also had Jenna's duck with her. Silas was not keen on the duck—the stubble gave him goose bumps when he looked at it and he thought the crocheted waistcoat was a sign that Sarah was going a little crazy.

"Oh, *there* you are," he said, heading along the neatly tended grass path toward the bed of mint that Sarah was absentmindedly poking at. "I've been looking everywhere for you."

Sarah gave Silas a wan half smile in reply, and as Silas and Maxie plowed through the defenseless patch of mint, she did not venture even a small protest. Silas, like Sarah, looked careworn. His straw-colored Heap curls had recently acquired a gray dusting of salt and pepper, his blue Ordinary Wizard robes hung loosely from him, and his silver Ordinary Wizard belt was pulled in a notch or two more than usual. Accompanied by the heady smell of crushed mint, Silas reached Sarah and launched straight into his prepared speech.

"You're not going to like this," he said, "but my mind is made up. Maxie and I are going into the Forest and we're not coming out until we've found him."

Sarah picked up the duck and hugged it tightly to her. It let out a strangled *quack*. "You are a pig-headed fool," she said. "How many times have I told you that if you would only get Marcia to do something about this horrible **Darke Magyk** that has trapped Nicko somewhere, then he'd be back in a moment. But you *won't*. You go on and on about the stupid Forest—"

Silas sighed. "I told you, Marcia says it's not **Darke Magyk**. There's no point asking her over and over again." Sarah glowered so Silas tried another tack. "Look, Sarah, I can't just do nothing, it's driving me crazy. It's been six months now since Jenna and Septimus came back without Nicko and I'm not waiting any longer. You had the same dream as I did. You *know* it means something."

Sarah remembered the dream she had had a few months after Nicko disappeared. He was walking through a forest deep in snow; it was twilight and in front of him a yellow light shone through the trees. There was a girl beside him, a little taller and older than he was, Sarah thought. The girl had long, white-blond hair and was wrapped in a wolfskin pelt. She pointed to the light ahead. Nicko took the girl's hand and together they hurried toward the light. At that moment Silas had started snoring and Sarah had woken up with a jolt. The next morning Silas had excitedly described a dream he had had about Nicko. To Sarah's amazement it was identical to hers.

Since that moment Silas had become convinced that Nicko was in the Forest and he wanted to go search for him. But Sarah had disagreed. The forest in the dream was not, she had told Silas, the Castle Forest. It was different, she was sure of that. Silas, in turn, had also disagreed. He knew the Forest, he said—and he was *sure* it was the Castle Forest.

In their time together Sarah and Silas did not always agree, but they would quickly resolve their differences, often when Silas brought home a few wildflowers or herbs for Sarah as a peace offering. But this time there was no peace offering. Silas and Sarah's arguments about forests became increasingly bitter and they soon lost sight of the real reason for their unhappiness: Nicko's disappearance.

But now Silas had just bumped into the departing Jannit Maarten, who was carrying Nicko's ex-Apprentice Indentures. He had made his mind up. He was going into the Forest to find Nicko and *no one* was going to stop him—particularly Sarah.

✠ 2 ✠
FREE!

*F*eed the Magogs, do not touch
Sleuth, and don't go nosing
around my room. Got that?"
Simon Heap told his scowling
assistant, Merrin Meredith.

"Yeah, yeah," sulked Merrin,
who was sitting listlessly on the
one comfortable chair in the
Observatory. His dark, straggly
hair hung limply over his
face, masking a large pimple
in the middle
of his forehead
that had sprung up
overnight.

"*You got that?*" asked Simon crossly.

"I *said* 'yeah,' didn't I?" mumbled Merrin, swinging his long, gangly legs so that his feet hit the chair with an irritating regularity.

"And you better keep the place tidy," Lucy Gringe told him. "I don't want to come back to a complete mess."

Merrin jumped up and made a mock bow to Lucy. "Yes, Your Ladyship. Can I do anything else for you, Your Ladyship?"

Lucy Gringe giggled.

Simon Heap frowned. "Come on, Lucy," he said irritably. "If you want to get to the Port before nightfall, that is."

"Wait a minute, I've just got to find my—"

"I've got your bag *and* your cloak. Come *on*, Luce." Simon strode across the Observatory, his footsteps sounding hollow on the black slate, and disappeared through the granite arch that led to the stairs. "And, Merrin—don't do anything *stupid*." Simon's voice echoed up the stairs.

Merrin kicked the chair angrily and a cloud of dust and disturbed moths flew out. He was *not* stupid. He was not, not, *not* stupid. Merrin had spent the first ten years of his life being called stupid by his old master, DomDaniel, and he had had enough of it. Merrin had been mistakenly known as Septimus Heap for all those years, but however hard he had tried, he had been a poor substitute for the real Septimus. DomDaniel never did realize the mistake—or the reason why his hapless Apprentice never managed to do anything right.

Scowling, Merrin threw himself back into the old armchair. He watched Lucy Gringe, plaits and ribbons flying, rush around, gathering up her last-minute bits and pieces.

At last Lucy was ready. She snatched up the multicolored scarf that she had knitted for Simon during the long winter evenings in the Harbor and Dock Pie Shop and ran after him. As she, too, disappeared under the gloomy granite archway, she gave Merrin a little wave. Merrin lost his scowl and waved back. Lucy always managed to make him smile.

Happy to be away from what she considered to be the creepiest place on earth, Lucy did not give Merrin another thought as he listened to the hollow sound of her boots beginning the long descent to the cold, damp, Wurm-slimed burrow where Simon's horse, Thunder, was stabled.

As the sound of Lucy's boots faded away into the distance and a heavy silence replaced it, Merrin sprang into action. He seized a long pole and quickly began lowering the black blinds that covered the skylight at the top of the room—it poked up from the rough grass and rocky outcrops at the top of the tall slate cliffs, the only part of the Observatory visible above-ground. As Merrin pulled down blind after blind, the huge room slowly darkened until a dim twilight reigned.

Merrin went over to the Camera Obscura—a large, concave dish that filled the center of the circular room—and gazed at it with a rapt expression. What had been a blank white dish in the early-morning sun streaming through the skylight was now transformed to show a beautifully detailed, colorful scene. Entranced, he watched a line of sheep silently amble along the cliff top above the ravine, the pink clouds of the sunrise drifting slowly behind them.

Merrin reached up, took hold of a long pole hanging down from the center of the skylight, and began to turn it. A protesting squeak started up from a small bonnet at the apex of the skylight, which held the lens that focused the scene onto the dish below. As Merrin slowly turned the bonnet through a full circle, the picture before him changed, showing a silent panorama of the outside world. Merrin took a turn through the whole 360 degrees just for fun and then sought out the spot he wished to watch. He let go of the pole, the squeaking stopped and, pushing his straggly black hair out of his eyes, Merrin leaned forward and stared intently at the scene before him.

The dish showed a long, winding path that snaked down between rocky outcrops. A deep ravine could be seen to its right, and sheer slate cliffs to the left, broken only by an occasional rock fall or cascade of gravel. Patiently Merrin waited until at last he saw Thunder come into view. The horse slowly picked his way along the path, carefully guided by Simon, his black cloak wrapped around him against the early-morning chill. He was muffled in Lucy's scarf, the end of which she had also wound around her own neck. Lucy sat behind Simon, swathed in her precious blue cloak, her arms clasped tightly around his waist.

Merrin grinned as he watched the horse travel silently across the dish. He was, he said to himself, seeing them off the premises. As he watched Thunder's slow progress, Merrin congratulated himself on having engineered the whole thing. From the moment Lucy Gringe had arrived a couple of weeks ago—accompanied by an immensely irritating rat that Merrin had also seen off the premises with a well-aimed kick—Merrin had started planning. His opportunity arose sooner than he had expected. Lucy wanted a ring—and not any old ring either. A *diamond* ring.

Merrin had been surprised at how quickly Simon had agreed to Lucy's way of thinking about many things—even diamond rings. Seizing his chance, Merrin had suggested that he could look after the Observatory while Simon took Lucy to the Port to find a ring. Simon said yes, as he had in mind a visit to Drago Mills's warehouse clearance sale, which the rat had talked about at length. It had started the week previously due to the death of the owner of the warehouse, and was apparently full of the most amazing bargains. Lucy Gringe, however, had other ideas. She had already decided on the perfect ring and it was definitely *not* from Drago Mills's warehouse clearance sale.

At last Merrin's patience was rewarded by the sight of Thunder carrying his two riders off the edge of the dish. As the horse's tail disappeared Merrin let out a loud whoop. At last, at long last—after spending his whole life being told what to do by someone else—he was *free!*

✢ 3 ✢
THE DARKE INDEX

From its hiding place under his mattress, Merrin pulled out a slim, dog-eared, leather-covered book with the title *The **Darke** Index* just visible in faded black letters. He grinned. At last he could read this without having to hide it from nosy-parker Simon Heap and the annoying Lucy. She was even worse than Simon and spent most of her time saying things like: "What are you *doing*, Merrin?"

and "What's that you're reading, Merrin? Show me. Oh, go on, don't be so *sulky*, Merrin."

Ever since Merrin had found the book at the back of a dusty cupboard that Simon had made him clean out, he had been fascinated by it. *The **Darke** Index* spoke to Merrin in his own language. He understood the spells, the rules—and he particularly liked the section that told him how to break the rules. Here was a book written by someone Merrin could understand.

At night, in his small cell, curtained off from the Observatory (because Jenna had once turned the door into chocolate), he would take a tube of Glo Grubs and read for hours under his covers. Simon had noticed the light and teased him about being afraid of the dark, but for once Merrin did not rise to the provocation. It suited him that Simon asked no more questions about the light that glowed on into the early hours of the morning. If Simon wanted to think that, let him. One day Simon Heap would find out that Merrin was most definitely *not* afraid of the dark—or, more to the point— the **Darke**.

Now, Merrin lit all the candles he could find—Simon was stingy with candles and only allowed one to be lit at a time— and he placed them all around the huge, circular chamber of the Observatory. The twilight he had caused by pulling down the blinds was replaced by the warm glow of candlelight. Merrin told himself that he was doing this because he needed the light to read, but Simon had also been a little bit right: Merrin did not like the dark—particularly when he was on his own.

Merrin decided to enjoy himself. He raided the tiny kitchen for the last of Lucy's pies—he found two steak and kidney, one chicken and mushroom and a squashed apple dumpling—then he poured himself a huge mug of Simon's cider. He put it all on the tiny table beside his narrow, lumpy bed and added a few musty chunks of the chocolate door that he had found in a dusty corner under the bed to his pile of food. Then he went and took the thick woolen blanket that Simon kept on his bed. Merrin hated being cold but he usually was, since the Observatory, being cut deep into the slate cliffs, always had a deep chill.

Looking forward to a whole day of doing exactly what he wanted, Merrin wrapped himself up in the blanket and, not even bothering to take his shoes off, he got into bed and started on his stash of food. By midmorning Merrin's book had fallen to the floor. He was fast asleep amid a sea of pastry crumbs, furry lumps of chocolate and discarded bits of kidney, because ever since Simon had told him what kidneys actually did, they had made Merrin feel sick.

One by one, the candles in the Observatory burned down but Merrin slept on until the dying splutters of the last candle jolted him awake. He woke in a panic. Night had fallen; it was pitch-dark and he couldn't remember where he was. He jumped out of bed and collided with the doorpost. As he reeled back, Merrin saw the white dish of the Camera Obscura illuminated by a thin shaft of moonlight that had found its way through a gap in the blinds. Panic subsiding, he took out his tinderbox and began lighting new candles. Soon the Observatory glowed with warm candlelight and felt almost cozy—but what Merrin had planned was about as far removed from cozy as it was possible to get.

Merrin picked *The **Darke** Index* off the floor and opened it to the last page, the title of which was:

Darkening *the Destiny of AnOther*
or The Ruination of Thine Enemy by Use of the
Two-Faced Ring
A Tried and Tested Formula Used with Great
Success by the Author

Merrin knew that part by heart, but he had read no further because of the next line, which said:

Read no Further until thou art Ready to Do,
Else shall be the worse for You

Merrin gulped. Now he was *Ready to Do*. His mouth felt dry and he licked his lips. They tasted of old pie—not nice. Merrin fetched a glass of water, gulped it down and wondered whether it might be better to put the whole thing off until the next night. But the thought of another bleak day in the Observatory on his own, plus the possibility that Simon and Lucy might return at any time, was not good. He had to do this *now*. And so, with a scared feeling in the pit of his stomach, Merrin read on:

First You **Summon** *your Servant* **Thing**

Merrin's heart thumped; this was *scary*. **Summoning** a **Thing** was something that even Simon had not dared to do. But now that he had started, Merrin dared not stop. Warily, as if he were pulling a particularly vicious spider out of its

lair, Merrin drew the **Summoning Charm** from its pocket at
the bottom of the page. The **Charm**—a wafer-thin black
diamond—felt as cold as ice. As instructed, Merrin held
the diamond against his heart and, with the cold of the
stone boring deep into his chest, he recited the **Summons**.
Nothing happened. No gust of wind, no disturbance in the
air, no fleeting shadows—nothing. The candles burned
steadily on and the Observatory felt as empty as ever.
Merrin tried again. Nothing.

A horrible feeling crept up on Merrin—it was true, he
really *was* stupid. Once again he read the words, saying them
slowly. Yet again nothing happened. Over and over Merrin
repeated the words, convinced that he must be missing something obvious—something that anyone else with half a brain
would have immediately noticed. But no **Thing** appeared, no
Thing at all. Getting angry now, Merrin shouted the
Summons—nothing. Then he whispered it, he pleaded,
cajoled—and in desperation he yelled it out backward, all to
no avail. Exhausted, Merrin sank to the floor in despair. He
had tried everything he could think of, and he had failed—
as usual.

What Merrin did not realize was that his **Summons**—

every single one—had worked. The Observatory was now actually seething with Things. The problem was he could not see them.

Things were generally not possible to see, which was fortunate, as they were not a pleasant sight. Most Things were some kind of human figure, although not obviously male or female. They were usually tall, thin to the point of being skeletal and extremely decrepit, their clothes no more than a collection of dark rags. They wore miserable, sometimes desperate expressions mixed with underlying malevolence that left sensitive people who were unfortunate enough to meet their gaze feeling desperate for weeks afterward. Merrin— although he did not know it—had an aunt Edna who fit that description pretty exactly, but even he would have been able to tell the difference between his aunt Edna and a Thing— because a Thing looked *dead*.

It was then that Merrin read the second part of the instructions:

> *Now Address the* Thing,
> *Demand to* See.
> *Remove its Invisibility.*

"Aaargh!" yelled Merrin, suddenly realizing to his horror
what had happened. Angrily, he hurled the book at the wall.
How was he supposed to know the Things were invisible?
Why hadn't the book said so before?

Half an hour later, Merrin had calmed down. Knowing that
he had no choice but to continue, he picked up the book,
found the crumpled page and began to follow the instructions.
He recited the See, closed his eyes and counted to thirteen.
Then, with a feeling of dread, he opened his eyes—and
screamed.

Merrin was *surrounded* by Things. Twenty-six aggrieved,
nose-out-of-joint, why-didn't-he-just-choose-me-aren't-I-good-
enough-for-him Things were staring at him, their lips moving,
mumbling and moaning but making no sound. They towered
above him and stared at him so intently that even Merrin, who
was not known for his sensitivity, felt a deep gloom rising
inside him. It was, he thought, all going horribly wrong.
Simon was right; everyone was right; he was *stupid*. But now
he was stuck. He had to continue or else it would, as the book
had said, be the worse for him. With a nasty feeling in the pit
of his stomach, Merrin read the next instruction:

Now Take with you your Servant **Thing**
To Find and Fetch the Two-Faced Ring

Merrin's heart sank when he read the words: *the Two-Faced Ring*. He still had nightmares about it.

A few months ago Simon had been grumpily cleaning up the Observatory, complaining loudly about Merrin's untidiness. Merrin, meanwhile, had hidden in the larder. He had been surreptitiously eating his way through a secret stash of cold sausages when he had heard Simon scream. Merrin had very nearly choked—Simon usually did not scream. Gasping and coughing, he had staggered out to see a truly terrible sight: a foul collection of rubbery-looking bones glistening with black slime was slowly stalking Simon across the Observatory. Clutching his garbage sack to him as though it were some kind of shield Simon was backing away with a look of utter terror on his face.

Merrin knew at once to whom the bones belonged—his old master, DomDaniel. It was the ring that gave it away. The thick gold and jade Two-Faced Ring that DomDaniel had always worn on his thumb shone out against the black sheen of the bones. "This ring," DomDaniel had once told Merrin, "is indestructible. He who wears it is indestructible. I wear it, therefore *I* am indestructible. Remember that, boy!" He had laughed and waggled his fat pink thumb in Merrin's face.

Merrin had watched the bones corner the terrified Simon. He had listened while, from somewhere deep within the bones, came a **Darke** hollow chant of destruction aimed directly at Simon. It had made Merrin want to curl up into a little ball, though he didn't know why. Luckily for him, he did not remember the time in the Marram Marshes when DomDaniel had directed the very same chant at him.

As the chant had progressed relentlessly toward its end— when Simon would be **Consumed**—Merrin saw Simon Heap change. But not in the way DomDaniel had planned. The fear in Simon's eyes was suddenly replaced by a wild anger. Merrin had seen that look before and he knew it meant trouble.

It did.

In one swift action—like a butterfly hunter after a prize specimen—Simon had brought his garbage sack down over the bones, yelling a **Darke** imprecation of his own. The bones had collapsed and some escaped across the floor, but the chant did not stop. Panicking now, Simon had scrabbled for the stray bones, throwing them into the sack just as he had been throw-

ing the garbage a few minutes earlier. Muffled by the sack, still
the **Darke** chant had continued.

Frantically, Simon had hurled the last bone into the sack.
Then, as if his life depended on it—which it did—he had
raced across the Observatory, pulled open the door to the
Endless Cupboard, hurled the sack inside and slammed and
Barred the door. Then, to Merrin's amusement, Simon's legs
had given way beneath him and he had collapsed onto the
floor like a wet rag. Merrin had taken advantage of the
moment to finish off the sausages.

But now Merrin was going to have to see those awful bones
once more. And, worse, take the ring from them. But even
worse, he was going to have to go into the Endless Cupboard
to find them, which really scared him. The Endless Cupboard
had been built by DomDaniel himself. It was a place to dump
Darke things that were no longer wanted and were impossible to **DeActivate**. The cupboard snaked deep into the rock
and, although it wasn't actually endless, it went on for miles.

Merrin swallowed hard. He knew he had to do it—there
was no going back now. Trembling, he muttered the **UnBar**,
grasped the innocent-looking brass cupboard doorknob and
pulled. The door opened. Merrin reeled. Ice-cold air laced

with the foulest smell—wet dog and rotting meat with a hint
of burned rubber—hit him. He retched and spat in disgust.

With a feeling of doom, Merrin peered into the darkness.
The cupboard appeared empty, but he knew it wasn't. The
Endless Cupboard shifted things about, taking the **Darkest**
deep into the rock. He dreaded to think how far it had taken
the bones.

Lifting the candle above his head, Merrin stepped inside.
The cupboard snaked deep into the rock like a tendril. As
Merrin walked in, the air became cold. After about a dozen
steps his candle flame began to gutter in the foul atmosphere,
but he pressed on, deeper into the cupboard. Now the flame
was growing smaller. It began to glow a dull red, and Merrin
became alarmed. If there was not enough air for the flame then
surely that meant that there was not enough air for him?
Feeling light-headed now, with a high-pitched buzzing in his
ears, Merrin took a few more steps and suddenly the candle
flame died, leaving for a brief moment the red glow at the end
of the wick, and then complete darkness.

Merrin's chest felt tight. He opened his mouth wide to try
to breathe more air, but nothing was there. He knew he had
to get out of the cupboard—fast. Gasping, he turned back,

only to run straight into an immoveable Thing. In a blind panic, he pushed past the Thing, only to find another in his way, then another. Horrified, Merrin realized that he was trapped—that the long, thin cupboard was *stuffed full* of Things, and that they were probably still trying to get in, which indeed they were. Outside, an agitated crowd of Things jostled, pushing, scratching and fighting to be the next one inside. A wave of fear engulfed Merrin; then the cupboard floor did something very strange. It rushed up to meet him and hit him on the head.

When Merrin came to he was back in the Observatory, lying on the cold slate floor.

Blearily he looked up, and twenty-six Things stared back. Usually the gaze of twenty-six Things would be enough to send someone into despair forever, but Merrin's eyes would not focus. All he saw was a wavy blur surrounding him, like a large, prickly hedge.

Slowly, Merrin became aware of something on the floor beside him. He turned his head—which *hurt*—and came face to face with a grubby canvas sack. A garbage sack. Inside, like a litter of kittens, something was *moving*.

Suddenly wide awake, Merrin leaped to his feet, grabbed

the sack and upended it. A tangle of soft, slimy bones slid out across the floor, the small fat bone wearing the ring skittering across the floor with a metallic *clink*. Merrin stared at it blankly—what was he meant to do *now*? A bone by his foot twitched. Merrin screamed. Like blind worms, the bones were beginning to move, each one searching for its neighbor—they were **ReAssembling**.

A bony finger poked his ribs and Merrin screamed. DomDaniel was poking him. He was going to *dieeeeee!* The *Darke* Index was thrust in front of his face and Merrin realized with relief that the bony finger belonged to a **Thing**. Obediently he read the passage that the **Thing**'s finger was pointing to:

> *Take the Two-Faced Ring*
> *From the Thumb*
> *Of the One*
> *Who wears It.*
> *Remove the Ring the* **Other** *Way:*
> *Your Possession now Holds Sway.*

Merrin went over to the small slimy black stick that wore the Two-Faced Ring and looked down at it with revulsion. He steeled himself to pick it up. One, two, three—no, he couldn't do it. Yes, he could—he *had* to do it. One . . . two . . . three—*eurgh!* He had it. The thumb bone was soft—like gristle. It was revolting. He was going to be sick.

Some seconds later, with a nasty taste in his mouth, Merrin grasped the Two-Faced Ring, knowing he had to pull it over the base of the bone—the *Other* way. He pulled. It stuck on the wider part of the bone where the joint had been. Merrin fought off panic. *It wouldn't come off.* Soon DomDaniel would **ReAssemble** and he'd be cat food. Desperation gave Merrin a kind of courage. He pulled out his pocket knife, put the thumb bone on the floor and sawed the end off the bone. Thick, black liquid oozed from the bone, and the Two-Faced Ring fell free.

Horribly fascinated, Merrin picked up the ring and stared at the broad, twisted band of gold with the opposite facing, evil-looking heads carved in jade. With shaking hands, he consulted *The* **Darke** *Index:*

> *On your left hand*
> *Upon the thumb*
> *You place the band—*
> *The Two-Faced One.*

Trembling, Merrin slid the ring onto his own thumb, pushing away the thought that one day someone might try to take it off *his* thumb the **Other** way. At first the ring sat loose on Merrin's thin, grubby thumb with its bitten nail and big knuckle, but not for long. He felt the gold become warmer and warmer until it was almost unpleasantly hot—and then the ring began to tighten. Soon it fit perfectly, but it did not stop there. Getting even hotter, the ring continued to tighten. His thumb began to throb.

Merrin panicked. He leaped up and down, shaking his thumb, yelling and stamping his feet with the pain. Tighter and tighter the ring swelled, turning the end of his thumb first red, then purple and finally a dark, deep blue. At that point, Merrin stopped shouting and stared at it in horror; he just *knew* that the end of his thumb was about to explode. Would it go *pop*, he wondered, or would it be a squelchy kind of *splat*? Merrin didn't want to know. He closed his eyes. And the moment he closed his eyes, the ring loosened its grip, the blood flowed back and Merrin's thumb deflated. The Two-Faced Ring now fit, although it felt tight—just tight enough to remind him of its presence. Merrin knew that it was his for life—or at least the life of his left thumb.

Merrin was beginning to realize that **Darke Magyk** was not necessarily on the side of those who practiced it. But he could not stop now. He was trapped, and now he must embark upon the last part of the Enchantment—*Darkening the Destiny of AnOther*. And that must be done in the Castle, for that was where the Other lived, at the top of the Wizard Tower, as he had once done. Using the same name that Merrin himself once had: Septimus Heap.

✛ 4 ✛
OUT OF THE BADLANDS

J*ust before dawn, Merrin roused* himself from his bed and staggered out, half asleep, into the gloomy Observatory, and headed for the Glo Grub tub. Blearily, he scooped out a fresh tube of Glo Grubs ready for his journey and it was only when he was jamming the lid back onto the tub that Merrin opened his eyes properly—and screamed. He had forgotten about the **Things**. A good dozen of them were clustered around the Glo Grub tub watching his every move. The rest were wandering aimlessly about as though blown by an invisible breeze.

Aware now that his every movement was being watched by the Things, Merrin padded into Simon's sparsely furnished room, unlocked a cupboard and took out a small black box on which was written: *Sleuth*.

Merrin elbowed his way back through his faithful cluster of Things and put Sleuth's box into a backpack along with a few other treasures. Then he shouldered the pack and took a deep breath. He knew it was time to go, but right then even the cold, creepy, damp and lonely Observatory stuffed full of Things felt a whole lot more inviting than the journey he had in front of him. It would be a steep climb down hundreds of dark, slippery steps cut into the rock, creeping past the old Magogs' chamber and then out along a long, slimy Wurm Burrow. But Merrin knew he had no choice; he had to go.

Any hopes Merrin might have had that the Things had finished their task and would stay behind in the Observatory were dashed when, after he had gone down the first few steps into the darkness, he turned and saw a line of Things. They shuffled forward, all elbows and knees, jabbing and kicking at one another, trying to get onto the steps behind him. Great, thought Merrin, just *great*.

Half an hour later, Merrin was at the entrance of the disused

Wurm Burrow, but he was not alone. He knew that there were twenty-six **Things** right behind him; he could feel them staring at him. They made the back of his neck feel prickly and icy cold. Nervously tapping his grubby fingers on the Wurm-slimed wall of the Burrow, Merrin shivered in the damp air. He stared intently at the dark skyline along the top of the cliffs on the far side of the ravine.

As much as Merrin longed to leave the Wurm Burrow, he was waiting for the first yellow streaks of dawn to show in the sky. Nighttime was a dangerous time to be out in the Slate Quarries of the Badlands. He had been told enough gory tales over the years to know that the most dangerous time of all was twilight. That was when the Land Wurms are on the move—in the evening breaking their day-long fast, or in the morning returning to their Burrows and looking out for one last tasty morsel to see them through the long day, which they would spend curled up deep inside the frosty slate cliffs.

Ten long, cold minutes later, Merrin was sure he could see the outline of the jagged rocks opposite him more clearly. And as he watched, a slow slither of movement just below the skyline told him that dawn must be near—a Land Wurm was returning to its Burrow. Fascinated, Merrin watched the seemingly endless cylinder of the creature pour into the cliff face on the far side of the ravine. He wondered how many were doing just the same thing at that very moment on *his* side of the ravine—maybe only a few feet away for all he knew, for Land Wurms were as silent as the night. The only sound heralding their arrival—if you were lucky—might be the clatter of a stone dislodging as they moved in for the kill. At that moment a shower of small stones fell from the cliffs above Merrin and, heart racing, he leaped back. Like a line of dominoes, twenty-six **Things** behind him did the same.

Merrin was spooked. As much as he was longing to escape the **Things**, he decided he would not set foot outside until he had seen the sun and *knew* that he was safe. However, the sun did not oblige. The sky remained a dull gray and Merrin waited . . . and waited. Then, just as he had become convinced that, typically, it would be his luck to pick the *one* day in the whole history of the world when the sun was not going to rise, he saw a watery white disc inching its way into the sky above the somber cliffs. At last—it was time to go.

But first he had to get rid of the **Things**. Merrin was not going to make the trek to the Castle dogged by a long line of dismal Things. No way. He turned to the first Thing in line. "I have left my cloak in the Observatory," he said. "Get it for me."

The Thing looked puzzled. His Master was wearing his cloak.

"Get it!" shouted Merrin. "All of you—*get my cloak!*"

A servant Thing may not disobey its Master. With reproachful looks—for Merrin's servant Things were not without intelligence—the creatures sloped off along the old Wurm Burrow. They were not surprised when a massive *thud* followed by a great rush of air told them that Merrin had slammed the huge iron Burrow plug closed. With a resigned air, the Things continued their task and all, bar one, were still searching for the nonexistent cloak when Simon and Lucy returned a few days later.

But unknown to Merrin, one of the Things—the one that he had Summoned with his backward Summons—was not bound to obey his Master. Which is why, after Merrin had set off down the track, the great iron plug to the Wurm Burrow opened once more. The Thing slunk out and began to follow the one who had Summoned him. And over the Thing's shoulder was slung a grubby canvas sack of bones. The Thing had rapidly come to the conclusion that its new Master was going to need all the help he could get. And a sack of **Darke** bones might be just the help he was going to need.

Merrin took the path that hugged the walls of the slate cliffs leading into the Farmlands. He knew this part of the track well and was not fazed when, on rounding the first bend, a landslip blocked his way. With a feeling of excitement—and a little trepidation—Merrin clambered up the slippery rocks. He took care not to hurry too much, for fear of dislodging one of the rocks and sending himself plummeting hundreds of feet down into the torrent below. He reached the top safely and began to slide carefully down the other side. But halfway down, his feet slipped and sent a cluster of small rocks clattering into the ravine. Merrin stopped and held his breath, waiting for the avalanche to begin and take him with it, but his luck held and very gingerly he set off again. A few minutes later his feet touched the firm ground of the path. Merrin let out a triumphant whoop and punched the air. He was free!

Accompanied by the roaring of the river flooding far below at the bottom of the ravine, Merrin traveled quickly down the ravine path. He did not look back even once. Even if he had, he probably would not have noticed the **Thing**, which blended into the shadows and took on the forms of the rocks in the way that Things do when they do not want to be noticed.

Before long Merrin was leaving the oppressive slate cliffs of the Badlands behind and heading into the scattered hill farms of the Upper Farmlands. This was unfamiliar territory now, but Merrin followed a wide track with a surface of dusty well-trodden earth. When he came to a fork in the road, he was rewarded by a sign-stone. The tall post of granite was carved with an arrow pointing him to the right and one word: CASTLE. Merrin smiled. With a confident stride, he set off along the right-hand fork.

It was a cool spring day and the sun gave off little heat as it slowly rose above the low-lying cloud, but Merrin's brisk pace kept him warm enough. Soon a familiar empty feeling gathered in the pit of his stomach. Merrin was used to being hungry, but now that he was a free agent he had no intention of letting that state of affairs continue.

As he walked jauntily down the track that meandered through fields of newly planted vines and tiny fruit trees, Merrin saw a small stone farmhouse. It was not far away, half hidden in a dip. He broke into a jog. A few minutes later he was walking into an overgrown yard surrounded by ram-shackle sheds, deserted except for a few bedraggled chickens pecking at the dirt. Before him was the long, low farmhouse, the front door half open. Merrin walked up to the door and the smell of baking bread hit him like a sledgehammer.

Merrin's stomach did something that felt like a double somersault—he *had* to have that bread. Taking care not to move the front door, which looked like it might have a nasty creak, he crept inside. He found himself in a long, dark room lit only by the glow of a fire from a stove at the far end. Merrin stopped and looked around. No one was there; he was sure of that. The baker of the bread obviously had other things to do, and while he or she was doing them Merrin would seize his chance.

Like a cat, Merrin padded silently across the earthen floor, past a large pile of hay and a stack of wooden boxes. But— unlike a cat—he stepped on a chicken. With a great squawk the old blind hen rose into the air flapping her wings. "Shh!" hissed Merrin desperately. "Shh, you stupid bird." The old hen took no notice and careened off, crashing into a carefully stacked pile of poles ready for bean planting. The poles collapsed with the loudest clatter Merrin had ever heard, and footsteps came running.

A large, motherly looking woman appeared, silhouetted in a doorway across the room. Merrin ducked behind the stack of boxes. "Henny!" cried the woman, running a few feet away from Merrin. She tripped over the hen in the gloom and hurriedly scooped her up. "You *silly* chook. Come now, time for your breakfast, my sweetheart."

Time for *my* breakfast, you mean, thought Merrin, annoyed that a moth-eaten old hen should get picked up, offered breakfast *and* called sweetheart, while he skulked hungrily in the shadows. He was pretty sure that if the woman had tripped over him instead of the chicken, the result would not have been the same. He held his breath as the woman walked right past him with the hen. His dark gray eyes followed her progress until she had disappeared out the front door and into the sunlight. Then, like a streak of black lightning, Merrin shot over to the stove, yanked his sleeves down over his hands, wrenched open the oven door and pulled out a great round loaf of bread.

"A . . . aah . . . *aaaah!*" Merrin gasped under his breath, hopping from foot to foot as the damp heat from the piping-hot bread quickly found its way through his sleeves. Juggling the loaf like a great hot potato, Merrin shot out of the nearest door, ran around the back of the farmhouse and found himself in the yard. His way was barred by a mass of chickens, which were being fed by the woman whose bread Merrin was still juggling. At the sound of the clucking and fussing among her hens, the woman looked up.

"Hey!" she shouted.

Merrin stopped, unsure what to do. Should he turn and run back into the farm, risking an encounter with the woman's husband or some burly farmhand? Or should he go straight ahead and get out onto the open road?

"That's my *bread*," said the woman, advancing toward him.

Merrin looked down at the loaf as if surprised to see it. Then he made a decision and ran—straight for the chickens. With much clucking and squawking the chickens scattered. Feathers flew as Merrin plowed through the flock, delivering a few well-aimed kicks as he fled.

In seconds he was out on the road and running fast. He glanced back once and saw the woman standing in the middle of the road shaking her fist at him. He knew he was safe. She was not coming after him.

What Merrin did not see, partly because it was daylight and Things do not show up well in bright light—but mainly because he was not expecting to see it—was the Thing. It flowed along the hedgerows some distance behind him, like a stream of dirty water.

Another thing that Merrin did not see as he jogged along, hugging the now pleasantly hot bread, was a brown rat sitting in the grass by the side of the road. But the rat saw Merrin well enough. Stanley, ex–Message Rat, ex–Secret Service Rat, had no intention of getting anywhere near Merrin, particularly near his right boot. But Stanley's old Secret Service habits died hard and he was curious to know where Merrin was going. The boy was, in Stanley's opinion, trouble.

Stanley had just spent a couple of weeks with Humphrey, his old Message Rat Service boss, who had fled the Castle some six months ago after the RatStranglers had formed. Although Humphrey was enjoying his retirement in an apple loft on a small cider farm and had no intention of returning, he had tried to persuade Stanley to start up the Message Rat Service again. Stanley had promised to think about it.

Stanley watched Merrin stop at a crossroads. The boy stared at the sign-stones for a few seconds and then jauntily set off in the direction of the Castle. The rat watched Merrin stride down the road. With people like *that* heading for the

Castle, he thought, a Message Rat Service might well be needed. He made a pact with himself: he would follow Merrin and if the boy did indeed go to the Castle, Stanley would take Humphrey's advice.

And so it was that two very different creatures followed Merrin as he made his way along the winding tracks that led through the Farmlands. Buoyed by his newfound freedom, Merrin made fast progress, and as night began to fall he saw the Castle in the distance. Weary now, he trudged past the last farm before the river. He looked longingly at the lit candles in the farmhouse windows and at a family sitting down to supper, but he kept going, following the track through a small wood. One sharp bend later Merrin suddenly found himself out of the trees and on the riverbank. Amazed, he threw himself down on the grass and stared. He had never seen anything like it in his life.

On the other side of the wide, slow river, a great wall of lights reared up into the night sky, casting their sparkling reflections in the dark waters of the river. Behind the lights the shadowy bulk of the Castle could be seen. Merrin knew there were thousands of people inside, each one belonging to one of the lights, all living their lives and going about their business without a thought for a boy sitting on the opposite bank. Suddenly Merrin felt very small and alone.

Merrin stared at the lights, resisting the urge to count them—he was much given to counting things—and soon his eyes began to pick out more details and make sense of the shapes behind them. He saw the high walls of The Ramblings, which seemed to stretch along the river for miles. And, in the silence of the riverbank, he heard the sound of chatter and laughter drifting across the water. He saw the deserted pontoons of the old docks and the outlines of a few rotting ships. And then as he looked, eyes wide as an owl's, Merrin picked out a ladder of lights that flickered purple and gold and reached impossibly high into the sky. At the top of the ladder was a golden pyramid, glowing with an eerie purple light and illuminating the underside of a bank of low-lying clouds.

A shiver ran through Merrin. He knew what that was—the Wizard Tower, a place where he had once spent an unhappy few months with his old master, DomDaniel. It was also, he thought with a sudden rush of anger, where that so-called Septimus Heap boy was right now, no doubt sitting by a warm fire, having supper and talking Wizard stuff and being listened to, as if what he said *mattered*. But not, thought Merrin, for very much longer. He ran his forefinger over the cold surface of the Two-Faced Ring that was wrapped—still a little too tightly—around his left thumb, and smiled.

Abruptly, Merrin jumped up from the damp grass and set off at top speed along the track. He knew that he would have to wait until dawn when the drawbridge was lowered to get into the Castle, and he needed somewhere to spend the night. The track took him away from the riverbank and through some muddy fields bounded by high hedges. As he emerged from the last field Merrin saw the lights of the Grateful Turbot Tavern appear. In his pocket his hand closed around the bag of Simon's secret stash of money that he had taken. Time, he thought, to spend some of my hard-earned cash.

Stanley watched Merrin push open the door to the tavern and walk into the warm, welcoming glow. There was no doubt about it; Merrin was headed for the Castle. The Grateful Turbot had a well-deserved reputation for being haunted. No one would choose to stay there unless they were waiting for the Castle drawbridge to be lowered the next morning.

As the rat scuttled off, the Thing loped up to the tavern door. But it did not venture inside. It sank into a dark corner of the front porch and huddled up on one of the benches that ran along the side with its sack of bones to keep it company through the night. The Thing did not exactly wear a look of contentment on its haggard face, but it was not displeased. If anyone had ever thought to ask a Thing what its idea of a fun night out would be—which strangely enough no one ever had—sitting outside a haunted tavern with a bag of Necromancer's bones for company would probably have been at the top of the list.

✠ 5 ✠
THE GRATEFUL TURBOT

Merrin did not know how old he was. He was in fact nearing his thirteenth birthday, but the guarded expression in his eyes made him look much older. Recently he had grown tall, and with the confidence of his new independence, plus the knowledge that he had enough money for many days to come, he strode into the Grateful Turbot Tavern. Making his voice as gruff as possible, he ordered supper and asked for a room for the night.

Some minutes later, Merrin was sitting by a crackling log fire with a tankard of the dark Turbot special on the table in front of him. He wished he had been brave enough to ask for lemonade. It was a quiet Sunday evening at the tavern and, apart from a couple of farmers haggling over the price of a cow, Merrin thought he had the place to himself. But what Merrin could not see, because he was not the kind of boy ghosts would normally choose to **Appear** to, was that the Grateful Turbot Tavern was stuffed full of ghosts. So much so that when Merrin had made his way from the bar to the fire he had inadvertently **Passed Through** half a dozen ghosts before they had had the chance to get out of his way, causing much ghostly grumbling.

As Merrin took what he thought was an unoccupied seat by the fire he was in fact surrounded by ghosts—who liked to stand by a blazing fire on a dark night as much as any Living person.

Next to Merrin were three fishermen, one of whom was somewhat grumpy, having been in the seat Merrin had just taken. Some fifty years ago, the fishermen had drowned right outside the tavern after an argument over who had caught the biggest fish, and they were still arguing. Sitting across the table from Merrin was an ancient and very faded tinker-woman endlessly counting her pennies. The tinker had died of old age at that very table and still did not understand that she was dead. Clustered around the fire was a party of six knights killed in a long-forgotten battle for the One Way Bridge. They were chatting with a couple of dairymaids who, only a few years back, had gotten lost in a blizzard on their way home from the market and had frozen during the night. Perched on the edge of Merrin's table was a Princess who had run away to meet her sweetheart, sheltered under a tree in a sudden thunderstorm and been struck by lightning. She studied Merrin with a mournful gaze until he shifted uncomfortably in his seat. He looked, thought the Princess, a little like her long-lost love—but only a little.

There was, not surprisingly, a bit of an atmosphere in the Grateful Turbot—which was why it was generally frequented only by those who were too late to get into the Castle and needed a bed for the night or by Northern Traders who were banned from most of the Castle taverns. And the first ghost that Merrin ever saw—although he never realized it—was the ghost of one of these Northern Traders.

Sitting in the shadows, some way back from the gathering by the fire, was the ghost of Olaf Snorrelssen, a Northern Trader who had once fallen asleep on the One Way Bridge and never woken again. Olaf sat in his shadowy corner and watched Merrin from across the room. There was something about the boy that caught his eye—here was a fellow traveler, a stranger in a foreign land as Olaf himself had so often been. In a sudden rush of fellow-feeling Olaf decided to make his first **Appearance** to a Living person.

As Olaf made his way toward Merrin, he glanced in one of the dark mirrors that lined the walls of the Grateful Turbot. He saw himself for the first time in fifteen years—or rather, bits of himself. It was a shock. Olaf stopped in front of the mirror and stared. It was very strange: all his edges were in place, but there was a nasty gap in his middle that he could see straight through. And the top of his head wasn't quite there either. Olaf concentrated hard, and slowly the rest of his head, with its old leather headband and thinning blond hair **Appeared**. Goodness, was he really that thin on top? He put his hand up to feel the top of his head, but nothing was there. Olaf felt suddenly depressed; for a moment he had forgotten that he was a ghost. The advice other ghosts had given him about **Appearing** for the first time came back to him now. Take care, they had told him. **Appearing** to the Living will stir old memories. The Living will seem too fast and too loud, and they will make you feel more of a ghost than you ever have before. Olaf took a deep breath and steadied himself. The rest of his stomach came into view. He had the beginnings of a paunch. He didn't remember that, either, but then he never had taken much notice of his appearance when he was Living.

By the time Olaf had reached Merrin's table the ghost looked, in the dim light of the tavern, as solid as if he were Living. Merrin looked up at him and Olaf felt flustered—no Living person had seen him as a ghost before.

"Greetings," said Olaf, uttering his first words to a Living being in fifteen years.

Merrin did not reply. Unsure what to do or say, Olaf sat down opposite the boy. He did not notice the faded ghost of the tinker-woman, who leaped squawking from her place, scattering her pennies all over the floor.

"Oh! I am sorry, Madam," said Olaf, jumping up and scrabbling around on the floor to try to retrieve the pennies for the woman—which was impossible, as they were part of another ghost—and causing even more offense. The tinker pushed Olaf out of the way. She gathered up her pennies and retreated, muttering, to a dark corner away from the fire, where she would spend the next one hundred years counting her pennies to make sure they were all there.

"Don't call me Madam. I am *not* a girl," Merrin growled, scowling at Olaf. He wondered why this stranger had come over to talk to him and then suddenly dived onto the floor. Something was odd about him, but Merrin could not quite figure out what.

"Why no, indeed you are not a girl," Olaf replied, confused. "You are a stranger here, I think?" he persevered, speaking softly in his singsong Northern accent.

"No," said Merrin sullenly. "I'm not. I was born in the Castle. I . . . am coming home."

"Ah, home," said Olaf wistfully. "Then you are lucky. There are some of us who can never return home."

Merrin looked at the man opposite him. His weatherbeaten face had a kindly look to it and his pale blue eyes were friendly. Merrin mellowed a little. It was the first time anyone had sought him out because they had been interested in talking to him, and the first time that anyone had ever spoken to him as if he were a grown-up, decent human being. It was a good feeling. Merrin risked a smile.

Encouraged by the smile, Olaf ventured, "You have family here?"

"No," said Merrin, quickly deciding that a possible mother in the Port did not count. "I . . . don't have *any* family."

Olaf, who had been one of a very large family, could not imagine what that must be like. "No family," he said. "Not one little piece of family?"

Merrin shook his head. "Nope."

"Then where will you stay? What will you do?"

Merrin shrugged. He'd been wondering that too but had put it to the back of his mind.

Olaf made a decision. Somewhere in the Lands of the Long Nights, he had a child who he had never seen and never would see. No matter that Olaf was sure for some reason he did not understand, his child was a girl. She would, he figured, be the same age as this boy. If he could not help his own, he would do another a good turn. "Tomorrow I shall take you into the Castle and I shall show you a good place where you can stay," he offered. "Tonight you are staying here?"

Merrin nodded.

"And today you have traveled far, I think?" Olaf was getting into his stride now and beginning to enjoy himself.

"All the way from the Badlands. Never want to go back."

"They were not your family there?" asked Olaf.

"No *way*. They treated me like a servant. Or worse. Took the first chance I could to get out of there."

Olaf nodded sympathetically. The boy, he thought, had had a hard life. It was time someone gave him a helping hand.

Encouraged by Olaf's attention, Merrin began to tell his story. "I got away once before but I ended up stuck in the marshes with a crazy old witch who made me eat eel and cabbage sandwiches."

"That is not good," Olaf murmured.

"It was *disgusting*. But to escape from her I took a job with Simon Heap, and that was even worse. I ended up back in the same horrible place I'd grown up. I couldn't believe it. Until a few weeks ago I thought I was stuck there forever with old Heap and that bag of bones."

"Bag of *bones*?" asked Olaf, thinking he had not quite understood.

"Yeah. Simon's old boss—and mine. DomDaniel. Lived in a sack till I tipped him out last night."

"Tipped him . . . *out?*" Now Olaf was sure he did not understand.

"Yeah. I got his ring—want to see?"

Without waiting for an answer, Merrin waved his beringed thumb in the ghost's face. "Mine now," he said, "and I *earned* it. It wasn't nice going through all those bones. Some of them had stuff on them like gristle. And slime. And they were *bendy.* Yuck. But I got it off his thumb. Chopped the end off, ha ha. *That* showed him. You know, thumb bones are just like toe bones?"

Olaf nodded warily. This boy was not turning out to be quite what he had expected; he was beginning to regret his earlier offer. It was true what they said about the Living— there were some weird ones out there. Trust him to pick one of them the very first time he **Appeared**. Olaf was saved from hearing any more about bones by the barmaid bringing Merrin his supper: a huge plate of sausages stuck into a mound of mashed potatoes.

"I will leave you to eat your supper," said Olaf, getting up quickly as the barmaid thumped the plate down in front of Merrin. Merrin nodded. He was pleased; he didn't want to share any of his meal with the stranger. Merrin stabbed a large sausage with his fork. Olaf winced. He thought the sausages looked like thumb bones. He could just imagine them in a sack. Wearing rings.

"See you tomorrow, then," said Merrin, his mouth full of sausage.

"Ah. Tomorrow. Yes, I will see you tomorrow," said Olaf gloomily. He never broke a promise.

"Good," said Merrin, looking up from spearing his second sausage. But the room was empty. The farmers had left, and so had the tall, blond stranger.

✝6✝
INTO THE CASTLE

While *Merrin was trying to get* comfortable in a lumpy bed under the eaves of the Grateful Turbot, Stanley was burrowing into some straw in the rat hole underneath the resting place of the Castle drawbridge. The rat hole was a popular location for rats returning to the Castle, as it was a safe place to sleep while waiting for the dawn lowering of the drawbridge.

Stanley had been concerned that he might find the rat hole already full. This had happened to him a few times in the past and he had been forced to spend an uncomfortable night up a nearby tree, which was preferable to the haunted kitchens. of the Grateful Turbot any day. Hoping he was not too late for a space, Stanley slipped down the bank and scooted into the well-hidden burrow. To his surprise, he realized that he was the only rat there. And then he remembered why—the RatStranglers.

Some six months ago Stanley and his wife, Dawnie, had narrowly escaped the RatStranglers. On reaching the relative safety of the Port, Dawnie had spread the increasingly dramatic story of their escape. There was nothing the rat community liked more than a bloodcurdling tale. Word had traveled fast, with the result that no rat in their right mind would now set foot in the Castle. But not all rats, thought Stanley, were as up-to-date on current affairs as he was, and *he* knew that the RatStranglers were long gone. Good riddance too, he thought. He made his way deep into the warm and musty rat hole until he reached the very end and burrowed down into some old straw.

The rat hole was no fun without company. Stanley was a sociable rat who liked nothing more than a good gossip with other Message Rats. He found it rather depressing to be on his own in what had once been such a convivial place. He tried nibbling at half a moldy turnip that some rat had left behind, but the thought of Dawnie and the RatStranglers had taken his appetite away. And so with a small groan Stanley, tired and aching after his long trek, stretched out his little legs, yawned and fell fast asleep. Soon the sound of rat snores were drifting across the Moat, but no one—not even the members of the Gringe household, who lived in the gatehouse opposite— heard them.

As the first streaks of dawn appeared in the sky, the tremen-dous *thud* of the drawbridge slamming down onto its resting place shook Stanley out of his straw and sent him rolling down to the mouth of the rat hole. Bleary-eyed, he peered out into the dull twilight. It was not a welcoming kind of day. The wind skit-tered across the slate gray surface of the Moat and large spots of rain dotted the surface of the water with widening rings. But the empty rat hole was no fun to be in either. Stanley hopped out and sniffed the early morning air. The scent of dead leaves, rain and Moat water was mixed with an unpleasant whiff of stale stew that drifted across the water from the gatehouse opposite. The rat balanced briefly on the flat take-off stone used by rats for generations and then made a well-timed leap. He landed lightly on a narrow metal shelf on the underside of the drawbridge and, careful not to look down at the deep water below, he crossed the Moat by running along the rat-run hidden beneath the massive planks of the bridge.

Safely on the other side, Stanley scrambled up the muddy bank. Keeping his head down against the biting wind, which was sending swirls of dirt into his eyes, he scurried along the track that went through the North Gate. Suddenly Stanley— to his horror—found himself running over the feet of Mrs. Gringe, the wife of the gatekeeper. Stanley was used to avoiding Gringe, who had large, heavy feet any rat could hear a mile away and a voice to match. But Mrs. Gringe, a small worried-looking woman, was sitting quiet and still in the shelter of the gatehouse, with her little feet stuck out of the door, just asking to trip up an unsuspecting rat. Which they did. The feel of rat feet running over her own delicate toes was not something that Mrs. Gringe took lightly. In one swift second she managed to scream, grab a broom and land it with a thump on Stanley's disappearing tail.

Stanley shot off and headed down the nearest drain, which was not, after a night's heavy rain, the most comfortable place to be. It also turned out to be blocked.

"Rat, rat!" he heard Mrs. Gringe yell.

"Where?" growled a voice from the gatehouse.

"In the drain—get it, Gringe!"

Trapped, Stanley listened to the heavy footsteps of Gringe thudding above his head. He took a deep breath and sank below the water just in time.

Gringe knelt down and peered into the drain. "I can't see nothin'. You sure?"

"'Course I'm sure. Saw it with me own eyes."

"Ah. Well, I dunno." Gringe stared at the filthy water. "You know," he said slowly, "when you scream, I still think . . . I still think it's you an' Lucy having a shout. Happy days . . ."

"We weren't *always* shouting," said Mrs. Gringe with a sigh. "Well, only about that Heap boy."

Stanley felt like his lungs were about to burst. A small bubble of air escaped from his mouth. "Ah," said Gringe. "I reckon the little blighter's hiding under the water."

"You want a shovel?"

"Yeah. Pass me that big one. I'll dig 'im out and whack 'im on the 'ead. Good practice if that Heap boy ever shows his face in 'ere."

Stanley could hold his breath no longer. A great shower of fetid water erupted from the drain—along with a sodden rat—and Gringe reeled back, spluttering. When he finally wiped the mess from his eyes, Stanley was gone—off into the warren of alleyways and sideslips that led from the North Gate deep into the Castle.

Just outside the Palace gates, Stanley took a quick and freezing cold bath in a horse trough. A bath was not the rat's favorite way of spending time—he couldn't remember when he last had one—but when a rat is off to the Palace, he has to make an effort.

Back at the Grateful Turbot Tavern, Merrin, however, was not making much of an effort at all. Olaf Snorrelssen had hung around for hours waiting for Merrin to wake up, spending the entire time being berated by the tinker-woman. The boy finally staggered downstairs just after ten, having been pulled out of bed by the landlady, who wanted her room back.

Mindful of his much-regretted promise, Olaf **Appeared** from the shadows. "I shall take you into the Castle, yes?" the ghost asked, hoping the boy would refuse. Unfortunately he didn't.

"Yeah. Let's get out of this dump," Merrin growled.

Olaf took Merrin over the One Way Bridge, the familiar feeling of gloom that the bridge gave him settling on him like a cloud. The cloud did not lift as, dutifully, Olaf showed the boy across the drawbridge. He mediated in the argument the boy picked with the gatekeeper—who was also in a foul temper and smelled pretty bad too. Then he headed for The Ramblings, a huge warren of a place that Olaf had a real affection for. As he guided Merrin through the narrow, sometimes crowded passageways, Olaf could not shake off a strange feeling that they were being followed. But every time he glanced back he could see nothing more than the occasional fleeting shadow, which was not unusual in the shadowy, twisting alleyways. Determined to keep his word, the ghost took Merrin deep into The Ramblings. He led him to a small guesthouse where he himself had happy memories of staying many years ago.

That, Olaf mused later, was a mistake. Merrin had not liked the place. It was, he had said, a disgusting dump. When told the price of the rooms, the boy had called the owner, who was a gentle woman, a grasping old bat. Olaf decided to **Appear** to the woman and apologize but that had been a mistake too. He had been flustered and got it wrong. At the sight of his sudden but incomplete **Appearance** the woman had screamed and slammed the door, which had **Passed Through** his foot and made him feel quite ill. By the time he recovered, Merrin had left. Relieved, Olaf had wandered off, unaware that he was half-**Appearing** to everyone and causing havoc. By the end of the day, safely back in the ghostly haven of the Hole in the Wall Tavern, Olaf had decided that he would never **Appear** to anyone again. It was madness.

Stanley scuttled up one of the many back stairs of the Palace. Although he had never actually been upstairs in the Palace before, as an ex–Message Rat, Stanley knew the layout backward—he had had to learn it as part of his higher exams. Avoiding the old ghost of a knight who was on guard—and who aimed a one-armed swipe at him with his sword—Stanley scuttled up the tapestry at the side of some big double doors. He pushed his way through the cobwebby rat-gap at the top of the wainscoting and looked down. It was a long drop on the other side. Stanley waited for a moment, gathering his courage for the jump. Far below, sitting by the fire, was Jenna Heap, Princess and heir to the Castle. Beside her lay a much-thumbed note.

Stanley could not read it from that distance, but Jenna already knew it by heart. The note read:

Delivered by hand from the Wizard Tower by B. Catchpole
Received at Palace: 7:30 A.M.
From: Septimus Heap, Apprentice to Marcia Overstrand,
ExtraOrdinary Wizard

Dear Jen,
    Can you meet me at Marcellus's place at midday today?
Have just had a note from him! It is really good. I think he
has remembered some things at last. He has some stuff of
Nicko's to show us and he says that there may be a way for
him to come back!!!! See you there.
Love,
Septimus xxxx

Jenna was so excited that she could hardly keep still, let alone wait for midday. After yet another depressing breakfast with Sarah Heap, she had escaped to her room and was trying to do something useful to pass the hours. Unaware that she was being watched by a teetering rat, she was determinedly reading a large book.

Far above Jenna, Stanley took a deep breath and launched himself into space. He landed on Jenna's bed, bounced high into the air, thumped down onto her hearthrug and turned his ankle. "Oof!" he grunted, rolling forward and banging his head on the coal-scuttle.

Jenna leaped to her feet. "Stanley?" she gasped.

Stanley jumped up, winced and saluted. "At your service, Your Majesty."

"Not 'Your Majesty' yet," said Jenna. "Not until I am crowned with *that*." She made a face and pointed to a very beautiful but simple crown sitting on a red velvet cushion on the mantelpiece.

"Ooh," said Stanley, a little overawed. "It looks very heavy. Wouldn't like to wear *that* all day."

"Neither would I," said Jenna. "And I don't intend to just yet either. You know, Stanley, you always turn up when I least expect it. How are you—and Dawnie?"

"I am fine," the rat replied. "I am sure that Dawnie is fine too. She makes a point of it, after all."

"Ah," said Jenna. "Things between you not good then?"

"No, Your Maj. But it was an amicable separation. Well,

when I left I thought she looked kind of amicable. Possibly. Although she was eating a pie at the time, which always puts her in a good mood."

"Oh, I'm really sorry, Stanley."

"I'm not," replied the rat tersely.

"So, er . . . what are you doing with your life now?" asked Jenna.

"Keeping busy. Can't complain. Visiting old friends, catching up, networking, you know how it is. Just done a bit of freelance actually—a mission to the Badlands."

Jenna shuddered. "Horrible place," she said.

"I'm with you there, Your Maj. And I wouldn't like to bump into those that live there on a dark night. Actually, I'd rather not bump into them at all. But I'm making my base here now; no place like home, as they say. And I have a little proposition of my own to put to you, if you wouldn't mind hearing me out. If you're not too busy, that is. But if you are I can come back later. No doubt the trials and tribulations of young Queenshipdom and royaltyness bear heavy on your youthful shoulders and I—"

"I'm only reading, Stanley. I'm meeting someone later—it's really important and I want to find out as much as I can before I go."

"Very wise. Always go prepared. Big book you've got there. Not a great one for reading myself."

"It is rather big." Jenna sighed. "And complicated, too. It's about Time."

"Yes, that's what I was thinking. It's about time I came back and—"

"No, that's what I am reading about. Time."

"Quite. Been away far too long. But like I said, I have a proposition to put to you that may indeed be to your advantage. Shall I go on?"

Jenna smiled. "Well, you generally do," she said, closing her book and putting it down on the rug. "Sit down. Perch on my book here."

"Ah. Thank you, Your Maj, but I think better on my feet," he said. "Now, my proposition is that if you would be so good as to let me reopen the East Gate Lookout Tower and reinstitute the much missed Official Castle Message Rat Service, I would be honored to offer you the first year's subscription at premium discount rates—"

"The Palace always got it free before," said Jenna.

"Really? Well free for the first year, then. I would also

throw in your own personal bodyguard rat and priority service at all times."

"Fine," said Jenna. "Go ahead."

Stanley sat down on the book. "You sure?" he asked.

"Yes. We could use the Message Rat Service; it's really missed. But where you'll find the rats I don't know. They've all disappeared. You're the first one I've seen in a long time."

Stanley jumped to his feet and saluted again—a habit he had recently picked up from an old ship's rat in the Port. "No problem," he said. "It takes a rat to find a rat. I'll keep you informed, Your Maj. Your bodyguard will be dispatched ASAP ohcrumbsyou'vegotacat." From underneath Jenna's bed a small, scraggy orange cat had emerged. Although the cat was not much bigger than Stanley, there was a steely glint in its blue eyes that the rat did not like the look of. Not one bit. Stanley, who never forgot a cat, was sure he had seen it somewhere before.

"Oh, well, yes. I'm taking care of him for someone. Calm, Ullr," said Jenna, noticing the cat was getting reading to pounce.

"I'll have to rescind the bodyguard offer," said Stanley, backing away. "Not with a cat in residence. Can't put my staff at risk."

Jenna picked up Ullr and held him tight. "Don't worry," she said. "Ullr's the best bodyguard I could wish for."

Stanley eyed the cat. "Bit on the small side for a bodyguard, isn't it?" he asked. Ullr unsheathed his claws and tried to wriggle out of Jenna's grasp. Stanley backed away hurriedly. "I'll be off, then, Your Maj. And thank you. Good-bye."

Jenna jumped up and let Stanley out of the door. "It's okay, Sir Hereward," she told the ghost who was about to aim another swipe at the rat. "He's a friend."

Stanley scampered along the corridor, leaped nimbly down the sweeping Palace stairs and, head held high, walked out of the main Palace door with Jenna's words ringing in his ears. He was a *friend*. A friend of Royalty.

If Dawnie could see him now.

✢7✢
IN CHARGE

Beetle, *Front Office and Inspection* Clerk at Number Thirteen Wizard Way, home of the **Magykal** Manuscriptorium and Spell Checkers Incorporated, was not having a good day. It was a blustery, rainy Monday morning and Jillie Djinn, the Chief Hermetic Scribe, had left him in charge.

At first Beetle had been thrilled. It was a real honor, since Miss Jillie Djinn chose her deputies carefully, even if it was only for an hour, and she usually gave the job to the most senior scribe. But that morning she had fixed Beetle with her disconcerting stare—which always made him wonder what he had done wrong—and said, "Beetle, you're in charge. Anyone comes about the job, fill out the form and I'll see them this afternoon. Back in an hour. No earlier. No later." Then, with a rustle of her dark blue silk robes Miss Djinn had bustled out of the door and was gone.

Beetle had closed the door against the wind and whistled a long low note. Resisting the urge to run amok yelling, "It's mine, all *mine!*" he had contented himself with peering into the Manuscriptorium itself and checking that all seemed well. It did. Twenty scribes—one short of the usual number—sat perched at their high desks under twenty dim pools of light, their pens scratching away, copying out various spells, formulas, charms, enchantments, indentures, diatribes, licences, permits, proxies and anything else that was needed by the Wizards—or indeed anyone in the Castle who had a few silver pennies to spare.

Beetle celebrated his temporary promotion by sitting on his swivel chair and spinning around and around in circles—which was not allowed—while practicing his I'm-in-charge look. For five heady minutes everything had been wonderful—and then it all went wrong.

Beetle was amazed at how much trouble could cram itself into such a short space of time. It began when a tall, thin boy dressed in a shabby black tunic and travel-stained cloak came into the front office, made Jillie Djinn's new—and extremely irritating—Daily Customer Counter click over to number three and demanded to see the Chief Hermetic Scribe.

"She's out," said Beetle snappily, deciding he did not like the look of the boy at all. "*I'm* in charge."

The boy looked Beetle up and down and sniggered. "Oh, yeah," he said. "I *don't* think."

"Obviously *not*," replied Beetle, surprised to hear himself sounding remarkably like Marcia Overstrand for a moment. Remembering, a little late, that a member of the Manuscriptorium must be civil at all times, Beetle hurriedly asked, "Well, um, can *I* help you?"

"I doubt it." The boy shrugged.

Beetle took a deep breath and counted to ten. Then he said, "I'm sure I can do something if you tell me what you want."

"I want that scribe's job," the boy replied.

Beetle was shocked. "The *scribe's* job?" he asked.

"Yeah," said the boy. He grinned, pleased at the effect he had had. "Like I said, the scribe's job."

"But—but do you have any qualifications?" Beetle stammered.

In reply, the boy leaned forward and clicked his finger and thumb in Beetle's face. A flicker of black flame appeared from the tip of his thumb. "*That's* my qualification," the boy said.

Beetle sat down in his chair with a bump. He'd heard about **Darke** tricks, although he'd never actually seen one before. It had not escaped his notice that the boy was wearing what he assumed to be a cheap copy of the fabled Two-Faced **Darke** Ring. The boy was obviously one of those weird kids who thought that if they dressed in black and bought pretend **Darke** trinkets from Gothyk Grotto in The Ramblings, they were the next Apprentice to old DomDaniel.

Beetle blamed Jillie Djinn. She had, much to his disapproval, put a notice up on the door to the Manuscriptorium a few weeks ago, seeking a new scribe. Beetle had objected, saying it would be an invitation to all kinds of weird people to apply. But Miss Djinn had insisted.

To Beetle's relief, up until that moment no one had applied for the job. He had been busy trying to persuade the notoriously stingy Miss Djinn to pay for an advertisement in *The Scribes and Scriveners Journal*. That morning he had, in fact, left a copy of their special-offer reduced rates on her desk. But now it looked as if his worst fears had come true.

With a sigh, Beetle got out the standard Manuscriptorium job application form, licked the end of his pencil and asked, "Name?"

"Septimus Heap," said the boy.

"Don't be stupid," said Beetle.

"No one calls me stupid!" the boy shouted. "*No one*. Got that?"

"Okay, okay," said Beetle. "But you are *not* Septimus Heap."

"How do *you* know?" the boy said with a sneer.

"Because I *know* Septimus Heap. And he's not you. No *way*."

The boy's dark eyes flashed angrily. "Well, that's where you're wrong. *I* know who I am. *You* don't. So where it says 'name' on your little form you can write down 'Septimus Heap.'"

"No."

Beetle and the boy stared each other down. The boy looked

away first. "Yeah, well," he said. "I *was* called that. Once."

Beetle decided to humor the boy in case he suddenly lost it—not that Beetle was concerned about coming off worse in a fight. Although the boy was a little taller than him, he was thin and had a weak look about him, whereas Beetle was sturdy and powerfully built. But Beetle did not want the front office trashed, particularly while *he* was in charge. "So what are you called now?" he asked quietly.

The boy did not answer right away. His black eyes, which Beetle noticed were flecked with green, flickered around like a lizard's. It seemed to Beetle as if the boy was making up a name on the spot.

Beetle was right. Merrin needed a name fast and he wanted something special. He didn't like being Merrin Meredith; it didn't feel like him. Besides, it was a stupid name. Meredith was a *girl's* name and he thought that Merrin was plain silly. He needed something scary. Quickly, Merrin chose the two scariest people he had known in his life—DomDaniel and the Hunter.

Beetle was getting impatient. "So what's your *name*?" he asked.

"Dom—er, I mean, Daniel."

"*DomDaniel?*" Beetle shook his head.

"Don't be *stupid*. I said Daniel. *Daniel*. Got that?"

Beetle concentrated on keeping calm and said, "Daniel what?"

"Daniel *Hunter*."

"Okay. I'll put down 'Daniel Hunter,' all right?" asked Beetle with exaggerated patience.

"Yeah."

"You sure? Don't want to change your mind again, do you?"

"Look, it's my *name*, right? So put it down," the boy said with a snarl.

Deciding that the best thing to do was to get rid of the boy as soon as he could, Beetle hurriedly filled out the rest of the form. He made no comment when the boy told him he had had at least ten years experience as an Apprentice to two Wizards and a working knowledge of White Witchcraft. Beetle did not believe a word of what the boy said and would have written down that he had flown to the Moon and back if it would have sped up his departure.

At last the form was filled in. With some relish, Beetle viciously impaled it on the spike of paperwork awaiting Jillie Djinn's return.

The boy showed no sign of leaving.

"That's it," said Beetle. "You can go now."

"So when do I come for my interview?"

Bother, thought Beetle. Merrin watched him closely as he looked through the Daily Diary, a hefty ledger that lived on Beetle's desk and was his job to keep up to date. "Two thirty-three precisely," he said. "Not a minute early, not a minute late."

"See ya then," said the boy with a smirk.

"Look forward to it," replied Beetle coolly. "Allow me to show you out." Beetle got up, held the door open and stared at Merrin until he was gone. Then he slammed the door with a *bang* that shook the office. At that the Rogue Spell Alarm sounded.

The Rogue Spell Alarm was designed to be particularly annoying—a series of loud screeches to the accompaniment of shrill, unremitting bell. Unsure whether it was another **Darke** trick or if there really *was* a rogue spell on the loose, Beetle sent four reluctant scribes down to the basement to check it out. But despite some serious thumping sounds echoing up from the basement, the alarm did not stop. Beetle was faced with a rebellion from the remaining scribes, who were trying to get on with the day's work. Exasperated, he sent two of the more beefy scribes down as reinforcements and suggested that the others find some earplugs. This was not received well.

At that point, a great crash shook the front office. Fearsome growls and thuds could be heard through the reinforced door that led from the office to the Wild Book Store. Beetle took a deep breath and peered through the inspection flap in the door. A big fight had broken out. The air was thick with fur and feathers. Beetle knew he had to get in there fast, before the whole bookstore got trashed. As he tentatively opened the door, a large—and very hairy—Spider Almanac tried to force its way out.

Unfortunately Beetle asked Foxy, one of the more highly strung scribes, to help him hold the door. It was not a good choice. Foxy screamed and fainted, knocking over two huge bottles of indelible ink, which spilled their entire contents over two weeks' worth of Jillie Djinn's calculations that Beetle was supposed to be copying for her.

Beetle put his head around the door to the Manuscriptorium and yelled, "**Erase** Spell! Quick!" Then, taking a deep breath, he plunged into the Wild Book Store.

Ten minutes later a disheveled, sore, but successful Beetle emerged from the store. Foxy was still flat out on the floor, being stepped over by the scribes as they hunted desperately for an **Erase** Spell before Jillie Djinn returned. The Rogue Spell Alarm was still ringing. And Beetle, who had taken his own advice and had two cork earplugs with twirly handles sticking out of his ears, was nursing some nasty scratches from an ambush by a Foryx Field Guide. It could not, thought Beetle, get any worse.

It could.

There was a sudden *ping* and the door counter clicked over to four. In strode Marcia Overstrand, ExtraOrdinary Wizard; her purple cloak flying in the wind, her dark curly hair wet and windswept from the cold spring rain. Marcia frowned at the shrieking of the Alarm, which drilled into her ears and seemed to meet somewhere in the soft and delicate middle of her head.

"Beetle!" she yelled. "What on earth is going on?"

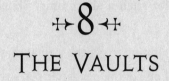

THE VAULTS

Tℏere was something about Marcia Overstrand that always seemed to fill the space she was in—and then some. Beetle instinctively stepped back to give the ExtraOrdinary Wizard more room.

"What on *earth* is this *awful din?*" Marcia shouted.

"She's not here," replied Beetle, who thought Marcia had asked, "Where on earth is the awful Djinn?"

"*What?*"

Beetle glanced desperately at the clock—had Jillie Djinn only been gone for such a short time? "Back in thirty minutes!" he yelled.

Marcia was beginning to get the feeling that she had stepped into the middle of one of the new-style plays that Septimus had taken her to see in the small Theater in The Ramblings. "And what *have* you got growing out of your ears?" she asked.

Beetle suddenly remembered his earplugs and pulled them out with a faint pop. "Sorry," he said, raising his voice above the Alarm, which chose that very moment to stop.

"No need to shout," said Marcia.

"No. Er, sorry," Beetle stammered. "Can I help you, Madam Marcia? I'm, um, in charge until Miss Djinn gets back."

"Oh, *good*." Marcia smiled as if relieved, which surprised Beetle.

"Been a bit of a morning," he said. He tried unsuccessfully to smooth down his thick black hair, which always stuck out at odd angles when he got flustered.

"So I see," said Marcia. "Well, it happens to us all."

"Does it?" said Beetle, surprised.

"All the time." Marcia sighed. "Now, Beetle, unfortunately I need to go down to the Vaults."

Feeling tremendously relieved that Marcia was taking things so well, Beetle led the ExtraOrdinary Wizard into the Manuscriptorium. As they stepped through the door there was a flash of green light. A huddle of scribes leaped back with a shout and then craned forward to see the results of their **Erase** Spell. A loud shriek came from the middle of the huddle. "Argh, my feet! Look at my *feet!*"

A collection of gasps rose from the group.

"I *told* you that spell was moldy but you wouldn't listen."

"Hey, those are *big* toadstools!"

"Yeah, *massive.*"

"Now your feet look like they smell, Partridge."

A loud laugh come from the group; then one of the scribes noticed Marcia standing behind them. He nudged the scribe next to him and seconds later an embarrassed silence fell.

"Good morning, Scribes," said Marcia.

"Good morning, Madam Overstrand," the scribes chorused like good schoolchildren.

"Having trouble?" asked Marcia with a smile.

The scribes nodded sheepishly.

Beetle was amazed at Marcia's good temper. He did not realize that Marcia was particularly fond of him ever since he had helped her with a difficult episode in her life not long before, which had involved an aggressive bunch of bones. Beetle watched admiringly as Marcia, with a flick of her fingers and a flash of **Magykal** purple light, wiped out the impressive crop of toadstools that had sprung up from Partridge's feet and burst through his boots in a spectacular array of red, orange and lurid yellow. Leaving Partridge gazing at his boots, which now had a random selection of holes dotted over them, Marcia **Erased** the spilled ink, **ReFilled** the ink bottles and **Restored** Jillie Djinn's calculations.

Amid the chorus of grateful "thank-yous" from the scribes—particularly from Partridge—Marcia stepped over the recumbent form of Foxy. Beetle showed her through a concealed door in the bookshelves that lined the Manuscriptorium, then he followed Marcia into a candle-lit, winding passage. The passage was long and sloped steeply downward until it came to a flight of stone steps. At the foot of these was a huge studded iron door—and the belligerent Ghost of the Vaults.

The Ghost of the Vaults was one of the Ancients—ghosts over five hundred years old—who inhabited the older parts of the Castle. But unlike all the other Ancients, he was not

particularly faded and his voice was still strong. He had a hec-
toring manner and was one of the most unpleasant ghosts in
the Castle. The Ghost of the Vaults refused to tell anyone his
name, although his old-fashioned Chief Hermetic Scribe
robes were somewhat of a giveaway. Marcia was well aware
who he was and Beetle had figured it out too—the ghost was
the very first Chief Scribe ever to hold office, Tertius Fume.
But although Beetle had searched for information about
Tertius Fume, he had found nothing—except a snippet hidden in a damp old tome that he had rescued from propping
up the rotten end of a bookshelf in a Manuscriptorium storeroom. The book, which Beetle guessed was part of an old
series for children, was called:

One Hundred and One Questions
You Have Always Wanted to Ask About: HOTEP-RA!
(Our Castle's very first ExtraOrdinary Wizard)
Deluxe edition with answers

Although the last few pages of answers were eaten away by
mold, Beetle had found out a lot of things he hadn't known.
One of the questions was: *Did Hotep-Ra have a best friend?*

The answer intrigued Beetle: *Yes, he did!!* (The book was much given to exclamation marks.) *But, boys and girls, he was not a good friend. He was an old friend who came to visit from far away, and his name was Tertius Fume. At first Hotep-Ra was pleased to see him. They had lots of fun! Hotep-Ra gave his best friend a house to live in on Wizard Way. Tertius Fume was very clever and soon his house became the Manuscriptorium! But although Hotep-Ra's best friend was clever, he was not nice! (Remember, boys and girls, that it is much better to be nice than clever.) Soon Tertius Fume was doing bad things that Hotep-Ra did not know about and so he came to a Bad End!*

That was the only place Beetle had seen Tertius Fume's name actually written down—apart from heading the list of all the Chief Hermetic Scribes inscribed on the honor board in the front office. It was as if everything about him had been expunged.

Tertius Fume glared at Marcia and Beetle as they came down the steps. He was not a pleasant-looking ghost. His deep black eyes were narrow slits in his pale face, which sported a long gray goatee. The ghost's thin white lips were drawn back into a mocking snarl and moved, Beetle realized, even when he was not talking. It looked as if he were chewing the cud.

"Password . . ." said Tertius Fume. His deep, hollow-sounding voice echoed off the damp stone walls and made the hairs on the back of Beetle's neck stand up. The ghost gave him the creeps.

Marcia sighed as if expecting trouble. "Tentacle," she said.

"No."

"Stop messing around," said Marcia. "Of course it is."

"Why?" Tertius Fume leaned back against the door, folded his arms and regarded Marcia with a superior air. Beetle, who was not a violent boy, felt like giving him a good kick.

"I have not the faintest idea why," said Marcia irritably, "but that is not the point. One doesn't have to know why; a password just *is*. Now let us through. Tentacle. *Tent-a-cle*."

"No. I've changed it."

"You can't change a password without clearing it first with the Password Committee, of which *I* am Chairwoman. And you haven't. Tentacle it was and Tentacle it remains."

But the great iron door to the Vaults stayed firmly closed. Tertius Fume looked at Marcia with an amused expression and started examining his ghostly fingernails as if Marcia was no longer of any consequence at all. Beetle began to think that there was some truth in the old story that Tertius Fume had been assassinated by a group of disaffected scribes.

"Very well," said Marcia. "You leave me no choice but to **OverRide** the password. Stand back, Beetle."

"Ah. Just testing," said Tertius Fume a little hurriedly. "You've passed. In you go now, and don't mess anything up."

"Idiot," said Marcia under her breath.

Beetle took a couple of lamps from the rack outside the door and lit them. Marcia gave the door a bad-tempered shove. It creaked open and the smell of damp earth and musty paper wafted into the stairwell. Inside the Vaults, Marcia locked the door and did an **Alarm** on it. If Tertius Fume was going to sidle up and eavesdrop she wanted some warning.

Marcia was still seething about the ghost. "He doesn't like women, that's his trouble," she told Beetle. "He *never* did that with Alther, but ever since I took over he's done that every time. *Every time.* It drives me crazy."

"We just call him Old Goat-Face," said Beetle.

"Do you?" Marcia laughed. "Well, I don't suppose he would like *that.* Now, Beetle, I would like *The Live Plan of What Lies Beneath*, please."

"Oh, right." Beetle sounded surprised. "Um, let me get you a seat." Beetle placed the lamps on a great lump of a table that

looked as though it was carved out of stone, and rubbed the
dust off the seat of the old chair beside it with the end of his
sleeve. Marcia sneezed. She sat down and wrapped her purple
cloak tightly around her against the damp air of the Vaults.
"Oh, and Beetle—could you bring the most recent
ExtraOrdinary Apprentice Urn?"

"No problem. I'll be back in a sec."

Marcia watched the flame from his lamp guttering in the
drafts that blew through the ancient ventilation system, as Beetle
disappeared into the farthest reaches of the Vaults. Beetle knew
his way around the Vaults with his eyes closed—something that
he had actually done for his Intermediate Manuscriptorium
Management Exam—and he was back quickly with his arms
clasped around a huge lapis lazuli blue and gold urn. The lamp
hung from a spare finger and on top of the urn a long cylinder
wrapped in cloth was balanced precariously.

Extremely carefully, Beetle set the urn and the cylinder
down on the table, and he placed his lamp beside it. In the
light of the flame the lapis lazuli gleamed a beautiful deep dark
blue and the streaks of gold that ran through it shone with a
warm glow.

"Would you like to take these up to the Hermetic

Chamber?" Beetle asked Marcia.

"No, thank you, Beetle," Marcia replied. "I have no wish to go to the Chamber. In fact I am glad that Miss Djinn is not here. I would like to speak to you in confidence."

"Me?" gasped Beetle.

"Indeed. In your capacity as Inspection Clerk. And because I trust you."

"Oh. Thank you." Beetle flushed.

"Of course I trust your Chief Hermetic Scribe *implicitly*," Marcia said. "But she does have a tendency to complicate matters, if you know what I mean?"

Beetle nodded. He knew exactly what Marcia meant.

"Would you take out the Plan, please?"

Beetle unwound the discolored cloth from the long silver tube. The end of the tube was sealed with purple wax, which was stamped with the imprint of the Akhu Amulet. The amulet, which hung around Marcia's neck, had been the symbol and source of the power of the ExtraOrdinary Wizards since Hotep-Ra himself.

From her ExtraOrdinary Wizard gold and platinum belt, Marcia unclipped what appeared to be a long silver lozenge. She muttered something under her breath and, like the claws of a cat unsheathing, a shiny, slightly curved silver blade silently shot out. Beetle watched, fascinated, as Marcia ran the razor-sharp blade around the wax on the end of the tube so that it parted like butter. She drew out a thick roll of paper and unrolled it. From a shelf under the table Beetle took four ornate gold paperweights with silver handles and placed one on each corner.

Marcia took out the tiny spectacles that she used for close work. She perused the complex diagram, running her finger along the path of the Ice Tunnels, muttering to herself. Beetle had politely stepped away but Marcia beckoned him over. "You know the two tunnel ghosts—the brothers who were trapped in the Emergency Freeze and have been looking for a way out ever since?"

"Eldred and Alfred Stone?"

"That's them. Well, apparently they *have* found a way out. Alther—you know the ghost of Alther Mella? You're too young to remember but he was our last ExtraOrdinary Wizard." Beetle nodded. He had met Alther many times recently while Septimus had been learning to use the Flyte Charm. "Well, Alther saw them a couple of nights ago."

"Actually," said Beetle, "now I think about it, I haven't seen them in the tunnels for some time."

"Really? This is not good news, Beetle. Not good news at all . . . *aha*. Now come and have a look. There is something going on here." Marcia stabbed a long finger at a fuzzy area on what appeared to be a tangle of worms, snaking and folding in and out of one another.

Beetle had never seen a Live Plan before. As he looked he was sure he saw something on the edge of the Plan move.

"Did you see that?" gasped Marcia. "It *moved*."

"It's doing it again," said Beetle. "I think it's the hatch under old Weasal's place."

"I *thought* you'd know what you were looking at," said Marcia. "Beetle, I need you to go and check this out. Urgently. That hatch and this fuzzy bit here . . . wherever *that* is."

Beetle whistled between his teeth. "That's under the old Alchemie Chamber."

Marcia frowned. "I think," she said, "that it might be a good idea if you take Septimus with you. There's safety in numbers. I'll send him over. You do understand that this is highly confidential, don't you?"

Beetle nodded.

"I particularly do not want the Ghost of the Vaults to know.

He is not to be trusted. You know who he is, I suppose?"

"Tertius Fume?"

"Quite. I thought you would have figured it out. Septimus did too." Marcia smiled fondly. "Very well, you can put the Plan away now. It's not good to have it out in the light for too long."

Beetle began rolling up the Plan. "Do you still want the Apprentice Urn?" he asked.

Marcia snapped out of her thoughts. "Oh! I'd quite forgotten. Yes, please, Beetle."

Marcia unsealed the urn and plunged her arm deep inside. She drew out a roll of vellum tied with purple and green ribbons and sealed with purple sealing wax, which also bore the imprint of the Akhu Amulet. Marcia checked the signature written along the length of the roll. Septimus's young, wobbly writing was unmistakable, but Marcia was amazed how it had changed in such a short time. Now, Septimus's signature was sprawling and confident—if a little overcomplicated. Satisfied that she had the right urn, Marcia replaced the roll of indentures. She took out from her ExtraOrdinary Wizard belt a beautiful tiny gold and silver arrow. For a moment she held it in her palm and both she and Beetle gazed at it.

"Sep's **Flyte Charm**," breathed Beetle.

"Half right, Beetle," corrected Marcia. "It *is* the **Flyte Charm** but it does *not* belong to Septimus. The **Flyte Charm** is one of the Ancient Charms; it belongs to no one." With that she dropped the **Charm** into the depths of the urn.

"Oh!" said Beetle. "Um . . . did you mean to do that?"

"I most certainly *did*," said Marcia. "Septimus needs to settle down and get on with his work. Recently he has been rushing around all over the place—which is, I understand, one of the effects of having the **Flyte Charm**. People become unsettled, always wanting to be off. Of course, he *says* he's been seeing his mother, but Sarah tells me she hasn't seen him for ages and I believe her. The **Flyte Charm** can stay here until he is old enough to handle it. It is *not* a toy. You may reseal now, Beetle."

One of the skills Beetle had learned in the Manuscriptorium was when to say nothing. He could tell that right then was just such a moment. He took the candle from his lamp and set it under a small tripod with a tiny brass saucepan perched upon it. From a drawer in the table he took out a knife and a great chunk of purple sealing wax, then he began to shave off some wax, allowing the shavings to drop into the pan. Marcia and Beetle watched the wax slowly melt into a dark purple puddle. Very carefully, Beetle poured half the wax over the end of the Plan and the other half so that it covered the ridge between the top of the urn and its gold stopper. When the wax was nearly set Marcia took off the Akhu Amulet and pressed it deep into the wax, leaving the unmistakable dragon imprint on the seals.

Marcia watched Beetle disappear into the depths of the Vaults. Somewhere surprisingly distant, she heard the faint scrape of lapis lazuli against stone as Beetle pushed the urn back into its place on a dark shelf far away from prying eyes, then the click of the lock as Beetle laid *The Live Plan of What Lies Beneath* back in its ebony chest.

"A *successful* visit?" said Tertius Fume grumpily as they left the Vaults. "I do hope you found nothing too *Alarming*?"

"I *knew* he'd try to listen," Marcia spluttered indignantly as she followed Beetle back along the zigzag passage. "Serves him right. I put a **Sting** in the **Alarm**."

Beetle chuckled. You don't mess with Marcia, he thought.

✠9✠
A Room with a View

A bored **Thing** *slowly chewed* the tops of its fingers, pulling at long bits of skin with its blackened teeth. It glared at its Master—a waste of space in the opinion of the **Thing**—and cursed its ill fortune at having been **Engendered** for such a fool. Its Master, blissfully unaware of the waves of loathing coming his way, was also busy chewing.

Merrin was leaning nonchalantly against the old clock tower opposite the Palace, eating a licorice snake, enjoying his first ever taste of a sweet. After his contretemps with Beetle in the Manuscriptorium, Merrin had wandered back through The Ramblings and had discovered Ma Custard's All-Day-All-Night Sweet Shop, tucked away on the far side of the Castle down Sugar Cone Cut beside the Old Dock. While the Thing and its sack of bones had loitered outside, creating an oppressive haze that put off other customers, Merrin had spent ages gazing at all the sweets. Ma Custard, who was used to people dithering for hours between lemon lumps and ferocious fizzes, had let him linger. Eventually Merrin had chosen the licorice snake because it reminded him of the black snake that Simon Heap kept, and Merrin had always wondered what snake tasted like.

Merrin savored his last sticky mouthful of licorice. He stared up at the windows that ran the length of the Palace—a long, low, mellow old building—and began to count them. It was then that the idea came to him. Why waste his money on renting a room? Just think how many licorice snakes he could buy with a whole week's rent. Anyway, he belonged in the Castle—it was his right to live anywhere he wanted. *So there.*

And where better than the Palace? Merrin swallowed the snake's tail with a decisive gulp. Problem solved.

Merrin was good at finding ways into places—especially places he should not go. So it was easy for him to sneak unnoticed along the narrow high-walled alleyway that led around the outside of the Palace grounds to the small door in the wall of the Palace kitchen garden. The door was open as usual. Sarah Heap liked to leave it open so her friend Sally Mullin could drop by and have a midmorning chat before she got back to the lunchtime rush in her café.

Although Merrin planned to one day have the entire Palace at his disposal—just as DomDaniel's deputy, the Supreme Custodian, once had—for now things were, regrettably, a little different. Closely followed by the Thing, he slipped in through the open door and found himself in the kitchen garden.

Merrin liked the kitchen garden; it appealed to his sense of order. It was the one place where Sarah Heap was tidy. The garden was bounded on all sides by a high redbrick wall. It was neatly laid out with close-mown grass paths running between well-tended beds where Sarah was in the process of planting early lettuce, peas, beans and all kinds of vegetables that

Merrin did not even recognize, let alone dream of eating. The paths all led to a large well in the center of the garden, where Sarah drew the water for her plants. At the far end of the garden was a low brick arch, which Merrin could see led into a covered way.

Keeping close to the wall, Merrin carefully walked the grass paths, resisting the urge to count the newly sewn lettuce seedlings. As he got near the arch, he could not believe his luck. At the end of the covered way was a half open door that led straight into the Palace. His new home beckoned.

It was then that Merrin felt *something* breathing down his neck. He had had the feeling of being followed for a while. He had felt it outside the Grateful Turbot, again when he had come out of the Manuscriptorium and particularly outside Ma Custard's—something had been Waiting for him, but every time he had turned around he had seen nothing. But now Merrin was sure. He spun around and caught the Thing unawares.

"Got you!" he yelled and then clapped his hand over his mouth in horror. Someone would hear. Merrin and the Thing froze, staring at each other, listening for footsteps. None came.

"You *stupid* Thing, I told you to look for my cloak," hissed Merrin. "What are you *doing* here?"

"I am come to help you, Master," the Thing replied in a low, mournful whisper.

"*Just* you?" asked Merrin suspiciously.

"Just me, Master," replied the Thing dolefully.

Merrin felt relieved. "Well, you can wait outside. I'm not having you tiptoeing behind me in the Palace—ohcrumbs-whydidyoubring*those*?" Merrin had caught sight of the sack of bones.

"For *yoooooou*, Master," said the Thing in its low, insinuating voice.

Merrin stared at the Thing. He hated the way he could not quite see the Thing's expression; it made him think it was mocking him. But Merrin knew that, whatever the Thing might think, it had to obey him. "I don't want those disgusting bones," he told the Thing. "You can . . ." Merrin cast around for somewhere to put them. His eyes lighted on the well. "You can chuck them down the well."

The Thing looked horrified but all Merrin saw was a faint flash of red from the lizard eyes. Leaving the Thing staring at its precious sack of bones in disbelief, Merrin slipped through the arch and crept along the covered way. He flitted from pillar to pillar until he had reached the half open door. The door looked as if it could have a nasty squeak, so he squeezed through the gap into the cool, musty shade of the old building. And there he was—*inside the Palace.*

Not long after, Sarah Heap came into the garden through a small gate near the old kitchens. She still wore Jannit's battered sailor's boater. Sarah rather liked it, as it made her feel quite jaunty and carefree, which was something she had not felt for some time. But as she walked past the well on her way to her greenhouse to collect the seedlings for that day's planting, a horrible feeling of gloom came over her. She stopped in her tracks—something **Darke** was by the well.

Sarah Heap had not been interested in **Magyk** for many years. She had trained as a healer and thought she had left **Magyk** far behind her. But she still had the telltale **Magykal** green eyes and knew quite enough to do a **See**. So when, to her horror, Sarah **Saw** the **Thing** perched on the edge of *her* well— her beautiful clean, clear, pure well—with a sack of something **Darke**, all Sarah's **Magyk** came flooding back to her. She looked the **Thing** in the eye—as much as that was possible with its flickering, evasive eyes—and chanted very slowly:

"Pure and clean this well shall stay
Shielded *from* **Darke** *for a year and a day."*

The **Thing** glared angrily at Sarah, but there was nothing it could do. It heaved the sack of bones over its shoulder and sloped off. Sarah waited until the **Thing** had left the kitchen garden, then the awfulness of what she had seen suddenly overcame her and she ran, trembling, back inside to sit with Ethel.

The **Thing** waited until Sarah had disappeared into the Palace, then returned to the kitchen garden. Unable now to put the bones where it had been instructed it chose instead the garden shed, where it carefully placed the sack among the piles of flowerpots and general garden clutter. Then the **Thing** loped up to the half-open door that led into the Palace and folded itself deep into a leafy bush to wait for its Master's eventual exit.

The Palace was not what Merrin had expected. It smelled funny—damp and old with musty cooking smells lurking in the corners. And as Merrin's eyes got used to the dimness, he could see it didn't look that great either. The plaster on the walls was cracked and crumbling and where he had brushed against it there was white dust all over his black cloak. Ahead of him was a seemingly endless stone-flagged corridor, known as the Long Walk. It was as wide as a small road, with a threadbare red carpet running along the middle. Warily, Merrin set off. Every few yards a door opened off the corridor and at first he stopped at each one, half expecting someone to come out. But now the Palace was occupied only by Sarah, Silas and Jenna Heap—and Maxie, the wolfhound. Employing staff did not come naturally to Sarah; she preferred to do things herself. That morning the few Palace servants Sarah had taken on were elsewhere—the Cook was in the kitchens chatting to the Cleaner, the WashingUp Boy was dozing in the pantry and the HouseKeeper had a bad cold and had stayed home.

Soon Merrin realized that the place was deserted and he became braver. He wandered along, poking at the strange array of objects displayed along the Long Walk. There were statues of all shapes and sizes—of animals, people and the kind of weird creatures that Merrin often had bad dreams about. There were tall vases, stuffed tigers, an ancient chariot, petrified trees, shrunken heads, ships' figureheads and all kinds of clutter. Hanging on the walls were ancient portraits of long-dead Queens and Princesses and as Merrin glanced up at them he was sure their eyes followed him. He half expected one of them to reach out, tap him on the shoulder and ask him what he was doing.

But they didn't. No one did.

After a while Merrin came across a tattered and faded red velvet curtain that was looped back, beyond which he could see a steep and narrow flight of stairs twisting up into darkness. This was more like it. He wanted a room right at the top of the Palace—somewhere where he could hide away, make his plans and look down on all the comings and goings. Quickly Merrin slipped past the curtain. Soon he was tiptoeing up the creaky stairs, past damp and peeling wallpaper, pushing through long, looping cobwebs and once—to his horror—having his foot disappear through a patch of rotten wood into the empty space below.

At the top of the stairs Merrin negotiated a landing piled high with old empty chests, then up two more flights of stairs, until at last he reached the tangle of tiny attic rooms that ran the length of the Palace. This was where, back when the Palace had been full of servants and courtiers, the more impor-

tant servants had lived, but now the rooms lay empty and for-
lorn, inhabited by only a few of the less sociable ghosts of governesses, ladies' maids and footmen. Most Palace ghosts
preferred the lower floors, where there was a chance to meet
old friends, talk about how things were so much better in the
old days and maybe catch a glimpse of the Living Princess if
they were lucky.

Merrin chose one of the governess's rooms at the front. It
was small, but there was a bed, a table, a small closet and a
fireplace that still bore the dusty remains of the last fire in the
grate. The room had a mournful atmosphere, helped along by
the faded rose-covered wallpaper, but it suited Merrin, who
noticed neither.

Merrin, however, did *not* suit the occupant of the room.
The governess, who was wearing the long gray dress with a
red stripe around the hem that all governesses to the
Princesses used to wear, leaped to her feet. With a look of horror she watched Merrin walking around her precious, private
space as if he owned the place. Twice he nearly **Passed
Through** her foot—which was not surprising as she wore the
long, pointy shoes fashionable in her Time. By the time
Merrin had sat down on her bed, testing the springs by

bouncing like a naughty three-year-old, the governess was in great distress. With a rush of freezing air, she fled from the room, leaving him wondering why the door had suddenly slammed shut.

Merrin took off his backpack and one by one he laid his precious possessions on the small table underneath the little dormer window in descending order of size. He then changed his mind and laid them out alphabetically and—finally—in order of importance. It took a while but eventually from left to right there was:

1 dog-eared book titled: *The* **Darke** *Index* by
   T.F.F. (Deceased)
1 small, square ebony box inscribed *Sleuth*
1 Magog claw
1 bottle of flies (mostly dead)
Small tub of Wurm Slime
1 pair of pajamas
1 toothbrush
1 bar of soap

Everything in order, Merrin rubbed the grime from the

inside of the little window in his attic room and peered out
through the smeared circle. It was a great view—all the way
down the old Ceremonial Way. The Ceremonial Way was
deserted, as usual, but to the left he could see the Wizard
Way, the wind sending the cloaks and hats flapping and flying
of those who were scurrying along trying to stay in the shelter of the low, yellow stone buildings. And almost at the end
of the Way, on the left, Merrin could just make out the purple
door of the Manuscriptorium. And outside the door was that
Septimus Heap boy—the bright green Apprentice tunic gave
him away.

Merrin could hardly believe that a chance to continue the
Darkening had happened so soon—and so easily. Quickly he
opened *The **Darke** Index*, found the page and began the next
stage of ***Darkening** the Destiny of AnOther*. He fixed Septimus
in his gaze and positioned his thumb so that the left-hand face
of the ring was looking out the window. Then he began to
chant a long, slow incantation under his breath. Merrin saw
Septimus stop, look back and then glance down at his shoe as
if he had stepped in something. Merrin chuckled to himself.
That Septimus Heap boy had no idea what was going on—no
idea at all. Merrin was getting good at this **Darke** stuff. And

he was going to get a lot better.

An amazing feeling of power suddenly swept over Merrin and he laughed out loud. He was the Possessor of the Two-Faced Ring—he was *indestructible*. For the first time in his life he felt important. But what, right then, felt best of all was the fact that he had his own place, and *no one* knew where to find him. No one could come and drag him from his bed and demand that he learn his lessons or eat up his cabbage sandwich. He could stay in bed all day if he wanted to. In fact, he might just lie down for a bit now. He had not slept well at the Grateful Turbot; the bed had been lumpy and he had heard the sound of someone else breathing in the room. And the night before that he had hardly slept at all. Merrin yawned. There was a letter he was planning to write, but he'd do it later. He lay down on the governess's equally lumpy bed and fell fast asleep.

Merrin woke groggy and in a panic, unsure of the time. He looked out of the window. There was a large clock on the tower above the clock repair shop at the end of Wizard Way, and he breathed a sigh of relief. It was all right. He had half an hour until his interview. Quickly, he stuffed The **Darke** Index into his pocket, strode across the little room and pulled at the door. It was jammed. Merrin pulled again, harder. It was stuck fast.

Twenty-five minutes later and in a total panic, Merrin desperately gave one last, enormous heave on the door. It flew open and sent him hurtling back across the room. Bruised, he picked himself up and rushed out.

Not caring who heard or saw him, Merrin flew down the stairs. He was determined not to mess up this chance. He would get there on time, whatever it took. And whoever got in his way had better look out.

✣ I O ✣
DRAGON MANAGEMENT

Septimus Heap stepped off the rotating silver spiral stairs that had taken him down through the Wizard Tower from the ExtraOrdinary Wizard's rooms at the top to the entrance Hall. As he hurried across the Hall, he was not surprised to see a message saying GOOD MORNING, APPRENTICE, YOUR DRAGON IS AWAKE appear in the multicolored floor, for the floor always greeted him and seemed to know what was going on before he did.

The next greeting was less welcome. "Good morning, Apprentice," came a voice from the Old Spells cupboard next to the pair of massive silver doors guarding the entrance to the Wizard Tower. Septimus jumped—as he always did. The voice belonged to Boris Catchpole, demoted from failed Wizard to night porter after a Final Warning from Marcia. Boris Catchpole's voice always startled Septimus. It gave him flashbacks to his days in the Young Army when Catchpole had been, for a while, the dreaded Deputy Hunter.

"Oh! Good morning, Catchpole," Septimus replied. "Did you deliver my message to the Palace?"

"Indeed I did, Apprentice. Always at your service, ha-ha. And *how* may I *help* you this morning?" asked Catchpole, who was on a self-imposed efficiency drive, determined to get back his sub-Wizard status. Catchpole was a beanpole of a man who still wore his treasured blue Ordinary Wizard robes with his old sub-Wizard flashes on the sleeves. It had been just Catchpole's luck not only to be given a set of robes too short for him, but also to get them shrunk in the wash, which meant that two thin white legs stuck out from the hem of the robes before they finally reached the safety of Catchpole's boots.

Like an insecure giant heron, Catchpole skipped in front of Septimus saying, "Allow me to open the doors, Apprentice."

"I have the password, thank you," Septimus replied.

Catchpole hopped back. "Oh, yes, of *course* you do. Silly me. Well, if there's anything else I can do, *anything* . . ." He suddenly stopped, remembering that there was something he definitely did not want to do. He did *not* want to help with Spit Fyre's breakfast.

But Septimus—to Catchpole's relief—did not take him up on his offer. He just murmured the password and let the giant silver doors silently swing open to reveal a gray, blustery spring day splattered with stray drops of rain. Septimus wrapped his green woolen Apprentice cloak around himself and set off at a brisk pace down the big marble steps that led from the Wizard Tower into the Courtyard. He skirted the base of the Tower and headed for a newly built wooden shed, which was neatly tucked in against one of the huge buttresses. Then, very quietly, in the hope that Spit Fyre would not hear and get overexcited, he opened the door and slipped inside.

Septimus clicked his fingers. Two candles sprang into flame, brightening the gray morning light inside the shed and illuminating the interior, which consisted of three big tubs of oats, a barrel of skimmed milk delivered that morning, one tub of windfall apples and, crammed into an old sack, an assortment of pies and sausages, the leftovers from the Meat Pie and Sausage Cart—also delivered early that morning.

With the practiced air of someone who did this every day—weekdays, weekends, holidays and feast days, come rain or shine—Septimus got to work. From outside the shed he wheeled in a large empty wooden tub on the side of which was written in multicolored letters:

SPIT FYRE

DO NOT REMOVE

If found please return to the Wizard Tower Courtyard

Septimus started to fill the tub. He took hold of a long-handled shovel and began to scoop out great quantities of oats and throw them into his wheeled tub. When it was about one third of the way full he emptied the sack of meat pies and sausages into the oats and mixed them in well; then he added two big shovelfuls of the apples. Finally he heaved up the barrel of skimmed milk, unscrewed the top and upended it over the mixture. The milk tumbled out with a loud glugging noise. When it had all disappeared into the oat and sausage mix, Septimus plunged in the shovel and, with some difficulty, stirred the glutinous mix. By the time he had finished, the oats had soaked up the milk and had expanded to nearly fill the tub. Septimus took out the shovel, shook off a few clinging pieces of steak and apple and regarded the mixture with an air of satisfaction. It was now a grubby brown color flecked with bits of broken piecrust, smashed sausages and bruised apples. Perfect.

Septimus wheeled the tub out into the Courtyard and took off, the wheels clattering and jumping on the cobbles. As he expected, as soon as the tub hit the cobbles, a loud thudding echoed around the Courtyard walls and the ground under his feet shook as though a stampede of elephants were on its way. Spit Fyre, Septimus's almost full-grown dragon, was *hungry*.

A stampede of elephants might well have been easier to manage than Septimus's next task, which was to let Spit Fyre out of the Dragon Kennel—a long stone building with a line of small windows set in just under the eaves. Septimus had recently had the Wizard Workshop make up a new set of doors with a huge iron bar inside each one. The trick was to open them without getting himself, or any passing Wizard, trampled into the ground. Septimus had noticed that it had been quite some time since any Wizard had actually dared to pass by during Spit Fyre's breakfast time, particularly since the notorious episode of Catchpole being mistaken for a large meat pie (or was it a sausage?) and hurled into the breakfast tub by a well-aimed swipe of the dragon's tail.

Septimus left the breakfast tub at the foot of a wide ramp that led up to the barn doors of the Dragon Kennel. He tip-toed up the ramp in the vain hope that Spit Fyre would not notice him coming, which of course the dragon did. And as the doors reverberated to great thuds of Spit Fyre banging them with his nose, Septimus calmly placed his hand on the doors and said, "UnBar!" Deep inside the thick doors he felt the whirr and rumble of the bar retracting. He immediately leaped to one side. No sooner had Septimus safely cleared the ramp then the doors sprang open under the force of a dragon, who now weighed the equivalent of 1,264 seagulls.

His claws sending up showers of sparks as they scraped along the stones, Spit Fyre skidded to a halt in front of his breakfast tub and began siphoning up the contents. The noise reminded Septimus of the sound his bathwater made when he took the plug out, only a hundred times louder. Catchpole, who claimed to have seen the elusive bottomless whirlpool in Bleak Creek, said that when he closed his eyes, he was hard pressed to tell the difference between Bleak Creek and Spit Fyre eating his breakfast, although he thought that Spit Fyre was probably louder.

The dragon did not take long to finish his breakfast. He scraped the barrel clean with his long, green, rasping tongue; then he licked his lips appreciatively and sucked up the last few shreds of sausage that had stuck to his scales.

"Hello, Spit Fyre," said Septimus, careful to approach the dragon from the front as he had had a few narrow misses with Spit Fyre's powerful tail. The dragon snuffled a greeting and put his head down so that his great green dragon eye, the iris rimmed with the red of Fyre, looked into Septimus's brilliant green eyes. Septimus stroked the dragon's velvety nose and said, "I'll be back later, Spit Fyre. Be good."

The dragon settled down outside the Dragon Kennel and closed his eyes. Now the usual late-morning chorus began— the crash of slamming windows as Wizard after Wizard tried to escape the low rumble of Spit Fyre's snores echoing around the yard.

Septimus jumped over Spit Fyre's tail, taking care not to trip over the barb at the end. Then he walked across the Courtyard and into the blue shadows of the beautiful lapis lazuli Great Arch. There, as he always did now, he stopped and looked down Wizard Way. Septimus still loved the feeling of being in the Wizard Way of his own Time, where he belonged. He breathed in the rain-misted air and as he gazed down the wide avenue something purple caught his eye at the far end. Septimus knew it was Marcia Overstrand; a gust of wind had blown the ExtraOrdinary Wizard's cloak out like a great purple sail behind her as she strode through the Palace gates.

Wondering what had sent Marcia to the Palace, Septimus checked in his pocket for a piece of paper and set off along Wizard Way to the Manuscriptorium. He paused for a moment outside the door, freshly painted in Jillie Djinn's new corporate color—a pinkish purple. He **Felt** someone **Ill-Watching** him. Slowly, Septimus turned and, to avoid the Watcher realizing he had been **Felt**, he lifted his foot as if he was looking at something he had stepped in. At the same time he tried, as best he could, to put up a **Shield** against the **Ill-Watcher**. While he energetically scraped the sole of his shoe against the curb he turned his eyes in the direction of the Ill-Watching. To his surprise his eyes were drawn to the Palace. Puzzled, Septimus stopped scraping. He must be wrong. There was no one in the Palace who would do *that*. He was getting jumpy. What he needed was half an hour of Beetle's company and a mug of FizzFroot.

Septimus pushed open the door to the Manuscriptorium. *Ping.* Jillie Djinn's counter clicked over to number seven.

"Wotcha, Sep," said Beetle, jumping up from his chair.

"Wotcha, Beetle," Septimus replied.

"That was quick. I wasn't expecting you so soon."

"I didn't know you were expecting me at all," said Septimus, puzzled. He took the piece of paper from his pocket. It was covered with his very best capital letters carefully drawn in various colors. "I need a space in your window."

Beetle looked at the Manuscriptorium front window—what he could see of it, at least, which amounted to no more than a few square inches. The rest was piled high with stacks of books, pamphlets, papers, manuscripts, parchments, bills, receipts and remedies that were randomly—and rather stickily—interspersed with old pies, socks, poems, peashooters, marshmallows (Beetle was a great fan of marshmallows), umbrellas and sausage sandwiches from the meat pie cart, most of which had been put down by absentminded scribes only to be instantly lost in the muddle and never seen again—although they were sometimes smelled.

"Can't I get you something else a bit easier, Sep?" asked Beetle. "Like an All My Dreams Come True Spell or something?"

Septimus looked at the piece of paper. "It's not *very* big," he said. "Couldn't you fit it in *somewhere*? It's really important. Marcia's threatening to send Spit Fyre away because she says I'm spending too much time looking after him and I'm not getting any work done. So I thought if I did this . . ."

Septimus handed the paper to Beetle. "'Dragon-sitter wanted,'" Beetle read out. "'Irregular hours but interesting work. Sense of humor an advantage. Apply to Septimus Heap, Wizard Tower.'" Beetle snorted with laughter. "They'll need a bit more than a sense of humor, won't they, Sep? How about cast-iron feet, no sense of smell and being able to run a hundred yards in two seconds flat—and that's just for starters."

Septimus looked downcast. "I know," he said, "but I didn't want to put people off. I've had people interested but as soon as I show them how to clean out the Dragon Kennel something weird happens. They suddenly remember that, oops, they *completely* forgot that they had agreed to look after their great-aunt or, oh *bother*, it escaped their mind that they had to take a long sea voyage the very next day. Then they look all embarrassed and say how really upset they are as they would have *loved* to have taken the job. I believed the first two but after that it got a bit predictable. Oh, go on, Beetle, *please* put my notice up. You get all sorts of unusual people looking in here; one of them might do the job."

"You're right, we get all sorts of unusual people in here," grumbled Beetle. "*Too* unusual for my liking. Tell you what, Sep. Since it's you, I'll make a space on the door. This advertisement for a new scribe can go. It's attracting the wrong kind of people, just like I told Miss Djinn it would. I'll stick yours there instead."

"Oh, *thanks*, Beetle."

With some enthusiasm, Beetle ripped down Jillie Djinn's notice, crumpled it into a little ball and hurled it into the wastepaper bin. Then he got a pot of glue, slathered it all over Septimus's paper, and stuck it on the grubby window. Septimus tried not to notice that the colored letters had run.

"I'm due a break now," said Beetle, licking the glue off his fingers. "Like some FizzFroot?"

"You bet," said Septimus. He followed Beetle out through the Manuscriptorium and into Beetle's den in the backyard.

Beetle set out two mugs, dropped a Fizz Bom cube into each one and lit a small burner. As the kettle began to boil, it let out the loud squeal that—ever since Beetle had once let it boil dry—it always made when the water got too hot for it. Beetle took the kettle off the burner and poured the water into the mugs, which immediately frothed up and began to overflow with chilled pink foam. He handed one to Septimus.

"Oof, that's a good one!" Septimus spluttered as the FizzFroot went straight up his nose.

"Funny thing happened this morning," said Beetle after a few restorative gulps of FizzFroot. "Someone said they were you."

Septimus took another gulp of FizzFroot and sneezed. "*Atchoo!* Me?"

"Yeah. Weird kid. Wanted the scribe job."

"So what did you say?"

"Well, I told him he *wasn't* you, and he didn't take it too well. But I had to tell him that he could come back later. Not my job to say who can apply to be a scribe. Hope Miss Djinn can see he's as nutty as a fruitcake. I shall tell her he knows a few **Darke** tricks, too. Don't want any of that stuff in here."

"**Darke** tricks?" asked Septimus.

"Yeah. You know, the flame coming out of the thumb one. Used to be considered highly insulting in the old days. Not nice even now."

"No. I wonder who he was."

"Hmm. Well, I'll let you know if he comes back."

Septimus and Beetle sat for a while, drinking their FizzFroot, until Beetle remembered that before everything had gone crazy that morning he had been hoping Septimus would drop by. "Hey, Sep," he said, suddenly jumping to his feet with a smile back on his face, "we can kill two birds with one stone. I've got something to show you."

"What?"

"You won't know unless you come and look, will you?" Beetle grinned.

✢✢ I I ✢✢
DRAGON·WATCHER

M r. *Pot!*" *yelled Marcia,*
striding across the
Palace lawns, her quarry
in sight. "*Mr. Pot!*"

Billy Pot did not
reply; he was pushing
a large wheelbarrow
of dragon dung and
was not in a good
mood. Billy had
completely forgot-
ten how pleased he
had been when Septimus
had allowed

him to start collecting Spit Fyre's dragon dung. But that had been in what Billy now considered to be the Good Old Days, when he had a regular job mowing the Palace lawns with his Contraption. Billy's Contraption worked on organic principles, which meant that it contained about twenty hungry lawn lizards in a box that Billy wheeled—extremely slowly—across the grass, while the lawn lizards ate the grass—or not.

Billy kept hundreds of lawn lizards in lizard lodges down by the river, and as the lizard population grew he began to have trouble keeping them under control. The dragon dung had worked miracles—at first. Fearing that a monster lizard had moved into their territory, the lawn lizards instantly became manageable. However, after some time passed and the monster lizard had not materialized, the lawn lizards, which were not stupid, realized something was up. And now they were just as uncontrollable as they ever had been and—having seen off a massive rival—they were arrogant too, and had taken to snapping at Billy's ankles. Billy was done with lawn lizards.

The last straw for Billy had come when, after a long day's mowing and several changes of lizards, the Contraption—never the same since it had been trampled by Simon Heap's horse—had finally fallen to pieces. Sarah Heap had seized her chance. Disgusted with the great piles of dragon dung littering the Palace lawns, Sarah had dispatched Silas to the Port with strict instructions to return with a state-of-the-art lawn mower. Silas was unusually efficient and came back on the return Port barge with an impressive machine.

Billy hated it. It had horrible sharp blades instead of lizards and had to be pulled by *horse*. Billy was a reptile person; he didn't like horses.

But the dragon dung had kept right on coming.

Sarah Heap, who was finally getting used to telling people what to do, provided Billy with a large field beside the Palace lawns and told him to shift the dragon dung into the field *now* and get to planting vegetables. Billy didn't like that. He didn't like vegetables, either.

Billy Pot now made a point of not talking to anyone who looked like they might be trouble—and the ExtraOrdinary Wizard yelling at him ticked all Billy's trouble boxes. But Marcia was not easily put off. She chased after Billy, who saw her coming and did his best to pick up speed, but was not entirely successful, hampered as he was by his heavy wheelbarrow.

"Mr. Pot!" Marcia jumped in front of the barrow, caught the heel of her pointy purple python shoe in an old rabbit hole and promptly fell over. Billy peered over the pile of dragon dung only to find that the ExtraOrdinary Wizard had disappeared, which was all right by him.

It was only when Marcia staggered to her feet, clutching the snapped heel from one of the pythons, hair awry and with an extremely irritable glint in her green eyes, that Billy thought it wise to set the barrow down.

He peered over the top. "What?"

"Mr. Pot . . . ouch . . . I have a job for you," said Marcia.

"Look, Your ExtraOrdinariness, I already collected the last lot and I ain't got room for no more until the end of the week. Got that?"

"Oh." Marcia was a little taken aback. After twelve years as an ExtraOrdinary Wizard she was used to a little more respect.

"I gotta get on now," Billy growled. He picked up the barrow handles and set off toward the vegetable garden at a slow trudge.

Putting on a fast hobble, Marcia waylaid the wheelbarrow again. "Mr. *Pot*," she said very insistently.

Billy sighed and let go of the barrow handles. "*What?*" he asked.

"As I said, I have a job for you. It's a new vacancy—Dragon-Watcher. I think you would be eminently well qualified."

"What d'you mean exactly, *Dragon-Watcher?*" asked Billy suspiciously.

"I've written out a job description," said Marcia, handing Billy a crisp piece of paper. He took it dubiously and stared at it. Billy didn't like paper very much either, especially fancy pieces of thick paper with writing on them. Actually it was the writing that Billy really did not like—he had no idea where to start with writing.

"Other way up," said Marcia.

"Oh." Flustered, as once again a piece of paper got the better of him, Billy turned the paper around. "You read it. Haven't got my specs," he mumbled. He handed the paper back to Marcia, who took it cautiously between finger and thumb, trying to avoid the thick, grimy fingerprints that now covered the edges.

"'Dragon-Watcher job description,'" Marcia began. "'Number one: Dragon to live out, i.e., at Dragon-Watcher's residence and or workplace.'"

"What?" Billy frowned, puzzled.

"Spit Fyre will live here," said Marcia.

"*Here?*"

"Yes, here. The vegetable field will be ideal."

"What about the veg?" asked Billy, suddenly discovering a new concern for vegetables.

"He's not fussy; he'll eat anything."

"That's what bothers me," muttered Billy.

"'Number two: Dragon-Watcher to have total responsibility for dragon when in his care. Number three: Apprentice may visit dragon on alternate evenings and weekends only, and is allowed one half-hour flight only at those times. Number four: rates of pay by negotiation—but I suggest double what you are currently getting from the Palace."

"Double?" Billy gasped, shocked.

"Very well, triple, then. But that's my final offer. Will you take the job or not?"

"Yes! Er, yes, ExtraOrdinary. I would be honored."

"My Apprentice will bring the dragon over later today. The builders will be arriving this morning."

"*Builders?*"

"To construct the dragon house. Good day to you, Mr. Pot.

I'll send a contract down for you to sign later."

"Oh. Right. Um, good day, Your ExtraOrdinariness."

As Marcia limped off, Billy Pot sat down on the riverbank and scratched his head in amazement. He immediately wished he hadn't. Dragon droppings were really hard to get out of your hair.

✛ 12 ✛

TERRY TARSAL

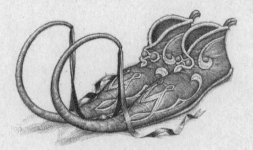

Terry Tarsal, *shoemaker and reluctant* keeper of a purple python, liked a quiet life. Most of the time he got it—and the times he didn't usually had something to do with purple python shoes.

Terry was a small, wiry man with large capable hands worn rough and callused after years of working with leather. He had a long, narrow shop down Footpad Passage just off Wizard Way, which smelled of dust, leather, waxed thread and, on that particular day, linseed oil. Terry enjoyed his work. What he did not enjoy was keeping a purple python in the backyard of the shop. But Marcia Overstrand was one of his best customers and over the ten years that Marcia had been ExtraOrdinary Wizard, Terry had steeled himself to look after the snake and collect its sloughed skins for when Marcia ordered her next pair of shoes.

That morning Terry had just fed the python, which always upset him. He was recovering with a cup of hot cider when through the frosted glass of his shop window he saw the purple blur of Marcia Overstrand's robes. The next moment the shop door—which was terrified of Marcia—sprang open.

Terry Tarsal was made of sterner stuff. "Good morning, Miss Overstrand," he said, not bothering to get up. He took another sip of cider. "Your new ones are not ready yet. I'm still waiting for the wretched python to slough."

"I haven't come for those," said Marcia, hobbling in. "It's an emergency." She bent down, pulled off her shoe and dropped it on the counter along with the broken heel. "Snapped, just like that. No warning. I could have broken my leg."

Terry picked up the offending shoe and held it at arm's length. "You've stepped in something," he said accusingly.

"Really? I was under the impression that was what shoes were for," said Marcia, "stepping on things."

"*On*, yes. But not *in*. Well, I suppose it will brush off. Do you want to wait or come back later?"

"I don't plan on hopping all the way back to the Wizard Tower, thank you, Mr. Tarsal. I'll wait."

"Please yourself. I am quite happy to lend you a pair of one-size-fits-all galoshes."

"I do *not* wear galoshes," said Marcia stonily. "And I most particularly do not wear one-size-fits-all galoshes, thank you very much."

Terry Tarsal picked up the shoes and disappeared into the back of the shop. Marcia sat down on the uncomfortable wooden bench beside the counter—Terry did not like his customers to linger—and gazed around the little shop.

Marcia enjoyed her visits to Terry Tarsal. She liked to sit in the quiet old shop in the dark alley where no one could find her. And if someone *did* stumble across her sitting there, she enjoyed the look of shock on their face at seeing the ExtraOrdinary Wizard sitting on the rickety bench in the shoemaker's shop, waiting for her shoes just like any other Castle inhabitant.

And so, while Terry Tarsal scraped off the dragon dung and set about making a new heel and finding a scrap of python skin to cover it with, Marcia contentedly sat and gazed at the shoes awaiting pick-up. They were a motley bunch. Most were run-of-the-mill boots of brown or black leather with thick laces and heavy leather soles. There was a collection of red and green workmen's clogs, the kind that many of those who worked in the craft rooms and small factories in The Ramblings wore to protect their feet. There was a troupe of small pink dance shoes festooned with ribbons, two pairs of fisherman's boots made from oiled leather—which Marcia realized were the source of the pungent smell of linseed oil that filled the shop—and a pair of the most bizarre shoes, with the longest, pointiest toes that Marcia had ever seen.

Intrigued, Marcia got up and went over for a closer look at the strange shoes. She could not resist picking them up. The shoes were beautiful, made from soft red leather, embellished with deep tooled swirls of gold leaf. Although the shoes were made for a normal foot size, the long, tapering toes stretched to at least two feet in length, and at the far end of each toe two long black ribbons were sewn onto the shoe. Marcia held them in her hands, marveling at how light they were, and at what good quality leather Terry Tarsal had used. She ran her finger along the lines of the gold tooling. The more she looked, the more she became convinced that the elegant swirls on each toe formed the letter M.

Still holding the soft red shoes, Marcia retreated to the bench with a feeling of excitement that she had not felt since she was a little girl on the eve of her birthday. It was, in fact, Marcia's birthday the following week and a suspicion had begun to form in her mind that maybe Septimus had actually put some thought into her present—rather than his usual hurried bunch of flowers picked from the Palace gardens. She remembered Septimus describing the shoes that they had worn in the Time that he had been kidnapped into by that ghastly Alchemist, Marcellus Pye. She had commented that the shoes sounded like they were about the only decent thing there. It would, thought Marcia, be just the kind of unusual present that Septimus would come up with if he put his mind to it.

Feeling a little guilty at seeing her present before her birthday, Marcia was hastily putting the shoes back on the shelf when Terry Tarsal reappeared. "Strangest shoes I've ever made," he commented.

Marcia spun around as though she had been caught doing

something she shouldn't. Unable to resist, she asked, "Who ordered them?"

"Your Apprentice, if I remember rightly," said Terry Tarsal.

"I thought as much," said Marcia, smiling. How sweet it was of Septimus, she thought. He could be so considerate at times; she *must* try to be less grumpy with him. She decided that if Septimus settled down and worked hard with his Projection, she would take notice of what Alther had told her—that Septimus was getting to the age where he needed more freedom—and she would try not to make a fuss about him going out and not telling her exactly where he was going.

Terry Tarsal's voice interrupted Marcia's good resolutions. "Are you paying for them?" he asked.

"Certainly not! And I don't want him to know I have seen them either. Is that clear?"

Terry Tarsal shrugged. "Don't know what it is about these shoes," he said. "That's exactly what your Apprentice said to me—don't let Marcia see them. He was very definite about that."

"I expect he was," said Marcia approvingly.

"Anyway, I've got to deliver them tomorrow. Though why he can't come and get them himself, I don't know. It's not as though Snake Slipway is miles away, is it?"

"*Snake Slipway?* What's Snake Slipway got to do with it?" asked Marcia.

"That's where he lives," said Terry patiently as though Marcia was being deliberately slow. "Now, about this heel—"

"That's where *who* lives?"

"The odd fellow who came in with your Apprentice—the one who the shoes are for. Look, the glue on the heel needs at least an hour to dry and—"

"*The one who the shoes are for?*"

"So are you sure you want to—"

"Mr. Tarsal, answer me. Exactly *who* are these shoes for?"

"I really can't answer that. It's confidential information."

"Balderdash!" exploded Marcia. "They're only a pair of shoes, for heaven's sake. It's hardly top secret, is it?"

Terry Tarsal would not give in. "Customer confidentiality," he replied.

"Mr. Tarsal. If you don't tell me who these shoes are for I will be forced to . . . to . . ." Marcia racked her brain for something Terry would find particularly galling. "I shall be forced to make all the shoes awaiting pick-up half a size smaller."

"You *wouldn't* . . ."

"I would. Now *who* are these shoes for?"

"Marcellus Pye."

"*Marcellus Pye?*" Marcia yelled so loud the door rattled in terror and a jar of tiny green buttons leaped from the counter and scattered across the floor.

"Now look what you've done," said Terry, getting on his hands and knees and hunting down the buttons. "I'll never find them all. They've gone everywhere."

Marcia stared at Terry scrabbling after the buttons as though he were from another planet. She could not make sense of anything; there were just three words going around in her head and they seemed to be taking up all the thinking space. The words were: "Septimus," "Marcellus" and "Pye."

"You could give us a hand instead of staring into space like a constipated camel," Terry Tarsal broke rudely into Marcia's spinning thoughts.

It was not every day that someone called Marcia a constipated camel but it did the trick. Marcia came to and joined Terry Tarsal in the button hunt, but still the thoughts whirled around her head. "You did say *Marcellus Pye*, didn't you?" she asked.

"*Yes,*" said Terry irritably. He levered a small green object out from between the floorboards with his fingernail only to discover it was a green sherbet pip. "Marcellus Pye. Remember writing it as 'Pie' as in apple and your Apprentice telling me it was 'P-Y-E.'"

"You are absolutely *sure*?" asked Marcia. All kinds of impossible explanations were going through her head. None made sense. And *all* involved Septimus.

Terry Tarsal straightened up with a groan and rubbed his back. "Yes, I said. Look, do stop going on, Madam Overstrand. I gotta concentrate here. These buttons are my best jade."

"*Best* jade?" asked Marcia.

"Yes. Never find their like again. Just my luck . . ."

Marcia stood up and brushed down her robes, which were covered in dust—Terry preferred shoemaking to housekeeping. She clicked her fingers and muttered a **Retrieve**. From hidden cracks and crevices in Terry Tarsal's floorboards the buttons gathered together, and as Terry watched open-mouthed, a fine green stream of buttons flew back into their jar.

Terry got to his feet, an expression of relief and amazement on his face. He had never actually seen any **Magyk** before and to have Marcia actually use it for something as mundane as finding his precious buttons touched Terry. "Thank you," he muttered. "That's . . . well, that's very kind of you."

"Least I could do," said Marcia. "Now, can I see the order book?"

"Order book?"

"Yes, please, Mr. Tarsal."

Bemused, Terry shook his head and went to fetch the order book. He returned with a heavy leather-bound ledger and thumped it down on the counter.

"I would like to see the order for those shoes," said Marcia. "Please."

Terry licked his finger and began leafing through to find the right day. "Here we are," he said, pointing to an entry from three weeks ago.

Marcia took out her spectacles and peered at Terry Tarsal's crabbed handwriting. The name *Marcellus Pye* jumped out and hit her. "I don't believe it," she muttered.

"Yeah. That's him."

"Was he very *old*?" asked Marcia, trying to make sense of things.

"No, he was young—about thirty. Quite good-looking if it weren't for the funny haircut. I remember now, I had to measure his feet as he didn't know what size he was. He kept giving me the old size—we stopped using those at least a hundred years ago. Even my old dad wouldn't have remembered *that*. He had an odd accent, too—not that he said much. Your Apprentice did most of the talking, if I remember."

"Did he really?" asked Marcia, suddenly sitting down on the bench. "Well, I don't know . . ."

"You all right, Miss Overstrand?" asked Terry. "You look a bit pale. I'll get you a glass of water."

Marcia was not all right. She felt strangely disconnected, as though the world was suddenly not quite what she had thought it was. Terry brought her a glass of water.

"Thank you, Terry." Sitting with her purple-stockinged feet resting on the dusty floor, Marcia sipped her glass of water. She knew that the real reason for her shock was not so much the presence of a young Marcellus Pye in her Time, which was weird enough, but the realization that Septimus— her trusted Septimus—had deceived her.

Watched by a concerned Terry Tarsal, Marcia drank the rest of the water and began to feel a little more like herself. "Terry," she said.

"Yes, ExtraOrdinary?"

"While you're waiting for the heel to dry, put those jade buttons on my shoes, will you?"

✢ 13 ✢
WIZARD SLED

Wile *Marcia waited for the* glue to dry, Septimus was doing something much more interesting—squeezing through a small trapdoor in the floor of Beetle's hut.

"I didn't know you could get to the Ice Tunnels through here," Septimus said, as his feet found the rungs of the ladder fixed to the wall of ice below him.

"Tradesman's entrance." Beetle grinned up at Septimus. His breath was misting on the freezing air and his face was an unearthly color in the light of the flickering blue lamp he had just lit. "Miss Djinn makes me use it. Close the hatch, will you, Sep?"

"Yep," said Septimus. He pulled down the heavy **Sealed** hatch—typical of all the **Sealed** entrances to the Ice Tunnels—that was hidden under the trapdoor, and heard the soft hiss as it settled onto its **Seal**. From beneath his Apprentice robes he took the Alchemie **Keye** that he wore around his neck and pressed it into a circular depression in the middle of the hatch. Then he climbed down the icy metal ladder into the depths below Beetle's hut and joined him on the slippery surface of the Ice Tunnel.

Septimus's dragon ring, which he wore on his right index finger, gave off a dim yellow glow. But it was Beetle's blue lamp that caught the beautiful white-blue sparkle of the ice covering the inside of the tunnel like cake icing and threw their distorted shadows across the icy vault of the high-arched roof.

"I'll just nip up and **Seal** the hatch," said Beetle. "Then we'll be off."

"It's all **Sealed**," said Septimus.

"No, Sep. I gotta use the **Seal**—see?" Beetle held up a wax disc—an exact copy of Septimus's solid gold **Keye**. In reply Septimus drew out his **Keye** and waved it at Beetle with a grin. Beetle shook his head in amazement. "*Sheesh* . . . I am not even going to *ask* how you got that, Sep."

"Marcellus gave it to me," said Septimus. "It's how Jenna and I got out."

"Ah," said Beetle, tactful enough not to mention Nicko, who had not gotten out and was still trapped in another Time. Mentioning Nicko upset Septimus, which Beetle did not like to see. Beetle took a simple wooden sled from a hook nailed into the icy wall. "Want to hop on?" he asked.

Beetle held the rope of the sled while Septimus climbed on; then he took his place at the front and fixed his lamp so that it became a headlight. Remembering what Beetle's sled driving was like, Septimus held on tight—and not a moment too soon. Before he had time to draw a breath the sled had shot off and was taking the first bend—a sharp right-hander—on one runner.

"Wheerrr . . . aaargh!" yelled Septimus. His shout was carried away on the icy air, traveling for miles joining with the many ghostly laments that lingered on the cold tunnel winds.

After almost two years as an Inspection clerk, Beetle was an expert sled driver—but unused to passengers. He took bends halfway up the icy walls, rounded corners using skid turns and if he had to stop he'd do what he called a double spin reverse whiz and end up facing the way he had come. After a few minutes Septimus was looking decidedly green. He had a brief respite as the sled trundled slowly up a long incline, but as it teetered at the top Septimus realized the worst was yet to come.

In front of him, in the light of Beetle's blue headlight, he could see a long brilliant white tunnel dropping into pitch-darkness, while above them the roof of the tunnel seemed to arch upward into a cavernous dome.

"This is my favorite part!" yelled Beetle over his shoulder. "Hold on tight!"

Septimus was already holding on so tight that he felt like his fingers had become welded to the sled. He took a deep breath and braced himself. The sled teetered as if it, too, were taking a deep breath. Then suddenly it went hurtling down the ice at breakneck speed, until Septimus felt a strange sensation, as though the ground was no longer there. He glanced down and realized to his horror that indeed the ground no longer *was* there. It was about twenty feet below them. They were airborne.

"*Beeeeee . . . tuuuuuuuul stop!*" yelled Septimus, his voice whisked away by the wind.

Beetle was oblivious. This was the very best part of his week. It was something that, ever since he had perfected the sled jump, he had wanted to share with Septimus. It never crossed his mind that Septimus might not feel the same way.

They landed surprisingly smoothly, whizzing across a wide, flat expanse of ice and shooting straight into a tunnel so narrow that Septimus was forced to stop holding on to the sled for fear of his knuckles scraping the walls of ice. The tunnel twisted and turned. Beetle slowed down to avoid the sled getting stuck, but as they bumped slowly along between two great walls of ice Septimus began to get a horrible closed-in feeling. At last the tunnel widened out into a circular chamber with a high roof. Beetle drew to an unexpectedly sedate halt.

"We're here," he said in a low voice.

"Where?" asked Septimus, looking around at the huge Chamber. It felt familiar but he could not quite think why.

"You *know*," Beetle said in a loud whisper. "The place that Marcia told us to check out."

"Marcia?" Septimus was puzzled.

"Didn't she tell you?" asked Beetle.

"Marcia doesn't tell me anything," Septimus replied gloomily.

Beetle got off the sled. "Well, anyway, we gotta check out something, Sep. Stuff's been happening down here. Come on."

Septimus gingerly stood up on the ice and followed Beetle as he set off, shining his brilliant blue light around the smooth ice walls of the Chamber. Suddenly Septimus knew where they were. "It's the Chamber of Alchemie!" He gasped. "I . . . I used to come here every day." Septimus sounded wistful. "Marcellus showed me tons of stuff. And *he* didn't nag me all the time."

"Yeah, well, I bet it was a bit warmer then too," Beetle said. "Ah, here we are. Look, it's melted and refrozen." Beetle's blue light had picked out the slab of ice that covered the old doorway to the Chamber. Unlike the rest of the hoarfrosted ice, this was clear, with hundreds of tiny bubbles trapped within it. It reminded Septimus of one of Beetle's FizzFroots—the lemon-flavored one that he did not like so much.

"That's new ice," Septimus whispered.

Beetle shrugged. "I know. But at least it's refrozen. I'll just check the **Seal**." Beetle pressed his wax **Keye** into the metal disc at the side of the ice. "Weird and weirder," he said. "It's been **ReSealed**. Come on, Sep, we've got one more to check—but first I've got something to show you."

Five minutes later, Beetle threw his sled into a double spin reverse whiz and stopped in a spray of frost. Septimus fell off and lay on the ice, staring up at the blue-white roof of a tunnel.

"Come on, Sep," said Beetle. He grabbed hold of Septimus's hands and pulled him to his feet. "I found it last week. I figured out a shortcut down one of the Narrows and I saw *that*." He pointed to a small piece of purple rope sticking out of the ice.

Septimus got down on his hands and knees to have a closer look.

"There's no color down here," explained Beetle. "So it stood out a mile. I tried to dig it out but it's no good; the ice has taken it in. It does that. I dropped my lucky scarf once and I found it the next week, trapped under two inches of ice. For a while I'd see it when I went by, but it got drawn down deeper and deeper until one day I couldn't see it anymore. So it's funny that you can still see the rope." Beetle scraped at the ice with his penknife and freed up a little more of the rope so that a few inches stuck clear. "Well—go on," he said.

"Go on, what?" asked Septimus, puzzled.

"Grab hold of the rope and pull. It won't come out for me, but I reckon it will for you."

"Why me?"

"Well, it belongs to you."

"*What* belongs to me?"

Beetle smiled a mysterious smile. "You'll have to give a tug and find out, won't you?" he said.

Septimus shook his head with a puzzled smile and then, humoring Beetle, he took up the frayed rope end and pulled. He couldn't get much of a hold, but to his surprise a long length of thick purple rope freed itself from the ice as easily as if he had been pulling it from newly fallen snow.

"It's coming!" Beetle yelled, excited. "I knew it would. Keep pulling, Sep!"

Septimus needed no encouragement. He pulled steadily until the ice began to crumble and two golden runners broke the surface. Amazed, Septimus gave a hefty tug and from the depths of the ice emerged the most beautiful sled he had ever seen. "The Wizard Tower sled," he breathed. "Beetle, you found the *Wizard Tower sled*."

"Yeah," said Beetle with the biggest grin Septimus had seen in a long time. "Good, isn't it?"

"Good? It's *incredible*." Septimus brushed the dusting of ice crystals off the sled and set it down on its golden runners. It stood waiting patiently on the ice—sleek, high and delicate like a racehorse compared to the donkey of a sled that Beetle had. The intricately carved wood, inlaid with strips of lapis lazuli, felt almost warm to Septimus's touch, and its purple, blue and gold paint sparkled in the light of Beetle's lamp. Hanging from the gold bar that ran between the front of the two curved runners was a silver whistle, tied on with a green ribbon.

"No wonder they lost it," said Beetle. "They left the whistle on the sled. That's a dumb thing to do. You should always keep it with you, Sep. Here." Beetle untied the whistle and handed it to Septimus. "It will come whenever you whistle," he said, "and you might find you need to. These highly strung sleds were notorious for wandering off. I bet that poor Apprentice spent a long time looking for it. Must have been a nightmare."

Septimus put the whistle in his tunic pocket. "Thanks, Beetle," he said. "You know so much stuff. Stuff that even Marcia doesn't know."

"I dunno about that, Sep. Marcia knows more than you think. She just doesn't want to *tell*, that's all," said Beetle.

"She certainly doesn't tell *me*," said Septimus.

"So," said Beetle, quickly changing the subject—aware that Marcia had told *him* rather a lot that morning—"are you going to get on? I can teach you how to do a double spin reverse whiz and even a triple spin if you like."

"Um. Well, maybe later, when I'm used to it." Septimus gingerly sat down on his sled, half expecting it to shoot off the way Beetle's sled did. But it just sat patiently beneath him as if waiting for instructions. "How do you work these things?" he asked, realizing he never inquired how Beetle got his sled to go up and down the ice slopes and do exactly as he wished.

"You just think about what you want it to do and it does it—but only if you're the right person to ride it. If you tried to ride mine it would just ignore you."

"Okay, then, I'll give it a try," said Septimus, and in his head he thought, *slowly—go slowly*. And so, very, *very* slowly, the Wizard Tower sled set off to the sound of Beetle's laughter.

"What did you tell it, Sep?" he shouted after him. "Make like a snail?"

"I'm just testing," said Septimus a little defensively.

"So test how fast it'll go," suggested Beetle. "I bet it's amazing. Much faster than this old thing." He kicked his own sled affectionately.

"Well, maybe later," Septimus replied.

"Okay, Sep," said Beetle, getting on his sled. "But there's one last thing Marcia asked us to check out."

Septimus smiled—what did Marcia matter when he had a beautiful sled like this? "Okay, Beetle," he said. "I can help you with your Inspection now. Like they did in the old days."

Beetle grinned. "Great," he said.

✛ 14 ✛
THE HOUSE ON SNAKE SLIPWAY

Beetle shone his light onto a hatch in the roof of an ice tunnel. It was no more than a few feet above their heads, almost near enough to touch if they jumped up high. The hatch formed an oval depression with the usual metal **Seal** beside it. All around it was a thin line of clear ice.

"See," said Beetle, "it's the same here. The ice

has melted and refrozen. And, let's see . . . yes, it's been **ReSealed** too. Weird."

"Hmm . . ." said Septimus, not totally surprised. He knew whose hatch this was.

Beetle peered up at the hatch. "Of course this one *could* just be a faulty **Seal** on the other side. Sometimes the domestic ones do that. It would be good to get in there and check, but some really weird guy moved in not long ago. Bit of a recluse, apparently. Won't even answer the door."

"I know," said Septimus. "I wish he would. But he's not really used to things yet."

"Do you know him, Sep?" asked Beetle, surprised.

Septimus made a decision—he would confide in Beetle. He was tired of keeping his visits to Marcellus a secret. "Well, yes, I do. But . . . er, Marcia doesn't know I come to see him. I keep meaning to tell her but she's so grumpy at the moment and—" Suddenly Septimus remembered something. "Oh, gosh—Beetle, have you got your timepiece with you?"

"Of course." Beetle grinned proudly. He had a state-of-the-art timepiece that had been found in pieces at the back of a Manuscriptorium cupboard and thrown out. He had rescued it and over several months, with the help of the Conservation

Scribe, had painstakingly put it back together. It was a beautiful piece of craftsmanship, completely silent due to a complicated flywheel mechanism and—most important of all—it kept very good time.

Proudly, Beetle took the timepiece from his pocket. It was made of a mix of gold and silver and was attached to a thick leather cord. On the top was a large handle with a winder in the middle. It sat covering Beetle's hand like a small, fat tortoise.

Septimus was impressed. "How did they make them so *small*?" he asked.

"Dunno," said Beetle. "You just don't get them like that anymore."

The hands on the timepiece were drawing close to midday. "Oh, rats," said Septimus. "I'm going to be *late*. Jenna will be really mad."

"*Jenna?*" Beetle seemed to have developed a squeak.

"Yeah. I'm meeting her here and I—"

"What—*here*, Sep?"

"No, not down here. I mean up there." Septimus pointed up to the hatch. "In the house."

"*Are* you?"

Septimus had an idea. "Would you like to come too? I could ask Marcellus if we could check the hatch from the inside."

"Marcellus—is that the weird guy who lives there?"

"He's not really weird," said Septimus. "Just a bit . . . unused to things."

"The name sounds familiar," said Beetle. "Hey, isn't he the one who kidnapped you through that Glass—the crazy old Alchemist?"

"Um, yes," admitted Septimus. "But he's not crazy. And he doesn't even look old anymore."

"Still an Alchemist though," said Beetle. "No wonder that hatch is a problem. Sheesh, I'm surprised we haven't had a total meltdown."

Septimus wondered if telling Beetle had been such a good idea, but it was too late now. "I'll open the hatch, then, okay?" he said. "It won't hurt for a few minutes. I can **ReSeal** it from inside."

Beetle looked shocked. "*Open* a **Sealed** hatch?"

"Well, yes. Then we can get in that way and meet Jenna—"

"Are you *really* meeting Princess Jenna up there?" Beetle asked.

Septimus nodded, jumping up and down to keep warm. His feet were beginning to feel like blocks of ice.

The temptation of seeing Jenna was too much for Beetle. "Okay, then," he said. "But I really shouldn't. Miss Djinn would throw a fit if she knew." From underneath his sled he took what Septimus realized was a telescopic ladder, opened it up and propped it against the wall. "I'll hold the ladder, Sep, and *you* can **UnSeal** the hatch. Probably better that way."

Ten minutes later Beetle and Septimus were making their way along the long, musty passageway that led from the hatch all the way to the house on Snake Slipway. Septimus knew the way well. He had first been there when it had belonged to Professor Weasal Van Klampff, whose ghastly housekeeper, Una Brakket, had taken him along the passage to Weasal's Laboratory. The passage had been dark and dusty then, but now it was well kept, with old-fashioned rush-lights placed in holders at regular intervals along the walls. It was just as it had been when Septimus had lived there for six strange months in another Time as Marcellus Pye's Alchemie Apprentice. Now Beetle followed Septimus as he set a brisk pace along the passage, passing the turning that led to the old Laboratory and following the long zigzag path underneath the houses that backed onto the Moat.

It was not long before Septimus and Beetle arrived at the end of the passageway and emerged into the large vaulted cellars below the house. Septimus strode through them and, worried that he was already late for Jenna, ran up the cellar steps and pushed open the cellar door under the stairs. "Marcellus?" he called out. "Marcellus?" There was no reply.

Septimus padded into the house, closely followed by a wary Beetle. The place smelled odd to Beetle. The waxy scent of candles was combined with a bittersweet aroma of oranges, cloves and something he could not identify. Beetle could not get rid of the feeling that he had somehow gone back in time. It had the same effect on Septimus. He was used to it now, but when he had first visited Marcellus just after the old Alchemist had moved in, Septimus had suddenly become convinced that he was still trapped in Marcellus's Time and his return to his own Time had been nothing more than a dream. In a terrible panic he had run out of the house, and to his joy he had seen Jillie Djinn bustling past. Jillie never did figure out quite why Marcia's Apprentice had thrown his arms around her and said how thrilled he was to see her, but she had gone back to the Manuscriptorium that morning with a spring in her step. People did not often throw their arms around Jillie Djinn.

The silence of the house fell upon Septimus and Beetle like a blanket. They walked along the narrow hallway, which was lit with more candles than Beetle had ever seen in his life. When they reached the foot of a steep flight of dark oak stairs, Beetle was amazed to see a lit candle had been placed on each step.

"All these candles, they're weird," whispered Beetle, feeling somewhat spooked.

"He doesn't like the dark," whispered Septimus. "Shhh, I can hear footsteps upstairs. Marcellus? *Marcell . . . us*," he called out.

"Apprentice?" came a wary voice from the floor above. "'Tis you?"

"Yes, it's me," Septimus replied.

Heavy footsteps sounded above and then Beetle saw a sight so strange he remembered it for the rest of his life. Coming slowly down the stairs, lit from below by each candle that he passed, was a dark-haired young man sporting an old-fashioned haircut. He was wearing what Beetle knew—from old engravings—were the black and gold robes of an Alchemist. The sleeves of the young man's tunic were what Beetle considered to be ridiculously long and they trailed down the stairs behind him. They were matched by the strangest shoes that Beetle had ever seen in his life—the points of the shoes must have been about two feet long and were tied up onto garters that the young man wore just below his knees. Beetle suddenly became aware that his mouth had fallen open and he rapidly closed it.

The young man reached the foot of the stairs and Septimus said, "Marcellus, this is my friend Beetle. He works at the Manuscriptorium. Beetle, this is Marcellus Pye."

A feeling of unreality stole over Beetle. Marcellus Pye was *five hundred years old*. He was the *Last Alchemist*. His writings were *banned*—even from the Manuscriptorium—and he, Beetle, was being introduced to him. It was not possible.

Marcellus Pye extended his hand and said in a somewhat strange accent, "Welcome. It is wonderful work you young scribes do. Wonderful."

Like a lost sheep, Beetle gazed in bewilderment and made a small baa.

A quick nudge from Septimus sorted the sheep out. "Oh . . . thank you," Beetle said, shaking the offered hand, which was, to his relief, warm—not ice-cold as he had expected. "But I'm not a scribe. I'm the Inspection clerk. I check the **Seals** in the ice tunnels."

"Ah," said Marcellus. "A necessary evil that I hope one day soon will be removed."

"Well, I don't know anything about that," said Beetle, back in professional mode. "But I do know that the hatch for this house has been **UnSealed** recently."

"Possibly. But not for long. I have **ReSealed** it. You have no need to worry."

"But—" Beetle was cut short by the tinkling of a bell far above his head.

Marcellus started at the noise. He looked panic-stricken. "'Tis the doorbell," he said, staring at the door.

"Shall I answer it?" Septimus offered.

"Must you?" asked Marcellus.

"You should try to be more sociable, Marcellus," Septimus scolded him. "It's not good for you to hide away like this."

"But the sun is so bright and the noise so loud, Apprentice."

There was another, more insistent, ring of the doorbell.

"I think it's probably Jenna," said Septimus, itching to open the door. "You said I could bring her here, remember? You said you were ready to tell us what happened. To Nicko."

Marcellus looked puzzled. "Nicko?" he asked.

Septimus's heart sank. For six months now he had been trying to get Marcellus to tell him what he knew about Nicko, and a few days earlier Marcellus had finally agreed. Now it seemed as though he had forgotten—*again*. Septimus found it hard to get used to the fact that although Marcellus Pye looked like a young man once more, he often behaved like an old man. Marcellus had centuries-old habits that were hard to discard—he would lapse into a shuffling old-man gait and adopt a querulous manner. But it was Marcellus's bad memory that annoyed Septimus the most. He had grumpily told Marcellus that this was just laziness, but Marcellus had countered by saying that he had five hundred years of memories in his head and where exactly did Septimus think he was going to find space for all the new ones?

Septimus sighed. He left Marcellus dithering in the hallway and went to answer the door.

"Sep!" said Jenna, sounding relieved. She stood on the doorstep, looking windswept and cold. Her dark hair was wet, hanging in tendrils around her face, and she had her thick red winter cloak wrapped tightly around her. "You took your time," she said, stamping her feet with the cold. "It's *horrible* out here. Aren't you going to let me in?"

"Password please," said Septimus, suddenly serious.

Jenna frowned. "*What* password?"

"Don't you know?"

"No. Oh, *bother*. Can't you let me in anyway?"

"Hmm . . . I don't know about that, Jen."

"Sep, I'm *freezing* out here. *Please.*"

"Oh, all right, then. Since it's you."

Septimus stepped back. Jenna rushed in out of the rain and stood shaking the drips off her cloak. Suddenly she stopped and looked at Septimus suspiciously. "There isn't a password, is there?" she said.

"Nope." Septimus grinned.

"*Horrible* boy!" Jenna laughed and gave Septimus a push. "Oh, hello, Beetle. Nice to see you."

Beetle blushed and found that, once again, he had forgotten how to speak—but Jenna did not seem to notice. She was occupied taking out a small orange cat from beneath her cloak and tucking it under her arm, which surprised Beetle—he hadn't thought of Jenna as someone who would have a cat.

Then for some reason Beetle did not understand, Marcellus said, "Welcome, Esmeralda."

"Thank you, Marcellus," said Jenna. She smiled; she had almost forgotten how she had once been regularly mistaken for Princess Esmeralda in Marcellus Pye's Time.

Then, with an old-fashioned half bow, Marcellus said, "Pray, Princess, Apprentice and Scribe, follow me."

A moment later Beetle was following Jenna, Septimus and Marcellus upstairs, weaving his way around dripping candles, wondering what he had gotten himself into. *And* how he was going to explain it all to Miss Djinn when she found out—which she always did.

✣I5✣
IN THE ATTIC

They followed
Marcellus up to
a small room right at
the top of the house—a
dark space, tucked in
under sloping eaves
and lined with wooden
paneling. The room
was sparsely furnished
with an old trestle table
with two benches, and a
few chairs lined up along
the walls—all left by the
previous owner, Weasal Van

Klampff. In the center of the table was a cluster of candles, lit earlier that morning by the housekeeper and already half burned down.

As Marcellus showed them in, a pang of recognition shot through Septimus—this had been his room not so long ago. Yet he knew it was *so* long ago that it seemed impossible. This was the room where, for the first few nights he had been in Marcellus's Time, an Alchemie Scribe had slept across the doorway to stop him from trying to escape. This was the room where he had desperately thought up all kinds of crazy plans to return to his own Time; the room where he had sat for hours looking out of the window longing to see a familiar face pass by in the street far below. It was not, all things considered, his most favorite place in the world—but now here he was, back again with Beetle and Jenna. *That* was something he had never dared to imagine. Suddenly Septimus felt very peculiar. He sat down with a bump on one of the benches at the trestle table.

Beetle and Jenna sat beside him, and soon three expectant faces were looking up at Marcellus Pye. Marcellus returned their gaze with a puzzled expression. "Now . . . why did we come up here?" he asked.

"It's to do with Nicko. You remember," said Septimus hopefully, although he had no idea why Marcellus had taken them all the way up to this particular room.

"Nicko?" asked Marcellus blankly.

"Nicko. My *brother*. He was trapped in your Time. You *must* remember," said Septimus, a trace of desperation surfacing in his voice. It had taken months for him to arrange this meeting and now, as Marcellus's memory did its familiar disappearing act, he felt it all slipping away again.

"Ah, I remember," said Marcellus. Septimus's spirits lifted. "It was my *spectacles*. I still need them; it is *most* annoying. Now, where are they?"

"They are on the top of your head," said Septimus wearily.

"Indeed, so they are." Marcellus reached for his spectacles and settled them on his nose. "Good," he said. "I shall need them for Nicko's papers."

Septimus felt excited—*now* they were getting somewhere. He smiled at Jenna, whose eyes looked suspiciously bright, as they always did when Nicko's name was mentioned.

Lapsing into his old man's shuffling gait—which Beetle blamed on the weird shoes—Marcellus went over to the chimney and pressed on a small panel high up on the side.

The panel swung open with an apologetic creak. Everyone watched as he took out a ragged collection of brittle, yellowing papers. Carefully, he brought them over to the table and gently laid them down.

Jenna gasped—they were covered in Nicko's distinctive scrawl.

"Nicko and Snorri left these behind," Marcellus said. "I put them in the chimney for safekeeping as I was afraid that someone might throw them away, for they appear to be but notes and jottings in an untutored hand. But, as the years went by—and there were many, many years—I forgot about the hiding place. Indeed, Apprentice, I did not remember again until some months after you asked me about your brother."

"When you said you *didn't* remember," said Septimus.

"'Tis true, I did not. But then things about my old life began to come back to me. And one day when I came up to this room I did remember. Briefly. After that I spent many weeks coming all the way up here only to wonder what it was I wanted. But when you last spoke to me about Nicko, I wrote it down. I carried the note everywhere and then, when I came up here again, I remembered. I even remembered the hiding place—which, to my amazement, I found undisturbed.

Which is why I sent you the message to come here today."

"Thank you, Marcellus," said Septimus.

"I owe it to you, Apprentice. I confess I cannot read much of what is in Nicko's hand, but perhaps you can understand your brother's writing better than I. It may be that the notes will tell their own story. But I will fill in the gaps as much as I can."

Jenna cautiously looked at the papers. The ink was faded to a pale sepia color, and the paper was thin and almost as brown as the ink. Even so, Jenna knew it was Nicko's work. There were doodles of boats, sketches of various sail rigs, numerous games of noughts and crosses, battleships, hangman, plus some she did not recognize and a lot of lists. But somehow instead of making her feel closer to Nicko, seeing his scribbles on such ancient, fragile things made him feel even farther away. Jenna found herself staring at a long, thin piece of paper with tears pricking the backs of her eyelids.

"What does it say, Jen?" asked Septimus.

"He . . . he's made a list."

"Typical Nicko," said Septimus. "Go on, Jen. Read it out."

"Oh. Okay. It says:

• 2 backpacks
• 2 bedrolls (if can find) or wolfskins from market

- Food for two weeks at least. Ask at market for salted stuff.
- Dried biscuits & fruit
- Tinderbox
- Candles
- 2 water bottles or flagon things
- Permit to travel? Ask M.
- 2 warm cloaks
- Boots with fur if possible
- Aunt Ells's lucky socks—remember
- 2 gold trinkets. For Toll-Man.
- Case for Snorri's compass."

As Jenna finished reading the list, the paper began to crumble in her fingers. She quickly laid it down on the table. "I . . . I wonder where he was going," she said.

"Somewhere cold. You can tell a lot from a list," said Beetle, who was a big fan of lists himself.

Jenna hated to think of Nicko—five hundred years ago— setting off for somewhere cold. It made her feel terribly bleak and empty. She sat slowly stroking Ullr for comfort. The cat was curled up on her lap, apparently asleep, but Jenna knew better. She could feel a watchfulness in the way Ullr lay very still and slightly tensed, as if ready to pounce.

Septimus looked at Marcellus Pye. He knew his old master well enough to know that Marcellus had something to tell—something important. "You know something, don't you?" Septimus said. "Tell us. Please, Marcellus."

Marcellus nodded but said nothing. He sat at the end of the table as if in a daydream, staring at the cluster of candles, watching their flames dance in the eddies that blew through the gaps of the ill-fitting windows. Shaking himself out of his reverie, he looked up. "First," he said, "some warmth." Marcellus got up and, striking a flint in the old-fashioned way, he lit the fire that was laid in the grate.

As the flames leaped up around the logs, the Alchemist leaned across the table and began to speak slowly—a habit Septimus remembered from his Alchemie Apprentice days, when Marcellus had wanted his full attention. But that afternoon Marcellus did not lack attention from his audience—all eyes were on him. Accompanied by a distant rumble of thunder—and embarrassingly for Beetle, a much nearer rumble from his stomach—Marcellus Pye began to speak.

✦16✦
SNORRI'S MAP

The Alchemist spoke in a low and measured voice. "As soon as you had gone through the Great Doors of Time the Glass liquefied," Marcellus said. "I cannot tell you what a terrible sight that was. My *Great Triumph* was nothing more than a pool of black stuff on the ground . . ." He shook his head as if still unable to believe what had happened. "Of course then I did not know that Nicko was your brother and, seeing as he had very nearly strangled me, I did not much care who he was.

But some hours later he returned with the girl Snorri and told me how they had **Come Through** another Glass to rescue you, Apprentice. I was impressed with his bravery, but when he asked if he and Snorri could **Go Through** the Glass of Time, all I could do was show them the ghastly black pool. If I had any bad feelings about Nicko, they vanished at that moment. He looked as though he had lost everything in the world— which of course he had. And Snorri too, but she did not react. With her everything was far below the surface, but Nicko . . . he was like an open book."

Jenna sat twisting her hair. She found it very hard to hear about Nicko, and could not help but imagine how he must have felt.

Marcellus continued. "I could do nothing for them except offer them a place to stay and help them in any other way I could. And so for some months—I cannot remember how many—they lived here with me. At first they looked much the way you had, Apprentice—haunted and restless. But after some weeks I noticed that this had changed—they gained a purposeful air; they smiled and even laughed sometimes. At first I thought they had adapted to our Time, and maybe even preferred it—for it was a good Time—but one evening they came and told me about Aunt Ells. After that I knew better, and that soon they would be gone."

"Aunt Ells," Jenna mused. "I'm sure I have heard that name before."

"'Tis likely, Princess," said Marcellus. "Aunt Ells was Snorri's great-aunt. They met her in the marketplace on the Way; she was selling pickled herring."

"They met Snorri's great-aunt?" asked Septimus. "In *your* Time?"

"Indeed. Nicko bought Snorri some pickled herring only to find that it was Aunt Ells who was selling it. The next thing I knew they were planning to leave for the deep forests of the Low Countries. It seems that Aunt Ells told them that there was—or is, I suppose—a place there where All Times Do Meet. It is called the House of Foryx."

There was silence around the table as this sunk in. Another rumble of thunder rolled in the distance and a gust of wind rattled the windows.

"Foryx—they're just in stories, they don't *really* exist," said Septimus.

"Who knows?" Marcellus replied. "I used to think that many things did not exist, but now I am not so sure."

"Nicko used to pretend to be a Foryx when we were little," said Jenna wistfully. "He used to pull his tunic over his head and make horrible growling noises. And he used to scare me with stories about how packs of Foryx would run and run and never stop, and how they would eat everything that was in their way—including little girls. And when we had to cross the road he used to make me look out for horses and carts—and Foryx." She laughed. "Wasn't he *awful?*"

Septimus felt wistful too. Whenever Jenna talked about what she called the old days in The Ramblings, when all the Heaps still lived as a family, it reminded him of all he had missed out on. It was not always a comfortable feeling. He changed the subject. "But what about Aunt Ells—how could she possibly be in *your* Time, Marcellus?"

"I remember what Snorri said now," said Jenna. "Her aunt Ells fell through a Glass when she was young. No one ever saw her again."

"I believe that is so," said Marcellus. "She said she fell through the Glass and came out into the House of Foryx. It was a dreamlike place, apparently, where most people lost the will to leave—but Aunt Ells was a determined child and decided to get out as soon as she could and go back home. She got out all right, but unfortunately she got out into the wrong Time. Nicko told me he was certain that if he and Snorri got to the House of Foryx they could find their way back to their own Time. Aunt Ells, I believe, was not so sure."

"So after they left," asked Septimus, "did you ever hear from them again?"

Marcellus shook his head. "Things were difficult then. It should have been Esmeralda's coronation, but she was in such a nervous state that she refused to come back to the Palace. She stayed in the Marram Marshes with my dear wife, Broda, for some years. I found myself in the position of Regent, running the Palace and also keeping my Alchemie experiments going. All too soon I realized that a whole year had gone by with no message. I was worried, as I had made a point of asking them to send word to let me know they were safe—the forests of the Low Countries were evil places then. I do not know how the forests are now but in my Time they were infested with monsters and monstrosities and all manner of foul things. Of course I told Nicko and Snorri all of this and more, but they would not listen. They were determined to go. I was very sorry. Well, I was sorry *then*, for I thought their young lives had been cut short. But now . . . well, who knows?"

Jenna sat up, her eyes shining with hope. "So *now* you know something else?"

Marcellus shook his head with a rueful smile. "I know a little more now than I did then," he said. "But who knows what it means? Let me tell you about Demelza Heap."

"Demelza?" said Septimus. "I didn't know there was a *Demelza* Heap."

"Not now, maybe," Marcellus replied. "But there was once. And Demelza told me that she had seen Nicko and Snorri. Two hundred years after they left me."

A silence descended in the room. *"Two hundred years?"* whispered Jenna.

A cold shiver went down Beetle's spine. This was creepy stuff. Jillie Djinn was right about Alchemists, he thought.

Marcellus noticed Beetle's expression. "You see, hungry scribe, I gave myself the curse of eternal life without eternal youth." Beetle's eyes widened in amazement. "I would not recommend it." Marcellus grimaced. "When I reached about two hundred and fifty years of age, I was so ancient that I could no longer bear the bright lights and fast chatter of the world. Things had changed so much that I felt I scarcely belonged and I longed to retreat to a place of darkness and silence. And so I made my plans to inhabit the Old Way, which runs between the Palace and my old Alchemie Chamber. It is a secret place belowground and it is not **Sealed** with ice. You look surprised, scribe. Ah, there are still some places untouched by the cold hand of the **Freeze**. Anyway, I decided to sell my house while I still had the wit to do so— and that was when I met Demelza Heap. I still remember it— the moment I opened the door I recognized her. She was a striking woman, tall with green eyes and that same hair that you have, Apprentice—although I believe it had seen more of a comb than yours has recently. In my time as a young man she had kept a shop selling the fine glass apparatus that I used for my experiments. I had gotten to know her well over the years, but she disappeared on a trip to the master glassblowers of the Low Countries. She had gone to search out some special flasks for me and I always felt bad about that.

"So there was Demelza Heap on my doorstep, more than *two hundred years* after she had gone to the Low Countries, and she was as young as ever. She did not recognize me, of course, for I was decrepit by then. When I told her who I was she would not believe me at first, but she humored an old man and we fell to talking over a glass of mead. I think she enjoyed speaking to someone who did not call her crazy when she spoke about what had befallen her. She told me she had become lost in a silent forest and to escape a marauding pack of Foryx—that *is* what she said—she had found refuge in a place where, she told me, All Times Do Meet—a place she, too, called the House of Foryx."

Jenna hardly dared ask the question. "Did . . . did you ask Demelza if she had seen Nicko?"

"I did."

Jenna and Septimus exchanged excited glances.

"And . . . ?" prompted Septimus.

Marcellus smiled. "Not only had she seen him—she had actually *talked* to him. She reckoned she was his great-great-great-great-great-great-great-great-aunt. So at last I knew what had become of them."

"Nicko made it to the House of Foryx," said Jenna, excited.

"So it seems," said Marcellus.

"So he can come back!"

"In a hundred years, maybe, so we'll never see him anyway," Septimus said gloomily. "Or he might have already come back a hundred years ago and now he's de—"

Jenna stopped him. "Sep—don't! Please, just . . . *don't*."

"Apprentice, *enough*," Marcellus chided. "You have a dismal turn of mind at times. We must hope that they quickly understood the Rule of the House of Foryx, which poor Demelza did not—until it was too late."

"What rule?" asked Jenna.

"She did not realize that you have to Go Out when someone from your own Time arrives. They have to remain *outside* the House—they may not enter. Once you step across the threshold you belong to no Time at all."

"Then that's what we'll do," said Jenna, jumping up in excitement. "We shall go to the House of Foryx and Nicko can Go Out with us."

"And Snorri. Don't forget Snorri," said Septimus.

Jenna looked unimpressed. "If it hadn't been for Snorri, Nicko would be here now," she said.

"Oh, *Jen*."

"Well, it's true," Jenna said. "Of course we'll get Snorri too," she added generously. "We might as well while we're there."

Septimus sighed. "You make it all sound so easy. We just catch a passing donkey cart to the House of Foryx, knock on the door and ask for Nik. I *wish*."

"Well, that's exactly what I *am* going to do, Sep, whatever you say. *You* don't have to come."

"Of course I do," said Septimus quietly.

With a small groan, Marcellus got up from his seat. He shuffled over to the cupboard in the chimney and took out a large, folded piece of paper, which he brought back to the table. "I was not going to show you this unless I was sure that nothing would stop you from going to the House of Foryx," he said as he very carefully began to unfold the brittle, brown paper—to reveal a map.

The map was neatly drawn. Along the bottom were the words: FOR MARCELLUS, WITH THANKS. FROM SNORRI AND NICKO. "This is a copy that Snorri drew for me," said Marcellus. "I thought that if I ever had a message that they were in trouble then at least I might have a chance of finding them."

Feeling in awe of the fragile sheet of paper, they looked at the faint pencil lines that Snorri had drawn so precisely, so very long ago. "So *this* is the way to Nicko . . ." Jenna breathed.

"You must treat this with caution," Marcellus urged, afraid that he had given too much encouragement. "Remember that Ells drew the original from her memory of things that had happened when she was only nine. She had had—although I

would not have dared say this to her face—at least fifty years
to forget the details. This may not be accurate."

They were peering closely at the map, trying to make sense
of the crowd of faded lines on the discolored paper when suddenly a loud clap of thunder sounded overhead. Marcellus
jumped in surprise and caught his long trailing sleeves in the
mass of candles in the middle of the table. The fine silk-edged
sleeve caught fire and a horrible smell of burning wool filled
the room. Marcellus yelled in panic and flapped his arms like
an unwieldy bird. He succeeded only in fanning the flames
and knocking over the candles, one of which set fire to the
edge of the map.

"No!" yelled Jenna. She grabbed the map and smothered
the flame with her hand, oblivious of the sharp sting of the
burn.

"Help!" yelled Marcellus, dancing around the room, the
flames licking up his sleeves. "Apprentice—*help!*"

"Bucket!" yelled Beetle.

"Bucket?" asked Septimus.

"Bucket!" Beetle grabbed the bucket of water he had
noticed beside the grate—Marcellus, who had a horror of fire,
had one in every room—and threw it over the Alchemist. A

loud sizzle and copious amounts of smoke filled the room. Marcellus collapsed onto a chair.

Marcellus sat sadly inspecting his ruined sleeves while Jenna refolded the precious map, and Septimus and Beetle retrieved Nicko's notes from the floor.

"Are you all right, Marcellus?" Septimus asked the damp, slightly smoking Alchemist.

Marcellus nodded and got to his feet. "Fire is a terrible thing," he said. "Thank you, scribe, for your speedy action."

"You're welcome," replied Beetle. "Anytime."

"I hope not," said Marcellus.

Jenna placed the last of Nicko's notes in a neat pile on the table and Marcellus went to pick them up. Jenna put her hand on them protectively.

"I'd like to keep them, please," she said.

"Very well, Princess. They are yours." Marcellus opened a drawer in the table and took out some tissue paper. With great care he wrapped up the brittle papers, tied them with a length of ribbon and handed them to Jenna. She tucked them under her cloak, then scooped up Ullr.

"Why don't I take the papers, Jen?" asked Septimus. "You can't carry them *and* Ullr."

"Yes, I can," Jenna insisted, and she set off purposefully out of the room as if she were already on her way to the House of Foryx.

As they clattered down the candlelit stairs in her wake, Septimus said, "Marcellus?"

"Yes, Apprentice? Oh! Watch your cloak on that candle."

"Oops. Um . . . Do *you* think Nik and Snorri are still in the House of Foryx—after all this time?"

"Maybe . . ." said Marcellus slowly as they reached the third-floor landing. Jenna sped off down the next flight of stairs, her boots tapping lightly on the bare wood, while Marcellus stopped and considered the matter. "And maybe I shall be taking tea with the ExtraOrdinary Wizard at the top of the Wizard Tower," he said. "Highly unlikely, but not totally impossible."

Septimus wished Marcellus had chosen a different example. Given Marcia's opinion of Marcellus Pye—and her complete ignorance of his present existence—totally impossible seemed more like it.

Jenna was waiting impatiently in the hallway. As Septimus, Beetle and Marcellus joined her, there was a furious knocking on the door. Everyone jumped.

"Prithee open the door, Apprentice," said Marcellus, flustered and reverting to Old Speak.

"I don't have to, not if you would rather not," said Septimus, who had a horrible feeling that there was only one person in the Castle who would ignore a perfectly serviceable doorbell and attack a door knocker like that.

Marcellus made an effort to compose himself. "No, no. You are quite right, Apprentice. I must not hide away from this Time," he said. "Open the door and we will be sociable, as you say."

Septimus gave the door a halfhearted pull. "I think it's stuck," he said.

"Here, let me," said Beetle, and he gave the handle a hefty tug. The door flew open to reveal Marcia Overstrand standing on the doorstep windswept, grumpy and soaked.

"Oh," said Septimus. "Hello, Marcia."

✠ 17 ✠
TROUBLE

Well," said Marcia icily. "Aren't you going to ask me in?"

Septimus looked around in a panic and caught Marcellus's eye. "With pleasure, Madam Marcia," said Marcellus, bowing one of his old-fashioned bows. "Please, do come in." He stepped to one side only just in time to avoid Marcia treading on his sodden shoes as she swept inside.

"Shut," she instructed the door and it did so with a loud slam that rattled the fragile walls of the old house—but it did not rattle Marcellus. In his own Time, Marcellus had had many dealings with belligerent ExtraOrdinary Wizards; he knew the best thing to do was keep a cool head and be polite at all times—whatever the provocation. And right now, as he looked at Marcia fuming in the hall, the rain dripping off her purple winter cloak and her green eyes flashing angrily, Marcellus reckoned he was in for a fair amount of provocation.

All of Marcellus's lack of confidence at living in a Time not his own suddenly left him. Some things in life were Timeless, and an ExtraOrdinary Wizard was one of them. Feeling quite at home, Marcellus said, "How kind of you to call. May I offer you some refreshment?"

"No," snapped Marcia, "you may not."

"Ah," murmured Marcellus, thinking that this was going to be one of the tougher ones.

Marcia fixed her gaze on Septimus much in the way a snake might look at a small vole at suppertime. "Septimus," she said icily, "perhaps you would like to introduce me to your . . . *friend*."

Septimus desperately wished that he could be somewhere—*anywhere*—else. Even the bottom of a wolverine pit in the Forest would be just fine with him right then. "Um," he said.

"Well?" Marcia tapped her right foot, which was encased in a pointy purple python shoe complete with new green buttons.

Septimus took a deep breath. "Marcia, this is Marcellus Pye. Marcellus, this is Marcia Overstrand, ExtraOrdinary Wizard."

"Thank you, Septimus," said Marcia. "That is *precisely* who I thought it was. Well, Mr. Pye, *my* Apprentice will not trouble you any longer. He will *not* be returning and I am sorry for any bother he has been over these last few months. Come, Septimus." With that Marcia made for the door but Marcellus got there first and barred her way.

"*My* old and *greatly valued* Apprentice has been no bother," he said. "It has been very kind of you to let me borrow him every now and then. I am most grateful."

"Borrow him!" exploded Marcia. "Septimus is not a library book. I have not forgotten that you *borrowed* him—as you put it—for six whole months and put the boy through absolute misery. Why he still wants to see you I cannot imagine. But I am not having him corrupted by your Alchemie claptrap any longer. Good-bye. Open!" The last word was addressed to the

door. It sprang open, nearly pinning Marcellus against the
wall. Reluctantly Septimus, Jenna and Beetle followed her out
into the rain and wind.

Septimus risked a tentative wave to Marcellus as Marcia
yelled, "Shut!" and the door slammed, shaking the windows of
the old house. A rumble of thunder rolled in the distance as
Marcia scolded all three of them. "Beetle," she said, "I am surprised at you. Let's hope for your sake that Miss Djinn does
not get to hear about you fraternizing with an Alchemist—
especially *that* one. And Jenna, I should have thought you
would have learned your lesson by now to keep away from
that man. He is Etheldredda's *son*, for goodness sake. Come,
Septimus, there are a few things I wish to discuss with you."

Jenna and Beetle shot Septimus sympathetic glances as
Marcia propelled her Apprentice rapidly along Snake Lane,
which led into Wizard Way. Beetle almost asked Jenna if he
could walk her to the Palace gate but to his annoyance he
didn't quite dare. Jenna gave him a brief wave and rushed off
along Snake Slipway toward the Palace. Beetle set off at a snail's
pace, taking the long way back to the Manuscriptorium—
and a possible encounter with Jillie Djinn, which he did not
relish at all.

Marcia and Septimus took the turn into Wizard Way. A sudden squall of rain blew in from the river and a gust of wind funneled up the broad avenue. They pulled their cloaks tight about them until they were wrapped up like a couple of angry cocoons. Neither said a word.

Halfway along the Way the green cocoon finally spoke. "I think you were very rude," it said.

"*What?*" Marcia could hardly believe her ears.

"I think you were very rude to Marcellus," Septimus repeated.

"That man," spluttered Marcia, almost lost for words, "has no right to expect anything else."

"He was very polite to *you*."

"Huh. Polite is as polite does. I do not think it is *polite* to kidnap my Apprentice and place him in extreme danger. Not to mention what he is up to now—exposing my Apprentice to all kinds of weird and dangerous ideas *behind my back*."

"He doesn't have any weird or dangerous ideas," protested Septimus. "And he didn't know I hadn't told you about him."

"But why didn't you tell me?" asked Marcia. "For *months* you let me think you were visiting your poor mother. No wonder she looked so puzzled when I asked her if she was enjoying seeing so much of you—I *thought* she was a bit snappy. If I hadn't gone to Terry Tarsal this morning I would never have found out. And incidentally, Septimus, I would like to know exactly how Marcellus Pye got to be looking so young again—*and* living in poor old Weasal's house."

"It was Marcellus's house first," said Septimus, ignoring the first question. "I lived there too, in his Time. I *told* you. And you didn't call him poor old Weasal last year. You said that he was lucky not to be sent into exile along with his housekeeper."

"And so he was," said Marcia.

Anxious to stop Marcia from pursuing the question of Marcellus's youthful appearance, Septimus quickly carried on. "So when Weasal left to go and live in the Port, Marcellus bought his house back with some gold pebbles he had hidden under the mud on Snake Slipway."

"Did he *really*? Well, Marcellus seems to have it all sewn up, doesn't he? But the point is, Septimus, that I shouldn't have to run around after my Apprentice like this just to find out the truth about what he is doing. I really *shouldn't*."

"I know. I'm sorry," muttered Septimus. "I . . . I wanted to tell you. I kept meaning to but, well, I knew you'd get upset and it just seemed easier not to."

"I only get upset," said Marcia, "because I want to protect you from harm. And how can I do that if you are not honest with me?"

"Marcellus is not harmful," said Septimus sullenly.

"*That* is where you and I disagree," said Marcia.

"But if you just talked to him for a bit. I know you'd—"

"*And* I would like an answer to my question."

Septimus stalled for time. "What question?"

"As I said, I would like to know exactly *how* Marcellus Pye got to be looking so young. The man is over five hundred years old. And don't try to tell me he's just kept out of the sun—no amount of face cream is going to do *that* for him."

"It was my side of the bargain," said Septimus quietly.

"What bargain?" asked Marcia suspiciously.

"The bargain I made to go back to my own Time. I agreed to make him the proper potion for eternal youth. There was a conjunction of the planets and—"

"What claptrap!" spluttered Marcia. "You don't really believe that ridiculous stuff, do you, Septimus?"

"Yes, I do," said Septimus quietly. "So the day after I got back to my Time I made the potion."

Marcia felt hurt. She remembered how amazed and thrilled

she had been to have Septimus back and how she had fondly left him to sleep all day in his room, thinking that he must have been exhausted. And all that time he had been quietly making a potion for that appalling Alchemist who had kidnapped him in the first place. It was unbelievable. "Why didn't you tell me?" she asked.

"Because you'd say it was ridiculous—like you just did. You might even have tried to stop me. And I couldn't let Marcellus go on being so unhappy. It was horrible. I had to help him."

"So you made a potion for eternal youth—just like that?" asked Marcia, bewildered.

"It wasn't too difficult. The planets were right—" Marcia suppressed a splutter. "And I just followed the instructions that Marcellus had left in the Physik Chest. I put it in the golden box he had left in the chest and I dropped it into the Moat by Snake Slipway so that he could pick it up. He used to like going for night walks in the Moat."

"In the *Moat*?"

"Well, under it, really. He used to walk along the bottom. It helped his aches and pains. I saw him once. It looked weird."

"He went for walks . . . *under* the Moat?" Marcia looked

rather like a fish that had just been dragged out of the Moat herself. Rivulets of rain ran down her face, and her mouth was open as if gasping for air.

Septimus continued. "So he picked up the box and I knew he'd got it because he put the **Flyte Charm** in it in exchange. I fished it out, although it took me weeks to find it. There's an awful lot of garbage in the Moat."

Marcia remembered Septimus's sudden interest in fishing. It all made sense now—well, not quite all. "What was *he* doing with the **Flyte Charm**?"

"He took it. But later he promised to give it back. Although he didn't know he'd taken it anyway."

"*What?*"

"It's a bit complicated. Um, Marcia . . ."

"Yes?" Marcia sounded a little faint.

"Can I have the **Flyte Charm** back now? Please. I won't fool around with it anymore, I promise."

Marcia's answer was what Septimus expected. "No, you may not."

Wizard and Apprentice walked in silence along the rest of Wizard Way, but as they went across the Courtyard of the Wizard Tower, Marcia's python shoes with their new green buttons slipped on something dragony. That was the last straw. "Septimus," she snapped, "that dragon is going *right now*. I am not having it pollute this yard a moment longer."

"But—"

"No buts. It's all arranged. Mr. Pot will be looking after him in the big field next to the Palace."

"Billy Pot? But—"

"I said *no buts*. Mr. Pot is very experienced with lizards and I am sure he will be absolutely fine with what is, after all, nothing more than one enormous lizard with an attitude problem. The rain's blowing over; you can take him there right now before more comes in."

"But Spit Fyre's still asleep," protested Septimus. "You know what happens if I wake him up."

Marcia did know—they had only just finished reglazing all the ground-floor windows of the Wizard Tower—but she didn't care. "No excuses, Septimus. You will take him over to Mr. Pot. Then you will come straight back here to make a start on your first **Projection**. It is high time you got some **Magyk** back into your head and got rid of all this Alchemie stuff once and for all. In fact, **Magyk** is what you are going to be doing *full-time* from now on, as you are not setting foot out of the Wizard Tower for the next two weeks."

"Two *weeks!*" protested Septimus.

"Possibly four," said Marcia. "I shall see how it goes. I expect you back in an hour." With that, Marcia Overstrand strode off across the Courtyard. She ran up the marble steps; then the silver doors of the Wizard Tower swung open and swallowed her up.

For once Spit Fyre woke without any trouble. He allowed Septimus to climb up and sit in his usual place, the dip behind the dragon's neck, and there was none of the usual snorting and tail thumping that Spit Fyre had recently taken to doing when Septimus climbed up. Today he was almost docile—apart from the quick burst of scalding hot air that he aimed at the passing Catchpole's cloak, which resulted in a foul smell of burned wool and old toast.

As this was a last chance for the Wizards to see the dragon take off at such close quarters, Septimus decided to give them a good view. On his command of "Up, Spit Fyre," the dragon beat his wings slowly and powerfully, sending a great downdraft of air whipping through the Courtyard. It was a perfect liftoff. Septimus took Spit Fyre up slowly past each floor, getting as near to the Tower as he dared. Windows were thrown open, blue-robed Wizards excitedly leaned out and the sound of applause rippled out from the Tower. As the dragon reached the twentieth floor a large window was thrown open and Septimus got a less appreciative response.

"Fifty minutes!" Marcia yelled and slammed the window shut. Spit Fyre wheeled away from the Tower in surprise but Septimus brought him back. They flew once around the golden pyramid at the top for luck, then set off. The storm had passed and clearer skies were coming in from the Port. The sun broke through the clouds and, far below, the rooftops glistened in the rain and glints of brilliant light sparkled from the puddles in the street. After six months of regular dragon-flying and three months before that of intense tuition with Alther Mella, Septimus was a confident flier. He decided to make the most of what would be his last flight for a while and take the long route to the Palace.

Septimus took Spit Fyre out over the North Gate and back above his favorite part of the Castle, The Ramblings. Entranced by the sight of so many peoples' lives going on below him, Septimus gazed down and let Spit Fyre choose his own way. He saw people out after the storm, hanging out their washing, tending their rooftop gardens or watching the rain-bow that had just appeared over the Farmlands. At the sound of the dragon wings beating far above, they stopped and waved—or just stared in amazement. Children, let out of stuffy rooms to play in the sun, ran along the open walkways of The Ramblings. Septimus heard their voices yelling with excitement, "Dragon, *dragon!*" But with Marcia's words ring-ing in his ears, Septimus knew he did not have much time for lingering and, reluctantly, he pointed Spit Fyre in the direction of the Palace. All too soon he was approaching Billy Pot's new vegetable field.

Septimus thought he made a good landing, but Billy Pot thought otherwise.

"Careful! Watch them lettuces!" Billy yelled as Spit Fyre folded his wings and set his tail down with a dull thud on some lettuce seedlings.

Septimus slipped down from Spit Fyre's neck. "I've brought Spit Fyre," he said rather unnecessarily.

"So I see," said Billy.

Billy Pot waited while Septimus patted the dragon's neck, rubbing his hand over the smooth scales, which were still chilled from the flight. After a minute or two he said, "Well, aren't you going to introduce us?"

"Yes," said Septimus, reluctant to leave his dragon.

"Dragons are sticklers for etiquette. They like to be introduced properly."

"Do they?" asked Septimus, surprised. "Well, Spit Fyre, may I introduce Billy Pot? And Billy, this is Spit Fyre, the best dragon ever. Aren't you, Spit Fyre?" Septimus gently patted the dragon's velvety nose.

Spit Fyre ducked his head and snorted a plume of air, which scorched some nearby carrot tops. Billy stepped up close. He met Spit Fyre's red-rimmed dragon eye and said, "I am honored to make your acquaintance, Mr. Spit Fyre."

Spit Fyre leaned his head to one side, considering what Billy Pot had said. Then he ducked his head once more and pushed his nose into Billy's rough tweed coat. Billy staggered back with the push and fell into a bed of parsley. But he jumped straight back on his feet and, after wiping his muddy hands on his corduroy tunic, he patted Spit Fyre's neck. "There," he said, "I can tell we'll be friends."

✦ 18 ✦
IN PIECES

Jenna was making her way back to the Palace. The squall that had caught Marcia and Septimus in Wizard Way had ambushed her, too. The driving rain stung her eyes and the wind sent her cloak flapping around her ankles as if it were trying to trip her up. Jenna put her head down and ran, one hand holding on to Ullr and her cloak, the other tightly clasping Nicko's notes and Snorri's precious map. She headed straight past the Palace Gates and ran for the relative shelter of the alleyway at the side of the Palace, which would take her to the kitchen garden. As she scoot-ed into the alley she was going fast—so fast that even if she had been looking she would not have had time to stop—when a dark, lanky figure dashed around the corner and hurtled toward her.

The collision with Merrin sent Jenna flying backward; she hit the wall with a thud that knocked the breath out of both her and Ullr. Merrin went sprawling to the ground but, like a gangly spider, he scrambled back onto his feet. He glared angrily at Jenna and raced off, determined not to be late.

Dazed, Jenna allowed Ullr to untangle himself from her cloak. She stood up and rubbed the back of her head, where a large bump was already beginning to form. For a moment she felt confused and, as she glanced down, she wondered about the strange brown confetti floating in the puddles at her feet. And then she knew.

Feeling suddenly sick, Jenna kneeled down and stared in disbelief. All Nicko's notes—and worse, Snorri's map—had been crushed in the collision and were now in hundreds of wet pieces on the ground. Their last chance of finding Nicko was gone.

Beetle was wandering slowly across the front of the Palace, oblivious to the rain, which was soaking through his woolen jacket and finding its way into his boots. The excitement of the last bizarre hour he had spent with Septimus and Jenna had evaporated in the downpour, and Beetle had begun worrying about what awaited him at the Manuscriptorium. He wondered if Marcia had already paid a visit to inform Jillie Djinn that he had been in the company of the Alchemist. Beetle was also worrying about how to get his sled back. Unlike the Wizard Tower sled, it did not respond to a whistle. It didn't even *have* a whistle. Even worse, the sled was prone to wandering off and Beetle could not remember if he had tied it up or not. He had been so keen to see Jenna that he had completely forgotten about his job. How was he going to explain *that*? Beetle felt very annoyed with himself and swore that he would never, *ever* again let the thought of Jenna get in the way of his work—and then he caught sight of her down the Palace alleyway kneeling in a puddle.

"Princess Jenna?" Beetle's concerned voice intruded on

Jenna's despair. "Are—are you all right?"

Jenna shook her head. She did not look up.

Feeling as though he was doing something he shouldn't, something that only someone who knew her well would do, Beetle kneeled down beside her. "Can I help?" he asked.

Jenna looked at him. Beetle was not sure whether it was raindrops or tears running down her face. He had a feeling it might be both. Jenna pointed at the flurry of paper floating in the puddle and said angrily, "I've messed up. It's *all my fault*. We'll never find them now."

Beetle had a terrible feeling that he knew what the bits of paper were. "Oh no," he murmured. "That's not . . ."

Jenna nodded miserably.

Tentatively, Beetle picked up a soggy fragment and laid it on the palm of his hand. "Maybe . . ." he said slowly, thinking very hard.

"What?"

"Maybe if we collected it all we could do something."

"Really?" A small note of hope crept into Jenna's voice.

"I—I don't want to promise too much, but the Manuscriptorium is good at this kind of stuff. It's worth a try." From his pocket, Beetle took a small packet and unfolded it until he had a large square of fine silk balanced on his knee. He licked his finger and thumb and rubbed the edges of the silk so that they parted. The silk square revealed itself to be a pouch with many compartments. "I always carry one of these," said Beetle. "You never know when you might find something you want to put in it."

"Gosh," said Jenna, who never seemed to carry anything useful with her.

With the rain still falling—and to the accompaniment of miserable mewing from a sodden orange cat—Beetle and Jenna spent the next ten minutes meticulously picking up the delicate scraps of five-hundred-year-old paper and laying them in Beetle's silk pouch. When they had satisfied themselves that they had found every last piece, Beetle carefully rolled up the silk and said, "Would you like to carry it under your cloak, Princess Jenna? I think it will keep drier there."

"I'm just Jenna, Beetle. *Please.*" Jenna smiled and tucked the roll of silk inside her cloak.

"Um. Shall I . . . ?" Beetle pointed to the shivering Ullr, faithfully waiting beside the puddle.

"Oh, yes *please,*" said Jenna.

Beetle picked up the cat and tucked the soggy animal inside

his jacket. Then together he and Jenna set off for the Manu-scriptorium. As they walked along Wizard Way, it occurred to Beetle that if it were not for the niggling fear that the Manuscriptorium would not be able to put Nicko and Snorri's papers back together, he would be completely and utterly happy just then.

All that changed when he pushed open the door to the Manuscriptorium. He was confronted by Jillie Djinn and Merrin Meredith, who were about to go into the Manuscriptorium itself. At the ping of the door and the click of the counter, both of them looked back.

"And *where* have you been?" demanded Miss Djinn.

"I—I was doing a hatch Inspection. Marcia—I mean Madam Overstrand told me to—"

"You are not employed by Madam Overstrand, Mr. Beetle. You are employed by *me*. I have had to take a scribe out to cover you. Which leaves precisely nineteen left for the Duties of the Day. Nineteen is not enough. Luckily for you, I have a promising candidate for the vacant post."

Beetle gasped.

Merrin smirked.

Jillie Djinn continued. "And what, pray Beetle, do you

mean by removing my advertisement, crumpling it up into a ball and throwing it in the garbage? You are getting above yourself. In fact I may well consider this young man for *your* post if you continue in this manner."

Beetle went pale.

"Excuse me, Miss Djinn," said Jenna, emerging from the shadows of a teetering stack of books by the door.

Jillie Djinn looked surprised. She had been so angry at Beetle that she had not noticed Jenna. In fact, Jillie generally found dealing with more than two people at one time confusing. The Chief Scribe gave a small bow and said, a little awkwardly, "How may I help you, Princess Jenna?"

Jenna put on her best Princess voice. She thought it sounded pompous but she had noticed it generally got her what she wanted. "Mr. Beetle has been engaged on very important Palace business. We have come to give you our personal thanks for allowing us to have the benefit of his expert knowledge. We do apologize if we have kept him too long. It is our fault entirely."

Jillie Djinn looked confused. "I was not aware of any Palace business this morning," she said. "It was not in the diary."

"Highly confidential," said Jenna. "As we are sure you are aware."

Jillie Djinn was not aware of any such thing, but she did not want to be shown up in front of her possible new recruit. "Oh," she said. "Well, yes. *Highly* confidential. Of course. I am glad we could be of service, Princess Jenna. Now, please excuse me, we are already two and three quarter minutes late for the interview." With that Miss Djinn ushered Merrin into the gloom of the Manuscriptorium, gave another small bow in Jenna's direction and was gone.

Beetle extricated Ullr and set him gently on the desk. "Phew," he said. "I don't know how to thank you, Prin— Jenna. I really don't."

"Yes, you do." Jenna smiled. She handed him the rolled-up silk pouch.

"Yes," said Beetle, looking at the pouch. "I guess I do."

+✛+ 19 +✛+
MR. EPHANIAH GREBE

F*oxy?" said Beetle in a hoarse whisper.*

Nineteen scribes looked up from their work and the sound of nineteen scratching pens ceased. "Yeah?" said Foxy.

"Would you watch the office for me? There's something I need to do."

Foxy was not sure. "What about *her*?" he

whispered, jabbing his thumb in the direction of a firmly closed door just off the Manuscriptorium, where Jillie Djinn was interviewing Merrin.

"She won't be out for twenty-two-and-a-half minutes," said Beetle, thinking that sometimes Miss Djinn's obsession with timekeeping had its advantages.

"You sure?"

Beetle nodded.

Glad of an excuse to stop copying out Jillie Djinn's calculations about the projected price of haddock for the next three-and-a-half years, Foxy slipped down from his high stool and padded out to the front office. At the sight of the soaking wet and disheveled Jenna he raised his eyebrows but said nothing.

Beetle gave Foxy a thumbs-up sign and said to Jenna, "I'd better go and take this down while I've got a chance."

"Can I come?" asked Jenna, to Beetle's amazement.

"What—with *me*?"

"Yes. I'd like to see what's going to happen to the map." Jenna was reluctant to let her only hope of getting Nicko back out of her sight for one moment.

"Well, yes. Of course. It's, um, through here." Conscious of Foxy's stare, Beetle held open the door that led from the front office into the actual Manuscriptorium, and Jenna walked through. Eighteen pens stopped their scratching and eighteen pairs of eyes stared as Beetle and *the Princess* walked past the rows of desks toward the basement stairs.

The basement was actually a collection of cellars. Over many hundreds of years the Manuscriptorium had annexed its neighbors' cellars, usually without any of them noticing, and it was now in possession of a long network of underground rooms in which Beetle hoped to find Mr. Ephaniah Grebe, the Conservation, Preservation and Protection Scribe.

Ephaniah Grebe not only worked in the basement, he lived there. None of the present scribes could remember ever seeing Ephaniah upstairs, although it was rumored that he did emerge at night when everyone had gone home. Even Jillie Djinn had seen him only once, on the day she was inducted as Chief Hermetic Scribe—but Beetle knew him well.

Usually anything in need of Conservation, Preservation or Protection was left in a basket at the top of the basement stairs every evening. In the morning it would be gone and in its place would be some of the Conserved, Preserved or Protected objects that had been left over the last week or so. Beetle would not have dreamed of leaving the precious fragments of paper in an unattended basket, so while Foxy kept an uneasy watch for Jillie Djinn—but no customers, as he had locked the door to prevent any danger of *that*—Beetle and Jenna set off in search of Ephaniah Grebe.

At the foot of the stairs was a long, dark corridor that ended with a door covered in green baize and big brass rivets. Beetle gave it a hefty push and the door swung open on well-oiled hinges. The appearance of the basement was not what Jenna was expecting; it was light and airy and smelled fresh and clean. The walls were painted white, the flagstone floor was scrubbed, and from the vaulted ceiling hung lamps that burned with a bright white flame and emitted a constant hiss—which was the only sound that Beetle and Jenna could hear.

The first cellar was the one Beetle was familiar with—this was where Ephaniah had helped him rebuild his timepiece. It was what the Conservation Scribe called his mechanical cellar, and it was peopled by tiny and not-so-tiny automatons. One of which—a rower in a boat followed by a circling seagull—suddenly sprang into action as Jenna walked by, and it was all she could do not to scream. But of Ephaniah Grebe there was no sign.

The next cellar was full of shelves that were stocked with a

large array of colored bottles, each neatly labeled. On a table
under a glass dome was a crushed **Remember Me** Spell that
Beetle remembered a distraught woman bringing in a few days
previously. This cellar too was empty.

Feeling as though they were intruding, Beetle set off with
Jenna deeper into the interlinked cellars, their footsteps echoing with the tinny sound that brick gives back. Beetle was
amazed at the mixture of work in progress. In one cellar was a
tiny book, laid out page by page, each one attached to a thick
piece of paper by a long, thin pin. To one side were a pair of
tweezers and a pot of newly collected paper beetle larvae.
Another cellar held a small snake, rearing up as though about
to strike. Beetle jumped back in shock and then, embarrassed,
realized it was actually a stuffed snake, and a box of assorted
snake fangs sitting beside it told him that its fangs were being
replaced.

But still there was no sign of Ephaniah Grebe. Worried
that time was ticking away, Beetle sped up. They scooted
through one cellar after another, each with an ongoing project
set out neatly on a table and each one devoid of Ephaniah
Grebe, until at last they arrived at the wide archway that
opened into the final and largest cellar.

Underneath Jenna's cloak, Ullr unsheathed his claws.

At first sight this cellar also appeared empty, apart from a round table in the center with a bright white, hissing light suspended above it. But as they stood in the archway a slight movement drew their attention to a figure, bent over a task that they could not see, sitting on a tall stool at a bench in the far corner. The figure was wrapped in a white cloak, blending in perfectly with the whitewashed wall behind him.

"Ahem," coughed Beetle quietly. There was no response. "Excuse me," he said. Still there was no reaction. The figure continued with whatever painstaking task he was busy with. Increasingly worried that Miss Djinn's interview would soon be at an end, Beetle hurried over and tapped him on the shoulder. The figure leaped with shock and spun around.

"Ephaniah, I'm sorry to bother you," said Beetle, "but I—"

"Argh!" Jenna screamed. Too late she tried to smother it, her hand flying to her mouth in horror. Half the man's face was that of a *rat*. Rat nose, rat whiskers and two long, yellow rodent teeth. The rat's mouth opened in shock, showing a pointed pink tongue. Quickly, the rat-man covered the lower part of his face with a long white silken cloth that had gotten loose and fallen around his neck. He readjusted it, winding it round and round until the swathes of silk covered the pointed bump of the rat nose.

"Oh," gasped Beetle, realizing he should have warned Jenna what to expect. "I am so sorry, Ephaniah. I didn't mean to interrupt like this."

Ephaniah Grebe nodded and squeaked something. Then he pushed his thick bottle-glass spectacles up onto the top of his head. Beneath the spectacles, Jenna saw a pair of sparkling, decidedly human, green eyes and she relaxed. Beetle began to apologize once more but Ephaniah Grebe held up his hand to stop him, wriggled off his stool and bowed deeply to Jenna. Then he took a long silver box from his pocket.

Inside the box was an index of hundreds of small white cards. Ephaniah Grebe leafed swiftly through it, took a card and laid it on the table. He beckoned Jenna and Beetle forward and pointed to a well-thumbed card. It said: DO NOT BE AFRAID. I AM HUMAN.

"Oh. What . . . *happened*?" asked Jenna.

Another, equally well-thumbed card took its place: PERMA-NENT RAT HEX. AMBUSHED AGE 14 BY DARKE HEX DIARY AND DARKE RAT REBUS IN WILD BOOK STORE.

Beetle gulped. He had never asked what had befallen

Ephaniah, but he wasn't surprised. He had always wondered what would happen if two **Darke** books got together and ganged up on him.

Another card: WITCH MOTHER MORWENNA SAVED ME. NOW PARTIAL HEX ONLY. He held out his hands, which were human—although Jenna thought the nails looked strangely long and thin, a little like rat claws.

Beetle realized he had not introduced Jenna. "Ephaniah," he said, "this is Princess Jenna."

Ephaniah Grebe bowed and, after some frantic leafing through the index, he placed an unused, pristine white card on the table: WELCOME, YOUR MAJESTY.

It was followed by another, well-thumbed card: WHAT CAN I DO FOR YOU?

In answer, Beetle laid his roll of silk on the table and unrolled it. He groaned, horrified at the sodden mash of paper that lay in its folds. He realized that he had been so busy comforting Jenna that he had not really taken in the enormous damage caused by not only the collision, but also the water. The ink had run, most of the pencil markings were rubbed off, and many of the fragile pieces were now stuck together. It reminded Beetle of the papier-mâché mix he used to play with at his nursery school.

Ephaniah Grebe made a long *aaaah* kind of sound, more like a concerned sheep than a rat, Beetle thought. The Conservation Scribe pulled his bottle-glass spectacles back down onto his long nose and peered at the disaster. Soon another card was placed on the table: WHAT IS IT?

And so Beetle explained as best he could what it was and how the papers had come to be in such a bad state. While he was speaking Jenna looked more and more agitated until she burst out, "Please, Mr. Grebe. Say you can put them all back together again. *Please.*"

Another card on the table: IT IS DIFFICULT.

Then, seeing Jenna's face fall, another: NOT IMPOSSIBLE.

"Those pieces of paper are my only chance of ever seeing my brother again," said Jenna simply.

Ephaniah Grebe's eyebrows were raised in surprise and he put his head to one side in a way that reminded Jenna—rather comfortingly—of Stanley. He reached for a pad and a pencil and wrote: *I will do my utmost. I promise.*

"Thank you, Mr. Grebe," said Jenna. *"Thank you!"*

They left Ephaniah Grebe poking at the sodden mess with a pair of tweezers. As they left the cellar, Jenna turned back for a last look at the precious fragments—and nearly screamed once more. Snaking out from under Ephaniah

Grebe's voluminous white robes was a long, giant pink rat's tail.

Beetle was heading fast through the cellars. "We've gotta run," he said as Jenna caught up with him. "Miss Djinn will be out any minute now." Jenna nodded. Together they raced back through the cellars, shot up the stairs—and were just in time to see a smiling Jillie Djinn emerging from the interview room, followed by a grinning Merrin Meredith.

The Chief Hermetic Scribe's smile faded as she saw Beetle emerge at the back of the Manuscriptorium. "*What* are you doing away from your post *again*?" she demanded. And then, noticing Jenna, a little irritably, "Good afternoon, Princess Jenna. We are honored to see you so *very* many times in one day. Can I *help* you?"

"No, thank you, Miss Djinn," Jenna replied in her Princess voice. "Your Inspection Clerk, Beetle, has already been most helpful. We are sorry to have kept him from his post. Naturally, Beetle ensured that it was not left unattended. We will take our leave now, as we have important business to attend to."

"Ah," said Jillie Djinn, feeling somehow wrong-footed once more, but not sure why. She gave a small half bow and watched the nearest scribe to the door jump down from his stool and hold the door open for Jenna, who swept out in the manner of Marcia Overstrand. Jillie Djinn turned to Beetle. "In that case, Beetle, now that the Princess no longer requires your services you can spend the rest of the afternoon showing our new trainee scribe the ropes."

"*What?*" gasped Beetle.

From behind the voluminous blue silk robes of his new boss, Merrin Meredith made a rude sign at Beetle. Beetle very nearly returned it but stopped himself just in time.

"B—but he hasn't taken the exams yet," Beetle could not help protesting.

"It is not your place, Mr. Beetle, to suggest the criteria I apply when appointing my scribes," Jillie Djinn replied icily. "*You* may well have needed to take the Manuscriptorium examinations, but Daniel has shown enough knowledge to convince me that the examinations would serve no purpose whatsoever in the selection process. Now, I would be grateful if you would do as I have requested and take our new scribe on his induction tour. You have one hour and thirty-three minutes. I suggest you make a start. I shall leave it to your own initiative to decide where."

Beetle grinned. He knew exactly where he would make a start—the Wild Book Store.

✠ 2 0 ✠
ReUnite

T hat *evening another gale came* in from the Port. It howled up the river, whisking slates off roofs and making everyone irritable and edgy.

Septimus was marooned in the Wizard Tower under the eagle eye of Marcia Overstrand. He was beginning the complicated preparations for his first **Projection**, which was an important milestone in an Apprentice's studies. A first **Projection** traditionally involved the Apprentice choosing a small domestic item and then trying to **Project** a realistic image of this object inside the communal areas of the Tower in the hope that it was believable enough to pass for the real thing. All **Projections** were mirror images of the original but, providing the Apprentice was careful not to choose something with lettering on it, this did not usually matter. Sometimes a seemingly innocuous "broom" would be propped up in a dark corner, a small "ornament" would sit high up on an inaccessible window ledge or a new "cloak" would hang in the closet. Throughout the time of the first **Projection**, an air of excitement would pervade the Tower as the Wizards, busy pretending they were doing something entirely different, went around prodding all manner of suspicious objects—and taking bets on what exactly the Apprentice would **Project**.

With Septimus shut away in the **Projection** room, Marcia made a start on removing the traces of Spit Fyre from the yard—or rather, she got Catchpole to do it for her. However, by that evening Catchpole had locked himself in the Old Spells cupboard and would not come out. Exasperated, Marcia sent a message to Hildegarde, the sub-Wizard on door duty at the Palace, to come to the Wizard Tower straightaway.

Hildegarde arrived windswept and out of breath, having

run all along Wizard Way, thrilled that at last she had received the summons to the Wizard Tower that she had long wished for. But instead of being offered a post as an Ordinary Wizard, Hildegarde was given a large broom and an even larger bucket. Hildegarde, determined as ever, rolled up her sleeves and got to work, telling herself sternly that any job at the Wizard Tower brought her one step nearer to her dream. The next morning Hildegarde was Terry Tarsal's first customer. She bought a sturdy pair of waterproof boots.

With the eagle-eyed Hildegarde gone from the Palace, Merrin began to get cocky. He no longer crept along the corridors but walked with a swagger. Twice he nearly bumped into Jenna coming unexpectedly around a corner. The second time he was tempted to walk past her and see if she noticed, but at the last moment he thought better of it and hid behind a curtain.

Jenna may well not have noticed Merrin even if he had walked past her. She was too preoccupied thinking about Nicko and the map. Unable to keep away from the Manuscriptorium, she stopped by to see Beetle at least twice a day. Beetle had mixed feelings about this. He loved to see her but every time the door went *ping*—or rather, *pi-ing*, in the particular way he was convinced it did only when pushed by Jenna—he braced himself to tell her that there was no news from Ephaniah Grebe. But on the third day that Jenna came by, Beetle did have news—and it was not good.

It was late in the afternoon and the dark clouds made it feel even later. Beetle had just lit a candle and placed it on his desk. He was getting ready to do the last round of the day—the LockingUp round—when *pi-ing*, the door flew open and Jenna was blown in. She pushed the door closed, pulled her windswept hair from out of her eyes, jammed her gold circlet securely down on her head and, with an anxious look, said, "Any news?"

Beetle had been dreading this moment. "Well, yes . . . but, um, not good news, I'm afraid. This note was on my desk this morning."

He handed the large piece of white paper to Jenna. On it was written: *Re: Ancient Paper Fragments. Vital piece missing. Please advise.*

"I suppose it's not surprising," said Beetle with a sigh.

"But we searched everywhere," Jenna protested. "And I looked again when I went back. And the next day just to make sure. There can't be . . ." Her voice trailed off. Now that she thought about it, she knew it would be a miracle if there *wasn't* a piece missing.

"I went to ask Sep what to do but they wouldn't let me see him," said Beetle. "Wouldn't even take a message. Said he was not to be disturbed. Marcia's as good as got him prisoner up there. I'm sure *he* could find the missing piece. There must be some kind of spell or something."

"We could ask Ephaniah," said Jenna. "He might know of a spell. Maybe we could get an Ordinary Wizard to do it for us."

It seemed like a long shot to Beetle, but he couldn't think of anything else to suggest. "Okay," he said.

The Manuscriptorium was empty. All the scribes had gone home, allowed to leave early before the wind became stronger at nightfall. Even Jillie Djinn had retired upstairs to the Chief Hermetic Scribe's rooms. As the wind rattled the office partition door, Jenna and Beetle crept though the rows of desks, which rose high above them like skeletal sentries and gave Jenna the creeps. At the top of the basement steps was a basket with that day's offerings—a couple of spells to be **ReSet** and an old treatise in need of rebinding. Beetle picked it up and took it down with them.

Beetle and Jenna pushed open the green baize door and set off through the cellars, which were almost blindingly bright in contrast to the shadowy Manuscriptorium. Once again the cellars were empty, but this time they walked briskly through and headed for the last one. There they found Ephaniah Grebe peering through a large magnifying glass and hunched over the table, which was covered with hundreds of tiny scraps of paper spread out like a huge, impossible jigsaw puzzle.

"I brought your basket," said Beetle, setting it down on the floor.

Ephaniah started and turned to greet them. Both Beetle and Jenna braced themselves for the sight of the rat face, but this time Ephaniah was swaddled in his wraps and all they saw were his green eyes, hugely magnified behind their bottle-glass spectacles. The Conservation Scribe made a low squeaking noise and beckoned them over. He handed them a piece of paper. On it was written: *I have succeeded in ReUniting all papers bar one.*

Ephaniah waved his hand toward a neatly stacked pile of papers on a shelf behind him.

"Well, look at those," said Beetle, trying to cheer up Jenna. "They're all back together. There's only *one* missing—that's not bad, is it? I bet the missing piece is one of those boat doodles, there were lots of those. Chances are it won't be important, just a scribble."

Jenna was about to say that all of Nicko's scribbles were important to her when Ephaniah placed another piece of paper in front of them: *I have strengthened all the papers but for future safekeeping I should like to bind them. Do I have your permission?*

Jenna nodded.

Ephaniah's eyes smiled—this was a job he loved. From a drawer in the table he took two thick pieces of card, covered in the new Jillie Djinn rebranding reddish purple Manuscriptorium cloth. Taking an eyelet punch, he made five holes down one side of each card and then picked up the sheaf of ReUnited papers and sandwiched them between them. Now Ephaniah took a long length of blue ribbon and deftly laced the covers together so that Nicko's notes and jottings were now safely bound between the thick red card. Next the Conservation Scribe tied the corners together with yet more ribbon; then with a final flourish he produced a large stamp and thumped it down onto the cloth. When he lifted the stamp the words CONSERVED, CHECKED AND GUARANTEED BY EPHANIAH GREBE were imprinted in gold on the red.

With his white wraps wrinkling as though underneath
them his rat whiskers were twitching with a smile, the Conservation Scribe proudly handed the beautifully bound papers
to Jenna. "Oh . . . *thank you*," she breathed. Now at last she
had Nicko's papers back in her hands; Jenna felt a huge sense
of relief. Everything was going to be all right. She would go to
see Sep, they would look at the map together and figure out
how to get to the House of Foryx, and then they would go and
get Nicko back. Her thoughts running far ahead, Jenna found
herself wondering if she could persuade Jillie Djinn to give
Beetle some time off—it would be great if Beetle could come
with them too. Just as Jenna was planning what she would say
to Miss Djinn when she refused to let Beetle go, Beetle's voice
broke into her thoughts.

"Have you seen what's missing?" he asked anxiously.

"Missing?" Jenna came down to earth with a bump.

"Yes. The one that wouldn't ReUnite. Which one was
that?"

"Oh." Jenna opened Ephaniah's beautifully bound book
and began to leaf through the papers, which were now clean
and strong, the writing clear and unsmudged with no signs of
any joins—the Conservation Scribe had done a wonderful job.

There were many things Jenna had not seen—lists for food
supplies, clothing, a messed-up application for two travel permits, numerous to-do lists and several urgent must-do lists.
Then there were the things she remembered seeing in
Marcellus's attic—the boat doodles, the knot diagrams, the
winter market list, the games that Nicko and Snorri had
played. They were all there except for one thing—*the map*.

Jenna looked at the mess on the table in despair. Tears
pricked the back of her eyelids as she took in the fact that the
key to finding Nicko lay strewn in a thousand pieces in front
of them, with a memo beside it in Ephaniah's neat hand:
Incomplete.

Ephaniah had seen Jenna's expression and was hastily
scribbling: *All is not lost. Maybe a Seek can be done for the missing piece. Ask EOW.*

"Who is Eow?" asked Jenna.

Ephaniah picked up his pen again, but Beetle said,
"ExtraOrdinary Wizard. It's the shorthand we use here. Like
CHS is Chief Hermetic Scribe or GFOAIC—that's me. But
nobody uses it because it's shorter to say Beetle."

"GFOAIC?" asked Jenna.

"General Front Office and Inspection Clerk."

"Ah," said Jenna. "Well, GFOAIC, would you come with me to find Marcia . . . please? She might listen to two of us." She turned to Ephaniah and said, "Thank you, Mr. Grebe. Thank you for giving me back Nicko's things." She clutched the beautifully bound book close to her.

Ephaniah nodded and produced a neatly written card, which he presented to Jenna with a flourish: *I have enjoyed your visits very much, Princess. I would be honored to see you again and hope I may be of service in the future.*

Jenna smiled. "Thank you, Mr. Grebe. I shall be back very soon with the EOW, and then you can do the final ReUnite," she said, sounding much more confident than she felt.

✛ 2 1 ✛
TERTIUS FUME

Jenna and Beetle left the bright lights of Ephaniah's realm and stumbled out into the darkness of the Manuscriptorium basement.

"I've got to check to see if the Vaults are secure and do the **LockUp**, but it won't take long," said Beetle.

Jenna was longing to rush and get Marcia but she realized

that Beetle had a job to do. "I'll come and help you check the Vaults if you like," she offered.

Beetle did like—very much. "Okay. Yep. Fine," he said, trying not to sound too pleased but overdoing it a little.

"But I don't want to get in the way."

"No! I mean no, of course you won't get in the way."

Jenna followed Beetle along the musty-smelling passageway that wound its way down to the Vaults, which were dug deep into the bedrock of the Castle below the cellars. As they reached the last turn of the passageway, the sound of voices could be heard—one of which had a low, booming resonance that Beetle knew was Tertius Fume. It was the other voice that surprised him. Beetle put his finger to his lips and began to move quietly. Jenna cast him a questioning glance.

"Trouble," Beetle mouthed in reply. He slipped into an alcove at the top of the steep flight of steps that led down to the Vaults. Jenna joined him. Beetle's heart was pounding so fast that at first he could not hear what the voices were saying. He took a few deep breaths and made himself calm down.

"Who is it?" mouthed Jenna.

Beetle risked a quick glance. It was exactly who he had thought it was. Sitting sprawled on the bottom step half hidden in the dancing shadows cast by the pair of rushlights outside the Vaults was Jillie Djinn's brand-new employee, gazing with rapt attention at the Ghost of the Vaults. The sound of the conversation drifted up the steps, the voices sounding hollow in the empty brick-lined passage.

"Of *course* it is difficult, boy." Tertius Fume's voice reverberated up to the two eavesdroppers in the alcove. The ghost sounded cranky. "That is why it is at the *end* of the book. You are meant to have done what goes before."

"But I didn't want to do *them*. I only wanted to do the end one."

"Practice perfect makes. A fool the shortcut takes," Tertius responded.

"But I did everything it said—and it worked. I even got the Thing. In fact I got *stacks* of **Things**."

"Stacks? What is *stacks*?"

"Lots. Lots and lots. Um . . . many."

"Many? How many?"

"I dunno. About twenty, maybe more."

"*Twenty* **Things**? Thou art more a fool than I took you for. They will dog thy life forever more."

"No, they won't. I locked 'em up. They can't get me now."

"Did you indeed? Then how angry they will truly be, when next they catch a sight of thee."

"Do you always talk in rhymes?"

"Yes. Now what do you want, boy? I am tired of this chatter."

"I wanted to ask you about the Darkening the Destiny thingy."

"*Thingy?*"

"I mean the Darke Hex. I did it on someone but I don't think it has worked. Nothing has happened to him yet and I'm sure I would have heard if it had."

Tertius Fume sounded amused and somewhat mocking. "So you've tried to Darken AnOther's Destiny, have you?" he asked. "And why would a young snake like you want to embark upon such a Darke journey, hmm? When I was your age I'd have chanced my luck with a sharp blade first. Much more satisfying." The ghost chuckled as though reliving fond memories.

The new scribe sounded taken aback. "Oh. Well, I don't really like knives," he mumbled.

"Ah, you prefer others to do your work for you, do you? Employ a little subterfuge, a little deceit, hey? I've seen your kind before. You prefer to be the puppet master pulling the strings. But, be warned, when you dabble with the **Darke** you may find that *you* become the puppet."

"Oh . . ." The boy's voice faltered and if Beetle had dared to take another look he would have seen him nervously fingering the ring on his left thumb. "But I thought that . . . well, as you wrote this book—and I think it's a really, *really* good book, the best I've ever read in fact and—"

"Don't waste your breath trying to flatter me, boy. I couldn't give a tinker's monkey whether you like my book or not," Tertius Fume snapped. "Just tell me what you want from me. Come on, out with it."

"I would like you to help me make the **Darkening** work. Big time."

"And why should I help you, boy? What's in it for me?"

"I could help you, too. We could work together."

Tertius Fume gave a loud snort. "Me—work with *you*? Me, the very first Chief Hermetic Scribe, *me* work with a jumped-up little pinchbrain—just give me one reason why on earth I would want to do that?"

There was a silence and then Jenna and Beetle heard the words, clear as a bell, "Because I am alive and you are *dead*."

Beetle raised his eyebrows at Jenna. That Daniel Hunter kid had nerve.

"Careful, boy," Tertius Fume growled. "That state of affairs is easily remedied."

"Oh. But I didn't mean to . . ." The boy's voice sounded thin and scared.

Tertius Fume ignored him and carried on. "However, it is true that I do miss some of the powers of the Living—and though I would not trust a lettuce leaf like you to do my bidding, I would trust your *interesting* companion here."

Beetle raised his eyebrows at Jenna as if to say *What interesting companion?* He risked a quick glance but could see only the ghost and the dark-haired boy in the shadows—no one else.

"You can have him." The boy sounded relieved. "He gives me the creeps, following me everywhere."

"Very well, **Transfer** his allegiance to me and I will make the **Darkening** work."

"And then—*then* will you help me?"

"I am a man of my word, whatever others may say," said Tertius Fume. "The Other whose destiny is to be **Darkened** will find himself cast onto the Precipice of Peril. How does that sound?"

"Great!" said the new scribe. "Really great. *That* will show him. That stuck-up, goody-goody Septimus Heap kid will wish he never stole my name."

Jenna and Beetle looked at each other. "Sep!" they both gasped, then clapped their hands over their mouths. But it was too late.

"What was that?" Tertius Fume's suspicious growl echoed up the steps.

"What was what?"

"I thought I heard . . . a rat. Or *rats*. Lurking at the top of the steps. Go and see, boy. Go on. *Now*."

Horrified, Beetle grabbed Jenna's hand and ran.

"There was no one there," said Merrin, returning to his place at Tertius Fume's feet.

"Very well," said the ghost. "So now we have a **Contract** to complete, do we not?"

Merrin nodded warily. Suddenly he felt very scared.

Tertius Fume fixed his dark eyes on Merrin and said, "Look at me, boy. Look . . . at . . . me."

Unable to resist, Merrin met the ghost's stare. "The **Contract**," said Tertius Fume, "is this: you will **Transfer** the

allegiance of your servant **Thing** to me in Perpetuity throughout the Universe and into the Great Beyond. In return I will make effective your pathetic attempt to **Darken** the Destiny of one Septimus Heap. Do you accept?"

Merrin managed a feeble croak. "How?"

"You just say yes, boy. It's not complicated," snapped Tertius Fume.

"But, um, *how* will you **Darken** his Destiny?"

"You *dare* to question me?" Wide-eyed with terror, Merrin shook his head. "If you question a **Contract** it must be answered, however *stupid* the question," Tertius Fume said. Merrin squirmed at being called stupid yet again. "I shall **Darken** the Heap boy's Destiny by sending him upon the **Queste**. No one returns from the **Queste**—*no one*. Do not look at me like an idiot, boy." The ghost sighed; the boy had seemed promising at first but was turning out to be a big disappointment. In the interest of making sure the **Contract** was valid, he continued his explanation. "To work its best, **Darke Magyk** must not be suspected. We must not give those who may wish to countermand it a chance to." Ignoring Merrin's puzzled look he carried on, "No one will suspect that the **Queste** is a **Darkening**, for over the centuries some twenty other Apprentices have also been dispatched. Has that answered your pre-Contract Inquiry?"

"Um . . ." Merrin mumbled.

"Oh, *give me patience*. Do you want to **Darken** the Heap boy's Destiny or not? Yes or no?"

"Yes."

"Very well." The ghost rubbed his hands in anticipation. "Now, to make the **Contract** binding you will need to give your servant **Thing** something precious from you in thanks for its services, something that it will wear as a symbol of the **Contract**. Though 'tis but a poor copy of the real thing, that ring on your thumb will do."

"But it *is* the—" Merrin stopped and thought the better of what he had been about to say. "It won't come off," he said lamely.

Tertius Fume smiled malevolently. "If I could still wield a knife it would."

Merrin went pale.

"So find something else, boy, before I am tempted to try."

In a panic, Merrin went through his pockets and was about to hand over Sleuth when he found his very last licorice snake. "This!" he said, pulling out the snake in triumph.

* * *

Beetle and Jenna were nearly at the end of the long, winding passage back up to the Manuscriptorium when Jenna realized something was missing. "Nicko's pin!" she said with a gasp, her hand flying to her cloak. "It's gone!"

Beetle stopped. In the candlelight he could see Jenna's tears welling. "What's it like?" he asked.

"It's a gold 'J.' Nicko brought it back from the Port. I always wear it in my cloak . . . always, and now *it's not there.*"

"You had it down by the Vaults. I remember."

"Did I?"

"I'm sure you did." Beetle had noticed how Jenna kept checking the pin and had wondered who had given it to her. "Wait here. I'll go get it."

"But that ghost—"

"I'll be really quiet. He won't know a thing. Be back in a sec."

Jenna leaned against the cold brick wall of the passageway and listened to the sound of Beetle's footsteps padding back to the Vaults. Without the reassuring presence of Beetle, the candlelit passage with its flickering shadows unnerved Jenna and she held Ullr tightly for comfort. Ullr mewed irritably and Jenna felt a tremor pass through the cat. Suddenly Ullr twisted out of her grasp and landed heavily in front of her. For a brief moment Jenna had an awful feeling that he was about to chase after Beetle and give them away—and then she realized what was happening. The sun had set. Ullr was **Transforming**.

Although Jenna had seen Ullr **Transform** many times now, it still fascinated her. She watched almost in awe as the black tip on the little orange cat's tail began to grow. She saw the fur rippling as the muscles below the skin grew thick and strong. Now the little cat grew fast, the black from his tail spreading across his body like the shadow of an eclipse running over the land, turning the scraggy mottled orange fur to a sleek shiny black and, finally, his blue eyes to a glittering green. Within the space of forty-nine seconds, the DayUllr had become the NightUllr and Jenna had a panther—with an orange-tipped tail—for company in the passageway.

Beetle found Jenna's pin in the alcove. Feeling very pleased, he picked it up. As he was about to rush back to Jenna, Tertius Fume's menacing laugh echoed up the steps. Beetle froze.

"You share the taste I once had for licorice, I see," he heard the ghost say.

What *was* the ghost talking about? Beetle wondered. Curious, he lingered for a moment.

"What is this . . . *thing*?" Tertius Fume sneered.

"It's a *snake*. My last one." The boy sounded aggrieved.

Beetle could not resist a quick look. The new scribe was clumsily trying to tie the snake into a circle. "See," he said sounding panicky, "I can make it smaller—I *can*. Then it can be a ring, a really *nice* ring." Beetle saw the boy close his eyes and guessed he was doing a Shrink Spell. To Beetle's surprise it appeared to work. The snake disappeared in a puff of black smoke and the boy held out his hand to show something to Tertius Fume.

"So be it," said the ghost. "Give the Thing its ring and we will proceed."

Beetle dared not stay any longer—he had left Jenna alone for long enough. He sped back up the twisting passage and, as he was nearing the end, his heart gave a fearful lurch. Two glittering green eyes were staring out of the shadows where he was sure he had left Jenna.

"Jenna?" he whispered, hardly daring to imagine what might have happened. "*Jenna?*"

Jenna stepped out of the shadows by the walls. "Did you

find it?" she asked anxiously.

"Shh," said Beetle. "Don't move."

"Why not? Oh, Beetle, wasn't it there?"

"Just . . . don't . . . move. Okay?"

Jenna froze. Something was wrong. She watched as Beetle stealthily crept along the wall, keeping to the shadows. A low rolling growl came from Ullr. "Ullr, shh," whispered Jenna.

Beetle pounced.

Ullr snarled.

"No! Stop! Beetle, it's only Ullr. Ullr *let go!*" There was a tearing sound as Beetle wrenched his sleeve out of Ullr's jaws and Jenna hauled Ullr away. "No, Ullr. *Leave.*" Ullr glared at Beetle angrily. He didn't like being pounced on—*he* was the one who did the pouncing. "*Leave,*" Jenna repeated sternly.

"Ullr?" gasped Beetle.

"Yes. You know he was Snorri's cat? He's a **Transformer**."

"Really?" said Beetle faintly. "Wow . . ."

"Beetle, um, did you—"

Beetle shook off the awful fear that something terrible had happened to Jenna. He uncurled his hand and showed Jenna a small gold 'J' lying in his palm.

"Oh, Beetle!" Jenna picked up the pin and fastened it back

in her cloak. "Oh, Beetle, *thank you!*" And she threw her arms around his neck. Beetle grinned. That was worth fighting a hundred panthers for.

Down by the Vaults, Merrin was not receiving such an enthusiastic response from the **Thing**. It peered at the licorice ring in disdain—what a *cheapskate*, it thought. The **Thing** sighed a hollow sigh; unfortunately it was no more than it would have expected. And things were not so bad; its new Master looked infinitely more promising. The **Thing** took the sticky black ring as though it were picking up a particularly disgusting insect, and placed it on its left thumb. The **Contract** was complete.

+‡ 22 ‡+
FIRED

B*eetle, Jenna and the NightUllr* stepped through the concealed door in the bookshelves into the shadowy Manuscriptorium, lit only by the windswept Wizard Way torches, which cast a red dancing light through the glass of the office partition.

"That boy," said Jenna as she followed Beetle through the towering ranks of dark, empty desks. "I think I know who he is."

"Yeah," said Beetle gloomily. "He's the new

scribe. Miss Djinn must need her head examined employing someone like him. You think she'd be able to see—"

"See what exactly, Beetle?" Jillie Djinn's voice came out of the dark.

"Argh!" yelled Beetle, still jumpy after the Ullr incident. "What . . . where?"

"Up here," said Jillie Djinn from somewhere above them. Beetle looked up and saw to his dismay that Jillie Djinn was perched on Partridge's seat, peering at a sheaf of papers through her tiny illuminated magnifying glass. Jillie Djinn turned her attention to Beetle and Jenna, not noticing the NightUllr in the shadows. She gazed down with a face like thunder. "I was occupied in checking Mr. Partridge's work. It has not been up to scratch these past three days. I have been examining his calculations for the increase in the rate of paper wastage by scribes of less than one year's experience averaged out over the past three-and-three-quarter years," she informed them. "I was just coming to the conclusion that they do not possess the standard of accuracy that I expect from my scribes, when not only do I hear the state of my head being so *insolently* discussed with a mere outsider but—"

"Jenna's not an out—"

"Do not interrupt. However important Princess Jenna may be, she is not a member of the Manuscriptorium, ergo, she is an *outsider*. And you, Mr. Beetle, have just taken an outsider through a Restricted Access passageway."

"But I—"

Jillie Djinn's tirade swept on, "Not only that, Mr. Beetle, you have been discussing sensitive Manuscriptorium business with the aforementioned outsider *and* insulted your Chief Hermetic Scribe, to whom you have taken an oath to show respect at all times. You have broken three of the sworn tenets of the Manuscriptorium."

"But—"

"Do *not* interrupt. I am not finished. In addition, Mr. Beetle, it has not escaped my notice that you have neglected to take due care of the Inspection sled."

A small groan escaped Beetle.

"My new scribe, Daniel Hunter, informed me of a conversation he overheard between you and Mr. Fox. I understand that two days ago you took Mr. Fox on an unauthorized errand into the Ice Tunnels to retrieve the Inspection sled, which you had neglected to secure in the approved manner. I also understand that Mr. Fox then spent the remainder of the day in the sick room after encountering the Ice Wraith and thus we were yet again one scribe short that afternoon. Is that correct?"

Beetle nodded miserably.

"Answer me!"

"Yes. It is correct," mumbled Beetle. Jenna gave Beetle a sympathetic glance, but Beetle, who was staring wretchedly at his boots, did not notice.

Unfortunately, Jillie Djinn was still not finished. "Normally, on receipt of a written apology and an undertaking to conform to the regulations of the Manuscriptorium at all times, I would be prepared to overlook such poor behavior."

Beetle glanced up at Jillie Djinn but she looked straight through him. Even in the red glow from the torchlight through the window, Beetle looked pale. He knew there was a *but* coming. A big but.

It came.

"*But*," said Jillie Djinn, "one thing I am *not* prepared to overlook is my Inspection Clerk colluding with a successful attempt to UnSeal a hatch. And then, so I understand, entering through the hatch into a forbidden area."

Beetle felt sick. Jillie Djinn had found out—just as he had known she would.

Jillie Djinn looked down from her lofty height. She seemed unwilling to get down from the desk—possibly, thought Jenna, because Beetle was a good six inches taller than she. But right then, Beetle could not have felt any smaller. He just wanted to curl up and disappear somewhere for a very long time.

"Mr. Beetle." Jillie Djinn drew herself up straight and, like a judge about to deliver a particularly harsh sentence, she announced, "I give you notice that I hereby terminate your employment at the Manuscriptorium immediately. Your Indentures shall be burned. You will leave now and take your personal effects with you."

Both Jenna and Beetle gasped. "*What?*"

"You're fired," snapped Jillie Djinn, who could be horribly concise when she wanted to be.

"You can't do that!" protested Jenna. "Beetle is *brilliant* here. This place couldn't run without him. You're crazy to get rid of him—he's the best person here." Jenna stopped, realizing too late what she had said.

"It is no concern of yours, Princess Jenna," Jillie Djinn replied coldly. "I shall run the Manuscriptorium as I see fit and will not be dictated to by anyone. Not even you."

Beetle could not speak. The great looming shapes of the desks seemed to dance mockingly around him as he struggled to take in what had just happened. Jenna took Beetle's arm and led him toward the front office. "Don't worry," she whispered. "She doesn't mean it. She *can't* mean it."

But Beetle knew better. He knew that once Jillie Djinn got an idea into her head that was it—nothing could change it.

As Jenna pulled open the door to the front office, Jillie Djinn's voice echoed through the empty Manuscriptorium: "You have five minutes to clear your desk, Mr. Beetle."

After that the Chief Hermetic Scribe said nothing more— for she had just caught sight of the NightUllr padding through the shadows behind Jenna. Jillie Djinn had a horror of wild animals. She remained motionless, marooned on Partridge's desk until well past midnight, when she finally plucked up the courage to make a run for it to the safety of her upstairs chamber.

Jenna propelled Beetle—who moved as if he were sleep-walking—into the front office and angrily slammed the door. One look at Beetle told her that he was not going to be doing any desk clearing. Beetle just stood and gazed around the office, taking in all the things he loved: the great stacks of papers and books piled up in the window, his desk, his swivel chair, the sausage sandwich that Foxy had bought him that morning and he had forgotten to finish—even the door to the Wild Book Store. All these things Beetle stared at, knowing that he would never see them again in the same way. Even if he ever dared to venture into the Manuscriptorium—which he didn't think he would—they would not be the same. They would belong to another clerk who would be sitting at his desk, eating Foxy's sausage sandwiches.

"Is there anything you want to take with you?" asked Jenna.

Beetle shook his head.

Jenna looked at Beetle's desk, which he had tidied and made ready for the end of the day. His Manuscriptorium pen sat in its pot along with other, more workaday pens. "I'll bring your pen. You don't want to leave that behind."

But Beetle didn't want to take anything to remind him. "Foxy," he croaked. "Give it to Foxy."

"Okay."

Quickly, Jenna wrote a brief note to Foxy, found some Spell-Binding twine and tied the note to Beetle's Manuscriptorium pen—a beautiful black onyx with an ornate jade green inlay that, if you looked closely, you could see that the complicated swirls spelled out BEETLE along the length of the pen. Jenna left it on the desk and hoped that Foxy would notice his name, which she had written on the outside of the note in her large, looping handwriting, which her essay tutor complained got bigger every day.

Gently, Jenna took Beetle by the elbow and steered him toward the door. She tugged the handle hard and the door flew open with a *pi-ing*. Outside the wind whined and spots of cold rain spattered onto the windowpanes. The evening was oppressively dark, almost untouched by the light from the torch flames, some of which had blown out. Eddies of litter and leaves came skittering into the Manuscriptorium and swirled around their feet. Beetle stood motionless on the doorstep until Jenna linked her arm through his and stepped outside, taking him with her.

Behind them the door slammed with a great *crash*.

✛ 23 ✛
THE PROJECTION

High on their silver torch posts, the last pair of torches at the end of Wizard Way struggled to stay lit in the wind, their flames thrown about like wet rags in a storm.

"Come *on*, Beetle, you've got to fight this!" Jenna yelled above the howl of the gale as they approached the Great Arch. "She can't just dump you like that. You wait—when Marcia hears about this Jillie Djinn won't stand a chance."

Beetle did not have the energy to reply. As Jenna propelled him through the Arch and into the Courtyard, all Beetle could think about was how he was going to break the news to his mother, who frequently told anyone who would listen that the proudest day of her life was the day that Beetle passed the Manuscriptorium entrance exam. But something his mother never mentioned was the fact that it was Beetle's weekly pay—a silver half crown—that paid the rent on their tiny rooms in The Ramblings and bought them a steady supply of potatoes and fish.

The Wizard Tower Courtyard was sheltered from the wind, and the light from the torches in their holders along the walls was steady and bright. Jenna thought the Courtyard looked unusually clean—gone were the nasty surprises, and even the precarious slippery feeling underfoot had disappeared. As she and Beetle approached the great white marble steps that led up to the Wizard Tower, the reason for this sudden attack of hygiene appeared carrying a shovel and a very big bucket.

"Hildegarde!" said Jenna in surprise. "What are you doing

here? I thought you were having some time off."

Hildegarde swept a grimy hand across her forehead, stopped and leaned wearily on her shovel. "I wish," she said.

Jenna noticed that the sub-Wizard's blue robes were soaked and splattered with mud—or worse—and her short brown hair had been blown into something resembling a bird's nest. "I suppose it's not quite the job you wanted at the Tower," said Jenna sympathetically.

"No, it's not," replied Hildegarde and then, realizing she had been curt, she said, "But of course I am happy to help out while the Apprentice is unable to look after his dragon and—"

"Why, what's happened?" Jenna interrupted, suddenly alarmed. "Is Sep ill? Has he had an accident?"

"Oh, it's nothing to worry about, Princess Jenna. He's doing his first **Projection**. It's tricky stuff; he mustn't be disturbed until it's finished. It will be ending soon and then we'll all find out what it was. He's obviously very good at it, as no one has guessed what it is, although"—Hildegarde's voice took on a disapproving tone—"some of the more elderly Wizards have been placing bets."

"Oh, thank goodness." Jenna sighed. "For a moment I thought we were too late."

"Too late? No, I think he has about ten minutes left until the end."

"The *end*?"

"Of the **Projection**. I suggest you try the Great Hall. I have a feeling all is not right in the Old Spells cupboard." Hildegarde winked conspiratorially. "But please excuse me, I must put these things away and I will join you there." She clattered off hurriedly.

Jenna and Beetle climbed the steps up to the massive silver doors that formed the entrance to the Wizard Tower. Jenna muttered the password and the doors silently opened. As they stepped into the Great Hall, the words WELCOME, PRINCESS ran across the floor in flickering, multicolored letters. It did not escape Beetle's notice that there was no WELCOME, INSPECTION CLERK to greet *him*—as there had been in the past. Beetle wondered how the Wizard Tower could possibly know. He felt even worse, if that was possible. Somehow it made it official.

There was a buzz of expectation in the Great Hall. A throng of Wizards was milling about, some clutching small pink slips of paper, others chatting or hanging around trying to look as if they just happened to come to the Great Hall for important business. Jenna had never seen so many Wizards in

one place. It was a colorful scene: the blue of the Ordinary
Wizard robes set against the backdrop of the bright, fleeting
pictures that moved over the walls showing fabled moments
from the Wizard Tower's past.

As always, Jenna felt a little overawed by the Wizard
Tower. Although as Princess she was always welcome—and
was even in possession of the password—the Tower was a
strange and intimidating place. It seemed to her as though it
were a living being. The pictures on the walls brightened and
faded as if the Tower itself were breathing in and out, in and
out. Light and dark, light and dark. The heady scent of
incense, and the odd smell of **Magyk**—of old Spells and new,
all combined to make Jenna feel unsettled. She wanted to
understand everything that went on in the Castle and did not
like the fact that she could not quite work out what the
Wizards actually *did*. She had once asked Marcia what she did
all day and, although it all seemed to make sense at the time,
later she could not remember a word of what Marcia had said.
It had even crossed her mind that Marcia had done a **Forget**
Spell on her, but when she had mentioned it to Septimus he
had laughed and told her that *he* never remembered what
Marcia said to him either. But even so, Jenna was beginning

to understand the old Castle saying: *A Queen and a Wizard shall never agree—what one calls two, the other calls three.*

Jenna's thoughts were interrupted by a sudden bout of shushing among the assembled Wizards. On the far side of the Great Hall, at the point where the silver corkscrew spiral stairs emerged through the high vaulted ceiling, Jenna saw the distinctive purple pointy python shoes of Marcia Overstrand appear. In order to make a more dramatic entrance, Marcia had placed the stairs on the slow nighttime mode. She had learned from bitter experience that spinning round at the relatively fast daytime speed was apt to give rise to some hilarity when a crowd of Wizards was assembled. And so, as though she were descending from the heavens, Marcia elegantly rotated down through the height of the Great Hall until she reached the ground. She jumped off and clapped her hands for silence.

"Word seems to have gotten around that my Apprentice, Septimus Heap, is about to finish his first **Projection**," she said. An excited murmur arose. "I do not entirely approve of this fuss," Marcia continued. "Frankly, I would have hoped you all had better things to do. But unfortunately it has become a tradition—in fact I seem to remember the same thing happening to me some time ago. Presumably, as you are all gathered here, you think that this is where the Projection has been placed."

A general muttering ensued and one brave Wizard shouted out, "Give us a clue, ExtraOrdinary!"

"I know no more than you," Marcia replied. "My Apprentice has made his own choice about what to Project. He has not informed me of his decision."

Excited murmurs spread as the Wizards propounded their own pet theories of what Septimus had actually Projected. Marcia raised her voice. "However . . . excuse me, can I have silence please? Now? Thank you. There are some things I must insist upon. One: until the Projection comes to an end, please do not move about more than necessary. Two: if, when the Projection is finished, it is not immediately apparent what has been Projected I do not want an undignified stampede around the Tower searching for it. If you haven't spotted it already, then you are hardly going to notice it once it has disappeared, are you?"

There was an outbreak of obedient nodding among the crowd.

"And three—positively no betting."

A stifled groan came from the Wizards. The little slips of pink paper that Jenna had noticed were hastily stuffed into deep pockets.

"I will now give a countdown to the end of the **Projection**. Five . . . four . . . three—"

A loud crash came from the Old Spells cupboard and the next moment Catchpole staggered out, pursued by a large, clattering trash can. The can proceeded to chase the unfortunate Catchpole around the Great Hall, to the great amusement of the audience. Marcia looked on in disbelief—if this was a **Projection** then she had never seen anything like it before. It had both substance and sound, something that was thought to be impossible. When she had been a young Apprentice, Marcia had once managed to coax a small *baa* from a troupe of dancing sheep she had **Projected** as a joke on Alther's birthday, but it had been a short and rather faint *baa* and Alther, who was getting hard of hearing by then, had not even heard it.

"Why's he so scared of an old trash can?" Jenna shouted to Beetle above the excited hubbub.

"I reckon Sep's done a double bluff," said Beetle.

"A what?"

"*We* see a trash can. *Catchpole* sees something else."

"Like what?"

"Probably the thing he fears most. That usually works. And it means that Sep didn't have to decide what Catchpole sees—Catchpole has done that for him." Jenna flashed Beetle an admiring look—how did he know all that stuff? Beetle caught the look and went red.

Pursued—or so he thought—by his old boss, the Hunter, Catchpole shot back into the Old Spells cupboard and slammed the door, leaving the trash can outside. The trash-can/Hunter retracted its legs, straightened up its lid, folded its little hairy arms and settled down outside the door, until it looked like any other can with little hairy arms left outside for the trash collection.

Amid the excitement, no one had noticed the stairs suddenly speeding up to emergency fast mode and a flash of green whizzing down them. A few seconds later, with perfect timing, Septimus leaped off the stairs and skidded to a halt next to Marcia, with the words CONGRATULATIONS, APPRENTICE, ON YOUR SUCCESSFUL FIRST PROJECTION swirling around his feet.

An outburst of applause greeted Septimus's arrival at

Marcia's side. Septimus grinned happily. He pointed to the can, clicked his fingers and, to a delighted chorus of *ooooooohs*, the can disappeared with a bang and a flash of green smoke.

Marcia was not amused. "There is no need for that, Septimus. We are not putting on some kind of cheap **Magyk** show. This is serious business."

Marcia did not know how true her words were. At that very moment the doors to the Wizard Tower swung open—to reveal Tertius Fume silhouetted against a blinding flash of lightning.

✛ 24 ✛
THE GATHERING

The excited hub-bub was replaced by an eerie silence.

"What's going on, Marcia?" A lone shout came from the Wizard who had been running the bets and, with this unexpected turn of events, could see a windfall coming his way. "Is this part of the Projection too?"

"Don't be ridiculous. Of

course it's not," Marcia snapped. And then, as a small flicker of doubt crossed her mind she muttered to Septimus, "This *isn't* still your **Projection**, is it?"

"No, it's not," replied Septimus, who wished that it were. He had a bad feeling about Tertius Fume.

On the threshold of the Wizard Tower, Tertius Fume regarded Marcia with a mocking gaze. "Well," he said, "aren't you going to invite us in? It is customary, you know. In fact, as I understand it, it is *obligatory*."

"Obligatory?" said Marcia, peering into the gloom behind the ghost, wondering why he had said *us*. And then she saw the reason—behind Tertius Fume was a sea of purple. It covered the white marble steps and flowed down into the Courtyard shifting like water in the dim light as hundreds of ExtraOrdinary Wizard ghosts floated about. Marcia went pale. "Oh," she whispered.

"Oh *indeed*." Tertius Fume said with a smirk.

With a shock Marcia recognized what this was—the **Gathering** of the Ghosts. It was something she had not expected to see until the very last day of Septimus's Apprenticeship—the day when the **Gathering** would arrive and the Apprentice must draw a stone from the **Questing Pot**.

That was a terrible moment. Everyone knew that if the Apprentice drew one of the **Questing Stones**, then he or she would be sent off on the **Queste** immediately—and no one had ever returned. Like all ExtraOrdinary Wizards before her—apart from DomDaniel, who had been rather looking forward to his Apprentice getting his comeuppance—Marcia dreaded that day; indeed it was one of the reasons why Marcia had hesitated in taking on an Apprentice for many years.

Marcia knew that the **Gathering**, which consisted of the ghosts of *all* previous ExtraOrdinary Wizards, must be admitted to the Wizard Tower at all times. She also knew that its unexpected **Appearance** only happened in times of peril in order to give the Living ExtraOrdinary Wizard the benefit of all her predecessors' collective wisdom. As she looked at the long line of ExtraOrdinary Wizard ghosts flowing down the steps, Marcia felt sick with apprehension—and Tertius Fume was pleased to see it.

Tertius Fume was hovering well above the broad white marble step—he had been short in Life and liked to float about eight inches above the ground to give an impression of height. He pressed his advantage, his booming voice echoing through the Great Hall of the Wizard Tower. "It is considered polite for

the Living ExtraOrdinary Wizard to invite the **Gathering** over
the threshold of the Wizard Tower," he informed Marcia. "But
it is not essential, for we have a right to enter. Indeed, there
have been some misguided ExtraOrdinary Wizards in the past
who have not invited us in and they always regretted it. *Always.*
I will ask you for the last time—are you going to invite us in?"

"Tertius Fume, you are no ExtraOrdinary Wizard," Marcia
retorted. "I have no obligation to invite *you* in."

The ghost looked triumphant. "I am afraid you are mistaken there, *Miss* Overstrand," he declared. "I held the office
in locum tenens for seven days, in honor of which I was given
purple to wear upon my sleeve. *There.*" He pointed to the
bands at the end of his sleeves. Reluctantly Marcia looked.
There, between the two gold strips set on the dark blue was a
color that could, she supposed, have been purple. "Added to
which, Miss Overstrand, it is *I* who have convened the
Gathering and as Convener I demand entry."

"*You* convened it? But why—what has happened?"

Tertius smiled, pleased that it was now Marcia asking the
questions. "You are forgetting procedure, Miss Overstrand.
First the **Gathering** is admitted. Then—possibly—we may
answer your questions."

Marcia knew she had no choice. "Very well," she said.

Tertius Fume smiled with his mouth but not with his eyes. "Very well *what*, Miss Overstrand?"

Marcia knew what she had to say. It was one of the many Articles of Conduct that she had had to memorize in the frantic few days following her sudden appointment as ExtraOrdinary Wizard. But she didn't want to say it, and Tertius Fume knew it. And she knew that he knew it. She could tell by his mocking smile and the way he folded his arms, just as he had done the morning she had paid a visit to the Vaults.

Marcia took a deep breath and began to speak, her defiantly confident voice filling the Great Hall. "As ExtraOrdinary Wizard I hereby invite the **Gathering** into the Wizard Tower. Upon your entry I do declare that I lay down my authority as ExtraOrdinary Wizard and become but one voice among many. We are all equals in this place."

"That's more like it," said Tertius Fume. He stepped over the threshold and waggled his forefinger at Marcia. "Remember, one voice among many. That's all you are now." The ghost strode in and gazed around the Great Hall as though he owned it.

Taking advantage of everyone's attention being focused on

Tertius Fume, Septimus slipped away from Marcia, into the shadows at the edge of the Great Hall. He made his way around to the doors, where he had just noticed Jenna and Beetle.

"Hello, Jen, Beetle," he whispered.

"Oh, *Sep*," said Jenna, "thank goodness you're okay. Tertius Fume is—"

"Shh . . ." Septimus laid a finger on his lips.

"But he's—"

"Shh! I've got to concentrate, Jen." Septimus looked so fierce that Jenna did not dare go on.

Septimus was rapidly running through his memory of the gigantic Rule Book that governed all aspects of being an ExtraOrdinary Wizard. Marcia made Septimus read a section each day and he had just gotten to *Gebblegons: Health and Safety Regulations part ii*. As he watched the river of purple ghosts begin to flow into the Wizard Tower, Septimus rewound some pages back to *Gathering: Rules of Convening*, concentrating hard on each ghost as it stepped over the threshold.

As the Great Hall of the Tower began to fill, the Living Ordinary Wizards respectfully drew back to make room for the ghosts—no one wanted to **Pass Through** an ancient ExtraOrdinary Wizard. Still the ghosts kept on pouring into the Great Hall, until the Ordinary Wizards were pressed against the walls, a thin rim of blue around a huge circle of purple. A surprising number of Ordinary Wizards were crammed into the various cupboards and alcoves that led off the hall. In fact the record for Wizards in the broom closet— set by eighteen Wizards at the end of a memorable banquet some years previously—was broken that night.

As each ExtraOrdinary Wizard ghost stepped over the threshold, as a matter of courtesy, he or she **Appeared** to all inside the Tower, and Septimus watched each and every one. Some were faded and extremely ancient; some were newer ghosts who looked quite substantial. Some were old, some young, but all wore an expression of wistfulness as they stepped inside the Wizard Tower once again.

Fascinated, Beetle watched too. At the sight of so many ghosts he could not help recalling some calculations that Jillie Djinn had once made. Although an individual ghost is always somewhat transparent, the combined density of a group of ghosts will soon add up to enough to block an object from view. The number of ghosts necessary for this will depend upon their age, for ghosts become more transparent over the years. Jillie Djinn had worked on a formula to predict this, but she had had trouble with it, as a ghost's emotional state can also affect how transparent he or she becomes. This, like emotional states in general, irritated Miss Djinn; but she had calculated that the number of ghosts of average range of years of age and stable emotional state needed to obscure a Living being was five and a quarter. Which was why, as the ghosts poured in, Septimus soon lost sight of Marcia at the far side of the hall, but he made sure he did not lose sight of any of the ghosts as they filed in one by one. There were two he was particularly looking out for—one that he wanted to see and one that he did not.

His job was made easier by the bottleneck that had begun to build up at the doors, as virtually each ghost stopped for a moment and gazed at the place he or she had left so long ago. A patient line formed on the steps, each ghost eventually floating through the doors, looking around and finding a place to be. The very last ghost was the one that Septimus had been longing to see—Alther Mella. A tall and relatively new ghost, Alther stood out. He still had a bright look to his robes, and a purposeful way of moving. He was neat and tidy, much more so than he had been when Living, due to the fact that—as he often joked—the upkeep was considerably easier. His hair stayed neatly tied back in its long gray ponytail and his beard remained a manageable length and no longer got bits of food stuck in it. Alther stepped almost reluctantly into the Wizard Tower, leaving the white marble steps behind him empty and glistening in the rain.

"Alther!" whispered Septimus.

Alther's face lit up. "Septimus!" Then his expression darkened. "You know what this is?" he muttered.

Septimus nodded.

Silence had fallen in the Great Hall and the huge silver doors were slowly closing. Marcia climbed up the first few steps on the **Stopped** spiral stairs so that she could look down upon the **Gathering**. Her mouth felt dry and her hands were shaking; she shoved them deep into her pockets, determined not to show any trace of fear.

A solemn, expectant atmosphere pervaded the Tower and all eyes were on the ExtraOrdinary Wizard. Marcia scanned the sea of purple, looking for Septimus—*where had he gone?* There was no sign of him, which annoyed her. At a time like this, her Apprentice should be at her side. She would, she

thought, be having words with him about his slap-dash attitude when all this was over. Marcia could see no sign of
Alther, either. She felt disappointed and a little hurt. She had
expected Alther to come find her, but he obviously hadn't
bothered. She was on her own.

Marcia was not completely on her own, however. Standing
close to her—far *too* close and deliberately invading her personal space—was Tertius Fume. The ghost had positioned
himself on the spiral stairs and was hovering a good ten inches
above the step in order to make himself taller than Marcia,
who was a tall woman. Marcia looked down and noticed that
the purple sea of ExtraOrdinary Wizards was parting to let a
speck of green through. With a feeling of relief she watched
Septimus make his way toward her—at least now she knew
where he was.

Tertius Fume surveyed the scene with an air of satisfaction.
"Aha," he said. "I do believe I see the very reason for our
Gathering approaching."

Marcia frowned. What did Fume mean—*the very reason?*

Septimus reached the foot of the silver spiral stairs and
Marcia looked at him, worried now. "Where have you *been?*"
she asked.

Septimus did not want to say what he had to tell her in front of Tertius Fume. "Could you come down here a moment, please?" he asked Marcia.

There was something in Septimus's voice that made Marcia **Pass Through** Tertius Fume's cloak with no hesitation whatsoever and join her Apprentice at the foot of the stairs. "Unauthorized communication is *not* allowed," boomed Tertius Fume as Septimus whispered something to Marcia.

Unauthorized or not, the communication was just what Marcia wanted to hear. "You're absolutely sure?" she whispered in return.

"Yep."

"Thank goodness. I was *so* worried. It's his ring—the Two-Faced Ring. You see, I never took it out of the sludge after I did the **Identify**. I looked for it after I did the **Deep Clean** and it wasn't there so I thought it was all right. But, well, I have sometimes wondered if the reason it wasn't there was because it had put him back together and he'd actually gotten away."

"But he was just a puddle of sludge," said Septimus. "And he was all over the place. How could he get back together after *that*?"

"Well . . . you never know. That ring's a powerful thing. Got him back together after the Marsh Brownies ate him.

Anyway, I was looking out for him coming in, but I couldn't tell from over here. They all look the same."

"*He* doesn't."

"No. You're right. That awful old hat—he'd be wearing that, wouldn't he?"

Septimus grinned. "I guess he would."

Marcia rejoined Tertius Fume with a spring in her step. "I do not need any *authorization* to talk to my Apprentice," she informed the ghost.

Tertius Fume smiled. "That, Miss Overstrand, is where you are wrong. For you are no longer mistress of your own domain."

"Indeed?" Marcia replied, raising her eyebrows as though amused by what the ghost had to say.

"Indeed, Miss Overstrand. Those are the Rules. Once the **Gathering** is in the Wizard Tower we are—as you so rightly said—all equals in this place."

"I understand the Rules perfectly well, Mr. Fume. It seems that you are the one who does not. There is no **Gathering** in the Wizard Tower. As such a stickler for procedure, Mr. Fume, you will surely be aware that for a **Gathering** to exist it must be Complete. This one is not."

"Of course it is."

"It is not."

"Prove it!"

"A certain DomDaniel is not here."

A faint cheer went up from the thin blue line of Ordinary Wizards. Tertius Fume looked furious.

"And, Mr. Fume, he never will be. I **DeepCleaned** him last year. The **Gathering** is not Complete—and indeed it never *can* be. So I suggest, Mr. Fume, that you and all these delightful ExtraOrdinary Wizards—whom it is a *great* pleasure to see, thank you all *so* much for turning out in such nasty weather— you can all go back to your haunts and do far more interesting things with the rest of the evening. Good night, all."

Outside the Wizard Tower, a thin figure wearing a brand-new scribe's uniform stood in the shadows of the old dragon kennel, sheltering from the rain. He was clutching a beautiful urn of lapis lazuli bound with gold bands. The urn was almost as big as he was. It was also extremely heavy and the muscles in his arms felt as though they were on fire, but Merrin didn't dare put down the urn, as he was not sure he would be able to lift it again. He felt miserable and more than a little annoyed—this was not what he had had in mind when

Tertius Fume promised him what the ghost had called a strategic role in the **Darkening** of Septimus Heap's destiny.

As the rain dripped from his hair and ran down his nose, Merrin knew that he could not hang on to the heavy pot much longer—he decided to dump it and go. Merrin was staggering across the Courtyard clutching the urn when a horribly familiar voice stopped him in his tracks. "Get *out* of my way, Apprentice. *How* many times do I have to tell you, *boy*?"

Terrified, Merrin dropped the urn; it landed on his foot. "Ouch!" he yelled. He grabbed hold of his foot and looked around in panic for the source of the terrifying voice from the past—where *was* he? And then, very slowly, the owner of the disembodied voice began to **Appear**. Merrin screamed. He couldn't believe it—the cylindrical black hat . . . the piggy black eyes. He thought he might be sick—it was all his worst nightmares come true. *DomDaniel had come back to haunt him.*

Quickly Merrin shoved his hands in his pockets. He didn't want his old master to see the Two-Faced Ring.

"Take your hands out of your pockets and stand up straight," growled the ghost. "You're a disgrace." With that, to Merrin's great relief, the ghost of DomDaniel continued on its unsteady way, floating haphazardly across the Courtyard and wobbling up the steps to the Wizard Tower. As DomDaniel reached the top step Merrin saw the silver doors open and a stream of bright light from the Great Hall illuminate the white marble steps. Even from where he was standing Merrin heard the collective gasp of surprise come from inside the Tower. He watched the doors slowly close and he smiled—he wouldn't want to be Septimus Heap in there now. *No way.*

Merrin's hand closed around a small bag of coins in his pocket—his advance pay for his first week at the Manuscriptorium. He brightened a little—the coins were enough to buy thirty-nine licorice snakes from Ma Custard's. The thought of Ma Custard's welcoming sweet shop and the memory of Ma Custard's kindly smile as she had watched him choose his first ever sweet made Merrin suddenly feel happy. Why stay where he wasn't wanted?

Merrin was not quite brave enough to completely disobey Tertius Fume so, with a huge effort, he lifted the urn and heaved it up the marble steps. As Merrin stood shakily on the top step, wondering how to drop the urn without it landing on his toes, two tall **Magykal** figures dressed in ancient chain mail stepped out of the shadows on either side of the door. In synchrony they each drew a dagger, took another step toward Merrin and then leveled their daggers at his throat, the purple lights from the Wizard Tower flashing on the sharp blades. Terrified, Merrin forgot any worries about his toes; he let the urn drop with a great *thud* and fled. The **Questing Guards** stepped back and melted into the shadows once more.

Merrin did not look back. He ran, leaping down the steps, tearing across the Courtyard, his footsteps echoing through the Great Arch. There he stopped and from his pocket he took what looked like a scruffy old tennis ball.

"Sleuth," he addressed the ball, "show me the quickest way to Ma Custard's." The tracker ball bounced slowly up and down as if thinking, then it shot off, taking a sharp left turn down Cutpurse Cut and then an immediate right into Dogbreath Dive. It was a three-mile run to Ma Custard's but Merrin didn't mind. The farther away he was from his old boss, the better. He followed the ball through rush-lit tunnels, over tall brick bridges and through countless back gardens, and then, tiring at last, lost sight of it down a narrow, dark cut. But he was lucky—the cut led straight to the sweet shop and as he arrived, puffing and panting, Sleuth was bouncing on the spot, impatiently waiting for him.

Merrin caught the ball, shoved it into his pocket and barged into the sweet shop. He was going to need a whole truckload of licorice snakes to help him get over the shock of seeing his old master again. And maybe some slug sherbets, too. And some spider-floss—*lots* of spider-floss.

✢ 25 ✢
SIEGE

The ghost of DomDaniel was enjoying himself. It had been a long time since he had been out anywhere interesting. The loss of the Two-Faced Ring had taken him out of a kind of limbo that he and his ghost had existed in after Marcia's Identify. The Call to the Gathering had been so strong that at last his ghost was set free—a little shaky maybe, but out in the world at last.

DomDaniel was particularly enjoying the dramatic effect of

his entry into the Wizard Tower. The look on the face of that awful woman, what was her name—Ghastlier Overland? Nastier Underhand?—well, *that* was worth waiting for. And it was good to see old Fume again. There were others he recognized too: that scruffy boy with the Dragon Ring—an Apprentice by the look of it. He'd seen him before . . . somewhere . . . what *was* his name? Oh, his memory was terrible. Almost wiped out by the . . . thingy. It was *so* unfair. What was that—what, *what*? Was someone saying his name?

Marcia Overstrand was indeed saying DomDaniel's name. "DomDaniel—it can't be! I do *not* believe it. It is absolutely *not possible.*"

Tertius Fume was triumphant. "Clearly, Miss Overstrand, it is perfectly possible. The **Gathering** is now Complete."

Pleased that all eyes were upon him, the ghost of DomDaniel bowed extravagantly to his audience and, forgetting that he was a ghost, he tried to sweep off his cylindrical hat but his ghostly hand went right through it. A little flustered, he straightened up and, aiming for the middle of the action, DomDaniel shuffled over to Septimus and Marcia, who were perched uncertainly on the spiral stairs, watching the crowd part to allow the rotund ghost room to advance toward them. DomDaniel favored the three occupants of the spiral stairs with another bow, this time remembering to leave his hat alone. Marcia returned his oily smile with a fierce glare.

Tertius Fume began to speak. "This **Gathering** has been Called on the momentous occasion of the Draw for the twenty-first Apprentice **Queste**."

A gasp came from the assembled ghosts—particularly loud from the nineteen who had lost their Apprentices to the **Queste**.

"Don't be ridiculous," snapped Marcia.

"I would not call the **Gathering** *ridiculous* if I were you, Miss Overstrand." There was a general murmur of agreement from the floor and Marcia realized she had to tread carefully.

"You deliberately misunderstand me, Mr. Fume. It is the very *idea* that Septimus should make the Draw for the **Queste** that is ridiculous. That—as even *you* must know, Mr. Fume— happens in the very last hour of the Apprenticeship. My Apprentice, Septimus Heap, is only just beginning his third year—thus he is *not* eligible for the **Queste** Draw."

Tertius Fume laughed. "It is no more than mere tradition that the Draw takes place at the end of an Apprenticeship. A Draw may be called at any time." The ghost raised his voice and called out the password for the doors. A gasp of dismay came from the Ordinary Wizards. No one *ever* shouted out the password to the Wizard Tower—it was considered highly unlucky and extremely rude. But the doors to the Wizard Tower did not have the finely turned sensibilities of the Wizards and they opened obediently to reveal—to Tertius Fume's surprise—the **Questing Pot** standing forlornly on the top step, like the last guest to arrive at a party. Suppressed giggles erupted from some of the younger Ordinary Wizards.

What, wondered the Ghost of the Vaults angrily, was the **Pot** doing there on its own? *Where* was that idiot of a scribe?

Tertius Fume jumped down from the stairs in an athletic leap he never would have dared make when Living. He strode through the **Gathering** and positioned himself in the very center of the Great Hall. "You!" he bellowed to Hildegarde, who was closest to the door. "Bring in the **Questing Pot**!"

"Not so fast, Fume," said Marcia. "You are forgetting something—*one voice among many*. Your voice may be extremely loud but it is still only *one*. What about the *many*? What does the **Gathering** have to say?"

Tertius Fume sighed loudly and reluctantly addressed the

Hall. "All ye Ghosts **Gathered** here—is it your wish that the **Questing Pot** be brought in?"

Over seven hundred and fifty ghosts had not left their cozy haunts on a windy evening—the one kind of weather that a ghost finds difficult—for nothing. There were only twenty-one against—the nineteen ExtraOrdinary Wizards who had lost their Apprentices to the **Queste**, plus Alther Mella and Marcia. The resounding vote was to bring in the **Pot**.

A large blue circle with a **Q** in the center began to appear in the illuminated floor right beneath the feet of Tertius Fume, who hastily stepped back. With an apologetic glance at Marcia, Hildegarde placed the **Pot** on the circle.

The **Questing Pot** was a beautiful thing. Tall and elegant, the blue lapis lazuli shone in the bright candlelight and the burnished gold bands that ran around it had a deep glow—as did the large golden stopper that sat in the top. With a shudder Marcia remembered drawing out the very same stopper on her last morning as Apprentice to Alther Mella—her whole future suddenly hanging in the balance. Marcia remembered her relief and joy as she had drawn out a plain lapis pebble with no sign of the gold **Q** that would have sent her away from the Castle forever.

"Now, boy," Tertius Fume said. He fixed his gaze on Septimus. "It is time for you to make the Draw. Come hither."

"No!" said Marcia. She put her arm protectively around Septimus's shoulder. "I will *not* allow Septimus to make the Draw."

"What you will or will not allow is of no consequence," Tertius Fume told her. "Each of us is—as you so rightly pointed out—but one voice among many. However, as Convener I am required to put it to the **Gathering** if you so wish."

Marcia did wish, although with little hope of success.

Tertius Fume addressed the Hall. "All ye Ghosts **Gathered** here—is it your wish that the Apprentice make the Draw?"

Again it was an overwhelming vote in favor, with, once again, the same twenty-one against. Septimus was to make the Draw.

"I'll do it," Septimus said to Marcia. "I probably won't get the **Questing Stone** anyway. Then at least I won't have to do it at the end of my Apprenticeship like you did."

"No, Septimus," said Marcia. "*No.* There's something not right about this."

"I'll be okay." Septimus smiled at Marcia. "Anyway, we'll

never get rid of this bunch if I don't do it." Without waiting for her reply, Septimus plunged into the crowd of ghosts, which parted respectfully. As Septimus drew near to the **Questing Pot**, a ghost with copious bloodstains running down the side of his face put his arm across his path. Septimus stopped, unwilling to **Pass Through**.

"Apprentice," whispered the bloodstained ghost, "I fear you will not be able to escape this **Queste**. But heed this: when you have the **Stone**, escape the **Questing Guards** and you will escape the worst of the Perils. I wish you well." The ghost let his arm fall to allow Septimus to pass.

"Oh," whispered Septimus, the danger of the situation beginning to dawn on him. "Um . . . thank you."

"You should not have told him that, Maurice," said a neighboring ghost as Septimus walked on, more hesitantly now, toward the **Questing Pot**.

Maurice McMohan—ExtraOrdinary Wizard some three hundred years ago, who had lost a much-loved Apprentice to the **Queste**—shrugged. "I don't see why not," he said. "There are too many secrets around here. I'd have told mine if I had known at the time. Give the boy a fighting chance."

"On your own head be it," replied his neighbor. "Oh,

sorry, Maurice. I didn't mean it like that." For Maurice McMohan had been killed by a candlestick that had fallen from a window on the eighteenth floor of the Wizard Tower, and he had a very nasty candlestick-shaped dent on the top of his head.

As Septimus moved through the now silent ghosts, Alther appeared beside him and told him all he could about the **Queste**—for Alther knew what would happen if Septimus Drew the **Questing Stone**. There would be no time *then* for talking.

As Septimus and Alther moved toward the **Questing Pot**, the walls of the Wizard Tower, which usually showed uplifting pictures of important events in the life of the Wizard Tower, began to show scenes of previous Apprentices setting off upon the **Queste**. These were anything but uplifting. Sad farewells were said as the Apprentice was escorted away by Tertius Fume and seven heavily armed **Questing Guards**. Some Apprentices went bravely, others were in tears, and one girl— forgetting in the heat of the moment that Tertius Fume was a ghost—had tried to punch him in the nose, which gave rise to a few sniggers from the floor. But at the sight of the pictures many of the ghosts remembered the reality of an Apprentice embarking on a **Queste** and began to regret their support of the Draw. However, it was too late to change their minds now.

Alther dropped back into the throng of ghosts and, to the accompaniment of excited murmers, Septimus reached the **Questing Pot**. The atmosphere in the Wizard Tower was electric. Septimus looked at the **Pot**, which was almost exactly the same height as he was, and it seemed to him that it looked back at him. He hesitated, remembering Marcia's words. Something *was* wrong—there was something **Darke** nearby. No—not nearby. There was something **Darke** inside the *Pot*.

Tertius Fume was losing patience. "Make the Draw," he commanded.

Septimus did not move.

"Are you deaf, boy?" demanded Tertius Fume. "*Make the Draw!*"

Septimus reached out as if to pull out the stopper of the **Questing Pot**, but instead he raised his right hand and made a circle with his index finger and thumb—the classic symbol that accompanies a **See** Spell—the advanced kind that can **See** through precious metals and stones.

"Cheat!" cried Tertius Fume. "You are trying to **See** inside the **Pot**. *Cheat!*"

"*I* am not the cheat," said Septimus, his voice carrying clear through the shocked silence. "It is not *I* who have placed a **Thing** inside the **Pot** ready to put the **Questing Stone** into my hand."

Tertius Fume was almost speechless with rage. "How *dare* you? I shall give you one last chance to redeem yourself. Remove the Stopper and *make . . . the . . . Draw!*"

"I will not."

"You *will!*" Tertius Fume looked as though he was about to explode.

"He will *not*." Marcia's voice came from beside her Apprentice.

"Are you telling me that you and your Apprentice are refusing the Rule of the **Gathering**?" Tertius Fume asked, incredulous.

"I am telling you that my Apprentice will not make the Draw. If that also means we refuse the Rule of the **Gathering**, then so be it," Marcia replied.

A loud muttering spread through the Great Hall—had this ever happened before? No one thought so. Many sympathized with Marcia but there was a core of Rule-loving ghosts who were outraged. The muttering grew into a hubbub of heated discussion.

"Silence!" shouted Tertius Fume. He glared at Septimus. "I

shall give you one last chance to accept the Rule of the Gathering or there will be serious consequences," he said. *"Make . . . the . . . Draw!"*

Septimus felt himself wavering. Maybe he should make the Draw. Would he be putting everyone in danger if he didn't? Then Marcia squeezed his shoulder and he heard her whisper, "No. *Don't*."

"No," replied Septimus, "I will not."

Tertius Fume's brief look of amazement was quickly replaced by fury. "Then I shall have no option but to put the Wizard Tower under Siege until you accept the Rule of the Gathering," he bellowed.

Marcia's green eyes flashed with rage. "You would not dare," she told Tertius Fume, her voice shaking with anger.

Tertius Fume mistook the shake in her voice for fear, and laughed. "I *do* dare," he said. He began to chant a fast and furious torrent of words. A cry of dismay rose from the Ordinary Wizards.

"Quick, Septimus," whispered Marcia, "you must get out of here. Out through the Ice Tunnels—you know the way. Get out of the Castle; go to Zelda's—or to your brothers in the Forest. When it's safe I'll come and Find you wherever you are—I *promise*."

"But—"

"Septimus—it takes only two minutes and forty-nine seconds to put us in a state of **Siege**. *Go!*"

"You *must* go," said Alther, suddenly behind him. "Now!"

Marcia **Extinguished** all the candles, and some of the more nervous Wizards screamed. The Hall was plunged into gloom, the only light coming from the depressing pictures flickering around the walls, but Tertius Fume did not even notice. Nearly halfway through the **Siege** Incantation now, his voice had an unstoppable rhythm as the ancient **Magykal** words filled the Wizard Tower and sent shivers down the spines of the Living and dread into some of the Dead.

"Sep!" Jenna grabbed Septimus's hand and pulled him into the crowd of ghosts. Some stepped back to let them go, but many did not and they were **Passed Through**, their complaints lost in the ever-rising volume of Tertius Fume's Incantation. Septimus was running now, behind him he could hear the heavy pad of Ullr's paws, and behind Ullr was Beetle, he was sure of that—he could smell the lemony hair oil that Beetle had unaccountably started using recently.

They reached the line of Living Ordinary Wizards and dozens of willing hands guided them into the broom closet.

The closet was packed to bursting, but a path was rapidly made for them—and even more rapidly for Ullr. With the help of the glow from his dragon ring, Septimus quickly found the catch that opened the concealed door to the Ice Tunnels. As he pushed open the door, to his surprise Hildegarde was there. She pressed something into his hand with the words, "Take my **SafeCharm**."

"Thank you," muttered Septimus. He shoved it into his pocket and rushed through the door, closely followed by Jenna, Ullr and Beetle. As the cold air from the Ice Tunnels hit them, Tertius Fume bellowed triumphantly, *"Siege!"*

At once the door to the Ice Tunnels slammed shut and they heard the *whirr-clunk* of the door being **Barred**—just as at that very moment the occupants of the packed Great Hall were listening to the huge iron bars inside the doors to the Wizard Tower slide across and make them prisoners. Then, as all the **Magykal** lights and sounds of the Wizard Tower were **Extinguished**, they heard a muffled cry of dismay.

The **Siege** had begun.

++26++
ON THE RUN

Beetle was back on his own territory and he knew what to do—he took out his tinderbox and lit his Ice Tunnel lamp. The blue light showed a steep flight of steps cut into the ice disappearing down into the darkness. Beetle and Septimus—who both knew the steps—started down, but Jenna and Ullr held back.

"But where—where does this go?" she asked.

Septimus had told Jenna so much about the Ice Tunnels that

he had forgotten she had never actually been in them before. In fact, at first he had had a lot of trouble persuading her that they even existed, and whenever he had mentioned them to her he always got the feeling that she didn't quite believe him. As he held out his hand for her to take, he could see the look of amazement on her face that they were real.

Jenna took the offered hand and, with Ullr padding behind, she followed Septimus down the steps, which were covered in a crisp frost and were not as slippery as she expected. At the foot of the steps they went through a tall, pointed archway where the ghost of an old ExtraOrdinary Wizard would normally sit guarding the entrance, but was now otherwise occupied in the Tower above. Glad that he did not have to explain himself to the ghost—who, to Septimus's annoyance, had formed the opinion that he was not the brightest of Apprentices—Septimus followed Beetle through the arch and into the tunnel that led from the Wizard Tower. Beetle's blue lamp shone down the long tunnel and lit up the glittery surfaces of the billions of ice crystals that stretched away into the distance. Septimus heard Jenna whisper, "*Wow.*"

He grinned. "I told you they were really something."

"But, not like *this*. I had no idea. So much ice. It's weird.

And *freezing*." Their breath hung in great white clouds on the icy air and Jenna thought she had never felt so cold in her life. She had, but she did not remember it.

There was something about the Ice Tunnels that gave Jenna goose bumps and it wasn't just the bitter cold—she was sure she could hear a faint moaning echoing somewhere far away. Her goose bumps were not helped by the blue light from Beetle's lamp, which gave their faces a deathly hue and made their eyes look dark and scared.

"Ullr," she whispered. "Komme, Ullr." She ran her hand along the big cat's warm fur, which was bristling and raised all along his back, and she could feel the watchfulness in him. "So, where's the way out?" she asked.

"Wait a minute, Jen," said Septimus. He took a silver whistle from his Apprentice belt, put it to his lips and blew. No sound came. He took the whistle out of his mouth, shook it and then tried again. Nothing happened.

"Careful, Sep," warned Beetle. "You only need to do it once, you don't want to upset it. The Wizard Tower sled is really sensitive. I heard it used to get frightened and run away if you blew too loudly."

"But the whistle didn't work," Septimus protested.

"You don't *hear* it, Sep. Only the sled hears the whistle. In fact, the only way you'd know it wasn't working would be if you *did* hear it. See?"

"Not really. But—"

"Shhh," Beetle interrupted. "Did you hear that?"

"No—what?"

"Oh, *bother*." The moan was no longer quite so faint or so far away. It was, in fact, getting louder and nearer by the second. "*Rats*. It's Moaning Hilda. I didn't think she came this way."

"Moaning Hilda?" asked Jenna, taking a firm grip on Ullr. She could feel the big cat's muscles tensing, getting ready to flee.

"Ice Wraith. Quick—back under the arch and whatever you do *don't breathe in as she goes past*. Got that?"

A wild wind came roaring down the tunnel, blowing the hoarfrost from the walls and spraying it into the air in a thick white mist. They dived for the safety of the archway. The shrill, hollow wail of the Ice Wraith began to fill the tunnel. Ullr howled and quickly Jenna put her hands over the panther's sensitive ears. A blast of frozen air shot past and Jenna was overwhelmed by the feeling of being dragged under ice-cold water. Instinctively she turned away, closed her eyes and held her nose as an ear-drilling *aaiiiiiieeeeeeeeeeeeeee* filled the tunnel. And then it was gone. The Ice Wraith went careening on her way, screaming through the tunnels as she had done for hundreds of years.

Jenna, Ullr, Beetle and Septimus emerged from behind the archway. "That was horrible," whispered Jenna.

"Hilda's all right, really," said Beetle airily. "You get used to her. Kind of a shock at first, though. Oh, look, here it is." Beetle shone his lamp along the tunnel and a glint of gold met the blue light. Silently coming along the tunnel toward them was the Wizard Tower sled, its fine runners skimming along the ice. With a soft swish, the sled drew up in front of them and nuzzled up to Septimus's knee like a faithful hound.

"*That* is beautiful," breathed Jenna, who was developing quite an appreciation of finely worked gold.

"It is, isn't it?" said Septimus proudly, picking up the purple rope. "It's my sled—well, it is while I'm Apprentice. However long *that's* going to be."

"Don't be ridiculous, Sep. You'll be Apprentice for ages," said Jenna, who felt considerably more chirpy now that the sled had arrived.

"You never know how long anything will last," said Beetle

gloomily. He thought how much he would miss the tattered old Inspection sled—and even more how much he would miss his double whiz reverse turns.

"Oh, Beetle, I'm sorry," said Jenna. "I didn't mean—"

"'S okay," mumbled Beetle.

"*What's* okay?" asked Septimus.

"Nothing. Tell you later," said Beetle grumpily. "Come *on*, Sep, you going to drive this thing or just stare at it?"

"Keep your hair on, Beetle. I'm *doing* it." Warily, Septimus climbed onto the front of the sled, half expecting it to shoot off like a rocket. But the sled sat patiently while Jenna insisted that Beetle get on next so she could sit in the back and make sure Ullr followed. There was scarcely room for three on the sled, let alone a large panther.

Slowly, the heavily laden Wizard Tower sled trundled off along the tunnel, closely followed by an obedient Ullr, and was soon crawling down what Septimus considered to be a dangerously steep slope.

"It's not actually *illegal* to go faster than your average snail," said Beetle, not taking easily to his new role of passenger.

"Be quiet, Beetle. I'm just getting used to it," said Septimus touchily, well aware of what Beetle thought of his sledding skills.

At the bottom of the slope Septimus carefully negotiated two easy bends, crawled up a gentle incline and took the sled slowly along a straight stretch with the smoothest ice Beetle had ever seen. Beetle heaved a loud sigh and tried not to think of the amazing speed he could get from the Wizard sled on such perfect ice.

They were now approaching a fork in the tunnel. "Hey, Beetle, which way?" Septimus asked.

"Depends where you're going," said Beetle a trifle unhelp- fully.

"Out of the Castle," said Septimus. "Like Marcia says— except not the Forest or Aunt Zelda's. We're going to find Nik and Snorri, aren't we, Jen?"

"Um, well, first we've got to—" Jenna mumbled.

But neither Beetle nor Septimus heard. "So which way d'you want to go out, then?" grumbled Beetle. "Make your mind up."

"Beetle, what *is* the matter?" asked Septimus. "You're like a bear with a sore head."

"Well, maybe it's because you're crawling along like a little old lady pushing a shopping cart," Beetle snapped.

"I am *not*. Shut *up*, Beetle."

"Go easy, Sep," said Jenna. "Beetle's really upset. Jillie Djinn sacked him this afternoon."

"*What?*" Septimus looked horrified. "I don't *believe* it. She couldn't have. Why would she do a stupid thing like that?"

"Exactly. But she did. Horrible old cow."

"But why didn't you tell me before?" Septimus asked Beetle.

Beetle shrugged.

"He doesn't want to talk about it," said Jenna.

"Oh. I see. I'm really, really sorry, Beetle," said Septimus.

"'S okay," muttered Beetle. "Let's just get going."

Jenna took a deep breath. She had been dreading this. "Um, Sep. Um, it's about the map . . ."

"Oh, yes. We've got to go to the Palace and get it, right?"

"No," said Jenna miserably. "There's something you don't know . . ."

Half an hour later, in the quiet, whitewashed cellars of the Manuscriptorium, Ephaniah Grebe was entertaining his second batch of unexpected visitors in one day. He had been very pleased to see Beetle and the Princess again so soon, and meeting the young ExtraOrdinary Apprentice was something he had wanted to do ever since Septimus had arrived in the Wizard Tower—but the panther had been a nasty shock, a very nasty shock indeed.

There was more rat to Ephaniah than met the eye. Morwenna had done her best to make him appear as human as possible, but the essence of Ephaniah Grebe was rat—and Ullr knew it. And now that the size difference was no longer to Ullr's disadvantage, he longed to take his chance against the giant rat. But Ullr was a faithful creature and Jenna had told him, very firmly, "No, Ullr. *No!*" And so the panther lay disconsolately at her feet—but the orange tip to his tail twitched and he did not take his glittering green eyes off Ephaniah Grebe for one second.

Well aware that he was being watched by the biggest cat he had ever had the misfortune to meet, Ephaniah did his best to concentrate while everyone clustered around the worktable, looking at the muddle of confetti that had once been Snorri's map.

"The **Seek** hasn't worked," Septimus was saying disconsolately. "I can't **See** the missing piece anywhere."

"Are you sure?" asked Jenna.

"Of course I'm sure. I always get a picture in my head of exactly where the thing is that I'm **Seeking**. Last week I did a **Seek** and found one of my socks in the coffee pot. I didn't

believe it when I got this weird picture of my sock floating in
the coffee but when I looked—there it was. My **Seeks** always
work, Jen. Promise."

Jenna sighed. "I know they do. It's just I was hoping—well,
I was *sure* you'd find it."

In front of Ephaniah was his usual pen and paper. He
wrote: *What is the range of your Seek?*

Septimus took the pen and began to write a reply but Jenna
stopped him. "Mr. Grebe can hear you, Sep. He just can't talk,
that's all."

"Oh," said Septimus, embarrassed. "I'm sorry. I didn't think."

Ephaniah Grebe placed a dog-eared card in front of
Septimus: DO NOT WORRY. IT IS A MISTAKE THAT MANY MAKE.

Septimus smiled and received in return a twinkling of
Ephaniah's green eyes and the twitching and rustling of the
swathes of white silk below. "It's about a mile," he replied.

*It would reach all places that the map has been while in your
possession?*

"Yes. Definitely."

*Then it seems that the piece is lost. Maybe a bird has taken it
far away for its nest. Or the wind has blown it into the river.
Who knows?*

"Ephaniah," said Jenna, "can you **ReUnite** the map *without* the piece? Then at least we would have most of it."

An incomplete ReUnion will generate much heat. There is a risk that the pieces may combust.

"It's worth the risk," said Jenna, glancing at Septimus and Beetle. They nodded.

Ephaniah's eyes smiled and he made a small bow to Jenna—he liked a challenge. *I have already coated every fragment with melding fluid, paying particular attention to the edges. I shall now select the Charms.* He uncorked a large glass flask; inside was a collection of yellow and black striped discs, which Jenna immediately recognized as **Charms**.

Stand well back, please.

They retreated to the doorway and watched. Delicately holding a **Charm** in each hand between the long nails of his finger and thumb, the Conservation Scribe moved them over each and every fragment of paper. As he did so a dull yellow haze appeared above the table and settled over the fragments of paper like a soft blanket of fog. Then, as if conducting an unseen orchestra, Ephaniah raised his arms and opened his long, scrabbly hands, palms down above the table. Like two large, lazy bumblebees, the **Charms** drifted down and began to circle in opposite directions above the haze while Ephaniah made long, slow gathering movements over the fragments.

The smell of hot paper filled the air and Jenna closed her eyes—if the map was going to burst into flames she didn't want to see it.

Suddenly Ephaniah let out a loud squeak and Septimus and Beetle applauded. Jenna opened her eyes just in time to see the yellow blanket rolling up to reveal a large piece of paper below—the map had ReUnited.

Ephaniah turned to his audience, bowed and beckoned them over. Jenna could hardly believe how good the map looked. It was smooth and flat, and looked as if it had never even been folded—let alone crushed into pieces and stamped into a muddy puddle. Snorri's neat lines were crisp, clear and full of detail. For a moment Jenna was convinced that Ephaniah had been mistaken and the map was complete, but Septimus set her straight.

"There's a hole in the middle," he said. "A great big *hole*."

It was true. And somewhere in the middle of the hole was the House of Foryx—the Place where All Times Do Meet.

Jenna refused to be downcast. "It doesn't matter," she said. "There's enough of the map to get us most of the way, and by the time we get to the hole in the middle we'll probably be able to see the House of Foryx anyway."

"But Snorri had drawn all sorts of stuff on the missing part, don't you remember?" said Septimus. "I bet it was really important."

"You don't know that for sure," said Jenna, exasperated and wishing that for once Septimus would look on the bright side. "Look, Sep, I'm going whether you come or not. I'm going to get the Port barge and find a ship and then—"

"Hey, wait a sec, Jen—of course I'm coming. Try and stop me. And Beetle's coming too, aren't you, Beetle?"

"*Me?*"

"Oh, please come, Beetle," said Jenna. "*Please.*"

Beetle was astonished—*Jenna* wanted him to come too. Suddenly Beetle felt liberated. He was no longer tied, day in and day out, to the Manuscriptorium. He could do what he wanted; he could live his life and do the kind of interesting things that Sep did. It was amazing. But . . . Beetle sighed. There was always a *but.*

"I'll have to tell my mum," he said. "She'll be frantic."

✛ 27 ✛
MESSAGE RATS

T*he East Gate Lookout Tower* was, strangely enough, on the west side of the Castle. It had been moved by a particularly fussy Queen so many years in the past that no one could now remember why. The small, round tower perched jauntily on top of the wide Castle walls. If you climbed to the top you could see for miles over the Forest that bordered the west and southwest of the Castle.

In the old days, when the Message Rat Service had been

thriving, the whole tower had been full of rats, but now it boasted just one solitary—and very disconsolate—rat. A dim light from a single candle shone from the tiny window on the lower floor of the tower, and on the battered old door were three increasingly desperate notices. The first read:

RATS WANTED FOR MESSAGE RAT DUTIES

NO EXPERIENCE NECESSARY

FULL TRAINING WILL BE GIVEN

APPLY WITHIN

The second read:

BEST RATES OF PAY

WE PAY DOUBLE THE PORT RATE!

DON'T MISS OUT ON THIS WONDERFUL OPPORTUNITY!!

And the third:

FREE FOOD!!!!!!

Stanley was settling down for his fourth night in the East

Gate Lookout Tower. He had set up camp in the old office on the ground floor. In front of him were the remains of his supper that he had salvaged from a very productive garbage can outside a little house a few doors along the Castle walls. That night the shepherd's pie had been particularly good, and Stanley had very much enjoyed its topping of cold custard and squashed tomatoes—although he was less sure about the crunchy bits, which he suspected of being toenail clippings. But overall it had been a good supper and he was pleased to discover he had not lost his scavenging touch when it came to other people's garbage.

Scavenging successes aside, things were not going well. The Message Rat Service was proving very difficult to get going, even though Stanley had done everything he could think of. He had even cleaned up the office, dusting down Humphrey's old desk and mending the wobbly leg, then rescuing the Message Ledger, Diary, Patent Rat Journey Scheduler and Pricing Schedules from a tin trunk under the floor. All was now set up, ready and waiting, but there was one big problem—no rats. Try as he might, Stanley could not find a single rat in the Castle.

But that night as Stanley sat behind his lonely desk with the unusual combination of a full tummy and a feeling of gloom, he suddenly—to his joy—smelled a rat. Stanley sniffed the air in excitement. It was a very strong rat smell— it must be more than one rat, that was for sure. At least a dozen, he reckoned—and *all* of them coming to answer his advertisement. What luck.

At the sound of the knock on the door, Stanley restrained himself from rushing to answer it. Instead he picked up his pen, opened the Message Ledger and began to peruse it as though he were catching up with a hectic day's work. Then, doing his best to sound busy and preoccupied—rather than brimming with excitement—Stanley called out, "Come in."

The door flew open and the biggest rat Stanley had ever seen in his life marched in. Stanley promptly fell off his chair.

Ephaniah Grebe waited patiently while Stanley picked himself up off the floor and, with as much dignity as he could muster, clambered back onto his chair. "Just testing," Stanley muttered. "We like our rats to be unflappable. You passed. Now when can you start?"

"I haven't come for a job," said Ephaniah, relieved to be able to converse out loud with someone who understood him.

Stanley was horribly disappointed. "Are you sure?" he asked. "How about a bit of part-time Messaging? We are tak-

ing on part-timers for this week only. I'd get in while you can.
It's a great opportunity."

"No doubt it is, but I am already fully employed, thank you.
I have come to send a message."

"Oh," said Stanley. He then realized he did not sound as
pleased as he should have been about what was, after all, his
very first customer. So much for his daydreams of sitting at
his desk while a team of fit young rats did all the Message-
running. He would have to do this one himself. "Where to?"
he asked, praying that it was not to the Marram Marshes.

Ephaniah Grebe took out a piece of paper and read Beetle's
writing with some difficulty. "'The blue arched door, Top
Turret, Echo End, The Ramblings,'" he read.

Stanley breathed a sigh of relief. "And the message is?"

"'Dear Mum,'" said Ephaniah, a little self-consciously. "'I
have been called away on urgent business but will be back
soon. There is some money hidden in the old jar in the window seat. Please don't worry. Love, Beetle xxx.'"

Stanley wrote the message in the Message Ledger with a
happy flourish. He could remember that. Short and sweet,
that's how he liked them.

"It's urgent," said Ephaniah. "As soon as you can, please."

Stanley sighed. All the frustrations of his Message Rat days were coming back to him. It was *always* urgent in his experience. No one ever thought ahead. No one ever said, "I'd like to send a message in three days time, please. Just fit me in when it is most convenient for your schedule." But a customer was a customer, and at least it meant some money coming in. Stanley made a big show of flicking through the Pricing Schedules, even though he knew perfectly well that The Ramblings was in Price Zone One.

"Now, let me see . . . that will be one penny outward message. Two pence for the rat to wait for a reply. Three pence for next-day reply collection. Terms are strictly cash, payment in advance."

"The message is sent on behalf of Princess Jenna," said Ephaniah Grebe. "I understand she has a special introductory offer—free messages for a year."

"Only for those messages originating from the Palace and placed in person," said Stanley briskly. "For all others normal rates apply. Now, is it outward only or return?"

Ephaniah Grebe left the East Gate Lookout Tower three pence poorer—he had also sent two other messages, one to Sarah

Heap and one to Marcia Overstrand—but underneath his rat whiskers was a happy smile. Leaving his face unswaddled and his rat nose free to sniff the night air, he took the wide path that ran along the top of the Castle walls and walked slowly back to the Manuscriptorium. He enjoyed the feeling of his sensitive tail trailing behind him as it was meant to do, touching the cool stones and balancing his upright gait. Sometimes it was a relief to be true to his real rat nature.

As Ephaniah wandered along the Walls—as he sometimes did when the confines of the Manuscriptorium basement became too much for him—he gazed down at the roofs of the little houses tucked in tight against the old stones. He saw the candles in their attic windows burning bright into the night, and inside the tiny rooms with their sloping ceilings Ephaniah saw people—fully human people with no trace of rat in them—going about their business. Whether they were sewing by the fireside, clearing away a meager supper, feeding a baby or just fast asleep in a comfortable chair, all were unaware that outside their very windows a shy half man, half rat, was wandering by, looking at a life he might have had.

Ephaniah shook off his sad thoughts as a rat will shake off a well-aimed bucket of dirty water and strode briskly on. As the tinny chimes of midnight drifted up from the Drapers' Court clock he arrived at the top of the flight of steps that led down to the Manuscriptorium. He stopped and took a last look at the broad sweep of the Castle below him before he descended once more into his bright basement. It was breathtakingly beautiful. The moon was riding high in the sky, casting its cool, white light across the rooftops and sending long shadows down the streets far below. A myriad of pinpoint candlelights glittered across the vast expanse of the Castle, in a way that Ephaniah had never seen before. Puzzled, Ephaniah stood for a moment wondering why he could see so many candles—and then he realized. The bright, **Magykal** purple and golden lights that lit up the Wizard Tower every night were *gone*. It was as if the Tower were no longer there. But as Ephaniah stared into the darkness he could just about make out the outline of the Tower against the moonlit clouds. But not a flicker of light came from it—the Wizard Tower was under **Siege**.

✢ 28 ✢

THE QUESTING BOAT

Marcia was stumbling around the Wizard Tower, unable to see. Desperately she called, "Septimus . . . Septimus . . . where are you?"

"I'm here, I'm here!" yelled Septimus.

"Go back 'sleep," mumbled Jenna.

"Wearghaahh," mumbled Beetle, who was in the middle of his own dream in which Jillie Djinn had locked him in a dungeon with a giant rat.

They were sleeping—or trying to—on the floor of a small storeroom at the entrance to Ephaniah's domain. Jenna and Beetle both slipped back into sleep, but Septimus

was wide awake, his dream of the blind Marcia still frighteningly vivid. He sat up, all the events of the previous evening
crowding in on him. What was happening at the Wizard
Tower? Surely Tertius Fume had discovered his escape by
now? And if so had he sent people, or—more likely—ghosts,
out to search for him? And what was happening to Marcia?
Was she all right? Septimus put his hand in his pocket to find
his last memento of the Wizard Tower and drew out the
SafeCharm that Hildegarde had given him. It was so nice of
Hildegarde to do that, he thought. By the comforting yellow
glow of his Dragon Ring, he looked fondly at the
SafeCharm—and a shot of fear ran through him like a knife.
No! No no no no *no*. It couldn't be. It couldn't *possibly* be.
Septimus stared at the heavy, oval lapis lazuli stone in his
hand, and the golden Q inscribed deep into it glinted back at
him mockingly. And, when he turned it over, the number 21
began to show and Septimus knew with a horrible certainty
what he had—*the* **Questing Stone**.

He stared at the **Stone**, trying to remember what Alther
had told him at the **Gathering**. But it was all a blur—only the
phrase *Once you Accept the* **Stone**, *your Will is not your Own*
came into his head.

Septimus tried to think clearly. But he *hadn't* accepted the **Questing Stone**, had he? He had accepted what he thought was a **SafeCharm**. So surely that was different—wasn't it? He stared hard at the **Stone**. It was a beautiful thing; silky smooth, slightly iridescent with delicate veins of gold winding their way through the brilliant blue. And the dreaded **Q**— that was beautiful too. The gold was set deep into the stone and polished to such smoothness that as he ran his fingers over it he could feel no join at all. In fact he could almost convince himself that the **Q** was not there. But as soon as he looked down at the stone in his palm there it was, winking up at him in the dim yellow light, refusing to go away.

Septimus shoved the **Questing Stone** back into his pocket. He would ignore it, he decided. He wouldn't tell Jenna or Beetle either. There was enough for them to think about without worrying about some stupid **Queste**, which he wasn't going on anyway.

Septimus threw himself back onto the hard bedroll and pulled the thin Manuscriptorium emergency blanket up over his head. He tried to block the **Questing Stone** from his thoughts, but it would not go away. He began to remember more of Alther's words—how the **Stone** was a **Magykal** thing and as the **Questor** drew nearer to his or her goal, it changed color. And at the **Queste**'s end it was the deepest blue, so dark that it looked black—except in the light of the full moon. Alther had gabbled a rhyme, trying to get across as much information as possible, but just then Septimus did not even want to think about it. He didn't need to, he decided. He was *not* going on the **Queste**. He closed his eyes and tried to sleep—with little success.

About an hour later from behind the storeroom door, Ephaniah watched the NightUllr change. As the panther slept, Ephaniah saw the orange tip on his tail expand and grow, the bright color traveling across the creature like the sun chasing away the shadows. And as it grew, the sleek panther fur became a mottled tabby orange and its muscled body shrank so fast that Ephaniah was sure that Ullr would disappear completely. Indeed, when the **Transformation** was complete it looked as though he almost had—the DayUllr was a small and scraggly cat, who looked as if he could use a real meal. The only reminder of his nighttime attire was a black tip at the end of his tail, ready for the moment that the sun would once again set.

Now that the storeroom was guarded only by a small cat,

Ephaniah dared venture in to wake its occupants. Sleepily, Jenna, Septimus and Beetle rolled up their bedrolls and stacked them back onto the orderly shelves. And then, at Ephaniah's insistence, they gathered around the big worktable in the first cellar and ate the oatmeal that he had cooked over the small burner he generally used for melting glue. Ullr, after some persuasion from Jenna, warily accepted Ephaniah's offering of a bowl of milk.

It was not a lively breakfast.

Jenna was anxious to get away to the Port. "If we hurry we can catch the early-morning barge to the Port," she said, scraping the last of the surprisingly good oatmeal from the bowl.

"Good," said Beetle, who had taken a lot of persuading to spend the night back at his old workplace and wanted to be off as soon as he could.

Ephaniah returned from putting the previous day's work in the basket at the top of the stairs. He flapped his hands, signaling them to wait, and laid a large sheet of paper down beside the bowls. It was covered with his now familiar handwriting. He ran his thin finger along the words: *The journey to the Forests of the Low Countries is long and perilous by ship. But there is another way. There is an old saying, "A journey to a Forest is best begun in a Forest."*

Jenna knew the saying but had never understood what it meant. "What do you mean?" she asked.

Ephaniah wrote: *In the Forest there are ancient Ways that lead to other Forests. Morwenna knows. I can take you safely into the Forest by the old charcoal burners' gulleys.*

"We used to use those in the Young Army," said Septimus. "The witches still do. Some of the Ways go to their winter quarters."

Ephaniah nodded and wrote: *We will find Morwenna. I will ask her to show you the Forest Ways.*

"What do you think, Jen?" asked Septimus.

Jenna shared Sarah Heap's mistrust of the Wendron Witches, but if it helped them to find Nicko—and get Septimus far away from the Castle, fast—then it was fine by her. "Okay," she said. "Let's do it."

"Beetle?" asked Septimus.

"Yep," said Beetle. "The sooner we're out of here, the better."

Ephaniah Grebe led the way down Lichen Twitten, a long, dank alleyway that went to the Manuscriptorium boathouse.

The boathouse was a tumbledown shed set a few yards down a hidden inlet off the Moat. Inside was the Manuscriptorium ferryboat, a little-used rowboat that had escaped Jillie Djinn's new colors. Septimus and Beetle offered to row, but Ephaniah insisted on taking the oars himself. Rowing was something he had enjoyed in his younger, pre-rat days and it was a long time since he had been out in a boat.

It was a cold, blustery morning, but it was good to be out in the open air once more. Ephaniah had lost none of his old rowing skills and he maneuvered the boat skillfully out of the cut. But as he rowed into the choppy, gray waters of the Moat an unexpected sight met them—an exotic, three-masted sail-boat was moored at the site of the old Wizard Tower landing stage. The landing stage had rotted away, as the great days of the maritime ExtraOrdinary Wizards were long gone, but the boat was tied to one of the few remaining gold- and lapis-covered poles. It rose and fell gently with the small Moat waves, and as the tide took the Manuscriptorium rowboat ever closer—despite Ephaniah's efforts to the contrary—they could see the faded blue and gold of the hull, the tattered azure ropes, and the peeling golden masts that must have once shone like the sun.

Only Septimus could see the dull, **Magykal** haze of purple that surrounded the boat, but as a sudden eddy pulled Ephaniah's oar from his grasp and sent the rowboat spinning toward the peeling blue hull, everyone could see the faded name in gold letters painted along the prow: QUESTE.

Beetle grabbed Ephaniah's lost oar just before it disappeared into the water. Ephaniah squeaked his thanks. He moved across to give Beetle space and together he and Beetle managed to get the rowboat back under control—but not before it had bumped into the hull of *Queste* with a loud, hollow thud.

As Beetle and Ephaniah frantically pulled away from the **Questing Boat**, there came the sound of running footsteps on the deck of *Queste*. Quickly, Jenna undid her red cloak and threw it over Septimus, hiding his distinctive fair hair and green tunic, so that when three **Questing Guards** peered over the side they saw a shivering Princess, with her arm protectively around a hunched little old lady, being ferried across the Moat. Where the Princess might be going with the little old lady was of no concern to the guards; they were more concerned about what had happened to the final **Questor**.

The final **Questor** stepped out of the rowboat and risked a quick glance back at *Queste*. She was not a bad boat, he thought. She looked fast and very maneuverable—the kind of boat that Nicko would like. The thought of Nicko made Septimus forget his own troubles.

Ephaniah led the way along the bank past the Infirmary with its early morning candles lighting up the small windows—it still had a few elderly victims of the Sickenesse regaining their strength. They took the footpath around the back of the Infirmary and were at last out of sight of the **Questing Boat**. Relieved, Septimus shrugged off his little-old-lady mode and handed Jenna back her cloak, which she carefully fastened with Nicko's precious gold pin.

Behind the Infirmary was an overgrown path, sunk between two deep banks, well-trodden long ago by generations of charcoal burners. They followed Ephaniah as he limped through the ferns and drifts of leaves that covered the old path, and soon they came to a low escarpment of rock, which seemed to block their way. Ephaniah turned and pointed to a narrow gap in the rock. With some difficulty, the rat-man squeezed through (he had been a little thinner when he had last made the journey as a fourteen-year-old) and Septimus, Beetle, Jenna and Ullr easily followed him.

In front of them stretched a deep and narrow cutting through the rocks, shaded by overhanging trees high above.

"The charcoal burners' gulley," squeaked Ephaniah proudly, pleased to have found the way after all the years. "The *best* way into the Forest."

"I wish Stanley were here," said Jenna. "He'd tell us what Ephaniah was saying."

"Eventually, he might." Septimus grinned. "But first he'd tell us all about his third cousin twice removed who followed a giant rat into the Forest and was never seen again and then he'd tell us all about the time that he and Dawnie had—"

"All right, all right," laughed Jenna. "Maybe I'm glad Stanley *isn't* here."

✢ 29 ✢
SILAS'S SEARCH

While Jenna, Ullr, Septimus and Beetle were setting off along the charcoal burners' gulley, Silas and Maxie were waking up in a cold, damp tepee in the Wendron Witches' Summer Circle.

Maxie had enjoyed his night in the Witches' Circle—Silas had not. The tepee had leaked and the bedding had gotten wet and begun to smell of rancid goat. To make matters worse, Silas had been kept awake by the giggling of a gang of teenage witches planning a raid on what they called Camp Heap, which was where Sam, Edd, Erik and Jo-Jo Heap lived. Silas, who had no wish to know what his four sons were up to when it came to the Wendron Witches, had stuffed his ears full of rancid goat wool—big mistake—and tried to get to sleep by counting sheep—even bigger mistake, as the sheep had turned into rancid goats and started chanting. After a while Silas had realized that the chanting was in fact the witches chanting around the campfire. Exasperated, he had thrown a pile of stinking goat fur over his head to drown out the noise and had finally fallen asleep.

As Silas lay staring blearily at the top of the tepee, a young witch put her head around the door flap and said, "The Witch Mother requests that you join her for breakfast."

Silas struggled to sit up, and the young witch suppressed a giggle. Silas's straw-colored curly hair looked like a bird's nest—the kind of nest that would belong to a large untidy bird with a hygiene problem. From the middle of the nest, Silas's green eyes peered out, trying to focus on the young witch. "Um, thank you. Please tell her that I would be delighted." Even though Silas felt as if he had spent the night with a wet goat sitting on his head, he knew that any invitation from the Witch Mother must always be treated with reverence and respect.

A few minutes later, Silas and Maxie were sitting beside a blazing campfire. A strong smell of damp dog with subtle notes of none-too-clean wool filled the air as Silas's Ordinary Wizard robes steamed in the heat. Behind him the young witch who had woken him poured out a cup of hot witches' brew and avoided breathing in too deeply.

Sitting opposite Silas was Morwenna, the Witch Mother—a large woman with piercingly blue witches' eyes and long graying hair held back with a green leather headband. Morwenna wore the Wendron Witches' summer tunic of green and, as Witch Mother, she had a broad white sash around her more than ample waist.

The young witch passed Silas a steaming cup of witches' brew and he warily took a sip. It was, as he feared, disgusting—but it was also strangely warming. Morwenna was watching him with a fond smile, so Silas slowly drank a few more mouthfuls. As he did so he felt the ache in his bones fade and his spirits begin to drag themselves up from the deep pit where they had spent the night.

The young witch passed Silas a wooden bowl containing what looked, at first impression, like cereal with caterpillars. Silas inspected it dubiously but, telling himself that that flecks of green were most likely some kind of fleshy herb, he took a spoonful. His first impression had been right. They were caterpillars. Silas swallowed with some difficulty—because you never, *ever* spat out food given to you by a witch. Gloomily he surveyed the enormous amount of caterpillar cereal that he still had left to eat and wondered if he could sneak any to Maxie. He decided not to risk it.

"I trust it is to your liking?" asked Morwenna, noticing Silas's expression.

"Oh. Yes. It's very, um . . ."—Silas bit through a particularly large caterpillar with *legs*—"crunchy."

"I am so pleased. They are a late spring delicacy and give great strength and will clear your head. I thought you looked in need of them."

Silas nodded, unable to speak right then due to a mouth full of caterpillars and a sudden inability to swallow. One ghastly gulp later Silas decided he had to be tough—he would herd all the caterpillars together and get it over with. Gathering his courage, he scooped up and quickly swallowed two large spoonfuls of caterpillars. With great relief he looked at the remains of his cereal, which was now caterpillar-free. But, as Silas was taking a great gulp of the witches' brew to wash

down the last resistant caterpillar that had got stuck between a gap in his teeth, the young serving-witch stepped forward with a small bowl full of writhing green tubes and dutifully added three more spoonfuls to his porridge.

"You seem preoccupied, Silas Heap," said Morwenna.

"Ahem," said Silas, overwhelmed by the latest caterpillar incursion.

"Thank you, Marissa, you may leave us now," said Morwenna, waving the young witch away. She took Silas's bowl from him with a smile and gave it to a deeply grateful Maxie. "Too many caterpillars this morning, perhaps?" she said.

"But, um, very . . . remarkable caterpillars. I feel much better, thank you." And it was true, Silas did suddenly feel better. In fact he felt very good indeed. Clear-headed, strong and ready for the day.

"Ever since I heard about Nicko's disappearance I have been expecting you," Morwenna said.

Silas looked amazed. "Oh. Oh, Morwenna, I Know Nicko is in the Forest. But I do not Know where."

"And I Know that he is not," said Morwenna.

"Are you *sure*?" asked Silas, who had great respect for Morwenna's knowledge.

Morwenna leaned forward and placed her surprisingly dainty hand on Silas's arm. Very gently she said, "Silas, I must tell you that Nicko is not in this world."

Silas went pale, the tepees surrounding him began to sway and he wanted to be sick. "You mean he's dead," he said.

Hastily Morwenna said, "No. He is no more dead than those who are not yet born are dead."

Silas put his head in his hands. He found what Sarah Heap scathingly called witchy-talk difficult at the best of times, and now was most definitely *not* the best of times. He needed to talk to his father. Silas's father had been a practical man—a good, honest Shape-Shifter Wizard who was now living as a tree somewhere in the Forest. He would know what to do.

"Morwenna," said Silas, "there's a tree I need to find."

"There are many trees in the Forest," Morwenna observed. Silas wondered if she was making fun of him but then she said, "And some are more tree than others. Some were born trees and some became trees. I believe the tree you seek was not a born tree, I am right, Silas Heap?"

"Yes," said Silas.

"To seek a tree not born of tree is no easy task. They grow in the Ancient Groves, which are dangerous places. Some are pleased with their choice to be tree and others weep and wail and wish to be as they once were. These are the ones that prey upon the traveler and lure her to her doom. Who is it you wish to find, Silas Heap?"

"Benjamin Heap. My father."

"Ah, your shape-shifter father. It is true what they say—your family runs deep and dark, Silas Heap."

"Do they? I don't know why. Dad just liked trees, that's all. He was a quiet man, very slow in his ways. I think it probably suits him. But . . . well, last year the boys—Septimus and Nicko—they *found* him. And I need to see him, Morwenna. He'll know how to find Nicko. He must. He *must*."

Morwenna had never seen Silas Heap so desperate. Remembering the time many years ago when Silas had saved her from certain death by the Forest wolverines, she made him a generous offer. "I will take you to your father," she said.

Silas gasped. "You know where he is?"

"Of course. I know each tree in the Forest. How could I be Witch Mother and *not* know this?"

Silas was speechless. He had spent the last twenty-five years searching for his father and Morwenna had *known all the time*.

"You are strangely silent, Silas. Perhaps you do not wish to see your father after all?"

"Oh . . . no, I do. I really *do*."

Five minutes later Silas and Maxie were following the Witch Mother down the spiral path to the Forest floor. They took a narrow track that Silas knew would lead them past Camp Heap, where Silas had spent the last few days—until both he and the occupants of the camp had become totally exasperated with one another. Quietly, they skirted Camp Heap which, at that time of the morning, was still a slumbering circle of what looked like great piles of leaves. These were in fact what the Heap boys called benders—simple shelters made from bent willow branches and leaves. The only sign of occupation was the smoldering of the campfire, which the boys always kept burning, and the sound of snoring drifting out of Sam Heap's bender. Silas felt the urge to go wake them all up and tell them to *get up and do something*—which was what had led to much of the trouble during his stay—but he resisted.

Silas, Maxie and Morwenna walked deeper into the Forest, through dark glades and gulleys and into hidden places where Silas had never been before. They traveled fast, with

Morwenna moving swift and agile through the trees. Silas concentrated hard on following the witch's Forest green robes, which took on the shadows and shapes of their surroundings and he knew would quickly disappear if he looked away for one moment. Maxie loped behind, his stiff old joints complaining at the long trek, but not letting Silas out of his sight for one second.

Suddenly, Morwenna dived into a thicket of giant ferns. Silas followed her but the thick stems would not let him pass. He pushed and shoved, he even insulted them under his breath, but they would not move. He succeeded in nothing more than getting an impressive collection of giant burrs and two sticky toads stuck to his cloak. Silas fought the temptation to call out Morwenna's name, for he knew that the sound of a human voice in the Forest, even in daytime, can draw the kind of attention a human does not necessarily want. So he waited, hoping that Morwenna would soon notice he was no longer following her. Maxie gratefully lay down and licked his weary paws, but Silas was not so patient. He kicked his heels, he scratched his itchy head and dislodged three tree beetles, he prized the sticky toads from his cloak and stuck them onto a nearby sapling, and then one by one he picked off twenty-five giant burrs that had stuck onto his cloak and threw them into the ferns. But still there was no sign of the Witch Mother.

Silas decided to risk a whisper. "Morwenna . . . *Morwenna* . . ."

A few moments later Morwenna emerged from the ferns. "*There* you are," she said. "Come on. Keep up." She plunged into the ferns once again but this time Silas followed her so closely that he was very nearly treading upon her heels. The thick stems made way for the witch—but not for Silas. As soon as Morwenna had passed through, the giant ferns began to close ranks again, forcing Silas and Maxie to be quick and slip through the narrowing gap. It was lucky, thought Silas, that Morwenna was so much wider than him.

As they moved through the ferns, the light faded to a green dimness. At last they stepped out into a great green cathedral of trees—the tallest trees Silas had ever seen in his life, their branches arching gracefully up into the canopy of the Forest hundreds of feet above him. An unexpected feeling of awe came over him. Maxie whimpered.

"Your father is here," Morwenna said quietly.

"Oh . . ."

"I shall leave you now, Silas Heap," Morwenna half-whispered. "I have business at our Winter Quarters. I will return for you on my way back."

Silas did not answer. He could not imagine ever leaving such a peaceful place.

"Silas?" Morwenna prompted.

Silas shook himself out of his trance and answered, "Thank you, Morwenna. But . . . I think I want to stay here for a while."

Morwenna saw the faraway look in Silas's eyes and she knew she would get no more sense out of him. "Well, take care," she told him. "Be sure to spend the hours of darkness off the Forest floor. The Ancient Groves are dangerous places at night."

Silas nodded.

"May the Goddess go with you."

"Morwenna?"

"Yes, Silas Heap?"

"Where exactly *is* my father?"

Morwenna pointed to the tangle of gnarled mossy roots below Silas's boots.

"You're standing on his toes," she said with a smile. With that she was gone.

✢ 30 ✢
PROMISED

After watching Silas—and a very bemused wolfhound— being slowly lifted up into the branches of Benjamin Heap, Morwenna headed straight for the Old Quarry. Morwenna's predecessor, Madam Agaric, had run the Wendron Witch Coven from the vastness of a large cave set high up in the walls of the Old Quarry deep in the Forest. Madam Agaric's reign had come to an unexpected—and generally unlamented—end one cold winter's night at a full moon when the old witch had taken a fraction of a second too long to **Freeze** a werewolf that she had found lurking in the heaps of mouldy clutter at the back of her cave.

One of the first things Morwenna had done when she became Witch Mother was to start the Witches' Summer Circle on the hill. It put an end to all the petty feuds and personal hexes that had been rife among the witches, which life in the oppressive Quarry had encouraged. Morwenna liked to oversee all the details of the move—and one of these details was making the Old Quarry safe and welcoming for their eventual return on the day of the Autumn Equinox.

Morwenna took the shortcut to the Old Quarry—a hidden path that descended into the secret valley of the Blue Star Firs, trees that grew nowhere but there. As she entered the valley a heady scent of Blue Fir resin filled the air, a scent that made unprepared travelers sleepy and easy prey for the blue snakes that infested the high branches of the firs. But Morwenna was well prepared. She took out her green-spotted handkerchief, shook a few drops of peppermint oil onto it and pressed it against her nose. Morwenna emerged from the valley and stopped for a moment by the Green Pool—an ancient pond cut deep into the stone floor of the Forest. She kneeled down, dipped her hands into the cold water and drank. Then she filled a small water bottle and continued on her way.

About half an hour later, Morwenna was clambering down the end of the steep, rocky path that led to the Old Quarry. She jumped nimbly from the last boulder and stepped onto the smooth Quarry floor. She stood for a moment to catch her breath and looked up at the expanse of rock rising up in front of her. The Old Quarry was roughly semicircular in shape. Although it was formed from the pale yellow stone that had built many of the Castle's older houses—and indeed, the Palace—the rough-hewn walls that stretched up into the tops of the trees were ominously dark, streaked and blackened with soot from the fires from hundreds of years of occupation by the Wendron Witches. The walls were also home to a local Forest slime-lichen, which was a nasty greenish-black color and gave off a dismal smell whenever it got damp. Dotted here and there in the rock face were the even darker shapes of entrances to various caves that had been exposed by the quarrymen all those years ago. Each cave had steps leading up to it that the witches had laboriously hacked from the rock when they first took over the Quarry. It was in these caves, safe from the marauding night creatures of the Forest—most of the time at least—that the Wendron Witches lived in winter.

Today Morwenna wanted to check and secure the lower caves. It was no fun to return to the Quarry on a cold, wet Autumn day, laden with grubby tepees and damp bedding, to find that a pack of Forest wolverines had decided that your caves suited them much better than you—and were ready to prove it.

The only thing Morwenna actually liked about the Old Quarry was that it was one of the few places in the Forest with some flat, open ground. She headed purposefully across its wide, yellow stone floor. She approvingly noted that all looked swept and tidy and nothing had been left outside—or if it had, something had already eaten it and saved her the trouble of clearing it away. As she neared the bluish-black shadows at the foot of the rock face, a sudden movement inside a large cave startled her. Morwenna stopped dead. Very, very slowly, she drew her green cape around her so that the mottled underside showed, making her blend into the shadows. And then she waited, chanting under her breath the witchy words,

"Though you may see, you see not me . . . not me . . . not me . . ."

But Morwenna made sure that *she* saw. Her piercing blue eyes took on a bright glow as she stared into the shadows, searching, scanning—and suddenly a flash of white caught her eye. Morwenna caught her breath—what was it? What great white creature was inside the cave?

Morwenna saw the white shape move toward the front of the cave. Quickly she did a basic **Safe Shield** Spell—one of the organic witch ones. She was preparing to do a **Freeze** on the creature as soon as she could see it properly when the large white shape almost fell out of the cave. Morwenna gasped and dropped the **Safe Shield**.

"Ephaniah!" she cried out. *"Ephaniah!"* For there was no mistaking the rat-man even from a distance.

Ephaniah Grebe stopped and blinked into the light. He looked startled at hearing his name, but he recognized the voice immediately. "Morwenna," he squeaked excitedly. "I had so hoped to find you. And here you are!" He set off toward the witch, limping as he went.

They met halfway. Morwenna hugged Ephaniah so tightly that the rat-man coughed, his little rat lungs squashed by the witch's grasp.

Morwenna stepped back and looked Ephaniah up and

down. "You're limping," she said, concerned.

"Oh, just my bumblefoot," muttered Ephaniah.

Morwenna, like many witches, understood Rat and Cat Speak. "Come to our Circle. I'll make you a compress," she said sympathetically.

Ephaniah's eyes smiled, but he shook his head regretfully. "Unfortunately I cannot stay. I have some small charges of my own to take care of," he said.

Morwenna raised her eyebrows. "You *have*?" She sounded surprised, although she had not meant to.

Hastily Ephaniah said, "No, no. Not my own children. No, something has occurred at the Wizard Tower. I have the ExtraOrdinary Apprentice with me who is fleeing from the **Queste**."

"The **Queste**?" said Morwenna. "So it is time again for *that*, is it? How very sad. Such a waste of young talent. What a terrible reward for seven years of hard work." Morwenna stopped, confused. "But surely the boy is too young? He has not been Apprentice for three years yet."

Ephaniah's squeak fell to a whisper. "Morwenna, I have come to ask for your help. Although they are escaping the **Queste**, they are also—"

"They?" asked Morwenna.

"I also have the Princess and an ex-member of the Manuscriptorium staff with me."

"Well, well. You don't do things by halves, do you, Ephaniah? The Princess in the Forest, eh? That must be a first."

"I need your advice. They have lost their brother."

"In another Time, so it seems."

"You *know*?"

"A witch must keep up with the gossip." Morwenna smiled.

"I . . . have a favor to ask," said Ephaniah hesitantly.

"There is no harm in asking."

Ephaniah took a deep breath. "I have come to ask you to show them the Forest Way."

"Ah." Morwenna's light-heartedness at seeing Ephaniah vanished. She took a step back as if to distance herself from him.

"Please."

Morwenna sighed. "Ephaniah, this knowledge is not mine to give. It must be paid for."

Ephaniah's eyes pleaded. "But it may save two young lives—or more."

"Then you have just raised the price."

"Morwenna—*please*."

Morwenna smiled, a little distant. "Ephaniah, enough," she said. "Spend the day at our Circle. I will dress your foot and then we shall talk. Yes?"

Septimus and Beetle enjoyed the Summer Circle that afternoon—Jenna did not. While Morwenna was fussing with a large green poultice on Ephaniah's swollen foot, Septimus and Beetle chatted with the young witches. Septimus even had some beads braided into his hair—much to Beetle's amusement. But Jenna sat at the door of the guest tepee, keeping a tight rein on Ullr and watching with a marked air of disapproval. Jenna did not take to the young witches. She mistrusted their talk of goddesses and spirits and their haughty, confident attitude. Compared with the sober Castle inhabitants they seemed so foreign—with their bright beaded tunics, fingers heavy with silver rings, the tangles of beads and feathers woven into their hair and their general air of sunburned grubbiness.

Ephaniah sat by the campfire with his foot covered in an uncomfortably hot poultice, trying to think how he could persuade Morwenna to show them the Forest Way. Having—foolishly, he now realized—promised Morwenna's help, he could not bear to let Jenna and Septimus down. He was willing to pay anything that Morwenna asked, but she would not name her price. "We will talk tonight under the moon," was all she would say.

Darkness began to fall and—with the **Transformation** of the DayUllr into the NightUllr—the atmosphere became electric. The witches crowded around Jenna and the panther. They said not a word but their bright blue eyes glittered in the darkness: everywhere Jenna looked two points of blue would meet her gaze briefly and then look away. Ullr seemed unconcerned. He lay down at Jenna's side and, apart from a watchful twitch of the end of his tail, he did not move a muscle.

At long last, the uncomfortable evening around the witches' campfire came to an end and Jenna, Septimus and Beetle threw themselves gratefully onto the pile of rancid goat furs in the guest tepee. Exhausted, Jenna fell fast asleep with her arm around Ullr. But Septimus lay wide awake, listening to the desultory chatter of the witches settling down for the night and the sporadic screeches and screams of the nighttime creatures far below in the Forest.

Septimus was angry with Morwenna. His mother was right, he thought, as he lay under a damp goatskin and sneezed for the umpteenth time. You never really knew where you were with a Wendron Witch. The events of the evening kept going through his head. It had started well enough, even though Jen had seemed a bit twitchy. Morwenna had made them guests of honor. Rugs and cushions were spread for them to sit on and the entire Coven had been introduced and had joined them in a large circle around the campfire. Huge logs—needing three witches apiece to carry them—were hauled off the woodpile and thrown onto the fire. He had watched the flames and sparks leap into the night sky and felt the surge of hope and possibilities that an evening around a blazing campfire brings.

The young witches on cooking duty had served an extremely tasty wolverine stew, and even the witches' brew had tasted good. All was going well, until Ephaniah had once more made his request to Morwenna. In an instant—as though someone had thrown a switch—a frosty silence fell. Suddenly Septimus felt as though he was surrounded by a circle of wolverines rather than witches.

Recklessly, Ephaniah had repeated his question. "But, Morwenna, I *beg* you to show us the Forest Way. Surely, for me, you will do it?"

Septimus had not understood the squeaks, but the replies were clear enough.

"Have I not done enough for you already?" Morwenna snapped.

Ephaniah looked shocked and hurt. "Yes," he squeaked. "You have done so much for me. I can never repay you. Never."

Morwenna's witchy blue eyes pierced the dark. "I never asked for payment, Ephaniah," she told him. "I freely gave what was mine to give. But the knowledge you ask is not mine to give. I am but the Guardian of the Forest Way. Therefore, I must exact a price."

"I shall pay whatever you ask," he recklessly replied.

Morwenna looked surprised. "Very well. I shall give you my price in the morning. And when I ask it, you *must* pay it."

Ephaniah nodded somberly. "I understand," he squeaked.

With that the Witch Mother got to her feet and the whole circle of witches had silently followed suit. And that was the end of the evening.

Septimus sat up and threw off the disgusting goatskin. He was, he decided, allergic to goats—especially rancid ones. He wondered if he could swap his goatskin for Beetle's blanket without Beetle waking up.

"You awake, Sep?" Beetle's whisper came from the other side of the tepee.

"No. I always sleep sitting up."

"Really?"

"Of *course* I'm awake, Beetle. You awake too?"

"Nah. Fast asleep."

"Ha ha. Hey . . . what's that?" Tall, distorted shadows had suddenly appeared in sharp focus on the side of the tepee. A bout of hastily smothered giggling gave the game away—a group of young witches were on the other side of the tepee.

"*No* . . . is that *really* what she's going to ask the rat-man for?" an incredulous voice was asking.

"That's what she said. She always tells me stuff when I help her get ready for bed. She likes to unwind and talk about things."

"You'll be Witch Mother-in-Waiting if you don't watch out, Marissa."

"Oh, ha ha. I don't think so."

An earnest voice chimed in. "But the rat-man doesn't *have* to give what she asks for, does he?"

"He does. He agreed, didn't he?"

A new voice said, "He *squeaked*. Could mean anything.

Could mean get off my foot you great fat—"

"*Shhh*. You're *crazy* calling the Witch Mother fat. You know how touchy she is about her weight. You'll end up a frog for a day—or worse."

The earnest voice chimed in again. "But why would she want the Princess anyway?"

Septimus's and Beetle's eyes widened in shock. They both strained to hear what was coming next.

"She wants the panther." This was Marissa. "Morwenna's always wanted a Day to Night **Transformer**."

"So why doesn't she just ask for the panther?"

"Two for the price of one," Marissa said, giggling. "If she asks for the panther that's all she gets. But if she asks for the Princess the panther comes too. Clever, huh?"

"Yeah . . ."

"And having the Princess would make her *really* powerful, wouldn't it? Morwenna says that the Palace is full of tons of old **Magyk** stuff that the Queens pinched from us in the first place. She just wants back what's rightfully ours."

"So she really *is* going to ask for the Princess?"

"Yep. She is. First thing tomorrow. So we'll have little Miss Royal Fusspot and her scrappy cat living here. She'll soon learn. Ho-ho."

There was another flurry of giggling—a little nastier this time—and to his dismay, Septimus felt another sneeze coming on. He grabbed hold of his nose and held his breath. *He must not sneeze.* He must not, not, *not*, ah . . . ah . . . *ah* . . . Beetle saw what was coming. He leaped up and shoved his hand over Septimus's nose and suddenly Septimus most definitely did not want to sneeze anymore. He just wanted to *breathe.*

The young witches' conversation continued, unaware of the listeners right next to them, divided only by a thick sheet of canvas. Marissa was speaking now. She sounded impatient. "Sam will be here soon. I can see his torch coming along the track. We can't wait for Bryony much longer."

"Give her a couple of minutes more, Marissa. She had to clean the cooking pot. Which is more than *you* did this morning. It's disgusting."

"Well, I *hate* cleaning the pot. No one notices a bit of breakfast in their wolverine stew. Oh, I'm tired of waiting. I'm going to go get her. She can come now or forget it."

"Okay. We'll come with you." The tallest shadow left the group and the three other shadows quickly followed.

Beetle and Septimus stared at each other, goggle-eyed. "Did you hear *that*?" mouthed Beetle.

Septimus nodded. "We've got to get Jen out of here," he whispered.

✛ 31 ✛
CAMP HEAP

Thirty seconds later a very drowsy Jenna was outside the tepee with Septimus and Beetle standing on either side of her like sentries. She blinked into the bright moonlight and looked around, puzzled. Ullr yawned and stretched, digging his claws into the damp grass.

Far on the other side of the Summer Circle an

argument about a cooking pot was developing. Under the cover of the raised voices Septimus whispered, "Jen—we've got to get out of here. Right now. Come on."

"But why? I'm so *tired*, Sep."

"Too bad, Jen. You can't stay here. Come on."

"But where *to*? I'm not going into the Forest at night. No *way*."

"Come *on*, Jen." Septimus gave Beetle a look—then they both grabbed an arm and lifted her off her feet.

"Hey!" Jenna protested.

"*Shhh . . .*" Septimus and Beetle hissed.

"Put . . . me . . . *down*," Jenna whispered, and then, veering into Princess voice, "Right *now*." Beetle and Septimus put Jenna down.

"Come on, Jen," Septimus pleaded. "You have to trust us. Please."

Jenna trusted Septimus completely, but what she did not trust was the Forest at night. Reluctantly, she walked down the hill with Septimus and Beetle, leaving behind the warmth of the campfire and the circle of illuminated tepees like upturned yellow cones on the hilltop, and headed to the dark uncertainty of the Forest. Even with the NightUllr by her side, Jenna felt fearful—and then she saw something that made her feel very afraid. Far below, half hidden in the trees, was a flickering flame coming toward just the point they were heading for. Jenna stopped and glared at Septimus and Beetle, daring them to even *think* about picking her up again. "There's a Forest Wraith," she whispered. "It's heading straight for us."

"It's not a Forest Wraith, Jen." The moonlight caught Septimus's grin and Jenna saw his green eyes shine. "It's *Sam.*"

"Jo-Jo will kill me," said Sam, sounding remarkably cheerful about the prospect.

"I'm really sorry," said Septimus as they followed him along the track between the tall Forest trees.

"*I'm* not," Sam replied. "I've had enough of those giggling witches keeping me awake at night. They're a pain. I don't know what Jo-Jo, Edd and Erik see in them."

Beetle thought he did know, but he didn't say anything. He was too busy trying to keep up. Sam set a fast pace. He was carrying a long branch of oak that had been dipped in tar and burned with a strong flame, and Beetle wanted to keep as close to it as he possibly could. The track narrowed and plunged into a particularly dark patch, and the group was forced to travel single file, with Beetle the last in line. Stories about wolverines picking off the weakest stragglers kept going through his head, and he was determined not to give the slightest impression of straggling.

Sam was a confident leader. He strode on steadily and slowed only once when a long, rolling growl rumbled out of the darkness in front of them. Despite an answering snarl from Ullr, the growl continued and on the path ahead Beetle saw the yellow glint of two pairs of eyes. Suddenly Sam jabbed his torch into the dark—there was a sharp yelp and a smell of singed fur. Quickly, they hurried on, with Beetle almost treading on Septimus's heels in an effort to keep up. But he kept glancing behind just in case the yellow eyes had decided to try their luck.

A few minutes later the track broadened and Beetle began to feel much better—he could see the dancing flames of a campfire flickering through the trees and he knew they must be approaching Camp Heap. As they followed Sam into the wide clearing, three gangly figures jumped up from where they had been lolling around the fire and ran to greet them.

Beetle had never met Septimus's Forest brothers before, although Septimus had told him all about them. Beetle was surprised; he realized he had been expecting larger versions of Septimus but they were all young men—tall, thin and gangly with a wild look to them. They wore an assortment of furs and colorful tunics, woven by various admiring young witches, and they looked, thought Beetle, as though they belonged in the Forest even more than the witches did. The only similarity between Septimus and his brothers was the **Magykal** green eyes and the Heap hair—straw-colored curls that the Forest Heaps had turned into long, matted rat tails.

"That was quick," said one with feathers woven into his rat tails.

"Yeah," replied Sam, "and a lot quieter than usual."

"Marissa . . . *Marissa*?" Another Heap with a collection of plaited leather headbands around his rat tails peered at the group behind Sam. "Hey, he's brought a load of *kids*. Where's Marissa?"

"For your information, Jo," said Sam, "this *load of kids* is your brother and sister, not to mention your sister's panther." Sam waved his hand at Ullr, who was almost invisible in the shadows. The boys whistled, impressed. "Oh . . ." Sam tried to remember what Septimus had called the older boy with the black hair. "Oh yeah, and there's Cockroach."

"No, actually it's Bee—" But Beetle's protests were lost in the argument that was rapidly developing between Jo-Jo and Sam.

Jo-Jo Heap looked angry. "So you haven't brought Marissa?"

"No."

"*Pigs*, Sam. It's been ages. All that time Dad was hanging around here I couldn't see her and then when he was up at the Circle I couldn't, and now he's gone and I can and *you haven't brought Marissa.*"

"Well, *you* go get her, then," said Sam, thrusting the burning torch into Jo-Jo's hands. "I'm tired of doing all the night stuff anyway. *You* can do it."

"All right, then, I *will*." Jo-Jo strode off with the branch and Sam watched him go with a surprised look.

"Will he be okay?" asked Septimus.

Sam shrugged. "Yeah. I expect so." Then he grinned. "He'll be fine on the way back that's for sure. Marissa will scare anything away."

The two remaining brothers—Edd and Erik—laughed.

Then one of them said, a little shyly, "Hello, Jen."

"Hello, Edd," said Jenna, equally shyly.

"Hey, you can *tell*."

"Of course I can. *I* never got you muddled up, did I? Not even when you tried to fool me."

Edd and Erik both laughed. "No, you didn't, not once," said Erik, remembering that they could sometimes fool even their mother—but never Jenna.

Sitting by the warmth of the campfire, with the comforting snap and crackle of the logs and the faint sizzle of a row of tiny fish cooking in the background, Jenna listened to Septimus and Beetle as they related what they had heard that night from the other side of the tepee.

"Well, that's just stupid," she said. "Ephaniah wouldn't do that. Anyway, he couldn't. No one can give a person to someone."

"It's different with witches," said Septimus.

"I'd like to see them try," said Jenna scornfully.

"He's right, Jen," said Sam. "It *is* different with witches. There are different rules—*their* rules. You think you are doing what *you* want, but then you find out that all along you've been doing what *they* want. Look at Jo-Jo."

"Jo-Jo's doing exactly what he wants," sniggered Edd and Erik.

"Yeah. He *thinks*," Sam muttered.

There was silence. Septimus picked up a stick and began to poke it into the fire.

"What about Ephaniah?" Jenna suddenly said.

"He'll understand," said Septimus.

"He *won't*. All he'll know is that we've gone."

"We had to go, Jen. You were going to end up as a Wendron Witch." Jenna snorted in disbelief. "Well, you *were*."

Jenna sighed. She, too, picked up a stick and jabbed at the fire angrily. She felt as if Nicko was forever just slipping out of reach. And somehow it was always something to do with *her*.

"You want some fish?" asked Sam, who had a great belief in the power of fish to keep the peace around the campfire. No one felt very hungry after the wolverine stew, but they nodded anyway.

Sam had his own system of cooking fish. He threaded each one onto a thin skewer of damp wood and laid it on the Sam Heap Fish-Cooker—a rickety metal tripod set up over the fire

that had an alarming habit of collapsing when least expected. Sam selected the three best fish and passed them to Jenna, Septimus and Beetle. Beetle took his fish-on-a-stick a little reluctantly; he was not a great fish fan and it didn't help that his fish seemed to be staring at him reproachfully. Beetle stared back at the fish and steeled himself to take a bite.

"Something wrong with your fish, Cockroach?" asked Sam.

"'S not Cockroach, Sam," said Septimus with a mouth full of what was, in fact, extremely good fish. "It's Bee—" He was interrupted by a sudden crashing through the trees behind them. With well-tuned Forest reflexes, Sam, Edd and Erik leaped to their feet brandishing sticks, ready to defend the camp. A small Forest leopard shot out of the trees, ran straight at the campfire in a blind panic, swerved to avoid it—and Ullr—and disappeared into the Forest on the other side.

"That's weird," said Sam. "What got into him?"

The answer to Sam's question emerged from the trees brandishing a torch, and strode into Camp Heap with a proud air. Beside him was the young witch, Marissa. Marissa was as tall as Jo-Jo with long wavy brown hair held back with a plaited leather headband that was identical to the one Jo-Jo wore. She allowed Jo-Jo to usher her to the campfire, where he tossed the burning torch into the flames with a triumphant flourish.

Jo-Jo threw himself down beside the fire and pulled Marissa down with him. Marissa settled, fussing with her dark green witch's cloak—over which she had sewn dozens of little bunches of colored feathers. She looked like an exotic bird roosting with a troupe of scruffy sparrows. Still on a high from his successful and scary—though he would be the last to admit it—trip through the nighttime Forest, Jo-Jo grabbed a fish and gulped it down in one bite. A little late, he remembered his manners and offered one to Marissa, but the young witch did not notice. Her eyes were fixed on Jenna, Septimus and Beetle on the other side of the campfire. "What are *you* doing here?" she asked suspiciously.

"Same as you," said Septimus, determined to give nothing away.

"But you're the Witch Mother's *guests*." Marissa was indignant. "You can't leave just like that. *No one* does that."

Septimus shrugged and said nothing, the ways of Camp Heap rubbing off on him. He was learning from his brothers that you didn't have to explain yourself if you didn't want to—and that sometimes, with a witch, it was better not to.

Marissa sat frowning at the fire. Jo-Jo offered her the fish once again but she angrily shook her head. "I ought to go back," she muttered.

"*Back?*" asked Jo-Jo, incredulous.

"Yes. Back. Take me back, Joby-Jo."

Jo-Jo looked stunned. "What—*now?*"

"Now." Marissa's lower lip stuck out crossly and her witch-blue eyes flashed in the firelight.

"But—"

Jo-Jo's protests were interrupted by Sam. "Jo-Jo is not going anywhere tonight. It's too dangerous. It's past midnight and it's time for bed." Jo-Jo flashed Sam a grateful glance but Sam ignored him. He stood up and said, "Sep, Jenna and Cockroach can have Wolf Boy's old bender. Come on, you guys," he said, looking in their direction. "I'll show you where it is."

Septimus was about to tell Sam that there was no need, he remembered where it was, when Sam caught his eye with a meaningful glance. "Yeah. Okay," muttered Septimus.

As soon as they were out of earshot of the campfire, Sam said quietly, "You'll have to be off at dawn tomorrow. Marissa will go straight back to Morwenna, you can bet on that. And if Morwenna wants Jen for the Coven she'll get her—one way or another."

"No, she won't!" said Beetle vehemently. "Not while me and Sep are here."

"Look, Cockroach," said Sam patiently, "you two don't stand a chance against a Witch Mother, believe me. You need to be out of here first thing before the witches realize you've gone."

"I suppose we could try to catch the Port barge," said Septimus doubtfully. "But it doesn't usually stop at the Forest."

"What do you want to do that for?" asked Sam, puzzled. "I thought you were taking the Forest Way."

"Yeah. Well, that was the idea. Until Morwenna got nasty and wouldn't show us where it is."

"You don't need that calculating old witch," said Sam. "*I'll* show you."

"You?" Septimus gasped.

"*Shh* . . ." Sam glanced at the group silhouetted around the campfire. "Don't give that Marissa any ideas we're planning something. I'll come wake you first thing. Okay?"

Septimus nodded. And then said, "Night, Sam. And thanks."

"'S all right. Got to look after my little brother and sister, haven't I?" Sam said with a grin.

It was warm and comfortable in Wolf Boy's bender after Sam had thrown in a pile of thick blankets. Feeling very, very tired, Jenna, Septimus and Beetle burrowed under the blankets and curled up on the bed of leaves.

"G'night," whispered Beetle.

"G'night, Cockroach."

"Night, Cockroach," came the replies.

✛ 32 ✛
NIGHT CROSSINGS

While Jenna, Septimus and Beetle slept dreamlessly in Wolf Boy's bender and the NightUllr listened to the sounds of the Forest, a small ferryboat was making a perilous crossing to the Castle. The ferryman had extracted a high fee for the trip but even so he was beginning to regret it—the tide was running fast against the wind, and as they reached the middle of the river, water was splashing into his boat with every wave it hit.

His passengers were beginning to regret it too.

"We should have waited till morning," Lucy Gringe moaned as the boat dipped alarmingly and her stomach seemed to go in the opposite direction.

"Don't worry, Luce," replied Simon Heap encouragingly. "I've known worse." He hadn't, but now was not the time for strict accuracy, he thought.

Lucy said nothing more. She thought if she did speak she would probably be sick, and she didn't want Simon to see *that*. A girl had to keep up appearances even in a rotten little rowboat. Lucy closed her eyes tight and sat concentrating on her thoughts. She could not get out of her head the expression of horror on Simon's face as they had walked into the Observatory that afternoon. "Luce," he had whispered in a panic. "Get straight back down those steps and get Thunder. Now!"

Lucy didn't like Simon telling her what to do—and he didn't usually dare—but this she knew was different. She had fled back down the steep, slippery slate steps, past the horrible old Magog chamber, and by the time Simon had joined her, Thunder was saddled once more and ready to go. She had asked Simon what was the problem, but all he would say was, "I did a **See**."

They were nearing the other side of the river now and the water was a little calmer. Lucy brightened. If what Simon had said—that they were never going to set foot in that awful Observatory again—was true, then she was very pleased indeed, but she wished they weren't going back to the Castle. She would much rather have been heading for the Port. Lucy liked the Port; it was much more fun than the Castle and there was no risk of bumping into her mother and father there, either.

However, the most pressing reason that Lucy did not want to go back to the Castle was Simon himself. Simon seemed to have forgotten the events that had led up to him fleeing the place almost a year ago. Lucy did not know exactly what had happened but she had heard all kinds of terrible things—most of which she did not believe but some, she knew, were true. Her brother, Rupert, had told her he had seen Simon throwing a **Thunderflash** at Septimus, Nicko and Jenna—and Lucy knew that Rupert did not tell fibs. And there were other stories too: that Simon had tried to do some horrible **Enchantment** on Marcia by using DomDaniel's bones and had very nearly succeeded, and that Marcia had let it be known that if Simon ever set foot in the Castle again she would put him in the lock-up forever.

Lucy looked at her beautiful ring—most definitely *not* from Drago Mills's warehouse clearance sale—and sighed. Why couldn't she and Simon be *normal*? All she wanted was for them to be like everyone else—planning to get married, looking for somewhere to live—just a room in The Ramblings would do. Why couldn't she take Simon to see her mother and father and have him and Rupert be friends? Why? It wasn't fair. It just *wasn't*.

The boat pulled in to the night ferry quay, just below Sally Mullin's Tea and Ale House. The ferryman, Micky Mullin, who was one of Sally's many nephews, tied the boat up with a feeling of relief and bid his soaked passengers good night. He watched them walk unsteadily toward the South Gate—which, if you knew where to look, had a small door that was open all night—and wondered what they were up to. Even though Simon had taken care to pull down his hood well over his face, Micky had noticed the distinctive Heap features. Simon, now that he was in his early twenties, looked remarkably like a young version of his father, Silas. Micky decided to

go see his aunt the next morning; she liked a bit of gossip—
and she made a good barley cake, too.

As they walked along the deserted streets, keeping out of
the worst of the wind, Lucy was still unusually silent.

"You okay, Luce?" asked Simon.

"I wish we weren't back here," Lucy replied. "I'm scared
they'll find you and lock you away forever."

Simon drew out a crumpled letter that had been waiting for
them on their return. Lucy heaved a sigh. She so wished she
had not seen it tucked under a rock beside the path leading up
to the Observatory entrance, but the envelope was stamped
with the words DELIVERED BY THE PORT PACKET POST COM-
PANY, and she had thought it sounded exciting. Lucy now
knew the contents of the wretched letter by heart, but she
listened once again as Simon read out the tiny, spiky handwriting.

The letter was written on official Manuscriptorium note-
paper and it said:

Dear Simon,
I expect you have noticed that I have gone.
   You may have noticed that something else has gone too. I have

~~Slooth Sluuth~~ Sleuth and it is MINE now. It likes being with me.

If you come to find it I will make sure someone finds _you_.

As you see from this writing paper, my ~~talants~~ talents have at last been recognized as I have a very good job here. Much better than the one I had with you.

I am back where I belong now but no one will have _you_ back again. Not in a ~~milloin~~ million years. Ha ha.

Your ex ~~faitful faithfil~~ faithful servant,

Merrin Meredith/Daniel Hunter/Septimus Heap

"I told you, Luce, he's not getting away with this," said Simon, shoving the letter back into his pocket. "He's teamed up with two other wasters—dunno who Daniel Hunter is but I always knew that precious little Septimus was no good—and now he thinks he can scare me into letting him keep Sleuth. He'll soon find out just how wrong he is."

Lucy shook her head. What was it with boys and their fights? "It's a long way to come just to get your ball back," she said.

When Sarah Heap got over her fright and realized that it was Simon tapping on her sitting-room window she did not know whether to laugh or cry. So she did both—at the same time. Lucy stood by feeling awkward, thinking that maybe she should go to see *her* mother. And then, as Sarah began to bombard Simon with questions—where had he been living, what was he doing, did he really do all those awful things everyone said he did and *why* hadn't he written to her—Lucy thought that it was probably better not to see her mother. Not yet.

Lucy and Simon sat and dried out in Sarah's sitting room beside the fire, eating the bread, cheese and apples that Sarah had found in the kitchen. Lucy liked the chaos of the sitting room, and she was fascinated by the stubbly duck with a crocheted waistcoat that Sarah had picked up from beside the fire and placed in her lap. Lucy liked the Heaps; they were so much more interesting than her own family.

"I don't know what Marcia will do if she finds you here," said Sarah, beginning to worry. "She's always in a bad mood nowadays. *Very* touchy. And not very nice, either. I *never* see Septimus and she *knows* that, but whenever she sees me she makes a point of saying that she hopes I am enjoying seeing so much of him. *Don't* make that face, Simon. I will not have you fighting with your little brother any longer, is that understood? *Well, is it?*"

Simon shrugged. "It's not *me* who's fighting. He's stolen

Sleuth," he muttered under his breath.

"Stolen *what*?"

"Nothing," growled Simon. "Doesn't matter."

Sarah sighed. She was thrilled to see Simon after so long but she wished he were not so angry. "No one must know you are here—*no one*," she told him. "You and Lucy will have to lie low in the Palace until we can work something out."

Lucy yawned and swayed sleepily. The yawn was not lost on Sarah. Carefully, she put down the duck and stood up beside the fire. "You must be exhausted," she said, giving Lucy a concerned smile. "Why don't we go find you a comfortable bed somewhere?" Lucy nodded gratefully. Simon's mum was nice, she thought.

Half an hour later, Lucy was fast asleep in a warm bed in a huge Palace guest room overlooking the river. Simon however— one floor up under the eaves of the attic—was moodily staring out the window. It was then he noticed that something was wrong . . . something was missing. *The lights of the Wizard Tower had disappeared.* Simon threw open the window and stared into the windswept night. Spread out below were the lights of the Castle. The torches of the Wizard Way flickered and danced in the wind but the great ladder of purple, **Magykal** lights that always lit up the Castle sky was *simply not there*.

Simon knew he could not stay in his tiny room wondering what was going on at the Wizard Tower—he *had* to find out. Feeling horribly like he was a little boy creeping out on an adventure when his mother had told him to stay in and do his homework, Simon eased open the creaky bedroom door and tiptoed down the darkened corridor. He was so intent on not making a noise that he did not notice Merrin—just returned from another late-night visit to Ma Custard's—emerge from the top of the stairs. Horror-struck at the sight of Simon, Merrin nearly choked on his last banana-and-bacon chew. He stopped dead in his tracks, then ducked behind one of the huge beams that lined the walls.

As Simon tiptoed past, Merrin stared at his former employer like a rabbit **Transfixed**. He could not believe his eyes. How had Simon tracked him down—how did he *know*? Not daring to even turn his head, Merrin watched Simon as he slunk down the stairs, treading as carefully as Merrin himself had during his first days at the Palace.

Simon snuck out of a side door and headed for the alley beside the Palace. He was soon striding up Wizard Way toward the darkness that he knew contained the Wizard

Tower. Despite all the things he had done—which now Simon could hardly believe, *what* had he been thinking of?—he retained a proprietary interest in the Wizard Tower. Deep down Simon Heap still wanted to be ExtraOrdinary Wizard. But he no longer wanted to do it the **Darke** way. That, he thought, was cheating. He wanted to do it properly, fair and square, so that Lucy would be proud of him.

Simon knew this was an impossible dream. But it didn't stop him from being drawn to the Wizard Tower and it didn't stop him wanting to know what was happening there.

As he approached the Great Arch at the entrance to the Courtyard, Simon saw a large but subdued crowd congregated outside, talking in low, anxious voices—he was not the only one to have noticed the absence of **Magykal** lights. Simon pulled the hood of his cloak over his head and, ignoring mutterings of protest, he pushed his way to the front. There he came face to face with two tall figures, surrounded by a **Magykal** haze. They were, although he did not know it, two of the seven **Questing Guards** who had come to escort the Apprentice away on the **Queste**. At Simon's determined approach the armed **Guards** crossed their pikestaffs in front of him with a loud *clack* and barred the way through the Arch.

"Halt!" they barked. Simon halted.

Mustering his courage, Simon asked, "What's going on?"

"Siege," was the terse reply.

Behind Simon an anxious muttering spread through the crowd.

"Why?" Simon asked.

The Guards' reply was swift and unexpected. They drew their daggers and brandished them at Simon, one of them catching his cloak.

"Go!" they barked.

The crowd scattered. Shocked, Simon ripped his cloak from the dagger, then walked away as slowly as he dared. Entertaining fantasies of storming the Wizard Tower, rescuing it from the Siege and being asked by a grateful Marcia Overstrand to be her Apprentice, Simon walked around the outside perimeter of the Courtyard walls, but the Courtyard gates were Barred. All Simon saw was the ghostly outline of the Wizard Tower in the moonlight and all he heard was the screech of an owl and the distant slam of a door as one of the crowd regained the safety of his home.

Simon trailed back to the Palace. This would not, he told himself, have happened if *he* had been Apprentice. Which was, of course, true.

✷ ✷ ✷

Back at the Palace, Merrin was angrily packing his backpack. Why, he thought, *why* did it always go wrong? Why, just when he had found a place of his own, did Simon stupid Heap have to come and spoil it all? As he left his room, several Ancient ghosts, including a very relieved ghost of a governess, watched him go. Merrin crept down through the sleeping Palace, slipped out and headed for the kitchen garden shed. At least, he thought, there would be no former employers *there*.

How wrong he was.

But Merrin was toughening up fast. Angrily, he grabbed the sack of DomDaniel's bones, dragged it out of the shed, and after getting a few rhythmic swings going, he heaved it over the kitchen garden wall. The sack flew over in a perfect arc and thumped down in Billy Pot's ex–vegetable patch, now home to a certain Mr. Spit Fyre, as Billy Pot respectfully called the dragon.

Spit Fyre slept on, unaware that breakfast had landed.

✢ 33 ✢
BREAKFAST

The next morning *Billy Pot* was up early mixing Spit Fyre's breakfast according to Septimus's strict instructions—but the dragon was not interested. Spit Fyre lay outside his new Dragon Kennel and regarded Billy drowsily through a half-open eye. As Billy approached with the breakfast bucket, a subterranean rumbling shook the ground and the dragon burped. Billy reeled.

He scratched his head, puzzled. If Billy didn't know better, he'd say that the dragon had already eaten. "I'll leave yer bucket o' breakfast here, Mr. Spit Fyre," he said. "You might like it later."

Spit Fyre groaned and closed his half-open eye. Deep in his fire stomach he could feel the old **Necromancer**'s bones lying heavy and **Darke**. He wished he'd never swallowed that nasty old sack. He didn't *ever* want to eat again.

As the dragon's fire stomach slowly geared up for the **Darke** task of dissolving the bones, the ghost of DomDaniel was reveling in being at the Wizard Tower once more. It had done him good to see old Nastier Underhand get her come-uppance at long last—it amused him to see her hanging around like any other common Wizard, waiting to be told what to do. And now he had cornered his old Apprentice, Alther Mella, who had pushed him off the golden pyramid at the top of the Wizard Tower. *That* memory was still there, clear as the day it had happened. DomDaniel was enjoying telling Alther in great detail all the **Darke** plans he intended to put into action now that, at last, he had become a ghost—when he began to feel a little strange. At that moment Alther noticed that DomDaniel's left leg had disappeared.

Alther watched, fascinated, as next DomDaniel's entire right arm faded from view, then his left knee . . . left forearm . . .

toes . . . both ankles . . . Astonished, Alther stared as, piece by piece, his old master disappeared.

DomDaniel did not like the way Alther was watching him—it was, he considered, extremely rude and did not show him the respect he was due. He opened his mouth to tell Alther to stop gaping and his head vanished, leaving a disembodied left hand gesticulating wildly and a large part of his stomach wobbling with indignation.

And then, as DomDaniel's last few bones dissolved in Spit Fyre's fire stomach, the old **Necromancer** disappeared completely—and forever. For there was no Two-Faced Ring with him in Spit Fyre's stomach to get him out of trouble *this* time. It was a moment that Alther would savor for a very long time—along with the memory of the next few minutes when he found Marcia and told her that the **Gathering** was no more.

Marcia, too, savored the memory of the end of the very last **Gathering**. She particularly enjoyed remembering Tertius Fume's reaction when she had triumphantly evicted him from her sofa—he had a nerve, she thought—and told him that not only was the **Gathering** at an end, but there could be no **Gathering** ever again and he could get out of her rooms *right* *now*. Tertius Fume had refused to believe her until Alther had backed her up. It was true what Marcia had said to Beetle— Tertius Fume had no respect for women.

Tertius Fume had instituted the **Siege** to force Septimus to make the Draw. When he had realized that Septimus was missing, he had sworn to continue the **Siege**—forever if necessary— until Marcia told him the whereabouts of her Apprentice, whom Tertius Fume was convinced was **Hidden** somewhere in the Wizard Tower. But now, without the power of the **Gathering** behind him, Tertius Fume had no means of continuing the **Siege**. The **Siege** was ended.

Marcia wasted no time. She got Catchpole to escort Tertius Fume ignominiously off the premises and, as the **Magyk** returned to the Wizard Tower, she stood at the door smiling through gritted teeth.

"Good-bye, good-bye. Thank you *so* much for coming," she said as the bewildered **Gathering** floated out.

Outside the Wizard Tower a wet, cold rat watched the huge doors open—*at last*. To his amazement a seemingly endless stream of purple ghosts spilled down the steps. He waited impatiently until the last ghost had wandered out, then he bounded inside, calling out, "Message Rat!"

While Stanley scuttled between the feet of an excited group of Ordinary Wizards surrounding the recipient of his message, Tertius Fume was in a huddled conversation in the shadows of the Great Arch with what appeared to be a young sub-Wizard.

"*Find* him," said Tertius Fume. "The **Queste** is begun and *must* be done."

The **Thing** nodded. It watched Tertius Fume stride angrily back to the Manuscriptorium and began to chew the ends of Hildegarde's fingers. It was bored with InHabiting the sub-Wizard. Her ordinariness—and her niceness—was irritating; it had seeped into the **Thing** and made it feel rather depressed. The **Thing** fancied InHabiting something a little more unusual, something maybe with a twist of **Darke** to it. It leaned back against the cold lapis lazuli walls of the Great Arch and, passing the time by seeing how far it could spit bits of Hildegarde's nails, it waited for something to turn up.

Some hours earlier that morning, Ephaniah Grebe had woken in a damp tepee feeling very strange. After Jenna, Septimus and Beetle had retreated to their tepee, Ephaniah had accepted a sweet, heavy drink from Morwenna. He knew as soon as he drank it that it was drugged and he had surreptitiously poured most of it away, but as the Witch Mother escorted him to his tepee, Ephaniah felt the ground sway beneath him and a bitter taste in his mouth. He had vainly fought against sleep— but his vivid dreams had woken him a few hours later. Determined not to fall asleep again, he had crept out of his tepee to breathe the fresh night air. There, in the middle of the Summer Circle, he saw Morwenna in a heated conversation with a young witch.

"Where is Marissa, pray?"

The young witch looked terrified.

"Tell me, Bryony. *Now.*"

"Um. She went to Camp Heap."

"I did not give her permission. She will regret it. *You* will take her place."

"*Me?* Oh, but I don't think—"

"You don't have to *think*, girl. Just do as you are told. I want a tepee made ready for the Princess and her familiar. We will need it in the morning."

"Oh. Then she really *is* going to be—"

"Stop babbling. And be sure to make the tepee **Secure**."

Bryony bobbed an awkward curtsy and rushed off. How did you make a tepee **Secure**? she wondered. *How?*

Ephaniah felt sick—now he *knew* what Morwenna would ask for the next morning. He guessed that the nightcap—as Morwenna had called it—had been designed to keep him quiet and amenable come the morning. Ephaniah cursed himself for being such a gullible fool and for promising what he could not give. Stealthily, he crept over to the other guest tepee, his head spinning. What was he going to tell them?

When Ephaniah found Jenna, Septimus and Beetle's tepee empty he felt a surge of relief—but it did not last long. All kinds of worries came into his head. Where had they gone? Why didn't they tell him? Didn't they trust him? Had he slept through their cries for help? In a daze, Ephaniah limped down the spiral path from the Summer Circle, his white robes shining in the light of the full moon. Bryony saw him go, but she dared not say anything to upset the Witch Mother. She watched Ephaniah disappear into the Forest where—left alone by the Forest night creatures, which preferred to avoid giant rats—he staggered back to the Castle.

By dawn Ephaniah Grebe found himself standing beside the Moat, watching Gringe lower the drawbridge. He paid his silver penny and hobbled across, oblivious to Gringe's inquisitive stare.

"You see all sorts in this job," Gringe mused later as he watched Mrs. Gringe warm up last night's stew for breakfast. "Saw a giant rat this morning. With specs on."

Mrs. Gringe broke a habit of not listening to her husband. She stopped stirring and peered into the brown depths of the saucepan. "I *thought* those mushrooms looked funny," she said.

"What mushrooms?" asked Gringe, confused.

"Last night. They were a funny color. Didn't eat any meself."

"But you let *me* eat them?"

Mrs. Gringe shrugged and poured the stew into Gringe's bowl. "Better pick the mushrooms out," she said.

"No, *thank you*," said Gringe. He got up and stomped back to the drawbridge. By midday Gringe thought the mushrooms were probably wearing off. Apart from being convinced he had seen Lucy peering around the corner—which was most upsetting—there had been no other ill effects.

✳ ✳ ✳

When Ephaniah had returned to the Manuscriptorium that morning, his feeling of gloom had not been improved by the sight of the new Front Office Clerk sitting with his feet up on the desk chewing a black snake with his mouth open. At the sight of the Conservation Scribe, Merrin had stared and insolently carried on chewing what was, in fact, his breakfast. It wasn't often that Ephaniah missed the power of speech, but as he watched the tail of the snake get noisily sucked into Merrin's mouth and looked at his boots messing up the desk that Beetle used to lovingly polish every morning, Ephaniah had an overwhelming desire to tell the boy, *Get your feet off the desk.*

And then, suddenly, he was glad he couldn't speak. For, as Ephaniah stared balefully at the offending pair of boots, he saw a small, round piece of paper stuck to the sole of Merrin's right boot. An instinct nurtured by years of putting things back together told Ephaniah that this *belonged* to something—and he was pretty sure he knew what. As he advanced upon the offending boots a flicker of fear ran across Merrin's face— what was the rat-man doing? And then, in a flash—like a rat after a rabbit—Ephaniah had the mangled scrap of paper in his hand and Merrin was on his feet, yelling, "Get off me, weirdo!"

Leaving the Front Office Clerk coughing up the remains of his snake, Ephaniah had rushed down to his basement, slammed the green baize door and locked it. And now, as he examined his find, he felt exhilarated. This was it—*this was the missing piece of the map.*

Painstakingly Ephaniah spent the next hour **Restoring** the fragile scrap of paper. It went well and before long he had in front of him a small, perfect circle with a finely detailed pencil drawing of an octagonal building encircled by a snake. In the middle was a key. Ephaniah carefully put the precious circle of paper into a secret pocket under his tunic. He pushed his spectacles up onto his forehead and sat back with a sigh. He had done it. The most painstaking—and maybe the most important—piece of **Restoring** he had ever attempted was finished.

Now came the difficult part—the **ReUnite**.

"No," said Stanley, his mouth full of breakfast. "Positively *not.* A Message Rat does not make deliveries. Mmm, nothing hits the spot like a cold bacon sandwich after a night out in the rain, does it? Care for a bite?"

"No, thank you," Ephaniah replied disdainfully.

"Suit yourself."

"It would be to your advantage."

Stanley laughed bitterly. "Oh, *ha*. They all say that. But it never is. You end up starving in some lunatic's cage or shoved under the floorboards and left for dead. You won't catch me like that."

"I can get you rats."

"*Rats?*"

"All the rats you want. I'll get them."

Stanley put down his cold bacon sandwich. "You mean *staff*?" he asked.

Ephaniah nodded.

Stanley considered the matter. He imagined the East Gate Lookout Tower once more being headquarters of a thriving Message Rat Service—with him in charge. He imagined the paperwork and the wages bills . . . and Dawnie hearing about his success and deciding to make another go of things.

"No," he said.

As Ephaniah walked slowly back from the East Gate Lookout Tower he saw something he had not expected to see—the **Magykal** lights of the Wizard Tower were back. He blinked in surprise—yes, they were still there. The familiar purple and blue flickering lights were once more playing around the Tower, the deep glow of the golden pyramid at the top of the Tower shone out into the dull gray day and the purple windows shimmered once more with their Magykal haze. All Ephaniah's worries left him. Everything was fine—he would go to the ExtraOrdinary Wizard and ask her to do a Send. All would be well. With a spring in his step—as much as he could manage with the painful bumps on the underside of his sore foot—Ephaniah wrapped his white cloths extra tightly around his face and took the next set of steps down to Wizard Way.

As he walked into the deep blue shadows of the Great Arch, Ephaniah bumped into Hildegarde Pigeon—and remembered nothing more.

✦ 34 ✦
FOREST WAYS

"Yᴏ̲ᴜ forgot your panther," Sam whispered.

Jenna, Septimus and Beetle stood outside Wolf Boy's bender in the gray-green light of the Forest dawn, blinking the sleep from their eyes. As far as Sam could see, they were minus the panther.

Too sleepy to get any words to work,

Jenna took Ullr from under her cloak and showed Sam the little orange cat. Sam looked puzzled for a moment, then he raised his eyebrows and grinned. Trust Jenna to get her hands on one of those **Transformers**, he thought admiringly. The kid may not have any **Magyk** in her but she had *something*—that was for sure. Queen-stuff, he supposed. Morwenna didn't know what she would have been taking on. But whatever the Witch Mother did or didn't know, it was time to get them out of the Forest before the Coven came **Looking**. It wasn't a good feeling when the Coven was **Looking**.

Sam had packed three backpacks. They had belonged to Jo-Jo, Edd and Erik during their foraging days, but now that the young Wendron Witches kept them supplied with most of their food—except for fish—Jo-Jo, Edd and Erik had given up foraging and preferred to hang around the campfire all day, much to Sam's irritation. Sam was an expert on traveling in the Forest and had made a good job of stocking all the things he thought the travelers could possibly need.

Jenna put Ullr down. From her pocket she took the precious book of Nicko's papers, carefully placed it in her backpack and then heaved the heavy pack onto her shoulders. "Ullr," she whispered, "you must follow me." Ullr meowed.

He understood Jenna's language now as well as he had understood Snorri's. He was a faithful cat and would follow Jenna
anywhere.

Three laden figures and a small orange cat followed Sam
out of the Camp Heap clearing. It was a damp, dull morning
and moisture dripped from the trees, finding its way into their
clothes and sending the Forest chill into their bones. Sam
strode out along the broad track that led up the hill from
Camp Heap. The long walking pole he grasped in his hand
measured out his loping, easy stride and Jenna thought how
much he looked like a man of the Forest.

They fell in and walked beside him but Sam's pace was
deceptively fast. They were all glad when, after about a mile,
he stopped by a large, round rock. Sam kneeled down and
tapped the rock, which gave a hollow, bell-like sound.
Satisfied, he nodded, then jumped up and plunged into the
close-knit group of tall trees with slim, smooth trunks.

Sam set off, weaving his way through the Forest, following
a path that only he could see. Septimus, Beetle, Jenna and Ullr
were in single file now, concentrating hard on following Sam
and trying not to lose sight of his brownish-blue cloak that
blended so well with the dappled bark of the trees. Luckily it

was easy-going underfoot—a soft mulch of a thousand seasons' leaf-fall mixed with tiny green fronds of bracken that were beginning to poke their heads up into the spring light like curious little snakes.

Suddenly Sam stopped. "We're here—at the Gateway," he said with a broad grin. "I *thought* I could find it again."

"You only *thought*?" said Septimus.

"Yeah," said Sam. "But it was a Forest thought. They're always right. You just have to trust your big brother, little bro. Okay, now we have to pass through. They'll let me through, as I smell of the Forest. But you smell of the Castle. They don't like Castle around here. You'd better put your cloaks on—they're in the backpacks."

From their backpacks each pulled out a wolverine-skin cloak. Ullr hissed as Jenna threw the cloak across her shoulders.

"Eurgh!" gasped Jenna. "It's so *smelly*. And it's still got *legs*."

"Smelly is the whole point, little sis," said Sam. "You need to smell right. And the legs are good for tying the cloak on. See?" Sam tied the legs of Jenna's wolverine cloak together tightly under her chin, just like Sarah Heap used to tie her cloak when she was little. "You've got two wolverines in that cloak," Sam told her. "You always leave the front legs of the top wolverine and the tail of the bottom wolverine. Forest tradition." Jenna looked down and saw that, sure enough, her cloak had a mangy-looking wolverine tail dangling from its hem.

"As long as they don't still have their teeth, I don't mind," Septimus muttered. He threw the cloak over his shoulders and was surprised by how warm it was—and how protected it made him feel. Suddenly he was part of the Forest, just another creature going about its Forest business.

Sam surveyed the three new Forest inhabitants with approval. "Good," he said. "They should accept you as Forest now."

"*Who* should accept us?" asked Jenna, glancing around.

"Them." Sam pointed at a pair of huge trees that reared up in front of them like sentries. The trees were the first in a long avenue of identical pairs of close-set trees. From each tree a thick branch looped down and barred their path. "Wait here," said Sam. "Don't say a word and stay very still. Okay?"

They nodded. Sam walked up to the trees and began to speak. "We are of the Forest as you are of the Forest," he said, his voice deep and slow. "We seek to go the Forest Way."

The trees did not react. Sam did not move. He stood, arms

folded, feet apart, staring unblinking up into the depths of the trees. Jenna, Beetle and Septimus waited expectantly. Ullr lay down at Jenna's feet and closed his eyes. The silence of the Forest enveloped them. Sam stood, immobile, waiting. The minutes passed slowly and still Sam stood waiting . . . and waiting. No one dared move. After about ten minutes, Beetle got a cramp in his leg and did a strange, slow pirouette to try and relieve it. Septimus watched him, his eyes laughing. Beetle caught the laugh and made an odd choking noise. Jenna flashed them a warning look and they both did their best to look serious once more—until, with a sudden crash, Beetle fell over and lay on the ground shaking with suppressed laughter. And still Sam did not move.

At last, just as Jenna was beginning to wonder if Sam had made the whole thing up, the branches barring their way began to move slowly upward and like a spreading wave, all the other trees along the avenue followed suit. Sam beckoned them forward and silently they followed him along the newly opened path between the trees. As they went the trees lowered their branches behind them once more.

At the end of the avenue they emerged into a small clearing dominated by what appeared to be three large and unruly heaps of wood partly covered with turf, each with a ram-shackle door in it.

"They're old charcoal burner kilns," said Septimus. "We used to really like those in the Young Army. They were always safe at night—and warm."

Sam looked at Septimus with new respect. "Sometimes I forget you were in the Young Army," he said. "You know the Forest too."

"In a different way," said Septimus. "It was always us *against* the Forest. You are *with* the Forest."

Sam nodded. The more he saw of Septimus the more he liked him. Septimus understood stuff—you didn't have to explain; he just *knew*.

"But actually," said Sam, "these aren't really charcoal burner kilns. These are the Forest Ways. Each leads to a different forest—so they say."

Jenna looked at the three heaps of wood with dismay—it hadn't occurred to her that there would be a *choice* of forests. "But how can we tell which one is the forest we want?" she asked.

"Well, I suppose we could open the doors and take a look," said Sam.

"Really?" asked Jenna. "We don't have to go in?"

"No, why should you? There are no rules in the Forest, you know."

Beetle wasn't so sure about that. There seemed to him to be a lot of rules—rules about wearing smelly wolverine skins and rules about keeping quiet, to name but two, but he didn't say anything. He felt like a new boy at school, trying to keep out of the way of creatures that were bigger than him and understand a strange place all at once. He watched the confident Sam pull open the door to the middle heap. A blast of hot air hit them.

"That one's desert," said Sam as a swirl of sand blew out over his feet.

"But I thought they were forests," said Jenna.

"These are Ancient Ways, and forests change," said Sam. "What was once a forest may become a desert. What was once a desert may become a sea. All things must change with time."

"Don't say that," said Jenna sharply.

Sam looked at Jenna, surprised—and then realized what he had said. "Sorry, Jen. Nik will be the same old Nik when you find him, you wait. Let's see if this is the one you want." Sam

closed the door on the desert and opened the door of the left
heap. A humid heat drifted out and the raucous sound of par-
rots invaded the Forest peace. "That one?" asked Sam.

"No," said Jenna.

"You sure?"

"Yep," said Septimus.

"Okay, must be this one, then." With a dramatic flourish
Sam pulled open the door to the last heap. A flurry of snow blew
into their faces. Jenna licked her lips; the metallic taste of a
snowflake from another land brought her a little closer to Nicko.

"That's it," she said.

"You sure?" asked Sam.

"I *know* it is. Nicko made a list. Of warm stuff and furs."

"Right. Okay . . . if you're sure." Suddenly Sam no longer
seemed his usual confident self. It was one thing for Sam to
guide the occasional lost stranger from a desert caravan or a
capsized jungle canoe back to their own forest, but quite
another to send his young brother and sister off into the
unknown. "Let me come with you," he said.

Septimus shook his head. This was something he wanted
to do without his older brother telling him how to do it. "No,
Sam. We'll be fine."

"You sure?"

"Really, Sam, we will," said Jenna. "And we'll be back soon with Nicko."

"And Snorri," added Septimus.

Another flurry of snow blew out. Sam undid the red ker-chief he wore around his neck. He tied it to the top of his walking pole and gave it to Septimus. "Put this in the ground to mark where you came in," he said. "I hear it's hard to tell once you're in there."

"Thanks," said Septimus.

"'S'okay," mumbled Sam.

"Oh, Sam," said Jenna, hugging him tightly. "Thank you, thank you *so* much."

"Yeah," said Sam.

They stepped into the kiln and their feet sank deep into the snow.

Sam waved. "Bye. Bye, Jen, Sep, Cockroach. Take care." And then he closed the door.

⊹35⊹
SNOW

Jenna, *Ullr, Septimus and Beetle* stepped out into the middle of a silent, snowy forest.

Septimus pushed Sam's walking pole into the snow to show where they had come in—Sam was right, there was nothing to mark the spot at all. The red scarf hung down limply. No breath of air disturbed it; all was still. The three looked at one another but said nothing—no one felt like breaking the heavy silence that covered them like a blanket. All they could see was snow and trees—so densely packed that their black trunks felt like great bars of a cage encircling them. The snow fell steadily, dropping from the branches high above and landing lightly on their hair and faces. Jenna brushed the snowflakes from her eyelashes and looked up. The trunks of the trees were thin and smooth and did not branch out until the very top, when they spread wide and flat like a snowy parasol.

Jenna realized that they had all expected to find themselves on a path, but there was nothing—just a featureless, flat wilderness of trees radiating in all directions. No footsteps led to where they stood and there was no way of knowing which direction was forward and which was back. It was, she thought, as if they had been dropped into the middle of the forest by a huge bird.

"Let's look at the map, Jen," Septimus whispered.

Jenna took off the backpack, pulled out Nicko's book and extracted the neatly folded map. Septimus held the map for the first time. It crackled with **ReStore** fluid, yet it felt flexible and strong. Septimus liked maps; he was used to them from his time in the Young Army when he had been a good map-reader. But as he looked at Snorri's finely detailed pencil lines, he realized that he had always taken one thing for granted—

he had started off knowing where he was.

"Where are we?" asked Beetle, peering over his shoulder.

"Good question," replied Septimus. "We could be any-where. There are no landmarks . . . nothing." He wiggled his finger through the hole in the middle of the map. "We could even be here."

"No, we couldn't," Jenna said. "*That* is the House of Foryx."

"That's what we think it is," said Septimus. "But we don't know for sure *what's* on the missing piece, do we?"

Jenna did not reply. She refused to even *think* that they were not heading for Nicko and the House of Foryx. She rummaged through the two deep silk-lined pockets in her red woolen tunic, hoping that, for once, she might have something useful with her. Jenna tried to remember if she had rescued it from the floor after she had thrown it across her room in a fit of temper when her real father, Milo, had told her he was off once more on his seafaring travels. Her hand closed around a cold metal disc and she grinned. "I've got a compass," she said.

"You've got a *compass*?" said Septimus.

"Yes. No need to sound so surprised."

"But you never carry *anything* with you, Jen."

Jenna shrugged irritably. It was true—she never took any-thing with her. When her tutor had pointed out approvingly that this was something Princesses and Queens were known for, Jenna had felt embarrassed. She didn't want to act all Princessy—and the idea of being Queen was still just plain *weird*. But after the tutor's comment, Jenna had deliberately tried to keep some things in her pocket—even if they were not obviously useful—just to prove her tutor wrong. And now Milo's compass, which had been no use whatsoever for paying for a packet of rainbow chewy turtles in Ma Custard's, came into its own. Jenna held out the small brass compass and they watched the needle spin round . . . and round . . . and round, like a watch on fast-forward.

"It shouldn't do that, should it?" said Jenna.

"No," said Beetle and Septimus together.

"That is just so *typical* of Milo," Jenna said grumpily. "All his stuff is useless—and weird."

"I'd say it was this *forest* that's weird," said Beetle, glancing around uncomfortably.

"Can I have a look, Jen?" asked Septimus. Jenna handed it to him, wondering if it would start to behave once Septimus held it. It didn't. Septimus kneeled down and laid the map on the icy crust of the snow, brushing away the soft, fat snowflakes that were drifting onto it. "I don't know where we are, but I'll put the compass . . . um . . ." Septimus waved his hand over the map as if hoping for some kind of sign. He didn't get one. "*Here*," he said, and placed the compass on the bottom left-hand corner.

"You going to do a **Navigate**?" asked Beetle.

Septimus nodded.

"But how're you going to do it without the part we're going to?" Beetle asked, pointing to the hole in the middle of the map.

"I thought maybe I could get it to take us to the edge of the hole," said Septimus. "And then, who knows, we might be able to see the House of Foryx from there."

"Yeah. Well, it's worth a try—anything to stop that needle whizzing around like crazy. Gives me the creeps."

Septimus took a fine wire cross from his Apprentice belt, straightened out a piece that had become bent and placed it on top of the compass. Jenna and Beetle peered over his shoulder. The compass needle continued to spin.

"It's not working," said Jenna anxiously.

"Give us a sec," muttered Septimus. "I've got to remember what the thingy is."

"*Thingy?*" asked Jenna.

"Technical term, Jen."

"Oh, ha-ha."

Septimus placed his finger on top of the cross, closed his eyes and muttered, "X shall mark the spot." Then he picked the fine wire cross off the compass and placed it on the edge of the hole in the middle of the map.

"About here?" he inquired. Jenna and Beetle nodded. Keeping his finger on the center of the wire cross, Septimus said,

> "Lead us here through dale and dell.
> Guide us true and guide us well."

"It's stopped!" Jenna gasped. The compass needle was now steady, its only movement being the slight tremble that a compass needle should have. "You're *amazing*," she said to Septimus.

"No, I'm not," he replied. "Anyone could do it."

"Don't be ridiculous," said Jenna. "I couldn't do it and neither could Beetle. Could you, Beetle?"

Beetle shook his head, but Septimus made a face. "It's nothing special," he said.

They set off with Septimus holding the compass, following the direction that the needle was pointing. Jenna carried the map, looking out for landmarks as they went, hoping to spot something. There were plenty on the map to choose from—criss-crossing paths, a winding stream with various bridges, standing stones, a well and a myriad of small huts scattered randomly across the map, neatly drawn with little pointed roofs and chimneys. Snorri had labeled these "refuge." Refuge from what? Jenna wondered. But all anyone could actually see in front of them was the wide, flat forest floor covered by a featureless blanket of snow.

They kept up a brisk pace, following the steadily pointing needle and keeping their eyes open for some kind of landmark, stopping briefly for some dried fish and spring water that Septimus had found at the top of his backpack. After that they kept doggedly on, three small figures in their wolverine cloaks and an orange cat threading their way through the trees, the snow crackling beneath their boots as, with each step, they broke through the delicate ice crust.

Every twenty steps Septimus glanced behind him. This was something he had had to practice for hours on end in the Young Army during long hikes through the Forest and now it came back to him like an old familiar habit—*Observe and Preserve* they had called it. Most of his glances revealed nothing except the great mass of trees ranked behind him and Jenna and Beetle struggling through the snow with a small flash of orange fur as Ullr bounded between them. But every now and then Septimus thought he saw something—a movement just on the edge of his vision. But Septimus said nothing. He didn't want to scare the others and he hoped that maybe he was imagining things. The trees made odd shapes at the edge of your vision, he told himself—like one of those optical illusions that Foxy used to draw.

They were walking up a hill where the trees were so densely packed they had to go in single file, when Jenna noticed that the washed-out whiteness of the forest was growing dimmer. She glanced down at the map but found it hard to see Snorri's delicate pencil marks in the dull light. "Hey, Beetle, what's the time?" she asked.

Beetle peered at his timepiece. It was hard to see in the gloom. "It's half past two," he replied.

"So why is it getting dark?" asked Jenna.

Beetle looked around, puzzled. Jenna was right—it *was* getting dark. It was *twilight*.

"Maybe your timepiece is wrong," suggested Septimus over his shoulder, increasing his pace. He wanted to get to the top of the hill fast.

"My timepiece isn't what's making it dark, is it?" Beetle puffed grumpily, trying to keep up. "The sun going down is doing that."

"It might be a storm coming," Septimus called back. "A snowstorm. Feels cold enough."

Jenna stopped, noticing that Ullr was no longer at her side. "It's not a snowstorm," she said flatly. "It's the sun going down. In fact it has just *gone* down. Look." There, coming toward them through the trees, was the NightUllr, blending in with the black tree trunks, his big panther feet stark against the white snow.

"Oh," said Beetle. "Bother."

"Come on, Beetle," said Jenna, grabbing his hand. "Let's catch up with Sep."

Beetle smiled. Suddenly nighttime in the forest didn't seem quite so bad.

At the top of the hill Septimus stopped and waited for Beetle and Jenna to catch up. He could hardly bear to look down. He murmured a witchy good luck mantra—the kind that Marcia deeply disapproved of—and forced himself to look. In front of him was a broad, gentle slope much more sparsely covered with trees. And in the distance, shining out of the darkness, was a light. He grinned—sometimes witchy stuff worked. As he watched, and as all around grew ever darker, the pinpoint of light seemed to get brighter. By the time Jenna and Beetle joined him on the brow of the hill, it was shining like a beacon.

They set off down the hill, leaping through the snow. The small pack of wolverines—pursued by a panther—rapidly covered the ground and as they neared the valley floor they heard the sound of running water.

"It's the stream on the map," Jenna whispered, afraid to speak out loud in the darkness. "Which means that light . . . it must be a refuge hut—mustn't it?" Her voice sounded almost pleading.

"It had better be," said Septimus. His witchy chant was still going around his head and he felt hopeful—more hopeful than he had felt all day. He linked arms with Jenna and Beetle and together they waded through the snow, which was deeper in the valley and came up almost to their knees. Ullr bounded through it, no longer skating over the icy crust, his black fur sprinkled with white, the snow turning the whiskers on his chin to an old man's beard.

Jenna and Beetle caught Septimus's good mood. The gurgling of the stream broke the oppressive silence of the forest, and the yellow glow of the lantern illuminated the frosty snow before them. The combination of snow and lanterns made all three feel happy. For Jenna and Septimus, it reminded them of the time they had spent the Big Freeze together at Aunt Zelda's—a time they both looked back on with happiness. For Beetle, it recalled Snow Days when he didn't have to go to school—days full of possibilities when he would wake up to find that snow had completely covered the windows and his mother had lit the lantern and was cooking bacon and eggs over the fire.

As they came closer they could see that the light did indeed come from a small wooden hut with a stovepipe chimney, just like the ones that Snorri had drawn. It shone from a lantern placed in the tiny window above the door, which cast long shadows from the few trees that still stood between them and the hut.

A few moments later they were pushing open the door to the hut. And as they stepped inside a strange, unearthly howl ululated in the distance.

Beetle slammed the door shut and Jenna shut the bolts—all three of them.

"Big bolts," said Septimus. "I wonder why."

"Don't," said Beetle. "Just *don't.*"

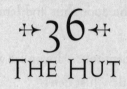

36
THE HUT

The inside of the hut was just as Aunt Ells had once
described to Nicko and Snorri. It was bare and basic but
after the chill of the snow and the bleakness of the forest it felt
warm and welcoming. On either side of the hut were three
sleeping platforms one above the other, with two neatly
folded blankets placed on each platform. Between these was
an old table and an iron stove with a good supply of logs piled
up on either side. At the back of the hut was a door. Jenna

opened it and peered in. Inside was a tiny room containing a jug, a frozen bowl of water and a scary-looking pit half covered with planks with a bucket of earth beside it. It didn't smell so great. Jenna quickly closed the door.

Septimus and Beetle set to lighting the stove and soon the logs were ablaze. They left the door of the stove open and all three crowded round the fire, warming their hands while the snow dripped from their wolverine skins and puddles collected on the earthen floor. Once their hands were thawed, they undid the buckles of the backpacks to find them stuffed full of packages that were neatly wrapped in leaves and tied with thin strands of vine. Eagerly, they tipped them out onto the table.

Ullr growled in a hopeful fashion—he could smell fish. Even in panther form Ullr kept a cat's taste for fish.

"Sam must have been up all night making these," said Jenna, surveying the pile of treasure heaped on the table. She felt as excited as if it were her birthday.

Septimus could tell that Jenna wanted to open all the packages at once. "We should only unwrap a few at a time," he said. "I think the leaves preserve things and . . . well, we don't know how long we're going to be here, do we? It could be *months.*"

"You are an old misery-bucket sometimes, Sep," said Jenna. "So which ones do we open?"

They decided to open two packages each, which resulted in four fish, a bag of dried leaves that Septimus thought was witches' brew and a flat, ash-covered loaf of bread that had obviously been cooked in the Heap campfire.

"We could open another one each," said Jenna, surveying the large pile of unopened packages that still remained.

"All right. Just one more," said Septimus grudgingly.

There was another fish and another loaf, but it was Beetle who drew the prize—a fat slab of toffee. The boat delivering Ma Custard's stock had run aground on the riverbank where Sam was fishing, and the skipper had been extremely grateful for Sam's help in pushing him free on a falling tide.

Beetle unwrapped the thick wax paper surrounding the sticky slab, and they all breathed in the warm, sweet smell of toffee.

"You know," said Septimus, "I really like Sam."

An hour later they were lying on the sleeping platforms, warm from the heat of the stove, full of toffee, fish and witches' brew. The hut was filled with an orange, drowsy glow from the stove and outside the snow glistened in the light of the virtually full moon. But it still felt like the middle of the afternoon—much too early to go to sleep.

"What does your timepiece say now, Beetle?" Jenna asked.

"Four o'clock," said Beetle, holding it up so that it caught the light of the fire.

"That's four in the afternoon and it's been dark for what—two hours?" said Jenna.

"Yerr," Beetle replied, trying to scrape off the remains of a lump of toffee from his back teeth.

"So that means . . ."

"Everything's weird," said Septimus.

"No, Sep. It means we are either much farther north or much farther east—or both."

"Which *is* pretty weird," said Beetle, "seeing as all we did was walk into a heap of charcoal. Not what you expect from a heap of charcoal, even though my old art teacher used to say, 'Charcoal can take you into a whole new world, Beetle.'"

"I wonder which it is?" said Septimus. "North or east?"

"We can work that out tomorrow," said Jenna. "We can see how long the days are. I reckon it's east and we've just lost a few hours. I don't think it would be getting this dark so early farther north. It's getting toward the summer now and the days should be really long."

Both boys were silent for a moment. Then Septimus said, "How do you know all that stuff, Jen?"

Jenna took a while to reply. "Milo," she said. "He told me all about his travels. He had a timepiece, too, and before I was born he said he always kept it on what he called 'home time' so that he would know what, um . . . my mother . . . was doing. And he said that when he traveled east he found that according to the timepiece the sun was setting earlier and earlier— even though it didn't feel like that to him. And it was Snorri who told me that in the Lands of the Long Nights in the summer the days are so long that the sun hardly sets."

Septimus thought about this. "So if we *are* farther east," he said, "that's a good thing. That's where the House of Foryx is, isn't it?"

"I'll see what Nicko says." Jenna picked up Ephaniah's beautifully bound book of Nicko's notes, which she had put safely on her bunk. She leafed through the notes, some of which were tiny scraps that Ephaniah had fused onto bigger pieces of paper, others were bigger and carefully folded, their edges reinforced. All of them felt smooth, almost resinous to the touch. Nicko's writing had a tendency to wander around like a lost ant, but Ephaniah had made it appear crisper and clearer and for once Jenna was able to make sense of most of it. "House of Foryx . . . House of Foryx," Jenna muttered, leafing through the pages. "Here's something. There's a note stuck to it from Snorri to Nicko—'Nicko, this is for you. For the parts you missed when Aunt Ells spoke in our language. Snorri x.' I think it's what Aunt Ells told them."

"Go on, then, Jen. Read it to us," said Septimus. Like a couple of children waiting to be read their bedtime story, Beetle and Septimus looked expectantly at Jenna.

She laughed. "Okay. But I'm not doing an Aunt Ells voice."

A chorus of disappointed protests filled the hut.

"Well, I'm not, so there. Here goes: 'I was nine years old. I was playing with my sister in my grandmother's house and we had a fight. I pushed her, she pushed me and I fell through the Glass. I know that now, but then I did not know what had happened. All I knew was that suddenly I was no longer in my grandmother's little house beside the sea, but in an octagonal room full of dark, heavy furniture. I was terrified.

"'When at last I dared to venture out of the room I found myself at the top of a long winding staircase. I went down and

came to the strangest place you could ever imagine. A great
hall full of candle smoke, filled with many people with different ways of speech and strange dress. I felt as though I had
walked into a never-ending fancy dress party. People wandered
through the corridors talking aimlessly, or sat around the
great log fires that burned constantly without ever seeming to
consume the logs. No one took any particular notice of me as
I roamed the house. I ate my fill in the great kitchens, I found
a soft bed in a beautiful room where a fire always burned and
the little tub of sweet biscuits was always full—but I was
alone and I longed to go home.

"'There was a great door that opened into the house, but
a visitor was a rare event. Some came to stay and Bide their
Time but most came searching for lost loved ones, although
I do not recall them finding any. I was surprised that so few
already there wanted to leave the House of Foryx. I do recall
one young woman wearing a beautiful white fur cloak. She
wanted to go, but she took pity on me and gave up her place
on the dragon chair in the checkerboard lobby by the door.
She said that I was but a child and should leave as soon as I
could, that no matter what Time I went into I was young
enough to adapt. And she was right—I will be forever grate-

ful to her. So I took her place on the chair sitting between the carved dragonheads, my feet resting upon the tail. I waited for many long weeks while she brought me food and kept me company. She told me stories of ice palaces and snow-swept plains, sleighs and roads of ice until even in the heat of the candles that burned day and night my knees knocked with the cold and I shivered inside my woolen cloak.

"'At last my chance came one morning when there was a loud knock on the door. To my surprise a little man jumped out of the pillar beside where I was sitting and ran to the door. Waiting outside were a man and a woman. The DoorKeeper would not let them come in and as the door began to close I took my chance and ran out, much to their surprise.

"'I was, I realize now, amazingly lucky. I do not know why my new mother and father went to the House of Foryx; they would never say. The next thing I remember was traveling across a great pit on a narrow bridge that swayed in the wind. My new papa led the horse while I rode, sitting in front of my new mama. Later Mama told me she had closed her eyes in terror as we crossed, but I was wide-eyed with excitement. There was a full moon rising through the mists below us and we were so high that I felt as if we were flying among the stars.

They brought me here to the Castle and were kindness itself. I grew to love them as much as I had loved my mother and father, but always at the back of my mind was the question, *What happened to me?*

"'I did not realize that I was in another Time for many years, until a traveling storyteller told a tale about the House of Foryx and I knew she was telling no story but the truth. I found her and told her my own tale. She told me that the House of Foryx is a place where All Times Do Meet. You can only leave when someone arrives and then you must enter their own Time. So when I ran from the House of Foryx I ran into my new parents' Time.

"'I believe the only chance you have of returning to your own Time is to find the House of Foryx and pray that some-one from your own Time comes to it. When I was a child I longed to return to my own Time, but when I finally under-stood what had happened I had already met my dear husband, my adoptive parents were old and frail and I did not wish to return. This is a good Time to live in—you could do much worse. But you are both young and I can see you are brave enough to try. May Odin and Skadi be your guides.' And then Nik has written . . . I think this is what he says . . . 'House of

Foryx—here we come.'"

"Sounds like Nik," said Septimus.

"I wonder if they are still there?" said Jenna.

"Only one way to find out," said Septimus.

No one found it easy to get to sleep that night.

The stove kept them warm and Septimus did a **SafeShield** Spell for the hut, but it was hard to ignore the noises outside— and there was a fine assortment to choose from. It was strange, Septimus thought, that a forest so silent by day should be so noisy at night. As the moon rose higher, the wind rose too; it funneled down the valley and did not take kindly to finding the refuge hut in the way. It moaned and howled; it rattled the shutters and shook the door; it ganged up with the trees so that their branches banged and scraped on the little hut's roof and its flimsy walls. There were other noises in the distance, sharp whooping cries and ululating howls that made Ullr's fur stand on end. Beetle put his fingers in his ears and wished that he was back in his cozy bed in The Ramblings.

Beetle and Septimus fell asleep first. Jenna sat up on her bunk wrapped in her wolverine skin, listening to the wind howl. She watched the snow pile up against the windows, the fire in the stove die down and the hut gradually become cold and dark. Suddenly she heard *scritch . . . scratch . . . scritch . . .* something was scratching at the door. Ullr, who was lying across the door, got to his feet and growled. Her heart racing, Jenna climbed down to Septimus, who was asleep on the bunk below, and shook him awake. "Sep . . . *listen!*"

Septimus sprang awake, thinking for one awful moment that he was back in the Young Army. "Wheerrr—wassat?"

"*Something's trying to get in,*" whispered Jenna.

"Oh. Oh, *crumbs.*" Ullr growled again. A gust of wind shook the hut and outside Septimus heard *scritch . . . scratch . . . scritch . . .* like long fingernails being dragged down the thin wooden door.

Wide awake now, Septimus sprang out of his bunk. He put both hands on the door, and muttered his **SafeShield** Spell once again. The *scritch . . . scratch . . . scritch* continued. Why wasn't it working? Flustered, Septimus tried an **Anti-Darke** incantation. At that, the scratching stopped.

Jenna and Septimus listened, hardly daring to breathe. Outside, the trees tapped their branches like long, impatient fingers drumming on the roof of the hut, but there was no more scratching at the door. Beetle stirred and mumbled in his sleep something that sounded like "Wotcha, Foxy," then with much creaking of his bunk he turned over and was quiet again. Ullr lay down once more and positioned himself across the doorway.

"It's gone," whispered Septimus.

"Thanks, Sep," whispered Jenna. She burrowed down beneath the rough hut blankets and her wolverine skin and soon fell asleep.

But Septimus lay awake. It wasn't the howl of the wind that kept him from sleeping, or the tapping of the branches on the roof of the hut, or even wondering what **Darke** creature had been outside. What kept Septimus from sleeping was the lapis lazuli stone with a golden **Q** inscribed into it. Every time he tried to get comfortable, the wretched thing somehow managed to stick into him. Irritably, he delved deep into his tunic pocket and pulled out the **Stone**. It lay warm and heavy on his palm. It was odd, he thought, how the light from the lantern made the **Stone** look so green—it didn't do that to anything else. And then a horrible feeling of dread shot through him like a dagger. It wasn't a trick of the light—it was the **Stone** itself. The **Questing Stone** had *turned* green.

Like a **Transfixed** rabbit Septimus stared at the **Stone**,

Alther's hurried whispered words at the **Gathering** spinning around his head like a dreadful nursery rhyme:

> *Blue to get ready,*
> *Green to go.*
> *Yellow to guide you*
> *Through the snow.*
> *Orange to warn you*
> *That over you'll go.*
> *Then Red will be the final glow.*
> *Now seek the Black; there's no going back.*

Green to go—that's what it was. Green to go on the **Queste**. Septimus lay down and gazed, unfocused, at the rough planks only a few inches from his face, panicky thoughts whirling around his head.

The first thought was bad enough: he was on the **Queste**—*he was on the* **Queste**.

The second thought was even worse: If he was on the **Queste**, how were they going to find Nicko?

But the third was the worst of all: *How was he going to tell Jenna?*

✢ 37 ✢
AN INVITATION

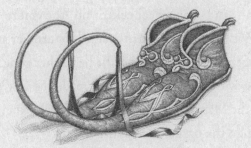

Marcia was enjoying being back in charge of the Wizard Tower.

As soon as the last of the **Gathering** had meandered off, somewhat confused at the sudden ending of their outing, Marcia had inspected the Wizard Tower from top to bottom, checking for any stragglers. She had had enough of Extra-Ordinary Wizard ghosts to last her quite a while and she had no wish to bump into one snoozing in a dark forgotten corner

in a few days' time. She found one asleep in an Ordinary
Wizard's larder and another wandering around the fifteenth
floor corridor looking for her teeth. It was, Marcia reflected, as
she checked the very last cupboard in the Hall, and flushed
out a sleeping Catchpole, not unlike fumigating mice.

Having reestablished her authority in the Tower to her
satisfaction—and having checked on the more elderly
Ordinary Wizards—Marcia had decided to turn her attention
to Finding Septimus. She assumed he had either gone into the
Forest to be with his brothers or had made his way to Aunt
Zelda's on the Marram Marshes. Either way, she knew a Find
Spell would do the trick and take her to him.

Marcia did not know that—at the very moment she had
closed the purple door to her rooms and breathed a sigh of
relief—Jenna, Septimus and Beetle were walking through an
ancient Forest Way into a silent, frozen forest. With a huge
sense of relief, she had climbed the narrow stone stairs up to
the library, which was housed in the great golden pyramid on
the top of the Tower, and sat down at her desk. Marcia
breathed in the smell of old leather, decayed spells and paper
dust (paper beetles were rampant in the library) and relaxed.
All was well with the world once more.

Ten minutes later Marcia was not entirely sure that all *was* well with the world after all. Her **Find** would not work. Aware that no **Magyk** is 100 percent reliable—although Marcia expected 99.9 percent recurring—she did the **Find** once more. Still it did not work.

Half an hour and three more attempts at the **Find** later, Marcia was worried. Septimus had apparently disappeared.

"Fume!" said Marcia, leaping to her feet and thumping her desk with her fist. "Blasted *Fume*. He's behind this. I just know it." Two minutes later, having put the spiral stairs on Emergency FastForward, Marcia staggered into the Hall of the Wizard Tower feeling very giddy and more than a little nauseous.

Outside, the cool air revived her and she strode across the Courtyard, the heels of her purple pythons clattering on the cobbles.

Underneath the Great Arch someone had, much to Marcia's disgust, left a pile of dirty washing. There was no excuse, she thought, for Wizards to go dumping their dirty old robes at the entrance of the Wizard Tower courtyard. What *would* people think? With an expression of distaste, Marcia picked up a corner of the robes, looking for the name tag. All Wizards had to sew name tags in their robes so that the Tower laundry could return them to the correct Wizard. It didn't always help. Once, a certain Ordinary Wizard by the name of Marcus Overland had received Marcia's robes from the Laundry and had promenaded around the Castle in them for three whole days, acting outrageously, before Marcia had cornered him. Marcus had left shortly afterward.

But as Marcia lifted the grubby blue cloth she suddenly realized that there was a body inside the robes. "Hildegarde!" she gasped. Quickly, Marcia pulled back the hood, which was covering the sub-Wizard's face. Hildegarde was ashen but still breathing. Marcia **Breathed** a small **Revive** over her and some color returned to Hildegarde's cheeks. She groaned.

"Hildegarde . . . what *happened*?" asked Marcia.

Hildegarde struggled to sit up. "Eurgh . . . I . . . Sep . . . timus . . ."

"*Septimus*?"

"Gone. **Queste**."

"You're delirious, Hildegarde," said Marcia sternly. "He most certainly has *not* gone on the **Queste**. Now, you wait there and I will go and get someone to—"

"No!" Hildegarde struggled to sit up. Her eyes fixed firmly on Marcia and she said, very deliberately, "I was **InHabited** by a **Thing**. I . . . *it* gave Septimus the **Questing Stone**. He accepted it. Said . . . thank you." Hildegarde smiled wanly. "So . . . polite . . . Septimus." And then, exhausted by the effort, she slumped down and fell into a deep, snoring sleep.

Marcia helped carry Hildegarde to the Wizard Tower sick bay—a large airy room on the first floor—then put the stairs on slow and rotated sedately down to the Hall, thinking about what Hildegarde had said. If it had not been for the failed Find, Marcia would have assumed it to be the delirious ramblings of a sudden fever, but now she was not so sure. What if it were true—what if Septimus *was* on the **Queste**? That did not bear thinking about. Deep in thought, Marcia wandered through the Courtyard and found her footsteps taking her along Wizard Way.

Distractedly, she answered concerned inquiries about the Wizard Tower from the braver passersby, while all the time her feet took her steadily toward the far end of the Way. Marcia's feet may have known where they were going—but Marcia herself did not realize it until she had turned the corner into Snake Slipway.

Outside the tall, narrow house on Snake Slipway, Marcia took a deep breath and politely rang the bell. She waited, nervously, rehearsing her speech.

Some minutes later, after two more rings, Marcia heard

hesitant footsteps shuffling toward the door. Then the bolts were drawn, a key was turned and the door opened a few inches.

"Yes?" said a hesitant voice.

"Is that Mr. Pye?" Marcia asked.

"I am he."

"It's Marcia here. Marcia Overstrand."

"Oh?"

"May I come in?"

"You want to *come in*?"

"Yes. Please. It's—well, it's about Septimus."

"He's not here."

"I know. Mr. Pye, I really need to talk to you."

The door opened a little wider and Marcellus peered out anxiously. His housekeeper was off for the day and she had told him it was about time he learned to answer the door. He had ignored Marcia's first two rings, telling himself that if the bell rang a third time he would answer it. Wondering what he had gotten himself into Marcellus opened the door wide and said, "Please come in, Madam Marcia."

"Thank you, Mr. Pye. Just Marcia will do," Marcia said as she stepped into the dark, narrow hall.

"And Marcellus will be perfectly adequate," Marcellus

replied with a small bow. "What can I do for you?"

Marcia glanced around, suddenly afraid of being overheard. She knew that the house was connected to the Manuscriptorium via the Ice Tunnels and that the hatch was possibly UnSealed. Anyone could be listening—and that anyone included Tertius Fume. She needed somewhere secure.

"Perhaps you would like to come to tea," she said. "At the Wizard Tower. In half an hour?"

"*Tea?*" asked Marcellus, blinking with surprise.

"In my rooms. I will instruct the doors to expect you. I look forward to it, Mr. Pye—um, Marcellus. Half an hour."

"Oh. Yes. I too shall . . . look forward to it. In half an hour, then. Good-bye."

"Good-bye, Marcellus."

Marcellus Pye bowed and Marcia was gone. He exhaled loudly, closed the door and leaned against it for support. What was going on? And *where* had he put his best shoes?

"So you see," said Marcia, pouring Marcellus his fifth cup of tea and watching, amazed, as the Alchemist added three large spoons of sugar to it, "I am so afraid that what Hildegarde said may be true. And if it is . . ." Her voice trailed off. She sighed.

"If it is true, then I must know all I can about the **Queste**. And you, Marcellus, are the only person alive who has had any experience of the **Queste**. Oh, there are plenty of ghosts, of course, but quite frankly I have had enough of ghosts at the moment."

Marcellus smiled. "And their concerns are not always those of the Living," he said, remembering what poor company the ghosts of his old friends had been as he had grown progressively more ancient.

"True. How very true," replied Marcia, remembering the horrors of the **Gathering**. She looked Marcellus in the eye as if checking whether she could trust him. Marcellus steadily returned her gaze. "I believe there were three **Questes** during your lifetime," she said—and then remembered that Marcellus's lifetime had lasted five hundred years or more. "Or, um, even more . . ."

"Many more," said Marcellus Pye. "But during my natural lifetime—as it were—you are correct. Indeed, my dear friend Julius Pike lost both his Apprentices to the **Queste**."

"Both!" gasped Marcia.

Marcellus nodded. "The first was a terrible shock. Syrah Syara was her name—I remember her well. I was at the Draw. In those days, you know, the Castle alchemist worked closely with the Wizard Tower. We were invited to all the important occasions."

With some difficulty, Marcia restrained a disapproving *tut*.

Marcellus continued. "I still remember the awful gasp from the Wizards as she Drew the **Stone**. Julius refused to let her go—Syrah was an orphan and he regarded her as his daughter. Poor Julius had a big fight with Tertius Fume. Then Syrah punched Fume in the nose—forgetting that he was a ghost— and got a huge cheer. Fume got angry and put the Tower under **Siege** for twenty-four hours and by then Syrah was gone. Had to be dragged on to the **Questing Boat** by all seven guards apparently—and landed a few punches on them too, we were told." Marcellus Pye shook his head. "It was a terrible thing.

"Julius didn't take another Apprentice for some years. He was an old man when it was time for the Draw once more, and no one could believe it when this Apprentice also drew the **Stone**. It finished Julius off. He died a few months later. And of course the Apprentice—a nice young man, very quiet— never came back. I always thought Fume did it to spite Julius. To show him who was really in charge."

"You mean Tertius Fume controls who gets the **Stone**?" asked Marcia.

Marcellus drained the last of his tea. "I believe so. Somehow he has taken control of the **Queste**. After Syrah had gone, Julius tried to find out as much as he could about the **Queste**, but all the ancient texts and protocols had disappeared. It was rumored that Fume had destroyed them because they tell a very different story. I have even heard that the **Queste** was set up to be an honor—a reward for talented Apprentices." Marcellus sighed. "But, alas, that has never been the case—quite the opposite in fact. All those who went have never returned."

Marcia was silent. This was not what she had wanted to hear. "But Septimus did not actually *Draw* the **Stone**," she said. "So surely he is not on the **Queste**?"

Marcellus shook his head. "The Draw is no more than a formality," he said. "It is, if you ask me, a way of ritualizing the unacceptable. The key moment is when the Apprentice accepts the **Stone**. By Drawing it, the Apprentice accepts it. And by taking it from an **InHabited** Wizard and saying "thank you," I fear that Septimus, too, has accepted it. And now he is on the **Queste**, which is why you cannot **Find** him. As the saying goes, 'Once you Accept the **Stone**, Your Will is not your Own.'"

Agitated, Marcia arose and began pacing the room. Marcellus leaped to his feet, for in his Time it was very rude to stay seated when the ExtraOrdinary Wizard was standing.

"This is terrible," said Marcia, tramping up and down her carpet. "Septimus is only *twelve*. How is he going to manage? And what is even worse, it seems that Jenna's gone with him *too*."

"That does not surprise me," said Marcellus. "She was a very determined girl. She reminded me of my dear sister—although less inclined to scream."

"Your *sister*? Oh. Yes, of course. I forget that you are the son of a Queen."

"Not a good Queen, unfortunately. I think Princess Jenna will be a better one. When the Time Is Right."

"Well," said Marcia, "it won't ever be Right if we don't get them back, will it?"

Without thinking, Marcellus placed his hand on Marcia's arm. Marcia looked surprised. "Marcia," he said, very seriously, "you have to understand. *No one* can get an Apprentice back from the **Queste**."

"Rubbish," said Marcia.

++38++
TRACKED DOWN

Merrin *Meredith was biting* the head off a licorice snake when Simon burst through the door.

"You *stupid* little *worm*," hissed Simon.

Merrin leaped to his feet in terror.

"Give me Sleuth before I bite *your* head off. You *thief*."

"Baaaaaah . . ." Merrin was paralyzed.

"Give me Sleuth. *Now*."

Desperately, Merrin

fumbled through the pockets of his new Manuscriptorium tunic. He had so many pockets—which one had he put Sleuth in? Simon Heap stared at Merrin, a fierce, greenish glint shining from his narrowed eyes. "Give . . . me . . . Sleuth," he intoned.

With relief, Merrin's trembling fingers closed around the tracker ball. He pulled it from his pocket, hurled it at Simon and shot off into the depths of the Manuscriptorium. Simon lunged to catch the ball but Merrin's terrified throw was wide and fast. It hurtled past Simon and, as the Manuscriptorium door opened with a sharp *ping*, Sleuth was deftly caught by the twenty-sixth visitor to the Manuscriptorium that day— Marcia Overstrand.

"Well caught," said Marcellus, the twenty-seventh visitor.

Simon Heap stood gasping. He opened his mouth and a bleating noise—surprisingly like the one Merrin had made a minute before—trickled out.

"Well, well," said Marcia. "Mr. Heap. Now remind me, Mr. Heap, about when we last met. Was it up in my rooms perhaps, after a little trouble with a particularly nasty **Placement**?"

"I—I, yes. It was." Simon Heap blushed. "That was kind of a mistake. I—I'm very sorry."

"Well, that makes it all right, then."

"Does it?" Simon said, brightening. Suddenly the possibility of being accepted back at the Castle lifted the burden he had carried ever since the night of Septimus's Apprentice supper, when he had been stupid enough to canoe off into the Marram Marshes and look for DomDaniel's bones.

But Marcia was scornful. "Of *course* it doesn't. How dare you show your face back here after all the trouble you have caused. How *dare* you!"

Simon stood staring at Marcia, who had Sleuth clasped firmly in her hand. Things were not going quite according to plan.

"You have five minutes to leave the Castle before I alert the lock-up. *Five minutes.*" Marcia's eyes flashed angrily.

Simon seemed unable to move. "Um," he said.

"Yes?"

"Um. Can I have my ball back, please?"

"No. Now go!"

Simon hesitated and then, thinking of how upset Lucy would be if he ended up in the lock-up—not to mention his mother—he fled.

With Marcellus in tow, Marcia strode into the

Manuscriptorium. All the scribes studiously carried on working, but Partridge looked up, glad of a break from his calculations, which he was laboriously quadruple-checking. "Can I help you, Madam Marcia?" he asked, jumping down from his desk.

"Thank you, Mr. Partridge," said Marcia. "You can escort me to the Vaults."

The other scribes glanced at one another with raised eyebrows. Two visits to the Vaults within the week by the ExtraOrdinary Wizard—what was going on?

A loud rustle of silk drew the scribes' attention back to their work. Jillie Djinn bustled out of the passageway that led to the Hermetic Chamber. "Yes?" she said peremptorily.

Marcia looked at Jillie Djinn crossly. The woman's social graces—never good—were rapidly disappearing, she thought. "We wish to be escorted to the Vaults," Marcia repeated.

"It is not convenient at present," replied Miss Djinn, eyeing Marcellus Pye suspiciously. "All my scribes are occupied."

"I'll go!" said Partridge.

Jillie Djinn glared at him. "You will not. You will finish your calculations."

Partridge sighed heavily and picked up his pen.

"If you would care to ask my new Front Office Clerk for an appointment, I will probably be able to fit you in sometime next week," said Jillie Djinn.

"*New* Front Office Clerk?" asked Marcia. "Where's Beetle?"

"He is no longer in our employment."

"What? *Why?*"

"His conduct was not satisfactory," replied Miss Djinn. "Allow me to show you out."

Speechless and spluttering with rage, Marcia and Marcellus were ushered out. If the Chief Hermetic Scribe chose to refuse access to the Vaults, there was nothing Marcia could do. Within her own small territory, Jillie Djinn wielded as much power as the ExtraOrdinary Wizard did in the Wizard Tower. And Jillie Djinn knew it.

Jillie Djinn closed the door firmly behind them and turned to her new protégé. "If she thinks I am allowing someone wearing the robes of an *Alchemist* down to the Vaults, she has another think coming," she told him.

Merrin nodded sagely, as though he understood exactly what Jillie Djinn meant and would have done the same himself. Then he put his feet up on the desk, tilted his head back and tried to fit a whole licorice snake in his mouth at once.

Marcellus had had as much excitement—and as much Marcia Overstrand—as he could stand for the day. After offering any help he possibly could with finding Septimus, he bade her a polite good-bye. Marcia let him go; she could see he was unused to company and quite exhausted by it. She watched as the Alchemist wandered off down Wizard Way, his footwear attracting amused glances from passersby. Marcellus may have done all he could, but Marcia was not about to give up on Finding Septimus. She had another idea up her sleeve—literally.

Marcia didn't like doing Magyk in public. She felt it was showy and she didn't like the way people would stop and stare. But sometimes it had to be done. And so those who had only just recovered from the sight of Marcellus Pye and his shoes were now treated to the astonishing spectacle of their ExtraOrdinary Wizard doing a Find right in the middle of Wizard Way. They stopped and gaped as Marcia—who was standing very still, chanting under her breath—became enveloped by a soft purple Magykal haze and very slowly

began to disappear. One brave child ran up to poke Marcia to
see if she was real, but by the time the little girl had reached
her, all that was left of the ExtraOrdinary Wizard was a purple
shimmering shadow. The child burst into tears, and her
mother stomped off to the Wizard Tower to lodge a complaint.

Simon Heap was waiting for the ferry with Lucy when a shimmering purple haze appeared beside him. Lucy screamed.
When Simon realized who it was, he felt a little like screaming too. "I—I'm just going, really I am," he stammered. "I had
to say good-bye to Mum and find Lucy and then we just
missed the ferry and—"

"Please don't put him in the lock-up. *Please*," begged Lucy.
"I'll do *anything*. I'll take him away and make sure he doesn't
come back *ever*. Ooooh, please, *please . . . Oooooh!*"

"Lucy, I am not going to put him in the lock-up," said Marcia
quickly. She could see that Lucy was working up to a scream.

Lucy subsided.

"Well, not unless—no, Lucy, it's all right—not unless he
deliberately withholds information. Which I am sure he
won't. *Will* you, Simon?"

Simon shook his head.

In the manner of a practiced conjurer, Marcia produced Sleuth from up her sleeve.

"Oh," said Simon, gazing mournfully at his much-loved Tracker Ball. Something told him that Marcia was not going to give it back.

"I presume this *is* a Tracker Ball?" Marcia said.

"Yes. Yes, it is. Its name is Sleuth. I trained it myself."

"Did you? Very good. Very good *indeed*."

Simon smiled. He thought it had been pretty good too.

"I want to find Septimus. I need you to **Instruct** it."

Simon's face fell. It was always about Septimus, wasn't it? Never about *him*.

Marcia ignored Simon's sullen expression and carried on. "Simon, I know for a *fact* that this Tracker Ball has a **Tag** on Jenna. Jenna is with Septimus, and I want you to **Instruct** it to follow the **Tag**."

"I can't," Simon said sulkily.

"Can't or *won't*?" asked Marcia icily.

"Si," said Lucy, "don't be awkward. *Please*. Just do it. What does it matter to you?"

"Luce, I can't do it—or rather Sleuth can't." Simon turned to Marcia. "I'm sorry, Madam Marcia, but Sleuth hasn't got a

Tag on Jenna anymore, so it can't do it."

"I'm warning you, Simon, don't lie to me," snapped Marcia.

"Si—*mon!*" wailed Lucy.

"Shh, Luce. Marcia, I—I'm not lying. I promise. Yes, Sleuth did have a **Tag** on Jenna, but that's all gone—every trace. I've reprogrammed Sleuth because . . . well, a few months ago something horrible happened. Something **Darke** came after me. I don't want anything more to do with **Darke** stuff—it just uses you up and throws you away. It's awful. And there was a lot of **Darke** in Sleuth, so I did a complete **WipeOut**. I'd left Sleuth **ReCharging** when that little tick took it. I'm sorry. I would have helped if I could have. I *really* would have." Simon was almost pleading.

Marcia sighed. She could see that Simon was telling the truth. It was just her luck, she thought, that just when she needed the help of a practitioner of **Darke Magyk**, he had decided to reform.

Marcia let Simon and Lucy go. As she watched the ferry take them across to the far side of the river she could not help but wonder what was in store for them. And, more to the point, what was in store for Septimus.

✳   ✳   ✳

The next morning, many thousands of miles away in a small hut, Jenna woke to find Ullr in his daytime guise, sitting on top of the stove. A dull gray light filled the hut and the air felt cold. She pulled the rough blanket around her and whispered, "Ullr, komme, Ullr." The cat's tail twitched. He looked at Jenna, considering whether to leave his warm place and decided not to bother. Jenna—who did not like being disobeyed, even by a cat—scrambled down from her bunk, grabbed hold of Ullr and took him back to bed with her.

"Blerrgh," mumbled Septimus from the bunk below. "I'm gettin' up, Marcia. Really yam."

"It's all right, Sep." Jenna laughed. "I'm not Marcia."

Septimus opened his eyes and found himself staring at the rough wood of Jenna's sleeping platform just a few inches away. He remembered where he was and sat up too quickly. He banged his head on the platform above. "Ouch."

"The fire's gone out," said Jenna. "Can you light it, Sep? It's freezing in here."

Septimus groaned and struggled out of his warm cocoon. "You may not actually *be* Marcia, Jen, but you're doing a very good impression." He put some more logs into the stove and, too sleepy to use his tinderbox, he cheated and did a

FireLighter Spell. Flames leaped up from the logs and a few minutes later the hut began to feel warm once more.

They ate the last of the dried fish for breakfast and Jenna handed out tin mugs of boiled witches' brew. To each one she had added a square of toffee that floated stickily on the surface of the cloudy green liquid. Septimus looked quizzically at the contents of his mug. "That's *weird*, Jen. Even Aunt Zelda could learn a thing or two from you."

"Well, I'll have it if you don't want it," Jenna replied.

"No, no. I *love* Aunt Zelda's stuff," said Septimus, draining the witches' brew in one gulp and chewing the toffee gratefully, as it took the bitterness away.

While Ullr finished off the bones and fish heads, they packed their backpacks and looked at the map.

"I figure we're here," said Septimus, pointing to a drawing of a hut beside a wiggly line that Snorri had helpfully labeled *STREAM*.

"We're getting near the edge, then," said Beetle, running his finger along the margins of the hole in the middle of the map.

Septimus nodded. "I hope when we get out into the light we'll be able to see something. Maybe even the House of Foryx—whatever that looks like."

✳ ✳ ✳

It was hard to leave the warmth and safety of the hut behind and open the door into an unfamiliar world. In fact it was a lot harder than they had expected, as the door would not budge. Septimus and Beetle leaned all their weight against it but it would not shift.

"It's the snow," said Beetle. "Look how much it's piled up against the windows. We're snowed in." He gave the door another hefty shove. "Oof! It's no good. It won't open. We're stuck."

"Let me try," said Jenna.

"Okay, come help us, Jen, but I don't think it will make any difference," said Septimus.

"I'll try it on my own thanks, Sep."

"On your *own*?" said Septimus and Beetle.

"Yes, on my *own*. Okay?"

"Okay." Septimus and Beetle shrugged and, clearly humoring Jenna, they stepped aside.

Jenna took hold of the latch and pulled the door. It opened with a rush and a pile of snow tumbled in. She grinned. "It opens inward," she said.

✳ ✳ ✳

Beetle was right about one thing: it had snowed so much during the night that the hut was very nearly completely covered
with snow. It lay where the wind had blown it, piled up against
the sides of the hut, a great heap of the stuff barring their way
out. Beetle fetched the shovel from the smelly little outhouse
and began digging the snow away very energetically, as if to
make up for the embarrassing door episode. After a few fast
shovelfuls had been thrown to the side, Beetle suddenly
stopped.

"Need a break?" asked Septimus.

"No! I mean, no thanks, I'm fine. Only just got started. But
there's something under the snow . . . something soft."
Carefully now, Beetle prodded at the snow with the shovel and
began to gently scrape it away.

"Look!" Jenna gasped. "Oh no, *look*."

Soaked and heavy with snow, a scarcely visible white woolen
cloth lay exposed by Beetle's digging. "Someone's under here,"
muttered Beetle. He dropped to his hands and knees, and along
with Jenna and Septimus, quickly scraped away the snow.

"Ephaniah!" Jenna exclaimed. "Oh no, it's *Ephaniah*.
Ephaniah, wake up!"

UNDER THE SNOW

I t took the combined strength of all three to haul the soaked and frozen figure into the hut. He lay on the floor taking up the entire space between the bunks, a great bulky mass of sodden white robes clinging to his strange rat-man shape. Ullr arched up, hissing, the fur on his tail sticking out like a bottlebrush and shot out of the hut. Jenna did not even notice.

"Oh, this is *awful*," she said tearfully, dropping to her

knees beside the rat-man. "That scratching last night was *Ephaniah*. We ignored him. And he couldn't even shout to tell us he was there—freezing to death. Oh, Sep, we've probably *killed* him."

Septimus thought Jenna might be right. Marcia had taught him to **Listen for the Sound of Human Heartbeat** and he could hear only Jenna's and Beetle's—both beating fast. But, thought Septimus, as he threw some logs into the stove and got the fire going once more, he didn't know if the **Listening** worked for the sound of rat-human heartbeat as well. It wasn't something he had thought to ask at the time.

Jenna looked at Ephaniah in dismay. He had lost his glasses and his eyes were closed, the long dark lashes stuck together with flecks of ice. His small amount of visible human skin was bluish-white and his sparse, short brown hair was caked with snow and plastered to his skull, which was surprisingly human in shape. Jenna knew she ought to unwind the cloth from his rat mouth and listen for sounds of breathing—or at the very least put her hand on him to check for the rise and fall of his chest—but she found herself very reluctant to touch the rat-man. She thought that maybe it was the nearness of his bulk, which was suddenly overwhelming in all its ratlike strangeness. When Ephaniah was conscious his humanity shone through, and Jenna hardly noticed the rat in the man—but now she found it hard to see the man in the rat. She glanced up at Beetle; he was standing in the doorway staring at Ephaniah. "Do *you* think he's still alive?" she half whispered.

Beetle nodded slowly. "Yeah . . ." he said, moving his timepiece from hand to hand—a nervous habit he had when he was worried. He thought he saw the rat-man's eyes flicker open for a moment, but he said nothing.

The fire in the stove was blazing now. Steam was rising from the white woolen robes and a musty, unpleasant smell began to fill the hut.

"He must have followed us," said Septimus, staring down at Ephaniah. "That must have been what I saw . . ."

"You saw him?" asked Jenna. "Why didn't you *say*?"

"Well . . . I wasn't sure."

"Poor Ephaniah," said Jenna. "He'd be camouflaged—like the Snow Foxes in the Lands of the Long Nights."

"Yeah. Well, it wasn't just that. I didn't want to say because it felt . . . **Darke**."

"Ephaniah felt **Darke**?"

Septimus shrugged. "Well, I—"

Beetle had been staring at Ephaniah intently. Now he spoke. "Sep."

There was something in Beetle's voice that sent a chill down Septimus's spine. "What?" he whispered.

Silently, Beetle pointed to his own left little finger and crossed the first and second fingers of his left hand—the sign scribes used for the **Darke**. Now Septimus understood—but Jenna did not. Frightened, she glanced at Septimus. "*Get out,*" he mouthed.

"Why?" asked Jenna, her voice sounding horribly loud in the silence.

No one replied. The next moment Septimus was beside her and before she knew it she was on her feet being propelled out of the doorway and over the pile of snow.

"But—" Jenna protested to no avail.

"Shh!" hissed Septimus. "You'll wake it."

"Wake *what?*"

Silent and fast, Beetle closed the hut door. Jenna watched as Septimus placed both hands on the door, just as he had done the night before, and muttered something under his breath. Then he gave a thumbs-up sign and scrambled over the snow. The next moment Jenna found herself grabbed by Septimus and Beetle and running from the hut as though it were on fire with Ullr bounding behind.

They headed down the valley, leaping over the snow and dodging through the trees like a trio of terrified deer. To their right a steep cliff reared up through the treetops and when they reached the base of the cliff, they stopped to catch their breath. They looked back up the valley, searching out the hut, which—if it had not been for the lazily rising wood smoke that was drifting up through the trees—would have been almost impossible to see.

"It's okay," said Beetle. "I can't see it. Of course it might be hiding behind the trees, but I don't think so."

"It?" asked Jenna. "What do you mean—the hut's *following* us? Are you crazy?"

"I mean Ephaniah," said Beetle. "Except it's not."

"Not *what?*" asked Jenna.

"It's not Ephaniah," said Beetle. "It's a **Thing**."

"A *Thing?*"

"Yep. The one from the Manuscriptorium. The one that came with the kid who got me fired and took my job."

"No. No, I don't believe it. It's *Ephaniah*."

Septimus glanced back up the valley anxiously. "Come on, let's get some distance between us."

They set off again, following the steady downward slope of the valley, keeping into the shadows of the cliff face. Every step that took them away from the hut made Jenna feel as if she were betraying Ephaniah. At last she could stand it no more. "Stop," she said in a deliberately Princessy voice. "I'm not going any farther. We've *got* to go back."

Septimus and Beetle stopped. "But, *Jen*," they both protested.

Jenna pulled her wolverine cloak around her as if it were a royal mantle and stubbornly stuck out her chin—just as her mother had done on the rare occasions her advisers had dared to disagree with her. "Either you two tell me exactly what's going on or I am going straight back to the hut. *Now*," she told them.

Septimus took a deep breath. He was going to have to make this good, he could tell. "Jen, last night the scrabbling at the door stopped after I did an **Anti-Darke** Incantation. And that only affects **Darke** stuff. It wouldn't have stopped the *real* Ephaniah."

"Maybe that was coincidence. Maybe he was getting

exhausted or his hands were too frozen . . ." Jenna stamped her feet through the snow in frustration. How could Septimus be so sure?

"No, Jen," said Septimus very definitely. "Beetle, tell Jen what you saw."

Beetle sat down on a snow-covered log—his legs ached after the unaccustomed exercise of the last few days. "I saw a ring. A **Darke** ring."

"What do you mean?" asked Jenna.

"It was when I went back to get your pin."

"*What* was?"

"The kid shrunk one of his precious licorice snakes and gave it to the **Thing** as part of a **Contract**."

"A **Contract**? Beetle, what are you talking about?"

Beetle found it hard to explain things to Jenna—the way she looked at him stopped him from thinking straight. But he had to try. He took a deep breath and began.

"That precious scribe of Jillie Djinn's who was in the Vaults—you remember?"

Jenna nodded.

"Well, it seems he had a **Darke Thing** with him. Because when I went back to find your pin I heard him transfer it to

Tertius Fume. The kid had to give the **Thing** a release token and he didn't have anything except a licorice snake. So he **Shrank** that and gave it to the **Thing**. And that's what I saw on Ephaniah's left little finger."

"*No*—but how?"

"The only possible explanation is that the **Thing** has **InHabited** Ephaniah. Because whatever form a **Thing** takes, a **Darke** ring will stay the same."

"I didn't see a ring," Jenna said stubbornly.

"You weren't looking, Jen," said Septimus.

Jenna shook her head in disbelief. She could not rid herself of the thought of Ephaniah lying abandoned in the hut. "I—I don't believe it. Poor Ephaniah. He must have followed us through that horrible forest. And with his limp he'd never have been able to catch us. And he couldn't shout, could he? So what did we do in return? We left him outside all night even though he was *begging* to come in, and now we've left him behind to freeze to death. Well, *you* might think that's okay, but *I* don't."

"But, *Jen*—" Septimus's protests fell on thin air. Jenna was already running back up the valley retracing their footsteps, followed by the faithful Ullr.

"Jen! *Stop!*" yelled Septimus.

"I wouldn't shout," said Beetle. "You don't know what's listening. Come on, Sep, we gotta get to her before the Thing does."

But Jenna, who could always run fast, had already put a good distance between them.

Beetle surprised himself by reaching the hut before Septimus. "Jenna . . ." he puffed. "Jenna?"

There was no reply. Heart beating fast, Beetle followed Jenna's scrambling footsteps through the snowdrift outside the door. He found Jenna alone, standing on the wet patch where the body of Ephaniah had lain.

"He's *gone*," said Jenna.

"Good," said Beetle.

"But . . . how? He was *unconscious*."

Beetle shook his head. "I saw his eyes open—just for a moment. He looked at me. Can't do that if you're unconscious."

"But how could he go so fast? Ephaniah can't even *walk* very well."

"Doesn't make any difference who they InHabit," said Beetle. "They can still shift it."

Jenna looked Beetle in the eye. "You really do think that

Ephaniah has been—what do you call it?—**InHabited**, don't
you?"

Beetle nodded solemnly.

"And you honestly, truly saw the snake ring on his finger?"

"Yep. Little pinky, left hand. Where they always wear
them."

"Okay," said Jenna reluctantly. "I believe it now."

Beetle grinned with relief and pleasure—Jenna had listened
to him. It was a good feeling.

Septimus appeared, out of breath. "I saw it at the top of the
hill," he said. "It's heading off."

"Good," said Beetle.

Jenna had something she wanted to say. "Beetle, I'm sorry
I didn't believe you."

"'S okay." Beetle shrugged.

"I know I should have."

"I don't see why—it's weird stuff. Why should you believe
it?"

"Because I know who that boy is. The one you call Daniel
Hunter."

"You *do*?"

"He was DomDaniel's Apprentice. You remember, Sep? I

know he's changed a lot—he's taller and his skin has gotten bad and his hair is long and horrible—but it *is* him, isn't it?"

Septimus wasn't too good with faces. But now that Jenna had said it, he knew she was right. "So *that's* why he said he was me—because for ten years he *was*. Well, he thought he was. Poor kid."

Beetle looked puzzled. "Tell you later, Beetle," said Septimus. "But we ought to get going." He held out the compass. The needle was still pointing steadily—but not in the direction he had hoped. "Darn. It's pointing the way the Thing has gone."

"We'll have to follow it," said Jenna.

"No, Jen. That's just plain dangerous," Septimus protested.

Jenna stuck out her bottom lip stubbornly. "I don't care, Sep. If that's the way to the House of Foryx, then that's the way we go."

Septimus appealed to Beetle. "It's *crazy* to follow that Thing. You agree, don't you, Beetle?"

"Well . . ." Beetle hesitated.

"Bee*tle*," Septimus protested.

"If it's going in the right direction we could do worse than to follow it. That way we keep an eye on it. Much better to have something like that in front of you than behind you where you can't see what it's doing."

"Yes," said Jenna briskly. "Just what I was thinking."

"You know, Jen," said Septimus as they set off following the Thing's tracks, "sometimes you really *do* remind me of Marcia."

⊹⊹40⊹⊹
THE EDGE OF THE ABYSS

T*hey followed the long, scuffling* tracks away from the hut. The tracks led over a small stone bridge that Snorri had marked on the map, then up a steep slope and down into another valley beyond. As they walked through the tall trees at the head of the broad valley, all around was silence and snow; not a breath of wind stirred the branches. Once or twice they caught a glimpse of the Thing far below, speeding down the slope with its odd, lurching gait, but the white of its robes made it hard to spot against the snow and it drew ever farther ahead until they lost sight of it.

Still following the tracks, the compass needle led them down to a frozen marsh on the valley floor. It was noticeably colder here. The mix of ice and marsh mud crackled beneath their feet and the tall, black spikes of reed that stuck up through the snow snagged on their wolverine-skin cloaks. As they continued on a downward slope, the marsh gave way to a wide frozen stream, along which the Thing had traveled in long, sliding strides. Jenna picked up Ullr and placed him on top of her backpack. The cat perched precariously and surveyed the scene in a disapproving manner. Slipping and sliding, they set off along the ice, leaning forward to balance their backpacks. Soon they got into a steady skating rhythm and picked up speed along the smooth ice of the stream.

The stream widened and led them into the lower reaches of the valley. Septimus, who was in the lead, suddenly saw a huge bank of thick white fog rising in front of them. He skidded to a halt and Beetle cannoned into him, closely followed by Jenna and Ullr, who toppled onto the ice with a loud *meow*.

"Ouch," said Beetle, dusting himself off and struggling to

his feet. "You might have warned us you were putting on the brakes."

"Didn't have time," said Septimus. "Look." He pointed to the fog.

Beetle whistled between his teeth. "Where did *that* come from?"

"I saw it," said Jenna, "but I thought it was snow."

It was true—the fog was exactly the same color as snow. It stretched from left to right as far as the eye could see and blended seamlessly into the gray-white snow-filled sky. Jenna did not like fog; it reminded her of the time when she had sat marooned inside a **Magykal** fog near the Marram Marshes, listening to the click of a pistol no more than a few feet away, aimed at her heart. "Do you think the **Thing** is in there, waiting for us?" she whispered.

"No," said Beetle. "Look—the **Thing** saw it before we did. There are the tracks." The lopsided tracks had left the frozen stream, doubled back on themselves and disappeared up the hill and into the trees.

As they scanned the tracks, a long low rumble began to shake the ground. Deep within the fog, something was coming.

"Can you hear that?" asked Jenna, wide-eyed and pale.

Septimus and Beetle nodded.

"Run?" said Beetle as the ground vibrated through the soles of his boots. *"Now?"*

"Where to?" asked Jenna, glancing around. Nowhere looked safe to her.

Septimus shook his head. "No . . . no. It's going away now. Listen. It's passed by. Whatever it was."

"Whatever it was," muttered Beetle, "I would not have liked to have been in the way."

Not so very far away, at the top of the hill, the Thing stopped and looked down on the three figures standing uncertainly on the edge of the fog bank. It grimaced, contorting Ephaniah's rat mouth into a vicious snarl. Just a few more careless steps, it thought, and the job would have been done. But no matter—let them take their chance with the Foryx on the precipice path. And if they miss the Foryx then it will do exactly as its new Master had instructed. The Thing respected its new Master. Slowly and clumsily, it turned away and, increasingly tired of the unwieldy body it had saddled itself with, lumbered off through the snow.

✳   ✳   ✳

Back at the frozen stream Septimus was looking at the compass, shaking it in irritation. "Bother, bother, bother. *Stop it.*" The needle, however, took no notice of being spoken to and carried on spinning wildly. "Jen," he said, "we'd better look at the map. I think we've reached the edge of the hole."

"Literally," Beetle said with a gulp. "*Look.*" The fog was a mixture of eddies and swirls that drifted up in the air. It was constantly shifting, in some places dense, in others almost clear—and it was in one of these clear patches that Beetle had seen that no more than a few steps away the frozen stream had become a waterfall of ice, plunging over the edge of an abyss.

"Oh . . ." Septimus swayed and closed his eyes. A horrible feeling of vertigo shot up from the soles of his feet and made his head spin.

Beetle and Jenna crept forward and warily peered over. The fog rose, swirling in long tendrils that wrapped themselves around their feet and chilled them to the bone. Beetle crept even closer to the edge; he picked up a rock from the pile of stones beside the waterfall and hurled it into the chasm. They counted the seconds, waiting for the sound of the rock hitting the bottom, but after one whole minute they had still heard nothing. A sudden gust of wind caught Beetle's cloak and sent it noisily flapping.

"Beetle!" Jenna gasped, grabbing hold of his sleeve. "You're too close. *Come back.*" This was exactly the kind of thing that Beetle's mother would have done. If it had been his mother, Beetle would have become extremely petulant and deliberately stood even closer to the edge—but not with Jenna. A decidedly unpetulant Beetle allowed himself to be pulled away.

Septimus, meanwhile, had no intention of going anywhere near the edge. He had found a nice, solid tree a safe distance away and was leaning against it, his head still spinning. He hadn't felt vertigo like this in a long time—certainly not since he had had the **Flyte Charm**. How he wished he had the **Flyte Charm** now. Trust Marcia, he thought, to take away the one thing that would have made this whole expedition actually easy. He took a deep breath. Not more than a few feet away was the deepest chasm he had ever come across. Septimus didn't need to look over the edge to know that—he could feel it all the way up from his feet, and he *knew*.

He remembered the Young Army saying: *On the brink, stop and think.* Now that he was a little older, the rhymes he had learned parrot-fashion seemed to make sense in a way they hadn't at the time. And so, leaning against the tree—as close to the brink as he was willing to get—Septimus began to think. He thought about the **Queste**. He thought he really should tell Jenna and Beetle about the **Questing Stone**. He should tell them to go on without him and leave him to do the **Queste**—wherever that would take him. But then he thought of walking away from Jenna and Beetle, of leaving them alone to find Nicko, and he knew he couldn't—he just *couldn't*.

Jenna's voice broke into his thoughts. "Look, Sep," she said, laying the map on the snow beneath the tree. Then, "No, Ullr, go sit somewhere else," she said, gently pushing the cat off the paper. Ullr looked unimpressed. He sat down in the snow and began to lick his paws. Jenna kneeled down and ran her finger around the edge of the hole where the missing piece should have been. "It's funny," she said, "that the edge of the hole in the map is at the edge of a chasm. It's almost as if it were a *real* hole, if you see what I mean. I figure the House of Foryx is over there." She pointed into the fog. "It all makes sense now. That must be what Aunt Ells called the great pit."

Suddenly Beetle said, "Look! There's the bridge." He whistled. "That is *some* bridge."

Far away to the left they could just make out the spindly
outline of a structure leaping high into the air and disappearing into the fog. It looked beautiful—a delicate tracery of fine
lines like a spider web suspended in space. And then the fog
closed over it once more and it was gone.

"That's it!" said Jenna, excited. "All we have to do is cross
that bridge and we're there. Isn't that great?

"Great," said Septimus with a sinking feeling that started in
his stomach and went all the way down to his feet. "Really
great."

They set off toward the bridge, following the edge of the chasm
but keeping—on Septimus's insistence—a safe distance away.
After a while it became apparent that they were, for the very
first time in this strange place, actually following a path. The
snow looked trampled by animals rather than humans and
Septimus could not help but wonder what *kind* of animals.
Whatever they were, they had the kind of droppings that
Septimus preferred not to step in.

As the morning wore on, the sun rose above the fog and
the heavy snow clouds in the sky began to clear. But the fog
remained, moving and shifting like a great brooding creature

beside them. Sometimes Septimus thought he heard distant voices far below, somewhere deep within the fog. Once, Jenna stopped, convinced she had heard someone cry out.

The thought that soon they would have to step onto a bridge and walk into this shifting, brooding bank of fog preoccupied all three—and Septimus in particular. He dropped back and let Jenna and Beetle move ahead. As he trudged behind the two wolverine-cloaked figures with their Forest backpacks—and a small orange cat with its fur puffed out—something else began to preoccupy Septimus. Very reluctantly, but unable to resist, he put his hand into his tunic pocket and drew out the **Questing Stone**. Hardly daring to look, he closed his eyes and then—remembering how near they were to the edge of the precipice—he opened them again fast. The **Stone** was *yellow*. Yellow to guide you through the snow, thought Septimus with a sinking feeling.

Jenna turned around suddenly. "Hey, Sep. You okay?"

Septimus quickly shoved his hand back in his pocket. "Yeah," he said, heavily. "Fine."

All along their journey beside the chasm, the path had steadily been curving to the right as it led them around in a great circle, but the fog had always obscured the bridge. But now, as they approached a thick-set, snow-covered tree standing close to the path, two tall, iron pillars appeared out of the fog. Tall, thin and strangely beautiful, the pair of pillars leaned slightly backward, glistening with damp from the mist, their tops tapering and disappearing into the swirls of fog that drifted up from the chasm below. With a feeling of dread, Septimus knew they had arrived.

"Wow . . ." breathed Beetle. "Look at that."

Septimus thought he would rather not.

The bridge itself was a precarious structure of wooden planks laid across two thick cables that rose in a curve and disappeared into the fog. How long did it go on for? he wondered. Was it just a few more yards or was it for miles? Septimus had a horrible feeling that the latter was more likely. There was something about the curve that made it look like a wide span. It was an odd structure; from the top of the pillars, four cables swooped down. Two stretched far behind them and were buried in the snow and the other two followed the curve of the bridge and vanished into the fog. Septimus searched for something that might reasonably be called "sides" or possibly "handrails," but all he could see was what seemed to him to be a couple of pieces of string. He'd had nightmares about bridges like this—but none of them had been *this* bad.

Septimus glanced at Jenna and Beetle, strangely relieved to see that they did not look exactly overjoyed at the prospect of the bridge either. He was about to suggest they have some of Sam's fish—anything to delay the awful moment when he would have to step onto what looked like no more than a piece of beginner's knitting—when he heard a movement in the tree behind them.

"That'll cost you," said a harsh voice from above.

They leaped into the air at the sound of the first new voice they had heard since Sam had said good-bye.

"I said, it'll cost you," the voice repeated.

Septimus looked up. "Where *are* you?" he asked.

"Up the tree. And I'm coming down."

✢ 4 I ✢
THE TOLL-MAN

A small, *wiry man clad* head to toe in an assortment of furs clambered down the trunk of the oak tree and jumped lightly onto the snow. His deep-set eyes, like two little black beads, quickly took in Jenna and Beetle and then fixed on Septimus as he came toward them. The man's brown, wrinkled face put Jenna in mind of an organ grinder's monkey she had once seen at a fair—she hadn't liked the look of the monkey then, and she didn't like the look of the man now.

The man waited until Septimus had joined them and then he spoke. "In case you was a'wondering, I be the Toll-Man," he said. "No one crosses the bridge without paying a price. Some pay more than others. It depends."

"On what?" asked Jenna sharply. She didn't like the way the man was looking at her.

"On whether I like 'em. And on how much gold they have." He smiled unpleasantly. The smile showed, to their surprise, two rows of gold teeth in bizarrely mismatched shapes and sizes. "Don't worry, Missy," he said, "I can tell you young 'uns still got your own teeth and they're no good to me. I'm a fair man. Don't ask folks for what they can't give." He shook his head as though amused. "But I is always surprised by what folks *can* give when they have to." He ran a long pale tongue over his uneven teeth and grinned.

"So, how much does it cost to cross the bridge?" Jenna asked.

"How much do you *want* to cross?" asked the Toll-Man.

No one answered because no one actually *wanted* to cross at all. All they wanted was to be on the other side.

"So are you crossing or just looking?" asked the Toll-Man

irritably. "I charge for looking, too. Can't have folks cluttering
up the place all day just *looking*."

"We're crossing," said Jenna decisively. "How much do
you want?"

The Toll-Man looked Jenna up and down. "Well, Missy.
That's a nice circlet of gold you have upon that pretty head of
yours. I'll take that."

Jenna's hands flew up to her gold circlet—the one that her
mother, the Queen, had worn as a girl. "You can't have *that!*"
she gasped.

The Toll-Man shrugged. "Then you can't cross."

With a heavy heart, Jenna reached up to take the circlet off.
It was only an object, she told herself. Nicko was worth more
than gold. *Much* more. But the Toll-Man did not notice; he
was already eyeing Beetle. "You, boy—I'll have your timepiece," he said.

Beetle looked shocked. "How do you know I've got a timepiece?" he asked.

The man paused, briefly wrong-footed. "I can hear it ticking,"
he said. "Got an ear for ticking, I 'ave."

Beetle frowned. He shot a questioning glance at Septimus,
who returned it with a slight nod of his head. "And you, boy,"

the Toll-Man said, turning to Septimus, "*you've* got a nice silver belt there with a few bits of gold on it. That'll do me well enough. I'll have the little trinkets inside, too." The man regarded them all with his bright yellow smile. "You see—I'm a fair man. I don't ask for what you haven't got." From his pocket he drew out a large velvet bag that hung from a collapsible wooden ring. With a practiced flick of the wrist he snapped the ring open and the bag hung down like an empty sock. Like the organ grinder's monkey, the Toll-Man pushed the bag toward Septimus. "You first, boy. Put your belt in there."

Very slowly, Septimus unbuckled his Apprentice belt, closely observed by the eager eye of the Toll-Man, who licked his teeth once again in anticipation. "'Urry up, boy. You won't get across in daylight at this rate." Septimus was fumbling with the last part of the buckle, partly because his cold fingers were clumsy and slow, but mainly because he needed time to think. Another Young Army saying was going around in his head: *To win the fight, time it right.* Time it right, he thought, gritting his teeth, time it . . . *right!*

With a *click*, the buckle finally snapped open and the Toll-Man leaned forward with his collecting bag. At that moment, to Jenna's shock, Septimus sprang at the Toll-Man and knocked him to the ground. The man fell back into a thick patch of snow. Before he had time to push Septimus off, Beetle had piled on top of them and Jenna watched in horror as, like a giant snowball, the struggling trio rolled toward the edge of the precipice.

The Toll-Man was not big, but he was strong, and without Beetle's weight—and willingness to land some good punches—Septimus would not have stood a chance. To Jenna's relief, the snowball stopped just short of the edge with Septimus and Beetle on top of the Toll-Man. "Shove him over, Sep—*now!*" yelled Beetle.

"No!" yelled Jenna, horrified at the thought of pushing someone to his death. "*No.* You can't do that. You *can't!*"

It seemed that Jenna was right. As if buoyed by her shout—and the boys' temporary loss of concentration—the Toll-Man found some extra strength. With an angry shove he threw Beetle off and sent him sprawling into the icy bank of the footpath. There was a sharp *crack* as Beetle's head met the wall of ice. He slumped down, a trickle of red running from behind his ear and staining the ice with a pinkish tinge.

Jenna glanced at Beetle. At least he was safe, and well away from the edge—Septimus was not. Septimus's head was in fact hanging over the edge of the precipice, and the Toll-Man was about to make sure that the rest of him followed.

Septimus stared into the abyss, trying not to imagine how far the ground was below the fog. While he struggled against the relentless pushing from the Toll-Man—whose sharp intakes of breath he could feel on the back of his neck—Septimus wished more than ever that he had the Flyte Charm. He could see it so clearly, he could almost *feel* it in his hand. The little white wings of his own Charm that Marcia had given him, which had become part of the Flyte Charm, were fluttering . . .

Then suddenly, Septimus *was* over the edge. As he began—incredibly slowly, so it seemed to him—to fall, he grabbed on to one of the bridge stanchions and there he hung, swinging above the abyss.

Uncaring now about whether the Toll-Man fell to his death or not, Jenna swung her fist at him and caught him by surprise. There was a thud as the man fell forward into the snow and knocked one of his gold teeth out. Blearily, he scrabbled in the snow to retrieve it.

Jenna's face appeared over the edge of the precipice, white and scared, afraid of what she would see. "Take my hand, Sep. Quick."

"No, Jen. I'll pull you over too."

Jenna looked fierce. "Just *do* it, Septimus!" she yelled.

Septimus did it. He grabbed Jenna's hand and to their

surprise he came up so easily that they both went staggering back into the snow.

The Toll-Man meanwhile had found his tooth, but when he picked up the bloodstained chunk of gold an expression of exasperation crossed his features and he threw the tooth away in disgust. This was not what he had come here for—what was he *doing*? But before he had time to answer his own question, two relentless forces met him and toppled him over the edge.

Jenna looked shocked at what they had done. "He's *gone*," she said.

Septimus was not so sure. Warily he leaned over the precipice to check. Suddenly a gloved hand shot up from the mist and grabbed Septimus's cloak. Septimus lurched back and wrenched the hand away—the Toll-Man was hanging from the very same stanchion that Septimus had been. His angry eyes glared at Septimus. "There's no escape, Apprentice," he growled. "The **Darkening** is done."

"Who . . . *what* are you?" asked Septimus.

The Toll-Man laughed. He pulled his left hand from his glove, which had frozen to the metal stanchion, and made another grab for him. Septimus caught the Toll-Man's wrist in midair. On the Toll-Man's little finger was exactly what he had expected to find: a small, black licorice snake.

"I'll take that," said Septimus. He pulled the band from the Toll-Man's finger, whereupon the Toll-Man began a loud rant in what Septimus knew was **Darke Tongue**. It was foul. The **Darke** imprecations flew into his ears, wormed their way into his brain and tried to unsettle his mind, but Septimus remembered his **Anti-Darke** chants and muttered them over and over again while he fought to pry the remaining hand off the stanchion.

But still the **Darke** shouts flowed and Septimus felt himself weakening. "Help me, Jen!" he yelled. The next moment Jenna was beside him, and together she and Septimus twisted the Toll-Man's hand out of his glove. And then, suddenly it was done. All that remained of the Toll-Man was a pair of brown woolen gloves stuck to the stanchion—and a rapidly disappearing scream in the mist.

Jenna slumped down onto the ice and put her head in her hands. "I can't believe we did that," she said. She looked at Septimus, a horrified expression in her eyes. "Sep, we've just *killed* someone."

"Yes," said Septimus simply.

"But that's *awful*," said Jenna. "I . . . I never thought I would . . ."

Septimus looked at Jenna, his green eyes serious. "It's a luxury, Jen," he said.

"What do you mean?"

Septimus stared at the scraped and bloody snow at his feet. It took him some moments to reply. "I mean . . ." he began slowly. "I mean that if you go through life and never face a situation where, in order for you to survive, someone else has to die, then you're lucky. That's what I mean."

"That's terrible, Sep."

Septimus shrugged. "Sometimes that is how it is. I learned that in the Young Army. It's either the chief cadet in the wolverine pit, or you."

Jenna shook her head very slowly, still not able to believe what she had done.

"Jen—look. Does this make you feel better?" asked Septimus quietly. He held out a small black licorice snake ring.

"Oh."

"It was on his left little finger. It was the **Thing**, Jen. It was him or us. And it had to be us—you know it did."

"It was the Toll-Man too," said Jenna.

"Yes. I know."

Slowly, Septimus got to his feet and gingerly approached the precipice. He stood as near as he dared then, and murmuring an **Anti-Darke** chant, he crushed the licorice ring between his fingers and sprinkled it into the void.

A low moan came from behind him. Jenna leaped to her feet. "Beetle!"

"Eurgh . . . wherrrmi?" came the answering groan.

It took a lot of persuasion to get Beetle up to the Toll-Man's tree house, even with the help of the steplike notches they found cut into the bark of the tree. Septimus pushed and Jenna pulled and somehow they all made it up to the ram-shackle collection of planks and skins on a platform wedged between the two main branches. Covering the entrance to the tree house was the hide of a large, reddish animal with huge curved claws that clattered when Jenna gingerly lifted the door flap. The inside of the tree house smelled musty—and strangely familiar. She peered in but the interior was pitch-black; all she could tell was that the floor, too, was covered with fur.

With a last heave and a push, Jenna and Septimus got the dopey—and very heavy—Beetle into the tree house, and then crawled in themselves.

There was someone already in there.

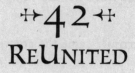

⁜42⁜
ReUnited

A half-rat, half-human face was eerily illuminated in the yellow glow of Septimus's Dragon Ring. Jenna suppressed a scream.

The body of Ephaniah Grebe was propped up in the far corner of the tree house, exactly where the **Thing** had left him for the more agile frame of the Toll-Man. Ephaniah's head lolled forward like a broken doll's, and his white robes looked like a pile of dirty sheets waiting to be washed. As soon as Jenna saw him, she knew he was **UnInHabited**—the difference between Ephaniah now and the last time she had seen him was obvious. *This* was Ephaniah—she felt no revulsion, no sense of overwhelming rat-ness and none of the feeling of pity and hopelessness that the InHabited Ephaniah had filled her with. And, she saw, his left little finger was ring-free. She rushed over to the rat-man and touched his hand. It felt cold.

"Oh, Sep, can you **Hear** . . . *anything?*" she whispered.

Septimus knew what Jenna was asking. He **Listened for the Sound of Human Heartbeat.** "I don't think so," he said, then he saw Jenna's expression and added hurriedly, "but I think that's because there's so much *rat* there. All I can **Hear** is Beetle's, which is slow and steady, and yours, which is really loud."

"Oh," said Jenna, surprised. "Sorry. What about yours?"

"You can never **Hear** your own," said Septimus. He thought for a moment. "We'll do it the old way," he said.

Septimus kneeled beside Ephaniah and took his emergency Physik tin from his pocket. The tin was crammed full of things that Jenna had no idea why he could possibly want. From it he selected a small, round mirror and held it close to Ephaniah's slightly open mouth from which two long, narrow teeth protruded. A light misting appeared on the glass. "Well, he's still breathing," said Septimus.

"Oh, Sep, that's *wonderful.*" Gently, Jenna stroked the rat-man's soft nose, intrigued at the way the human features merged so well with the rat fur. As she stroked the fur, Ephaniah's eyes

fluttered open for a brief moment. "He saw me," whispered
Jenna. "His eyes smiled. He's okay. I *know* he is."

"It'll take a while to be sure about that," said Septimus,
who knew enough Physik to know that nothing is certain.
"But at least he's got a chance."

The tree house was surprisingly comfortable, if a little strange.
It was completely lined with a coarse reddish fur, and once the
door flap was closed no light entered at all. In the opposite corner from where Ephaniah lay, his head resting on a pillow that
Jenna had made from the Toll-Man's blankets, there was a
small stove set on a thick piece of slate. After several attempts
to light it with Beetle's tinderbox, Jenna finally coaxed a large
yellow flame from the big round burner. Septimus took the
battered old pan that hung from a hook above the stove,
climbed down the tree and scooped up some snow. With his
pan piled high with snow, poised to climb back to safety, he
stopped for a moment and listened. A bloodchilling ululating
howl—the same one that they had heard the night before—
pierced the air and Septimus felt the ground tremble beneath
his feet.

Startled, he looked up and saw a long, dark shape moving

along the path around the chasm. It was coming toward him—fast. With a sudden certainty Septimus knew what it was—and what had gone past them earlier hidden in the fog. He did not waste a moment; he dropped the pan and shot back up the rope ladder. As he threw himself into the tree house, the whole tree began to shake.

"Earthquake!" cried Jenna.

Septimus shook his head. "No," he said. "Foryx!"

Terrified and fascinated at the same time, Jenna peered out of the door flap. A phalanx of Foryx was hurtling through the snow, so fast that Jenna's only impression was a long, red streak of galloping fur and tusks as the Foryx thundered past on the path below the tree house.

"They're real!" said Jenna.

"A bit too real," said Septimus.

A few minutes later, pointing to the walls of the tree house, Jenna said, "You know what fur this is, don't you?"

"Foryx," said Septimus with a grimace.

Jenna smiled. "Which means, if you think about it, that we are already in a House of Foryx."

"Well, I wish Nik were *here*," said Septimus glumly.

"I know. So do I."

✳ ✳ ✳

Jenna made Septimus go back for some snow. "We'll hear
them if they're coming back," she said when Septimus had
objected. "And make sure you get the snow from a clean
patch. We don't want Foryx dribble for supper."

Septimus broke the record time for snow collection. While
Jenna boiled up some witches' brew, Septimus sat next to
Beetle and looked through his Physik tin with a feeling of
anticipation. At last he was getting a chance to try out the
Physik he had learned on a real patient. Beside him his unwit-
ting patient dozed peacefully on the floor of the tree house,
pale but breathing steadily. The thick yellow flame of the stove
filled the tree house with a comforting glow and the warmth
began to bring out the pungent smell of the Foryx skins.
Septimus decided it was time Beetle woke up and drank some
witches' brew. He took out a small phial labeled Sal Volatile
and was about to waft it under his new patient's nose when
Beetle suddenly opened his eyes. Foryx skin reek was as effective as any phial of Sal Volatile.

Beetle had a nasty gash behind his right ear and now that
he was warming up it was beginning to throb painfully.
"Ouch!" he protested as Septimus cleaned up the dried blood
with some sphagnum moss dipped in antiseptic.

Jenna looked up as she was dropping three squares of toffee into the boiling water. "You're turning him purple, Sep." She laughed.

"Purple?" said Beetle. "Wotcha *doing*, Sep?"

"It's Gentian Violet," Septimus explained. "It will stop the cut from getting infected. But we need to keep the edges together. Wait, I've got something here." Septimus picked up a large needle.

"What's that for?" asked Beetle suspiciously.

"Oh, that? Well, when I was learning about Physik, Marcellus took me to watch a surgeon at work," said Septimus. "Someone came in with a deep cut and he sewed the edges together."

"He did *what*?" Jenna asked, wide-eyed.

"You're joking," said Beetle.

Septimus shook his head.

"Eurgh, Sep, that's *disgusting*," said Jenna. "You can't sew people up like . . . like bags of flour."

"Why not? It works."

"Well, you're not doing it to *me*," Beetle told him. "So you can put that needle away right now."

Septimus smiled, pleased that Beetle sounded like his old self. "I wasn't going to sew you up, Beetle," he said. "Your cut's not big enough and it's in an awkward place for stitches anyway. I was just looking for a bandage. Ah, here it is."

Beetle allowed Septimus to put a clean piece of moss over his cut and wrap a bandage around his head. He obediently drank all of the witches' brew that Jenna had made and was soon asleep on the Foryx skin floor.

"Marcellus would say that we ought to wake him every few hours to check that he's sleeping and not unconscious," said Septimus.

"But he won't be sleeping if we wake him, will he?" Jenna objected. "He'll just be grumpy and tired tomorrow."

"I know," said Septimus. "Anyway, I think he's fine. His breathing is good."

Jenna smiled. "You know," she said, "even though it was horrible, you being trapped in Marcellus's Time, you've come back really different—in a good way. You know stuff. Stuff that no one else does. Not even Marcia."

"Yeah," said Septimus glumly. He was silent for a while and stirred his witches' brew, watching the toffee whiz around faster and faster. Then he said, "I'd be a better Physician than a Wizard."

"Don't be ridiculous," said Jenna. "You'll be a great

Wizard. One of the best. You *know* you will."

"Marcia doesn't think so."

"She didn't say that."

"No. But I can tell she thinks it. She says I just mess around with stuff. It's true, really. I . . . I don't think I want to be a Wizard really, Jen."

Jenna nodded. "Sometimes I think I don't want to be Queen," she said. "It's horrible to feel you *have* to be something. At least you can decide not to be a Wizard if you don't want to be."

Septimus did not reply. He put his hand in his pocket and felt the **Questing Stone**. He didn't think there was going to be much chance of deciding anything anyway. "Jen," he said.

"What is it, Sep?" Jenna looked concerned.

"Oh . . . nothing." He couldn't say it.

Later, when night had fallen and Jenna and Beetle were sleeping, the NightUllr was lying across the doorway, and even Ephaniah was breathing peacefully, Septimus took out the **Questing Stone**. Jenna stirred and he quickly shoved it back into his pocket—but not before he saw that the yellow had deepened to a dull orange: "Orange to warn you that over you'll go." And now Septimus knew exactly what that meant.

✳ ✳ ✳

Septimus woke the next morning feeling groggy from the musty fumes of the Foryx skin. It was still dark inside the tree house and the only way that Septimus could tell it was morning was by the presence of a small orange cat mewing impatiently to be let out. He lifted a corner of the Foryx skin door and, tail up, Ullr stalked out into the morning air. A moment later the cat landed with a soft thud in the snow below the tree and set about hunting for a more interesting breakfast than dried fish.

Unskilled in the art of hunting tree voles, the occupants of the tree house had to make other arrangements for breakfast. They set to heating some water and wondered if dried fish could be made more interesting by boiling it up with toffee. Jenna thought not, although Septimus liked the idea. Beetle woke with a headache and a stiff neck and grumpily refused both fish and toffee, either separately or together.

Septimus put an end to the fish-or-toffee discussion by using the pan of boiling water for an infusion of strips of willow bark from his Physik tin. He made Beetle drink it. It was bitter and made Beetle gag, but half an hour later his headache and stiff neck were better and he was helping Jenna open three more of

Sam's packages. They discovered some tiny sticky raisin cakes that Melissa had made for Jo-Jo, and a long strip of dried bacon. Suddenly breakfast seemed a lot more interesting.

Septimus decided to take Ephaniah's pulse; he wondered if it would be in the usual place. It was, even though his wrist was covered with soft rat fur. The pulse was weak but regular and Septimus was sure that Ephaniah was now in a deep sleep and not unconscious, but he could think of nothing in his Physik tin that would be of any help to the rat-man. It was, he thought, a question of time and, later on, something to stop the recurring nightmares that always afflicted those who had been InHabited.

About midmorning—according to Beetle's silent, tick-free timepiece—they had finished breakfast and decided that the only thing they could do was leave Ephaniah in the tree house to recover, and call for him on the way back. "Nik's really strong," said Jenna. "It will be so much easier with him to help get Ephaniah back to the Forest."

Septimus said nothing. He didn't think they'd be coming back at all, let alone coming back with Nicko, but Ephaniah was as safe in the tree house as anywhere—safer, in fact, than they were going to be.

Jenna kneeled beside the rat-man, covering him with their

wolverine cloaks and making him comfortable. "Good-bye, Ephaniah," she said. "We've got to go, but we'll be back soon." Ephaniah's whiskers twitched and Jenna stroked his forehead. "You'll be fine," she said. Ephaniah half opened one eye. "He's waking up!" Jenna gasped.

Ephaniah seemed to be trying to focus on Jenna. He groaned and lifted his hand restlessly. Jenna took his hand and laid it gently back on his chest, but Ephaniah resisted. Jenna let go and watched his long, bony fingers scrabble inside the folds of his robes around his neck. "What is it?" she asked. "Does your neck hurt?"

In answer, Ephaniah drew out something from a hidden pocket and pressed it into Jenna's hand. Then, with a long sigh, he closed his eyes and fell into a deep sleep.

Jenna stared at her hand. On it lay a slightly shiny circle of paper covered in a mass of finely detailed pencil lines. For a moment Jenna wondered what it could possibly be, but only for a moment. And then she knew—it was the missing piece of the map. It was the *House of Foryx*.

✛43✛
THE BRIDGE

They *spread the map out* on the snow below the tree. As they unfolded it the stiffened paper crackled and looked yellow against the frosty whiteness.

"No, Ullr," said Jenna. "You are *not* sitting here." She held up the missing piece. "Do I have to do anything special?" she asked. "Like say the **ReUnite** or something?"

"No," said Beetle. He grinned. "It's ready to go."

Jenna let go of the circular piece of paper and slowly it

fluttered down. Ullr went to bat at it with his paw but Jenna grabbed the cat and held him tight. The missing piece hovered for a few seconds above the hole, turning this way and that, deciding which way to go—and then, to the accompaniment of "Yaaay!" it slipped into place. Snorri's map was complete once more.

"That's amazing," said Jenna. "You can't even see the join."

Beetle inspected the map with a professional air. "Nice work," he said.

Septimus took his Enlarging Glass from his Apprentice Belt and held it over the center of the map. As the glass passed across, they watched the minutely annotated details rendered in Snorri's neat hand spring into focus. They saw an octagonal building shaded a delicate gray. In heavy letters over the gray, Snorri had written HOUSE OF FORYX. In the middle of the octagon Snorri had drawn a key, and wrapped around the outside of the octagon was a huge snake. The House of Foryx was on what seemed to be an island, connected to the surrounding land by a spidery contraption of a bridge. Beside the bridge was a tree and a small figure with an arrow pointing to it. Snorri had written in tiny writing, BEWARE THE TOLL-MAN. She had also written the words BOTTOMLESS PIT across the gap that the bridge spanned, but Septimus did not care. He was so relieved that the Queste had not taken them away from the House of Foryx after all that he felt he could walk over a hundred bottomless pits if he had to—although he would rather not. One was quite enough.

With Ullr securely ensconced in her backpack, Jenna stood for a moment between the two soaring pillars that formed the gateway to the bridge. She looked up and saw it rise, black and spiderlike into the white air, its thin wire ropes shining with damp. The fog swirled around her feet and a long, low wail came from somewhere far below.

Jenna swallowed hard. This was the way to Nicko, she told herself, and this was the way she would have to go. She stepped between the pillars and onto the icy dusting of unmarked snow that lay on the first precarious plank. Ahead of her the line of planks rose up into a curve and disappeared into the fog. Jenna put out her hands to take the wire handrails. They were taut, cold, and felt frighteningly flimsy. Aware that Septimus was right behind her, Jenna gathered her courage and took another step forward. The bridge gave slightly under her weight. She froze, horribly aware that there was nothing but a thin plank of wood between her and a plunge to oblivion—but she was determined not to show how scared she was. "It's fine," she said brightly. "Come on, Sep."

Septimus did not move.

"Go on," said Beetle. He gave him a gentle shove and Septimus stepped onto the bridge. Jenna moved up a couple of paces. Once again the bridge swayed. In a panic, Septimus grabbed the wire handrails.

"Wait for me," said Beetle, sounding more confident than he felt. He stepped onto the bridge, which moved once again. Septimus felt sick. He had been determined to walk across the bridge calmly, as though it was no more than a few feet above the ground—but suddenly he knew he couldn't.

Jenna glanced back and saw that Septimus's green eyes were wide with fear. "It's okay, Sep," she said. "The trick is to just take one step at a time. One foot in front of the other is all you have to think about. It doesn't matter how long it goes on for because we *know* we are going to get to the other side. All we have to do is put one foot in front of the other, okay? It's easy."

Septimus nodded. His mouth was too dry to speak.

Like a trio of snails creeping along a washing line, they set off up the bridge with Jenna counting out the steps. "One . . .

two . . . three . . . four . . . five . . . that's it, Sep, you're doing great. Look how far we've gone already—oh no, I didn't mean that, no *don't* look—keep going, keep going, ten . . . eleven . . . twelve . . . thirteen . . ."

Septimus obeyed, putting one foot in front of the other like one of Ephaniah's automatons. Unblinking, he stared straight ahead into the mist. The scene before him was oddly unchanging—always a few feet of bridge in front of them, rising in a gradual curve and disappearing into the whiteness. Sometimes a gust of wind blew some of the mist away and revealed a little more of the stretch in front but Septimus did not see it, as whenever that happened he closed his eyes until the bridge stopped swaying.

But closing his eyes did not take away the terrible wails and despairing cries that issued from the bottomless pit. As they progressed along the wobbling planks, clinging onto the ice-cold handrails with numb fingers, the cries became louder and ever more desperate. These bothered Beetle more than the bridge and he began to sing his own very special tuneless version of an old Castle favorite, "How Much Is That Weasel in the Window?" For the first time ever, Septimus did not object.

And so, to the accompaniment of Beetle's drone—which

was at times hard to distinguish from the moans far below—they put one foot in front of the other and climbed the ever-ascending curve. They had probably been no longer than a quarter of an hour on the bridge when Jenna said, "It's flattening out. Can you feel it? We must be nearly at the top."

At the mention of "top" Septimus had a sudden vision of them suspended in the middle of nowhere. The dizzying absence of earth traveled up from the soles of his feet and made his head spin. He swayed backward—Beetle caught him and the weasel song stopped. "Hey, steady, Sep. Easy does it."

Septimus could not move. His hands gripped the wires, his knuckles white. Jenna felt his fear seeping into her, too. A long, desolate lament drifted up from the chasm, rising and falling as if telling the lonely tale of the lost souls who inhabited the fog. Septimus listened, entranced. He felt an overwhelming urge to let himself fall into the soft pillow of fog and join the voices below. He loosened his grip on the handrails. At that moment a patch of fog lifted and Jenna saw a large black bird fly across their path. She gasped in surprise..

Septimus woke from his trance. "Jen . . . what is it?" he croaked.

"Nothing, Sep." But the flight of the bird had triggered her thoughts. "Sep, the **Flyte Charm**. Remember?"

At Jenna's words, Septimus felt as if the fog had cleared from his mind. He remembered the feeling of the **Charm** in his hand, the silver flights on the golden arrow fluttering like the wings of a tiny bird, the **Charm** buzzing in his hand. And as he remembered, his feet began to feel lighter and less anchored to the rickety planks of the bridge. His legs no longer felt like jelly and the keening voices from below no longer invited him to jump into the fog. To the accompaniment of a renewed burst of the weasel song behind him, Septimus took a step forward.

"Come on," he said. "We'll soon be there."

Septimus didn't see the end of the bridge—his head was full of the image of the **Flyte Charm** and nothing else. But as Jenna and Beetle walked down the last few yards of the bridge, the gaunt shape of the House of Foryx slowly materialized out of the fog.

"It's *massive*," whispered Jenna.

Beetle replaced the weasel song with a long, low whistle.

With a huge feeling of relief, Jenna stepped off the bridge. As she kneeled to set Ullr free from the backpack, she found

her eyes drawn up to the House of Foryx. It was a daunting
sight. It towered above them—more of a fortress than a
house—a forbidding mass of granite blocks perched on top of
a rocky escarpment. True to Snorri's drawing, it consisted of
a central octagonal column flanked by four octagonal towers
that disappeared into the milky white sky, the tops of their
crenulated battlements hidden by a low snow cloud. A few
small windows broke up the smooth gray surface but a strange
swirling sheen—like oil on water—covered them. They
reminded Jenna of the eyes of a blind old cat that she and her
friend Bo had once adopted.

Spurred on by the resumption of the twenty-first rendition
of the weasal song, Septimus had at last reached the end of the
bridge. He stepped from the final wobbly plank and, with a
feeling of exhilaration—he had *done* it—he let go of the image
of the Flyte Charm. His feet felt heavy once more and his
boots settled firmly back onto the ground. Painfully, Septimus
tried to uncurl his fingers, which had been clamped tight to
the freezing wire handrails, but they would not move. He
shoved his frozen hands into his tunic pockets and the
Questing Stone slipped into his right hand and nestled into
his palm. "It's hot!" he gasped.

"What are you talking about?" said Jenna. "It's *freezing*."

Septimus did not reply.

Gently, Jenna took Septimus by the arm and led him away from the edge of the chasm. "Come on, Sep," she said, "let's get going."

But Septimus had something to say and he didn't know where to begin. So he took his clenched hand from his pocket and opened it—in his palm lay the **Questing Stone**. It was glowing a brilliant orangy-red now, and it shone out in the white, muted surroundings like a beacon.

"What's that?" asked Beetle suspiciously.

"Huh," said Jenna. "It's a **Magykal** hand-warmer. You might have told us, Sep, we could have all used that."

"It's not a hand-warmer," muttered Septimus.

"No, it's not, is it?" said Beetle, peering down at the **Stone**. "You kept this quiet, Sep."

"Kept *what* quiet?" asked Jenna.

"The **Questing Stone**," said Beetle. "He's got the *Questing Stone*. Sep—why didn't you *say?*"

"Because we were looking for Nik and Snorri, that was the important thing. And, well, at first I didn't think it mattered."

"You took the **Questing Stone** and you *didn't think it mattered?*" Beetle was aghast.

"Give me a break, Beetle. I didn't know it was the **Stone** when I took it, did I? I wouldn't have taken it if I *had*. Hildegarde gave it to me just before we escaped from the Wizard Tower. She said it was her **SafeCharm**."

"Well, it's obviously *not* her **SafeCharm**," said Beetle snappily.

"And *she* wasn't Hildegarde," said Septimus.

"What's going on?" asked Jenna crossly. "*Who* wasn't Hildegarde? *Tell* me."

"Hildegarde wasn't Hildegarde," replied Beetle, a trifle unhelpfully.

"*Beetle*," protested Jenna, fixing Beetle with a Princessy stare.

"Beetle's right, Jen," said Septimus, coming to Beetle's rescue. "I've been going over and over it—the moment when I took the **Stone**. I know Marcia says never accept **Charms** from strangers, but I didn't think Hildegarde *was* a stranger. But she had been standing next to the **Questing Pot**, hadn't she? And I **Saw** the **Thing** in the **Pot**. So when Tertius Fume started putting the Tower into **Siege**, I reckon the **Thing** must have got out of the **Pot** and **InHabited** Hildegarde. It was so dark and crazy anything could have happened."

Jenna looked at Septimus, puzzled. "But why didn't you tell us?" she asked.

"Well . . . when I first found out I had it, I really thought that if I got away from the Castle and the **Questing Guards** like Marcia told me, then it would be okay. And we could all go and find Nik and Snorri and forget about the **Queste**. And then when it turned green—"

"When *what* turned green?" asked Jenna.

"The **Stone**. It started off blue but then, when we were in the hut, I saw it had turned green, just like Alther said it would. And then I realized I was on the **Queste**."

"So why didn't you *tell* us?"

Septimus took a while to answer. "I couldn't. I just couldn't. I'm sorry. We were following Snorri's map and everything seemed okay so I thought . . ." Septimus ran out of words. He felt terrible, as if he had betrayed his closest friends.

"But Sep, it *is* okay. We're still rescuing Nik, aren't we?" said Jenna.

"No," snapped Beetle suddenly. "This has nothing to do with Nicko now. We are with Sep, and Sep is on the **Queste**. He has no choice. *Once you Accept the Stone, Your Will is Not Your Own.* Isn't that right, Sep?"

Septimus nodded miserably.

Jenna shook her head in disbelief. "No! No *way*. We are on *our* quest—for Nik. And, look, we've done it." She pointed up to the great octagonal towers looming out of the mists.

"Because *there* is the House of Foryx."

Beetle was adamant. "We don't know that," he said. "We don't know *anything* anymore. Like I said, all we know for certain is that we are with Sep, and *Sep* is on the **Queste**. Oh yes—and one more little detail . . ."

"What?" asked Jenna quietly, surprised at Beetle's angry torrent of words.

"That no one has ever come back from the **Queste**."

There was silence as this sunk in.

Septimus felt awful. "I . . . I'm sorry," he muttered. "I'm *really* sorry."

A few stray snowflakes drifted down from the sky. Fiercely, Jenna brushed them from her eyes. She looked up at the great granite fortress looming out of the mist far above them, hoping somehow to find a clue that Nicko was indeed there. As she stared at the blind windows, a flight of ravens flew out of one of the towers, cawing. Jenna shivered and pulled her cloak tighter. Ullr mewed miserably and rubbed against her leg, his hackles raised.

At last Jenna spoke. "Well, if we're on some stupid **Queste**, then that's okay. We'll do it *and* we'll come back—with Nik. *That* will show them." With that, Jenna marched off up the steep zigzag path, with Ullr at her heels.

Beetle and Septimus followed in her wake.

"I'm sorry," said Septimus after a few minutes. "I should have told you about the **Stone**."

"Yes," said Beetle. "You should have." A few minutes later he said, "Wouldn't have made any difference. I would have still come."

"Thanks, Beetle."

"Jenna would have too," said Beetle.

"Yeah," said Septimus. "I don't think I could have stopped her."

"I don't think you could stop Jenna from doing *anything*," said Beetle with a grin. "Not once she's made up her mind."

Halfway up the path Jenna stopped and waited for Septimus and Beetle to catch up. Snow was falling steadily now and it seemed as if the only color in the whole world was the fiery orange of the **Questing Stone** that shone in Septimus's hand as he and Beetle emerged from the mist.

"You know," said Jenna, "this place reminds me of a story Dad used to tell us about the weary travelers who climbed up to a huge tower in the mist. They got to a door with weird creatures carved all around it and pulled the bellpull. *Ages* later it was opened by a little hunchback figure who stared at them for *hours* and then said in a really creepy voice, 'Yeeeeeeeees?' You remember that, Sep?"

"Nope," said Septimus. "I was in the Young Army at the time—probably at the bottom of a wolverine pit while you were listening to bedtime stories."

"Oh sorry, Sep. Sometimes it feels as though you were with us all the time."

"Wish I had been," said Septimus quietly. Sometimes he tried to imagine what he had missed but it wasn't a good thing to do. It gave him a feeling of heaviness that was hard to shake off.

They set off once more walking together, but soon the path narrowed and they were forced to go on in single file. The path became steeper, winding in and out of rocky outcrops, and as they climbed the air grew colder. Beetle had a feeling that they were near the top. He braced himself for the sight of the snake that Snorri had drawn wrapped around the tower.

It must, he thought, be enormous. He wondered what it ate—and then he decided to stop wondering. It wasn't making him feel good.

Now the path widened and began to level off. With their boots crunching on fine gravel, they approached the smooth white marble of the wide terrace that surrounded the House of

Foryx. On the terrace they stopped to catch their breath. In front of them a bank of mist rose, rolling and swirling with the snow, and behind that they could just make out the gray granite of the House of Foryx. They glanced at one another. Where was the snake?

Stealthily, they crept across the terrace, their feet slipping on the damp smoothness of the marble. Septimus held out the **Questing Stone** and like a beacon it guided them through the whiteness to the foot of a flight of wide, shallow steps.

"Wait there," Septimus whispered. "I'll go check out the snake."

"No," said Jenna. "We'll *all* go. Won't we, Beetle?"

Beetle nodded reluctantly. He hated snakes. "Okay," he said.

Cautiously, they crept up the steps, Septimus holding the **Questing Stone** before him to guide the way. "There's no snake," said Septimus from the mist. "Just a big old door with lots of strange carvings around it."

"No snake?" asked Beetle just to make sure.

"No snake," came Septimus's voice, "not even a tiny licorice one."

✛44✛
THE DOORKEEPER

The huge door to the House of Foryx was almost as tall as the Wizard Tower doors. It was made out of great planks of ebony, fixed together with blackened iron bars and long lines of rivets. Around the door was a heavy frame carved with monsters and bizarre creatures that stared down at Jenna, Septimus and Beetle. They stood with the snow settling onto their wolverine cloaks, plucking up the courage to ring the long bellpull that emerged from the mouth of an iron dragon poking through the granite beside the door.

"Now, you remember what we decided?" Septimus asked Beetle.

"Yep. You and Jen go in and I'll wait outside. I'll give you three hours on the timepiece and then ring the bell. If you don't come out, I'll ring every hour until you do. Okay?"

"Great." Septimus gave Beetle a thumbs-up sign.

Jenna reached up and yanked hard on the bellpull. Deep within the House of Foryx a bell jangled. Silently they stood in the steadily falling snow and waited . . . and waited.

After what felt like hours, the door creaked slowly open. A small, bent figure peered out. "Yeeeeeeeeees?" it said.

Jenna stared at the DoorKeeper. She remembered Silas hunched over the storybook, putting on his funny, squeaky voice in which he pronounced the "R" as a "W," and making silly faces at her and her brothers. An attack of giggles overcame her.

The DoorKeeper looked somewhat affronted at Jenna's laughter. Usually no one laughed when they arrived at the House of Foryx. He reminded Jenna of a brown bat. He was small, with tiny hooded eyes, a close-fitting brown moleskin cap and a long brown cape made of some kind of closely

cropped fur. Like a roosting bat, he clung to the doorknob as
if he were afraid of being blown away.

"Um, may we come in, please?" asked Jenna.

"Dooooooooo you have an appointment?" asked the
DoorKeeper, standing in the gap made by the open door, barring their way in.

"An appointment?" replied Jenna. "No, but—"

"Noooooooooo one enters the House without an appointment."
The DoorKeeper said in his swooping, bat-squeak of a voice. He
stared at Jenna reproachfully, his eyes like little black beads.

"In that case I would like to make an appointment, please,"
Jenna told him.

"*Veeeeeeeewy* well. You may enter when you have made it.
Good-bye."

"But how do we make—" The DoorKeeper began to close
the door. "No—*wait!*" Jenna yelled.

Beetle leaped forward and put his foot against the door.
The DoorKeeper pushed hard against Beetle's boot. A battle
developed between Beetle's boot and the door, but inch by
inch the DoorKeeper pushed Beetle's boot back. Beetle added
his shoulder to the pressure of his boot and leaned against the
door, but the strength of the DoorKeeper was out of propor-
tion to his small size. Jenna began to panic. They had to get

inside—they *had* to. It was unthinkable to be so close to Nicko and to have the door slammed in their faces. She threw herself at the door, adding her weight to Beetle's, but still the door kept closing.

"Stop!" yelled Septimus. "We don't need an appointment." He thrust the **Questing Stone** under the nose of the DoorKeeper. "We've got this."

The DoorKeeper stopped pushing and looked at the **Stone**. He peered up at Septimus and said suspiciously, "What, are *all* of you on the **Queste**?"

"Yes," said Septimus defiantly.

"Typical. You wait thousands of years for one Appwentice and then thwee come along at once."

Jenna stared at the DoorKeeper in amazement. He spoke exactly as Silas had done—he couldn't pronounce his Rs. Did Silas know about the House of Foryx, she wondered? Had *he* been here once?

The DoorKeeper scrutinized them more closely, taking in the fact that only Septimus wore a green tunic. "*You* can come in," he said to Septimus, "but the other two can't."

Jenna panicked at the thought of Septimus going into the House of Foryx on his own. If he did, she was sure they would never see him again. She imagined herself and Beetle waiting outside for days, for weeks—months even, and then going home without him. *That* was unbearable. In desperation— remembering the next part of Silas's bedtime story—she said, "We demand the Right of the Riddle."

The DoorKeeper looked at her in amazement. "You *what?*" he asked.

Aware that Septimus and Beetle were staring at her as though she had gone crazy, Jenna repeated, "We demand the Right of the Riddle."

"*The Wight of the Widdle?*"

"Yes," said Jenna very firmly, determined to keep a straight face—despite a suppressed splutter from Beetle.

"Vewy well," the DoorKeeper replied grumpily.

"Go on, then," prompted Jenna.

The DoorKeeper sighed and began to chant in his high-pitched voice,

"I spit like bacon,
I am made with an egg,
I have plenty of backbone, but lack a good leg,
I peel layers like onions, but still wemain whole,
I am long like a flagpole, yet fit in a hole,
What am I?"

Now Jenna understood Snorri's drawing. "A snake," she replied with a grin.

The DoorKeeper looked surprised and not particularly pleased. "Vewy well. You have two more. I think you will not be smiling *then*." Once more he began his chant:

> "What force and stwength cannot get thwough,
> I with a gentle touch can do.
> And many in the stweet would stand,
> Were I not a fwend at hand.
> What am I?"

Jenna knew at once. "A key," she said.

Now the DoorKeeper was irritated. "Cowect," he said very reluctantly. "But you will not find *this* one so easy." He began once again, this time chanting much faster and in a whisper. They leaned forward to catch his words.

> "I am only one color, but not one size.
> Though I'm chained to the earth, I can easily fly.
> I am pwesent in sun, but not in wain,
> I do no harm, I feel no pain.
> What am I?"

This time Jenna was stumped. What else was on the map? There was nothing she could remember.

"I'm *wait*—ing," said the DoorKeeper in a singsong sneer. "You have one minute to answer and then I shall let the **Questor** in. Alone. You two can go home—if you pay the Toll-Man enough." He gave a horrible chuckle.

In a panic, Jenna unfolded the map.

"No cheating. *I said no cheating!*" The DoorKeeper screamed excitedly. He snatched the map and began tearing it into shreds.

"No!" yelled Jenna, lunging forward to grab the map. "Give it back!"

"Jen, Jen, we don't need it anymore," said Septimus, pulling Jenna back. "We've got to keep calm and *think*."

"Twenty seconds," came the DoorKeeper's taunting squeak. "Fifteen seconds . . . ten, nine, eight, seven—"

Septimus summoned up Snorri's drawing in his mind—the snake, the key, the shaded House of Foryx.

"Four, thwee, two . . ."

And then he got it.

"One—"

"Shadow!"

The DoorKeeper glared at them. He said nothing, though

the door spoke for him as he heaved it open with a chorus of groans and Septimus stepped over the threshold. But as Jenna went to follow the DoorKeeper began to push the door closed.

"No!" yelled Beetle. "You let Jenna in." He leaped forward and threw himself at the door. The DoorKeeper staggered back, the door flew open and Jenna, Beetle and Septimus fell into the House of Foryx.

The door slammed behind them with a bang.

"Oh no!" Beetle gasped, suddenly realizing his mistake. "Let me out, *let me out!*"

It was too late. Time was suspended.

✢45✢
THE HOUSE OF FORYX

O*h, pigs,*" said Beetle. "*Pigs pigs pigs.*"

"Oh . . . *Beetle,*" whispered Jenna, feeling sick.

"I don't believe I could be so *stupid.* How are we going to get back into our Time *now?*"

The DoorKeeper looked up at Beetle. "Time?" he said with a lopsided grin. "What is Time now that you are here? Welcome to the House of Fowyx."

They were in the checker-board lobby that Aunt Ells

had described—but the tall dragon chair that Aunt Ells had so resolutely sat on was empty. Jenna felt overwhelmed by disappointment. She had expected Nicko to be sitting on the chair waiting for them just as Aunt Ells had done, and *he wasn't there*.

"Leave your bags here," said the DoorKeeper, pointing to a large cupboard.

Jenna took out Ullr from her backpack and tucked him firmly under her arm—much to the DoorKeeper's surprise. The DoorKeeper threw the bags into the cupboard, and then turned to watch the new arrivals.

In front of them was a pair of silver doors—a smaller version of those in the Wizard Tower, although much more ornate, as they were covered with hieroglyphs. The DoorKeeper pushed them open and ushered Jenna, Septimus and Beetle into the House of Foryx. They stood stock still, three small figures dwarfed between two huge marble pillars, the snow on their boots melting in the warmth and making puddles on the white marble floor. Before them was a great space lit with thousands of candles and yet still shadowy and dim.

Jenna felt dizzy, as though she were standing on the edge of a whirling carousel in a foggy, silent fairground, waiting for her turn—and she did not want her turn to come. Septimus was reminded of the Wizard Tower. There was a certain sense of things not being quite what they appeared to be, a feeling of things shifting slightly whenever you tried to focus on them, giving the sensation that the more you looked, the less you saw. Beetle was reminded of something too—the inside of the Dangerous Bin in the yard at the Manuscriptorium. On a dare he had once taken off the lid and seen a deep, foggy whirlpool inside that had made him want to dive in and swim around and around forever—until Foxy had grabbed his collar and pulled him away.

The DoorKeeper regarded their expressions with amusement. He generally made a point of being unamused by everything, but he made an exception for the expressions on the faces of newcomers as they tried to make sense of the Eddies of Time. After some minutes, having had his fill of fun for the day—indeed for the next few months—the DoorKeeper scuttled off through a tiny gilded door in the pillar next to Jenna and slammed it shut.

The slamming of the door brought them back to reality. "Come on," whispered Septimus. "Let's go in." They linked arms and together they stepped into the slow, muggy vortex of candle smoke and Time.

They walked hesitantly forward, feeling as though they were wading through treacle, forcing themselves through an invisible barrier. Septimus held out the **Questing Stone**, which sat, hot, in his hand, glowing a brilliant fiery red. It shone like a beacon, clearing a path through the haze. As they pushed their way deeper into the House of Foryx, shadowy shapes that they had at first taken for drifts of candle smoke and disturbances in the air became clearer. Figures began to emerge from the miasma and circle around them.

"There are ghosts in here," Beetle whispered. "Tons of 'em."

"They're not ghosts," said Septimus. "They're real. I mean . . . alive. I can hear them. I can **Hear the Sounds of Human Heartbeats**. Hundreds of them."

"What are they doing?" Jenna whispered.

"The same as us, I expect," said Septimus. "Trying to get back to their own Time."

"But we're not doing that."

"We will be."

Jenna said nothing. Beetle felt awful.

The figures around them became increasingly solid; their robes took on colors and shapes and their faces became clear. There were farmers, hunters, women in fine clothes, serving

men and women in rough tunics, knights in all kinds of armor
and finery, a large family of exotic-looking people festooned
with gold with an interesting line in pointy headgear.

Ullr was restless. He struggled in Jenna's arms, trying to
jump down. But Jenna clutched the cat even more tightly. The
last thing she needed right now was to lose Ullr.

Jenna and Septimus were scanning the crowd, hoping to see
the familiar sight of Nicko's fair curls and Snorri's white-blond
hair. They began to realize that they, too, had become visible,
and that they—and the **Questing Stone** in particular—were
the center of attention.

Suddenly the crowd parted and a young woman in a threadbare green cloak and tunic made her way to the front, heading
straight for Septimus. She fixed Septimus with her surprisingly
brilliant green eyes and pointed a long, delicate finger at the
Stone. "You have the **Questing Stone**," she said in amazement.

Septimus nodded.

"And what are you called?"

"Um. Septimus. Septimus Heap."

The girl looked at Septimus with a puzzled expression.
"Well, Septimus Heap, you are very . . . short," she said as if
searching for the right words.

"*Short?*" asked Septimus indignantly.

"I mean . . . young. You are very *young*. Surely you have not finished your Apprenticeship?"

"No . . . I haven't," he replied, puzzled.

"So what, pray, are you doing on the **Queste**?" demanded the girl, sounding a little like Marcia.

"I—I'm not really on the **Queste**," stammered Septimus. "Or rather . . . I didn't *mean* to go on the **Queste**. Someone gave me the **Stone** and I took it by mistake."

"By *mistake*?" The girl now sounded completely like Marcia. "How *very* foolish. Still, we can't be choosy. My Master will just have to make do with you. We were expecting great things but now . . ." The girl looked Septimus up and down with an expression that said she had no expectations of any kind—let alone great ones—when it came to Septimus.

Jenna had been impatiently waiting for her chance to ask the girl if she had seen Nicko, but as she opened her mouth to speak, a tall, important-looking woman swept up to them. She was wearing a dark blue fur-edged robe and her long face reminded Beetle of a horse he used to feed apples to on the way to school. She pushed aside the grumpy girl in green.

"Welcome to Eternity," said the woman.

"Eternity?" Beetle gasped. "Are we *dead?*"

"You are alive in all Times, and yet dead in all Times," she replied. "Welcome."

Beetle thought it was not the best welcome he had ever had. He glanced at Jenna and Septimus. They did not look too thrilled either.

"I am the Guardian of this House," the horse-faced woman continued. "This House is a Place of Waiting. Here you will want for nothing, for here you will want nothing. Many arrive but few wish to leave."

A dark-haired young woman wearing a long white fur cloak and a large amount of gold jewelery pushed forward. "*Some* of us wish to leave," she interrupted the Guardian. The young woman looked at Jenna, Septimus and Beetle. "I can smell the snow on you," she said longingly. "I come from the Palaces of the Eastern SnowPlains. All I wish is to go home to my family. But *you* have Come In and told no one your Time. No one has had the chance to go."

The girl in green who, Septimus now realized, was wearing a very ancient Apprentice tunic—one of the full-length ones with the old hieroglyphs—was getting impatient. "Madam Guardian," she said. "I have come to take the Apprentice boy to our Master."

"My friends must come too," said Septimus.

The girl looked at Beetle and Jenna in surprise. "You have brought friends with you—on the *Queste?*" she said, and then she noticed Jenna's red robes and gold circlet. In a flurry of embarrassment she made a low bow. "I beg a thousand pardons, Princess. I did not realize." She turned to Septimus, even more disapprovingly. "Why did you bring the Princess, Apprentice? It is *most* foolhardy. Who will protect the Castle now?"

"I didn't *bring* her," said Septimus, feeling exasperated. "It was *her* idea. We are looking for our brother; we think he is here."

The ancient Apprentice looked shocked. "You are a Prince. Forgive me." She bowed once again.

"No—no, I'm not a Prince," said Septimus quickly.

The Apprentice stopped in midbow. "Follow me," she said curtly. She set off through the crowd, like a mother duck with three wayward ducklings. The crowd parted to allow them through, staring at them as they went.

They followed the mother duck up a broad flight of stairs that took them higher and higher until they were surrounded by the waxy haze of candle smoke that hung over the hall far below. At last, coughing and spluttering in the smoke, they came to a wide balustraded landing lined with marble benches along the walls and a hundred tiny alcoves containing yet more candles. Now that they were away from the crowd, the ancient Apprentice relaxed a little. She stopped and turned to them in the manner of a tour guide. Pointing through the haze, she said, "Here you see four stairways. Each of these leads to a tower. In each tower is an ancient Glass."

Septimus glanced at Jenna—*now* they were getting somewhere. "What kind of Glass?" he asked.

"I will not explain. You are too young to comprehend," she replied, lapsing into Marcia-speak once more. "Follow me." The girl pushed open a concealed door in the soot-stained white marble walls. "Take a candle," she instructed, pointing to a collection of lit candles in brass candleholders lined up in an alcove by the door. She took one herself and stepped through the door.

They took their candles and followed the girl into a narrow passage, which was cut into the marble walls so that the sloping sides met at a point not far above their heads. It wound steeply upward and as they followed the girl's practiced steps, they slipped and slid on the smooth marble underfoot.

"Where are we going?" asked Septimus.

The girl did not reply.

Breathless from the climb, some minutes later they arrived at the end of the passageway. The candles flared and cast distorted shadows across the smoke-blackened marble. For a moment, Septimus thought he was seeing things: in front of them, barring their way, was the big purple door that led to Marcia's rooms.

"That's Marcia's door!" Septimus gasped. He looked around at Jenna and Beetle. "It is, isn't it?"

"Looks like it," said Beetle. "Can't be though, can it? Must be a copy."

"No. It's identical. Look, there's where Marcia caught Catchpole scratching his initials when he was on door duty." Septimus pointed to a B and an unfinished C. "And that's where Spit Fyre chewed the edge, and that's where the Assassin kicked it. It's the *same*."

At Septimus's approach it did what Marcia's door always did—unlatched itself and began to swing open.

"Weird," said Beetle, trying to peer inside. "Do you suppose we'll find Marcia in there too?"

"*You* will find no one in there," the girl said to Beetle, stepping in front of him. She grabbed hold of the door handle. "Because *you* are not coming in."

"Yes, he *is*," said Jenna. "Where Sep goes we all go."

"Your Majesty," the girl began.

"*Don't* call me that," blazed Jenna.

"I am sorry. I did not wish to offend. Princess, I will give you a few minutes to say farewell to the **Questor** and then you and your servant must leave. I realize this is a sad occasion but I wish you Good Speed in returning to the Castle and Good Fortune in finding a Time that is Right. You are lucky, you have the key to this House. May your freedom to roam take you where you wish. Farewell." The girl bowed; then—taking everyone by surprise—she pushed Septimus inside, ran in after him and slammed the door in Jenna and Beetle's face.

Shocked, Jenna and Beetle looked at each other as they heard the unmistakable sound of the door **Barring**.

"Oh, *pigs*," said Beetle. "Pigs pigs *pigs*."

✢ 46 ✢
ULLR'S QUEST

Jenna *banged on the purple* door. "Sep!" she yelled. "Sep!"

Seizing his chance, Ullr wriggled out from under her arm, but Beetle grabbed his tail as he shot past. Furious, Ullr screeched. Ignoring the cat's sharp claws, Beetle picked him up and stuffed the struggling animal under his arm. "Jenna—we're going to get Septimus out. Whatever it takes," Beetle told her. "Ouch. Stop it, Ullr."

Jenna slumped against the **Barred** door in despair. "But how?" she wailed. "*How?*"

"I shall find an ax and break down the door," said Beetle quietly, looking Jenna in the eye.

Jenna returned his gaze. She knew Beetle meant what he said. "Okay," she said.

They set off down the marble passage. As a parting shot, Beetle yelled, "We'll be back!" The door stared back at them, impervious.

Waiting on a bench on the candle-filled landing was the horse-faced Guardian. As Jenna emerged through the concealed door, the Guardian got to her feet. "Princess," she said, planting herself in front of Jenna and barring her way.

"Yes?" Jenna snapped.

The Guardian smiled smoothly. She had an expression bordering on smug that irritated Jenna. "Whither do you go?"

"To find an ax," Jenna replied sharply—and then wished she hadn't.

However, the Guardian did not react. "I have some business with you," she said. "You can send your servant for what you need."

"My servant?"

The Guardian waved her arm at Beetle, who was stuck in

the passageway behind Jenna, occupied with Ullr.

Jenna was indignant. "He's not my *servant*," she said.

"What is he, then?"

"He is not a *what*; he is a *who*. And it is none of your business. Would you let me pass, please? We have things to do." Jenna tried to sidestep the Guardian but once again her way was barred.

"Whatever it is you wish to do," the Guardian told her, "there is no need for haste. You have Eternity in which to do it. You are no longer on the donkey cart of Time, forever trundling onward."

"Thank you," said Jenna icily. "But I quite *like* the donkey cart. At least it gets you somewhere. Now *excuse me*."

"You are young, so I *will* excuse you. Now give me the key."

"*What?*"

"The key." The Guardian indicated the key to the Queen's Room—a beautiful gold key set with an emerald—that hung from Jenna's belt.

"No!"

"Yes!" The Guardian grabbed Jenna, digging her nails into her arm. "You *must*," she hissed. "It belongs to the House. You have stolen it."

"I have *not*!" Jenna was furious. "Let go of me!"

The Guardian shook her head. "Not until you give me the key." She smiled, her horse teeth glinting in the candlelight. "I am patient. Time is nothing to me, although it still has meaning to you, it seems. I will wait. We can stand here as long as you like." The nails sunk deeper into Jenna's arm.

"Let go of her." There was an edge of menace in Beetle's voice that Jenna had not heard before.

"Your servant is very *loyal*," the Guardian said with a sneer.

Suddenly, a long, rumbling growl began somewhere by the Guardian's knees. She looked down and the NightUllr, ready to pounce, stared back with angry eyes. "Let go of the Princess," said Beetle quietly, "or she will set her panther on you."

The Guardian let go. A panther was a panther, whatever Time it was.

Beetle grabbed Jenna's hand. "Come on," he said, "we've got an ax to find."

Too afraid to move, the Guardian watched them walk swiftly across the landing and then—as the panther suddenly veered off and raced up one of the turret stairs—saw them break into a run.

"Ullr!" yelled Jenna, racing off in pursuit. "Come back! *Ullr!*"

Unused to such excitement, the Guardian resumed her place on the bench and waited—knowing that all things in the House of Foryx come to those who wait.

The turret stairs were steep, narrow and seemingly endless. Jenna and Beetle pounded up after Ullr and came to a halt at a small stone archway. The stairs carried on upward but through the archway Jenna could see a long, dark corridor lit by a few sparse candles. She stopped and tried to catch her breath. Which way had Ullr gone?

Beetle caught up with her. "Can you see him?" she puffed.

Too breathless to speak, Beetle shook his head. Then, in the light of the very last candle at the end of the corridor he caught a glimpse of the orange tip of Ullr's tail. "There!"

With a new burst of energy, Jenna lifted up her long tunic and hurtled down the corridor, with Beetle close behind. The corridor followed the shape of the octagonal turret, each 135-degree bend turning just enough to obscure their view of the next. The turret was rougher than the marble opulence of the main part of the House of Foryx and their feet echoed on bare stone flags as they ran. So intent were Jenna and Beetle on catching up with Ullr that they paid no attention to the little rooms that led off from the corridor. Each one was lit by a

single candle and occupied by shadowy figures slowly per-
forming their familiar everyday routines, as some of them had
been doing for thousands of years.

As Jenna and Beetle rounded each corner, they caught a
brief glimpse of Ullr's tail disappearing around the next—then
the next and the next. A few of the inhabitants of the turret
glanced up, first at the panther and then at the hurried footsteps of Jenna and Beetle, but none paid them much heed.

As they rounded yet another corner Jenna realized there
was no sight of Ullr's tail. She stopped to catch her breath.
"Can't see . . . him," she puffed as a few seconds later Beetle
caught up with her. "Gone."

Beetle leaned against the wall, gasping. He had led a seden-
tary life up until the previous few days and the last few minutes had just about finished him off. "Haaaah . . ." was all he
could manage in reply.

Suddenly, from somewhere down the corridor, there was a
scream and then a yell of joy. "Ullr! Ullr, Ullr, *Ullr!*"

Jenna looked at Beetle, half excited, half afraid. "It's Snorri,"
she whispered.

"Is it?"

"Yes. It is. Oh, Beetle—Snorri is *here*. So Nicko . . . Nicko must be too." Then an awful thought struck Jenna. What if Nicko wasn't there—what if something had happened to him and it was just Snorri? Jenna looked at Beetle. "I'm scared," she whispered. "Scared we've come all this way and he won't be here."

Beetle put his arm around Jenna. "There's only one way to find out," he said. "Come on, let's go see."

It felt like the longest walk Jenna had ever taken. She and Beetle went slowly, looking inside each dimly lit room. In the first room were two beds and a simple table. Two girls were sitting at the table chatting quietly, a bottle of wine between them. The second room was sparse and barracklike; at the end of a narrow bed with folded blankets a man sat polishing a gleaming suit of armor. In the third room a hammock was slung from one wall to another. The only piece of furniture was a large trunk, on which an old man with a full white beard and a tattered sailor's uniform sat knitting. The fourth room was lined with books; in the shadows Jenna saw the outline of a woman in a long, dark dress hunched over a desk, writing. The fifth room was empty. The sixth contained three members of the pointy hat contingent sitting around a table, playing a board game. The seventh contained Snorri Snorrelssen.

Clutching Beetle's hand, with her heart beating so loudly she was sure Snorri could hear it, Jenna walked softly through the doorway and stood in the shadows. All she could see was the candlelight reflecting off Snorri's white-blond hair and the dark shape of Ullr enclosed in Snorri's arms. There was no sign of Nicko. And then—

"Jen?" A voice came from the shadows beside Jenna. "Jen! Oh, *Jen!*" She heard the sound of a chair being pushed back from a table and clattering to the ground, felt a whirlwind enveloping her and then she was lifted off her feet and spun around and around—as if she were a little girl once again.

Nicko set Jenna back on her feet, but Jenna would not let go. Beetle saw her head buried in her brother's grubby sailor's tunic, her shoulders shaking with—Beetle was not sure if it was tears or laughter. He was still not sure when Jenna looked up, her eyes bright and her smile the biggest he had ever seen.

"We found him. We *found* him!" laughed Jenna.

✣ 47 ✣
SEPTIMUS'S QUESTE

Septimus heard nothing of Jenna's shouts and thumps through the thick purple door. Angrily, he instructed the door to **UnBar**.

The girl laughed. "You will not succeed, Septimus Heap. Though 'tis true, the door is a **Twin**, but all identical twins have some differences. You have just discovered one of them." The Apprentice appraised Septimus with a disappointed air. "I have spent a long time waiting for a **Questor** to arrive. I had

hoped for someone more . . . mature to pass some days with.
Do you play cards?"

"*Cards?*"

"I could teach you a few games. I expect you could manage
Snap."

"*Snap?*"

The girl sighed. "Possibly not," she said.

Septimus said nothing. The girl reminded him of Lucy
Gringe—although she was *much* more irritating. He gave up
any hope of a reasonable conversation and turned his attention to his new surroundings. He was in a huge octagonal
chamber. Above him was a beautiful glass dome through
which he could see the darkening sky suffused with the last
pinkish rays of the sunset. He was, he guessed, at the very top
of the House of Foryx. Watched by the eagle eyes of the
ancient Apprentice, Septimus wandered around the chamber.
It was a vast place, and the furnishings—the rugs, the lapis
chests, the rich tapestries—reminded him of Marcia's rooms.
But that, thought Septimus, did not completely explain the
oddly familiar feeling. There was something else . . . something more essential—*the smell of* **Magyk**.

"What *is* this place?" Septimus asked the grumpy
Apprentice.

"The House of Foryx," came the reply.

"I know that," Septimus replied, trying not to betray his impatience. "But *this* place. This *room*—what *is* it?"

"You will find out soon enough."

Septimus sighed. He tried one last question. "Who *are* you?"

To his surprise the girl actually answered his question. "I am Talmar," she said.

Talmar. The name was familiar. Septimus tried to remember why—and then it came to him. Suddenly, he felt very odd indeed. "Not . . . Talmar *Ray Bell*?" he asked.

A look of amazement appeared on the girl's face. "How do you know?" she asked.

Septimus grinned, pleased with the effect of his question.

Somewhere in the distance came the silvery sound of a bell. Talmar assumed her air of superiority once more and pronounced, "My Master is ready. Follow me, Septimus Heap."

With the setting of the sun, the glass dome had darkened. As Septimus followed Talmar through the chamber, candles sprang into flame one by one to light their path. At the far end of the chamber, Talmar drew back some heavy curtains to reveal a figure sitting by a fire on a low, comfortable chair not unlike the one that sat close to the fire in Marcia's rooms— the one she always insisted was *hers*.

Talmar beckoned Septimus inside. He stepped through the curtains and the figure—a frail, elderly man with long, wavy white hair held back with an ExtraOrdinary Wizard headband—looked up. The light of the candle flames shone in his brilliant green eyes, making them seem almost on fire.

"This is our **Questor**, Septimus Heap," said Talmar.

"Welcome, **Questor**," the old man said with a smile. He started to get up and Talmar rushed to his side to help him. As he stood, a little bent and unsteady on his feet, Septimus saw that he was dressed in an archaic set of ExtraOrdinary Wizard robes—from the ancient days when they were embroidered with hieroglyphs in gold thread. Leaning on Talmar's arm, the old man walked slowly toward Septimus.

"From the Old to the New," he murmured in an accent Septimus had not heard before. "Greetings."

"Greetings," Septimus replied, taking the thin old hand.

The old man looked down at Septimus's right hand. Septimus followed his gaze and saw the Dragon Ring, which was shining brighter than he had ever seen it do before—like a tiny lamp on his right index finger. "You have my ring," murmured the ancient ExtraOrdinary Wizard.

"*Your* ring?" said Septimus. "But I thought it had only ever belonged to . . . Oh. Oh, *of course*."

"Ah. You know who I am?" asked the old man.

Septimus nodded. *Now* he understood. "You're Hotep-Ra," he said.

As the stars shimmered through the dome and the full moon traveled across the sky, Septimus, Talmar Ray Bell and Hotep-Ra sat picking at a feast of delicacies, which had appeared on the long, low table that Talmar had set in front of the fire. Talmar poured mint tea into three small colored glasses.

Hotep-Ra raised his glass and said, "Let us celebrate the end of your **Queste**." He downed the tea in one gulp. Septimus and Talmar followed suit.

"There is but one thing left for you to do before your **Queste** is ended."

"Oh?" Septimus feared the worst.

"You must give me the **Questing Stone**."

Septimus smiled—there was nothing he would like better. He took the fiery red stone from his pocket.

Relieved to be rid of the **Stone**, Septimus put it in the outstretched hand. Hotep-Ra placed his other hand over the **Stone** and Septimus saw the bright light shine through, showing the bones of the hand beneath the skin like dark red shadows. And then the light began to fade and Hotep-Ra's hands became opaque once more. He uncupped his hands and the **Questing Stone** was now an inky black. "You have completed the **Queste**." Hotep-Ra smiled at Septimus. "Now for the reason I have brought you all this way: come sit beside me and tell me all that has happened at the Castle in my absence."

"*All?*" asked Septimus, wondering how he was supposed to know.

"As Apprentice you will know such things. Now, before you begin I shall place my sign on the back of this stone and return it to you as a memento of your journey."

Septimus was not sure that he actually wanted a memento of the journey but he said nothing. Hotep-Ra turned the stone over and his expression clouded.

"What is it, Master?" asked Talmar.

"I do not understand. I numbered these **Stones** with a **Hidden** tally. As each one was Drawn the number would show itself. This is number *twenty-one*. This is the last **Stone**," muttered Hotep-Ra.

"I *thought* something was wrong," said Talmar, glaring at

Septimus. "He is far too young. He has not even finished his Apprenticeship."

"Has he not?" asked the Wizard, puzzled. "But this is an honor reserved for the last day of the Apprenticeship."

"Exactly. He must have stolen it. He is no more than a common thief."

Septimus had had enough of Talmar's rudeness. He exploded with indignation. "How *dare* you call me a thief! Anyway, what would anyone want to steal *that* for?" he asked. "It has been nothing but trouble. And I can tell you that I *am* the last **Questor**—it was the last **Stone** in the **Pot**. And I can tell you something else—all the others who went on the **Queste** never returned. It is not an honor—it is a curse. Every Apprentice *dreads* their last day because of it. And Tertius Fume is—"

"Tertius Fume?" Hotep-Ra gasped. "Has that lying, under-handed, double-crossing streak of Wurm Slime returned?"

"Well, his *ghost* has," said Septimus.

"His *ghost*? Ha! At least he is no longer Living. But what effrontery—I **Banish** him and he sneaks back as soon as I am gone. When did this happen?"

"A long time ago. He's *ancient*."

"How ancient?"

"I—I don't really know. He's one of the oldest in the Castle."

"One of the *oldest* . . ." Hotep-Ra fell silent for some minutes. Neither Talmar nor Septimus dared speak. Finally the ancient ExtraOrdinary Wizard said very quietly, as if expecting bad news, "Tell me, Apprentice—how many ExtraOrdinary Wizards have there been since Talmar and I left the Castle?"

"Seven hundred and seventy-six," Septimus said.

"*You jest!*" exclaimed Hotep-Ra.

"No. I had to learn it when I first became an Apprentice. My ExtraOrdinary Wizard made me write it out and stick it on the wall. Anyway I counted them all last week."

Hotep-Ra swallowed hard. "I thought it was maybe five or six at the most," he said quietly. "Things are not as they should be."

"How—how should they be?" asked Septimus.

Hotep-Ra sighed. "Eat, fellow Dragon Master," he said. "Tell me about your **Queste** and I will tell you about mine."

And so Septimus sat under the moonlit dome and told Hotep-Ra how he had come to the House of Foryx. And then, while he hungrily ate from the dishes of fragrant fruits, spicy meats and fish and drank mint tea, he listened to the soft, melodious frail voice of the Castle's very first ExtraOrdinary Wizard.

"When I was a young man," said Hotep-Ra, "and I *was* a young man once, it was forbidden to dabble with Time. But, like many young men, I did not always obey the rules. And when I discovered the secret of suspending Time I knew I had to find a place where I could keep my secret and make it work. I traveled far and wide until I came across a beautiful forest in the center of which was an abyss. From the middle of this chasm rose a tall rock and when I saw it I knew I had found the perfect place to build my secret House of Time.

"And so I set to work. First, I **Caused** a bridge to be made—it is a beautiful bridge is it not?"

Septimus nodded. Hotep-Ra spoke the truth: the bridge was beautiful.

Hotep-Ra smiled. "Beautiful but terrifying. Now, among the more **Magykal** Wizards, there is an unfortunate tendency to be afraid of heights. I have to admit, I wished to keep my fellow Wizards away from my House of Time—I wanted no interference and no scheming. Wizards can be jealous of true

talent, Apprentice. They are not above sabotaging projects of
the more gifted. Remember that. And so, to make doubly sure
of being left in peace, I enticed the Foryx, which many now
think are mythical beasts, for they are no longer seen—except
here. I **Caused** them to forever run around the precipice path
to guard my House of Time. I soon noticed that those who
came began to call this place the House of Foryx and I was
pleased, as it gave no clue that this was a place where All
Times Do Meet.

"When I became old I left the Castle, the dear Queen and
my poor Dragon Boat, and I came to my House of Foryx. I
wish now that I had come earlier, when I still had my
strength, but I wanted to see my Dragon Boat restored. Never
get a boat repaired by the Port men, Apprentice—they are lag-
gards and thieves. As I made my way to the House of Foryx, I
comforted myself that although I would miss the Castle terribly, I would still know what was going on, because I had set
up the **Queste**.

"The **Queste** was to be a great honor. I had toyed with the
idea of having only the most talented Apprentices go on my
Queste, but then I realized that this would be unfair, so I
devised a lottery. I filled a huge urn with hundreds of lapis

stones, of which twenty-one were inscribed with a golden Q,
and which each Apprentice had a fair chance of drawing. I
thought it would be a wonderful culmination to seven years'
hard study to be picked to go on the **Queste**—to visit the
founder of the Wizard Tower, to bring him the news of the
Castle and to return with new knowledge and understanding.
In order to make it safe—for I did not want to risk the lives of
anyone—I **Engendered** a boat to take the chosen Apprentice
safely across the sea and up the great river right to the edge of
what was a beautiful forest. I also **Engendered** seven
Questing Guards to escort them on their journey, to guide
them past the Foryx and across the bridge. Their most important job was, of course, to wait outside my House so that the
Questor would Go Out into his or her own Time. I made sure
the **Stone** would also guide them here for safety, should the
Guards fail. That was my plan. But that is not, so it seems,
how it is?"

"No," said Septimus sadly.

"There have been *twenty* **Questors** before you, you say?"
said Hotep-Ra.

Septimus nodded.

"*All* perished?"

"Well, no one came back. And they would have if they could, wouldn't they?"

Hotep-Ra nodded slowly and lapsed into thought. "It is Fume," he said. "He has **Darkened** this **Queste**. All you tell me: the frozen forest, the silence, the foul and moaning fog, the murderous **Questing Guards**—do not look so shocked, Apprentice, how else could he make sure that no one reached me? It is him. I *know* it."

Septimus knew it too.

"He was my closest friend," said Hotep-Ra sadly. "Once I trusted him completely. I loved him like a brother. But one time while I was away on the marshes attending to my dear Dragon Boat, he took over the Tower and sent his guards out to kill me." Hotep-Ra shook his head in disbelief. "He had been planning that for years—and all the while showing me nothing but friendship. Think how you would feel, Apprentice, if your closest friend did this to you."

Septimus nodded in sympathy. He couldn't even *imagine* Beetle ever doing anything like that.

"Tertius only had the Tower for seven days, but it took seven *years* to repair the **Darke** damage he did. I **Banished** him, of course." Hotep-Ra sighed. "And I have to admit that I missed him, even after he had betrayed me. As he left, he said that I might think I would control the Tower forever, but it would not be so. He swore he would return and that I would be sorry. I remember I told him there was nothing he could do that would make me sorrier than I was then, but now I think that is not true, for twenty young lives have been lost, and I never knew. And all those years I have been alone, waiting . . ." Hotep-Ra's voice trailed off sadly into the night.

As Talmar busied herself with rugs and blankets for the nighttime chill, Septimus sat quietly, watching his **Questing Stone** shimmer a deep iridescent blue in the light of the full moon, which shone through the dome above. He had done it, he told himself in amazement. *He had completed the **Queste**.* But then a feeling of sadness came over him—twenty others had not. Septimus thought about what they had missed. Not only the rest of their lives, but also a **Magykal** night talking to the first-*ever* ExtraOrdinary Wizard. Septimus shivered. He smelled the **Magyk** in the air and, for the first time since he had started reading the works of Marcellus Pye, he felt content. This was good. And Marcia—Marcia would be proud. If he ever saw her again.

✳ ✳ ✳

Early the next morning, his head spinning, Septimus bade
farewell to Hotep-Ra and walked out of the octagonal chamber.
The Twin of Marcia's door closed gently behind him. With a
candle in his hand, provided by a marginally more friendly
Talmar Ray Bell, he wandered down the steep narrow marble
passage and emerged onto the smoky balustrade landing.

Septimus knew it was morning—he had seen the sun rise
through the glass dome—but there was no way of knowing
that inside the blind House of Foryx. Wearily, he sat on one
of the benches—avoiding the horse-faced Guardian, who still
sat and waited—and like her, he too waited. All who inhabit
the House of Foryx will pass by the landing if you wait long
enough, Hotep-Ra had advised. Septimus was prepared to wait
for as long as it took for Jenna and Beetle to pass by. But the
combination of the warmth of the muggy atmosphere and his
restless night soon began to have an effect, and it was not long
before Septimus had lain down on his bench and fallen asleep.

He dreamed the strangest dreams: Hotep-Ra and Tertius
Fume dancing down Wizard Way, Marcia flying Spit Fyre
through a thunderstorm, Talmar playing cards with a crocodile
and Nicko shaking him, saying, "Wake up, you lazy lummox!"
The shaking continued past the dream and blearily

Septimus opened one eye to find himself face to face with—
Nicko. In a split second Septimus was wide-awake. "Nik!" He
threw his arms around his brother. "Hey, you're *real*."

"And so are *you*." Nicko laughed.

"Sep—oh, Sep, you've *escaped*!" Jenna cried happily.

"Well, it wasn't really like that but—"

The tall, horse-faced woman pushed between them and
clamped a heavy hand on Jenna's shoulder.

"When you have finished your touching reunion, I will
have the key. *Now* please."

Beetle sprang forward and pulled the hand away. "Leave her
alone," he said.

But in the absence of a panther, the Guardian was not to be
deterred. She grabbed Jenna's arm. Jenna yelped in pain. "*Give
me the key*. If I have to take it I shall use it to lock *you* away. For
Eternity."

Nicko loathed the Guardian. She had once called Snorri a
witch and **Hidden** her in another turret for—how long?
Nicko did not know. Days, weeks, centuries—he had no idea.
Now it was payback time. Using more force than he knew was
necessary, Nicko grabbed the Guardian's wrist and angrily
wrenched her arm away. Suddenly there was a loud scream

and the Guardian was cradling her wrist, her hand hanging limp.

"Nik!" gasped Jenna. "You've broken her arm."

"Desperate times, desperate measures," said Nicko, heading for the stairs down the hall. "Let's get out of here. Who is waiting outside? I bet it's Sam, isn't it?"

Jenna ran to keep up with him. "No."

"Or Dad. Must be Dad. I can't wait to see him. And Mum."

Jenna couldn't bear it. "No! Oh, Nik, I didn't tell you. There's no one outside."

Nicko stopped dead. *"No one?"*

"No."

Beetle stared at his feet and wished he could disappear forever—until it occurred to him that that was exactly what he was *going* to do. He felt terrible.

"Then we're *all* stuck," said Nicko angrily. "Just like me and Snorri. We'll never go home. *Ever.*"

"Not necessarily," said Septimus. "I have an idea."

✢4 8✢
DOOR TO DOOR

S omeone," *Marcia told Catchpole,*
"has defaced my door."

Catchpole jumped up guiltily,
his sparse sandy hair standing up
in surprise. Marcia had caught
him taking a quick nap in the
Old Spells cupboard. "Oh," he said.

"If this is your idea of a joke I don't
think it is very funny," said Marcia icily.

Catchpole balanced on one leg like an
embarrassed heron. He wasn't sure what
Marcia was talking about but it sounded
like trouble—again.
"Oh, dear," he said.

"Well, is it?"

"Is it what?"

"Is it your idea of a joke? I know your penchant for drawing on doors."

The penny dropped. "Oh, no. It wasn't me, I promise. Absolutely not. Honestly—*it wasn't.*"

Marcia sighed. She believed him. The bizarre scribbles were far too complicated for Catchpole to have done. "Well, go get a bucket and a scrubbing brush. I want them cleaned off. I'm off to see Sarah Heap and I expect a nice clean door by the time I return. Got that?"

"Got that, Madam Marcia. Will do." Reprieved, Catchpole shot off to find a bucket and a scrubbing brush.

"No!" Jenna gasped. "It's disappearing! Stop. *Stop!*" In front of them the map was vanishing.

"Quick, tell it to stop," said Nicko.

"Stop!" yelled Jenna.

"No—no, I mean write on it. Quick, Jen, before it all goes."

Jenna picked up the piece of chalk and scrawled: STOP! DO NOT ERASE.

✳ ✳ ✳

Catchpole screamed and dropped the bucket of hot soapy water on his foot. Huge, looping letters were writing themselves across the door as he watched. It was worse than when he had started—what would Marcia say? Catchpole picked up the scrubbing brush and got to work with a vengeance, but even as he scrubbed, more words appeared in the very spot he had just cleaned. Suddenly Catchpole understood—this was a test. Marcia had set it so that he could prove himself worthy of being reinstated as a sub-Wizard. Catchpole was determined not to fail. As more and more words came into view telling him STOP! THIS IS AN URGENT MESSAGE! Catchpole sped up, catching each one with his scrubbing brush as soon as it appeared, splashing water everywhere. Soon the landing outside Marcia's rooms was a large, chalky puddle.

"More chalk!" yelled Jenna. "Quick!"

Snorri handed her a stub of chalk. "It's the last one," she said.

Jenna stopped, her hand poised above the door. She could not risk wasting this precious last piece of chalk. They watched MARCIA, WE ARE HERE! disappear from the door, followed by the rest of the precious map until nothing remained of Jenna's messages. "It's not going to work," she said miserably. "The door just gets rid of it."

Everyone fell silent, a feeling of despair hanging in the air. Suddenly Septimus said, "It *did* work. But someone is washing it off."

"Who would do that?" asked Nicko.

"Marcia wouldn't," said Jenna, "or any of the Wizards. They'd *know* it was important."

"So who would be so *stupid*?" said Nicko.

Septimus knew exactly who. "Catchpole," he said.

"*Catchpole?*"

"Yep. It has to be. No one else in the Tower would *dream* of doing that. Jen, give me the chalk. I know what to write."

Jenna handed over the chalk. She hoped Septimus knew what he was doing.

IS THAT YOU, CATCHPOLE? Septimus wrote in very clear letters.

"Is that you" was quickly erased, but the rubbing out stopped at the "C" of "Catchpole."

"I'll wait for him to reply," said Septimus. "There's no point wasting any more chalk until we know he's figured it out."

Outside the Twin of Marcia's door five people watched with

bated breath. Seven long minutes passed while Catchpole threw the spiral stairs into fast mode and zoomed down to the Old Spells cupboard to get his pen.

He returned to find an irate Marcia accompanied by an anxious Sarah Heap—who Marcia had bumped into under the Great Arch. Marcia was staring at the door, her robes gathered around her ankles, her purple pythons soaking up the chalky water like a couple of pointy sponges. Catchpole jumped off the stairs, skidded across the soapy floor and careened into his bucket, sending the rest of the water flying over Marcia. "What do you think you are doing?" she exploded. "I ask you to perform the simple task of removing graffiti from my door and you have the *cheek* to daub it with your own name. Catchpole, this is the last straw. You are *fired!*"

Sarah Heap looked shocked. No wonder Septimus had run away if Marcia spent so much time yelling like this.

Catchpole was horrified. "No!" he pleaded. "No, it's not what it looks like."

"Ha!" said Marcia. "I've heard that one before. Believe me, Catchpole, it generally is *exactly* what it looks like—and then some."

Catchpole produced his pen and waved it desperately. "But I was just—"

"I have no need to see what you've been writing with, thank you," said Marcia. "I have better things to do. Stand aside, will you?"

"No! No, you don't understand." Catchpole threw himself in front of the door to stop Marcia from going inside. "Please, Madam Marcia, *please*. I didn't do it. I can prove it. *Please*." There was a break in Catchpole's voice that caught Marcia by surprise.

"Very well," she said. "Prove it."

"Oh, thank you, thank you, *thank you!*"

"For heaven's sake, stop groveling. Just get on with it."

Oblivious to the soapy water, Catchpole kneeled down and wrote on the door, IT IS I, BORIS CATCHPOLE. WHO ARE YOU?

Marcia tapped her foot impatiently, making little splashing noises. But as the words SEPTIMUS (BOY 412) appeared, the splashing noises stopped. Sarah Heap screamed.

"See?" said Catchpole. "It does it on its own. It's said lots of things."

"Like what?" asked Marcia.

"I don't know," Catchpole replied. "I was too busy washing them off."

"You idiot! You *washed them off?*"

"But you *told* me to."

"Oh, for goodness sake, give me your pen." Marcia snatched the pen from Catchpole's trembling hand and wrote: SEPTIMUS, IT'S MARCIA HERE. WHERE ARE YOU?

Far away in the House of Foryx a loud cheer went up.

✝49✝
IN TIME

As they emerged, *jubilant*, *onto* the balustrade landing, a reception committee was waiting. Two huge body-guards leaped forward and grabbed Nicko. Snorri screamed. These were the very same bodyguards—known as Fowler and Brat—who had taken her away after a neighbor had accused her of Ill-Wishing his cactus.

"Let go!" yelled Nicko, struggling furiously. A furor broke out. Snorri aimed a kick at Fowler—a huge man with a gleaming bald head—who had Nicko's arms pinned behind his back. Septimus and Beetle weighed in, rapidly followed by Jenna. Brat, who was much the smaller of the guards but was surprisingly strong and sported a pair of impressive cauliflower ears, swatted them away like irritating flies.

The Guardian stood in the background, half obscured by the candle smoke, her arm swathed in bandages. "Take him to the fortified room," she called out. "I do not wish to *ever* see him again!"

"Don't worry, Madam Guardian, you won't." Fowler laughed. "You can be *sure* of that. *Oof*—get *off*, boy," he snarled. This was addressed to Beetle, who had succeeded in getting him in a headlock.

The bodyguards dragged Nicko across the landing, accompanied by Snorri yelling and kicking their shins, and Jenna hanging on to her brother like a limpet. Beetle still had Fowler in a headlock—but to no discernable effect—and Ullr followed the melee, hissing.

But Septimus had stepped back from the fray. From his Apprentice belt he took a small crystal shaped like a shard of ice. Holding it carefully between finger and thumb he pointed the thinnest end at Fowler, who was now trying to drag Nicko and his entourage through a dark archway on the far side of the landing.

"**Freeze!**" yelled Septimus.

Beetle **Froze**. Horrified, Septimus realized his mistake. However, having a **Frozen** Beetle dangling from his neck like a dead weight had put Fowler off his stride, and Nicko seized his chance. He struggled free, grabbed Snorri and in a moment they were running for the stairs. Furious, Fowler shrugged Beetle off, and Beetle toppled onto the floor like a felled tree. "Beetle!" cried Jenna. "Oh, *Beetle!*"

Nicko hurtled past Septimus, pulling Snorri behind him. "Come on, Sep!" Nicko yelled. "Let's get out of this place. I've had *enough*—I don't care *what* Time we end up in."

"No, Nik!" shouted Septimus. "No—*don't.*"

But Nicko and Snorri were racing down the wide, sweeping stairs, with Fowler and Brat in hot pursuit.

Septimus ran to Jenna. "You've got to stop Nik," he told her. "He's flipped. Stop him before he's gone *forever.*"

Jenna leaped to her feet. "But, Beetle . . ."

"He'll be okay. I'll fix it. Now, *go!*"

Jenna sped off, pushing her way past the Guardian, who made a half-hearted grab for her, and raced down the stairs.

Septimus left the **Frozen** Beetle and leaned over the balustrade. He saw Jenna flying down the stairs, her red cloak streaming out behind. Far below through the candle smoke, he could see the hazy outlines of Nicko and Snorri reach the crowded hall and begin to push their way through, heading for the silver doors. Closing fast were Fowler and Brat.

Mistaking Septimus's apparent lack of concern, the Guardian joined him. "We will soon have the troublemaker." She smiled. Septimus did not reply. The Guardian felt suddenly uncomfortable and moved away. She didn't like the strange unfocused look in Septimus's eyes and she particularly did not like the peculiar purple mist that was beginning to surround him—she was afraid it might be catching.

Down in the Great Hall of the House of Foryx, Brat had overtaken Fowler and was within an arm's length of Nicko. He reached out to grab him but at the last second Nicko eluded him by darting behind a large man in a tall, pointy hat. Suddenly Fowler stopped, looked puzzled, then yelled, "Idiot—he's over there!" Brat wheeled around to see his quarry heading back up the stairs—how had the boy managed *that*?

Leaning over the balustrade, Septimus was concentrating

harder than he had ever done before. To **Project** a living person is one of the hardest **Projections** to do. Septimus was struggling using **Magykal** powers he never believed he had but, like all **Projections**, it was not totally perfect. There were fuzzy edges and momentary gaps. Luckily the candle smoke covered up any imperfections and Septimus was careful to make sure the **Projected** Nicko was running just far enough ahead of the guards for them not to get too close a look. Exhilarated now by his mastery of **Magyk**, Septimus took the **Projection** up the stairs. As the mirror image of Nicko came closer, he stepped back to give himself some distance—for the nearer a **Projection** was, the harder it was to maintain. The Guardian noted approvingly that Septimus watched the young thug rush past but did nothing; she had misjudged the Apprentice, she thought. Her long nose shone with excitement as she watched her faithful Fowler and Brat—sweating profusely and bright red in the face—close in. They would have the boy any moment now.

Septimus sent his **Projection** racing into Nicko and Snorri's turret and then relaxed. All he had to do now was **Project** the sound of running footsteps and let the guards exhaust themselves. He looked down to see if Jenna had managed to stop Nicko from leaving, but the candle smoke obscured his view. Septimus longed to rush down and talk some sense into Nicko, but he knew he had to trust Jenna to do it. He had something else to do—something that could not wait. Beetle needed **DeFrosting**.

The Guardian watched Septimus lead a shaky Beetle down the long sweeping staircase and as they disappeared into the haze of candle smoke she heard Fowler and Brat thudding back down the turret steps. She smiled the kind of smile that you might expect from a horse that, determined to unseat its rider, sees a low tree branch come into sight.

Jenna had caught up with Nicko and Snorri in the checker-board lobby. "No, Nik!" she yelled. "No, don't go. Please. Not on your own. *Please.*"

"I'm not staying here," said Nicko. "I'm not spending the rest of my life—and then some—locked in a filthy hole under the ground. They took Snorri there for ages. It was awful."

"It was only a few days, Nicko," said Snorri.

"Who *knows* how long it was," Nicko growled. "This place messes with your head. No one knows how long *any* Time is—it's crazy. *I can't stand it anymore.*" He lunged for the door to the outside Time but Jenna caught his hand in midair.

"Nik! Just promise one thing. Please."

"*What?*"

"That you'll wait for Sep and Beetle."

"*If* they turn up. You don't understand, Jen. It's weird here. People disappear."

"They will turn up. They *will.*" As if in answer, the silver doors to the lobby suddenly flew open and Septimus and Beetle rushed in.

"They're coming!" gasped Septimus. "My **Projection** broke down when I **DeFrosted** Beetle."

"Okay, that's it," said Nicko. "I'm off."

"Nik—*wait!*" said Jenna. She unclipped the key to the Queen's Room that hung from her belt and shoved it into a small keyhole almost hidden in the middle of a hieroglyph on the right-hand silver door. As soon as she turned it they heard the sound of the doors **Barring.**

"That won't stop her," said Nicko. "*She's* got a key too."

"It will if I leave it in the lock," said Jenna with a smile.

"Good one, Jen," Septimus said with a grin.

✳　　✳　　✳

They sat in the checkerboard lobby, poised between two worlds. Like her Aunt Ells before her, Snorri was seated on the tall dragon chair. She rested her feet on the thick, curled tail, and her thin frame almost disappeared into the carved dragon wings that formed the back of the chair. Nicko perched on the broad dragon-head arms. Both he and Snorri looked tense and worn.

Jenna, Septimus and Beetle had retrieved their backpacks and were sitting on the cold marble floor, leaning against them.

Nicko looked at them, shaking his head with amazement. "I still don't believe it—that you're really here. I just don't. We've waited so long, haven't we, Snorri?"

Snorri nodded.

"I'm just very glad *you're* here," Jenna said quietly. "I was so afraid you wouldn't be."

"I very nearly wasn't," said Nicko. "There were so many times when I decided to leave. The doors are open and they don't stop you, you know. But they tell you that you could go out into any Time at all. Even a time before"—Nicko shuddered—"before there were any people around. Before the House of Foryx existed—so you could never get back. Snorri always said we should wait. She was right—but then she usually is." Snorri blushed.

"Yes," said Jenna, thawing a little toward Snorri. "She was right."

A pensive silence fell in the checkerboard lobby, but it did not last long. Suddenly there was a loud rapping on the silver doors, followed by a frantic rattling—someone was trying to put a key into the lock.

"It won't go!" came the Guardian's angry voice. "Guards, break down the doors!"

At once Nicko was on his feet, his eyes wild. "They won't get me," he declared. "I'll Go Out and take my chance rather than that."

"I will come with you," said Snorri. She picked up Ullr. "Ullr, too. He will come."

"And so will we," said Jenna solemnly. She looked at Septimus and Beetle. "Won't we?"

Septimus glanced at Beetle. "Count me in," said Beetle.

"And me," said Septimus.

"*Really?*" asked Nicko. "But it's me they're after, not you."

"We're in it together now, Nik," said Septimus. "Whatever happens."

Now rhythmic thumping began. Fowler was hurling himself at the doors. Soon the lock, which was the weakest point, began to give.

"I'm Going Out now," said Nicko, very composed and sure, his hand rested on the heavy iron latch that fastened the great ebony door of the House of Foryx. He looked at Jenna, Septimus and Beetle. "But I want you to stay," he told them, raising his voice against the rhythmic thudding behind him. "You still have a chance to go home, to see Mum and Dad and tell them what has happened. To tell them I'm sorry . . ."

Septimus took a deep breath. "No, Nik. We're coming with you," he said, glancing around at the others. Four pairs of terrified eyes met his—the enormity of what they were about to do had just hit them.

Thud.

Nicko's eyes felt blurry. He blinked. "Okay," he said, "here we go."

Thud. Thud.

Nicko went to lift the latch of the ebony door, which would take them to the outside Time—whatever that might be. And as his hand touched the latch, there came a furious knocking on the door that drowned out the thuds behind them. Everyone jumped.

Septimus gave a loud whoop. There was only one person he knew who ignored a perfectly serviceable doorbell and attacked a door knocker like that. He threw open the door to the House of Foryx.

"Well," said Marcia with a broad smile, "aren't you going to ask me in?"

"No way," Septimus replied. "*We* are coming *out!*"

From the wide sweep of the marble terrace, Sarah Heap watched her two youngest sons and her daughter walk out into the white, misty air and break into whoops of joy. She watched them envelop Marcia Overstrand in an onslaught of hugs and she hardly dared to believe what she was seeing. Sarah leaned against a solid dragon neck for support and Spit Fyre thumped his tail tiredly. It had been a long, cold flight.

The thud of the tail drew Nicko's attention. "Mum?" he said, ignoring the dragon and seeing only a thin windswept figure wrapped in an old green cloak. "Mum?"

"Oh . . . *Nicko*," was all Sarah could manage.

ENDINGS AND BEGINNINGS . . .

ALICE AND ALTHER

The ending of Alice's life was in fact the beginning of Alther and Alice's long and happy time together. During both their Living times, Alther in particular—but Alice too—had each been too busy with their own careers to be together. Now Alther was determined that this would change.

Twenty-four hours after she was shot, Alice's ghost **Appeared** on the Palace Landing Stage to find Alther waiting for her. All ghosts must spend the first year and a day of their ghosthood in the very place where they became a ghost. This is known as their **Resting Time**. It can be a difficult time for a ghost who has met an unexpected end, and Alther was determined that he would stay with Alice for the whole of her

Resting Time and help her through it. He may not have been there for Alice when he should have been while they were Living, but he would be there for her from now on.

It did not matter to Alther and Alice whether they were indoors or out. Weather does not generally matter to a ghost—except blustery winds, when a ghost feels Blown Through. Even though Jenna knew this, she hated the idea of Alther and Alice spending a whole year and a day just drifting around the Palace Landing Stage, so she got Billy Pot to help her set up a large red-and-white-striped tent—or the Pavilion, as she liked to call it—on the very spot where Alice had been shot.

Jenna was glad she had. There were some bad storms that year, but the inside of the Pavilion was always an oasis of calm. Jenna was determined to make Alice—and Alther—feel at home. The planks of the landing stage were strewn with a thick layer of patterned rugs from the Palace and she filled the Pavilion with furniture, cushions, books and various mementos. There was an ornate inlaid wooden chest, whose open lid revealed many of Alice's favorite treasures from her old warehouse aerie—a marble chessboard with ships for chessmen, a hand-knitted scarf from one of her many nieces, some letters from Alther tied up in a red ribbon and her old judge's wig from many years back. There was Alther's favorite chair—a moth-eaten old leather thing that Jenna had taken from Sarah Heap's sitting room and placed in a corner, next to the pink and gold overstuffed sofa that Sarah had insisted Alice would love. Alice didn't, but a tacky sofa no longer mattered to her in the way that it once would have.

Knowing that Alther and Alice would have many visitors, Jenna had set a low table with a jug of fresh juice, a plate of savory biscuits and a bowl of fruit for the Living.

The most regular visitors were Jenna and Silas Heap. Silas could no longer talk to Sarah about Nicko and he needed to talk to *someone*. Alther, his old tutor, listened for long hours to Silas, and they had endless discussions about Nicko, Time and more recently, forests. Late at night Silas would stagger back across the long lawns to the Palace, feeling as though his head were stuffed full of cotton wool. Alther did not always look forward to the moment when Silas would stick his head out through the tent flap and say, "Um, Alther. Can you spare a few minutes?" But he never refused.

Jenna loved the Pavilion. Most mornings she would pay a short visit and talk quietly to Alice, who had saved her life. They would chat about Alice's Living time and how much she had enjoyed being a judge at the Castle Courts in what every-one now called the Old Days. Alice would tell Jenna about her apartment at the top of the warehouse—which she had loved—and recount the interesting cases she had dealt with as Chief Customs Officer at the Port. But sometimes Alice would suddenly get up and say that she *must* get back to work now, and Jenna would have to gently remind Alice that she was no longer Living. Those times were difficult—Alice would grow sad and thoughtful and Jenna would leave her and Alther in peace for a few days.

The night that Alther was **Gathered** was the first time he had been away from Alice. Being **Gathered** was a shock to Alther. All ExtraOrdinary Wizard ghosts expect it at the end of an Apprenticeship, but an unexpected **Gathering** was extremely rare and did not bode well. To Alice's amazement, Alther was suddenly whisked out of the Pavilion and, although her sense of time was still not good, it felt like a few days before she saw him again.

Alice loved Alther and was touched by his sudden devo-tion, but in Life she had been a solitary person who had enjoyed her own company. Alther's absence gave Alice time to think her thoughts once more and to begin to understand what had happened to her that afternoon on the Palace Landing Stage.

When Alther returned from the Siege—frazzled and very apologetic—Alice was, of course, pleased to see him. But that evening she persuaded him to return to his old habit of visiting the Hole in the Wall Tavern. It would be good for them both, she said.

MRS. BEETLE

Pamela Beetle-Gurney was not, to her great sadness, married to Brian Beetle for very long. A year after they were married, Pamela gave birth to a baby boy with a shock of black hair and a mischievous smile. The couple had not even registered the birth when Brian Beetle—who worked at the Castle Dock, loading and unloading the Port barge—was bitten by a snake that had crawled out of a box of exotic fruit. Brian—as Pamela would sadly tell people many years later—blew up like a balloon and turned blue. No one could save him.

A few weeks after Brian Beetle died, the Registrar paid Mrs. Beetle a call to inform her that the time limit for registering the baby's name had expired and she must do so there and then. Mrs. Beetle was in a bad state. The baby cried all night, she cried all day and the last thing on her mind was what to call her baby boy. So when the Registrar got out the Ledger of Names, dipped her pen in the ink and very gently asked Mrs. Beetle for the baby's name, all Mrs. Beetle could do was wail, "Oh, Beetle . . . *Beetle!*"—which was what she had called Brian. Beetle was duly registered as O. Beetle Beetle.

Without Brian Beetle's wages coming in, Mrs. Beetle had to move to two small rooms at the end of a dingy corridor in The Ramblings. Her family—and Brian's too—lived at the Port and did not offer any help. Mrs. Beetle considered moving back to the Port, but she liked The Ramblings, and her neighbors helped her more, she thought, than her family ever would. And Mrs. Beetle had ambitions for her son. She wanted him to do better in life than work on the docks, and the Castle schools provided much better opportunities for a good education than the rough schools in the Port.

The young Beetle went to one of the many small, good schools in The Ramblings and Mrs. Beetle worked extra hours as a cleaner to pay for a tutor on Saturday mornings. Beetle was a bright boy, and Mrs. Beetle's ambitions were fulfilled even sooner than she had expected, for he was the youngest person ever to pass the Manuscriptorium entrance examination.

After Brian died Pamela had stopped using Gurney, her maiden name, and soon she stopped even using Pamela. Everyone knew her simply as Mrs. Beetle—except for Beetle, who still called her Mum and didn't care if the scribes teased him. All the scribes referred to their mothers as Mother—if they referred to them at all. But Beetle would often talk about his mother; he worried about her and wished she could be happy once more.

JANNIT MAARTEN AND NICKO

When Jannit Maarten got back to the boatyard after her visit to Sarah Heap she looked—as Rupert Gringe put it—as though she had had the wind spilled from her sails. And she was wearing a very peculiar hat. Jannit was not known for sitting around or gazing into space, but for the rest of that day Jannit did both. Even when Rupert showed her the perfect brass fittings he had finally discovered for Jannit's pet project that season—the restoration of a rare Port Sloop—Jannit just smiled wanly.

Rupert Gringe knew what the problem was. When he had seen Jannit set off that morning carrying the Indentures, he had guessed what she was doing. Rupert was not a great fan of the Heap family, particularly now that his sister Lucy had run off with Simon blasted Heap—as Rupert always called him—but he, too, was unhappy about Nicko's disappearance. Rupert was not sure he believed all the stories that were going around the Castle about Nicko being trapped in another Time, but it was plain that something nasty had happened to him and Rupert was very sorry about that.

Although at first he had been extremely dubious about Jannit taking on a Heap, Rupert had grown to like and respect Nicko. He was fun to have around and always willing to sail down to the Port and have a laugh. And since Nicko had gone, Rupert had realized how much work Nicko had done—more than two yard hands' worth put together, he told Jannit. But even though they could never replace Nicko, they needed a new apprentice before the summer season began.

That afternoon, when Jannit had returned from the Palace, Rupert watched her wander slowly over to her ramshackle hut at the entrance to the boatyard. There was a small shed attached to the side of the hut where the junior apprentice slept, and Rupert saw her gingerly push open the door and go inside. Half an hour later Jannit came and found him.

"Need a hand," was all she said.

What Jannit needed a hand with was tin trunk with NICKO HEAP painted on the top in spidery writing. Rupert helped her carry it over to the old lock-up.

"Keep it in there until he gets back," said Jannit.

"Yeah. Until he gets back," Rupert said. Then he went and sat on the bowsprit of the Port Sloop for half an hour and watched the muddy waters of the Moat drift by.

SIMON AND LUCY

Simon and Lucy made it safely over the river, paid a small fortune to get Thunder out of the Ferry stables and then set off for the Port. It was a subdued journey—being back in the Castle had upset them both.

Simon had been shocked to see the Wizard Tower in a state of **Siege**. It had made him realize how important the place was to him and how much he cared that it continued unharmed. And with this insight had come the unwelcome realization that through his actions of the last three years he had thrown away any chance he might have had of one day becoming an Ordinary Wizard (which Simon would have gladly settled for now) and actually being able to live and work in such a wonderful, Magykal place. Now he was unlikely to even *see* the Wizard Tower again.

Lucy sat behind Simon and looked back mournfully. Thunder trotted briskly along the riverbank path and, as the Castle disappeared behind Raven's Rock, Lucy wished she had been brave enough to say hello to her father when she had gone to the gatehouse the morning after they had arrived. He had looked tired and careworn—and so much smaller than she had remembered. Lucy didn't really know why she hadn't dared to tell him she was there. Well, she did know—it was the thought of a full-blown Mrs. Gringe tantrum. But now she really wished she had. How long would it be before she saw her parents again? Years probably, she thought. And she would *never* be able to bring Simon to meet them. Not that they would want to, she thought gloomily.

As Thunder trotted along, in high spirits after leaving the

damp and dingy stables, Lucy made an effort to brighten the
gloom. "At least Marcia didn't put you in the lock-up," she
said. "She can't be *totally* mad."

"Huh," was Simon's response. But then, later, "I hope she
looks after Sleuth. That blasted Merrin took it before it was
completely **ReCharged**. I think I'll send her the instructions."

"Si, you *can't!*"

"Why not?"

"Oh, *Simon*. You don't give up, do you?"

"No, Luce. I don't."

MERRIN

The beginning of Merrin's employment at the
Manuscriptorium was not the best. After the shock of being
confronted by Simon—and the unexpected loss of Sleuth—
Merrin ate his entire licorice snake supply. By mid-afternoon
he felt sick and very irritable. When Foxy asked him to fetch
a copy of the Cameloleopard Conundrum Pamphlet from the
Wild Book Store, Merrin—who was terrified of the store after
Beetle's lurid tales—told Foxy to get it himself. Foxy looked

shocked. Beetle *never* would have done that. Foxy then proceeded, in Merrin's opinion, to get very unreasonable. Merrin promptly told Foxy what he could do with his precious Camelthingies and Foxy stomped back to his desk in a huff.

Merrin listened at the door for a while, but like all listeners, he did not hear anything good about himself. He decided to leave them to it and go stock up on snakes. He snuck out, locking the door behind him to make sure that no customers could get in, then he crossed Wizard Way and headed into the tangle of alleys that would take him—he hoped—to Ma Custard's All-Day-All-Night Sweet Shop.

But the alleys were not as Merrin remembered them—someone had changed them just to annoy him. By the time Merrin eventually found Ma Custard's, he was very hungry. Which was probably why he bought three dozen licorice snakes, two bags of spider floss, a box of toffee termites and a whole jar of banana bears. Ma Custard asked Merrin if he was having a party. Merrin wasn't quite sure what a party was, so he said yes. Ma Custard gave him a tub of crumbly cocoa crumbs "for his little friends."

Merrin decided it was too late to bother going back to the Manuscriptorium that day. After eating three snakes dipped in cocoa crumbs and ten banana bears, Merrin felt quite brave. He went to the Palace kitchen garden, retrieved his things from the horrible shed and, safe in the knowledge that Simon Heap had been thrown out of the Castle, he reclaimed his room.

The ghost of the governess fled sobbing to the old schoolroom.

At the Manuscriptorium at half past five precisely, the scribes leaped from their desks and rushed to the front door. It was locked. The Manuscriptorium had a **One and All** Spell on the outside doors—if one was locked, all were locked. The scribes had to wait until Jillie Djinn emerged from the Hermetic Chamber some two hours later before they could get out. They spent the time discussing in some detail what they intended to do to Merrin when they finally got him.

When Merrin turned up the next day he had some explaining to do, but he had a good line in tall stories and Jillie Djinn (unlike the scribes) believed him. Jillie was not about to admit that she had made a bad choice—and who else but Merrin would be perfectly happy counting the entire stock of Manuscriptorium used pencils and arranging them according to Miss Djinn's new cataloging system, which depended on the number of teeth marks on each pencil?

STANLEY

The beginning of Stanley's Message Rat Service was not all that he had hoped for. After he had turned down Ephaniah Grebe's offer of staff, Stanley found that word had spread about the reinstated message rat service and soon a steady trickle of customers found their way to the East Gate Lookout Tower.

Stanley was somewhat irritated by the sudden craze for silly birthday messages among the younger Castle inhabitants, and after—for the third time that day—he had flatly refused to *sing* a birthday greeting, he began to seriously consider packing in the whole enterprise.

The night after he had not only been asked to sing a message but also to perform a *dance*, Stanley went for a late night scramble along the Outside Path to clear his head. Stanley liked the Outside Path. It ran along the Castle Walls and was at some points—as Septimus had once found out—nothing more than a narrow ridge. Stanley didn't believe the tales about Things walking the path; in fact, he didn't believe in Things at all. But it was a dark night and when, at a particularly narrow and crumbly section, he heard scrabbling and a high-pitched squeaking right in front of him, Stanley suddenly discovered that he did believe in Things after all. It was not a good moment, and he very nearly jumped into the Moat there and then.

But Stanley hated getting wet and the Moat looked dark and cold. He decided that the Thing would not be interested in a mere rat, and if he kept very still it would probably go away. But the noises did not go away. And the more Stanley listened, the more he realized how much they sounded like rat squeaks—baby rat squeaks.

Dawn was breaking by the time Stanley was back in the East Gate Lookout Tower—and he was no longer alone. With him were four cold, hungry and very small orphan ratlets.

SYRAH SYARA

When Syrah saw the long knives of the Questing Guards, she knew she was in trouble. With no time to say a proper farewell to Julius Pike, whom she loved like a father, Syrah was bundled onto the Questing Boat. As soon as she set foot upon the deck, Syrah felt her Magykal powers drain away.

Seen off by a triumphant Tertius Fume, the **Questing Boat** set off fast. A **Magykal** wind filled its sails, and soon they were sailing past the Port and out to sea. Syrah refused to go below. She sat, shivering in the wind and the rain as the **Questing Boat** cut through the waves. Syrah stayed awake all through the first night and the following day, eyes wide—hardly daring to even blink—keeping a close eye on the **Questing Guards** and their sharp knives.

Syrah knew that as soon as she fell asleep, she was as good as dead. And as the second night on the deck of the **Questing Boat** drew on, Syrah felt her eyelids droop and the lure of sleep become irresistible. As she gazed out across the calm sea, watching the distant loom of a lighthouse, the rhythmic movement of the boat lulled her into a brief sleep. She woke with a start to find three **Guards** advancing on her with their knives drawn.

Syrah had no choice. She jumped overboard.

The sea was a shock. It was cold and Syrah could not swim. Her heavy robes dragged her down, but as she struggled away from the **Questing Boat**, Syrah felt her **Magyk** return. She **Called** a dolphin, which arrived just as the water was closing over her head for the last time. Lying exhausted on the dolphin's back, Syrah found herself heading toward the lighthouse on the horizon. Dolphin and Apprentice arrived safely as dawn was breaking.

Syrah began a new life far away from the Castle. She never dared return, but she sent a coded message to Julius Pike to tell him she was safe. Unfortunately, Julius thought it was a final demand for some **Magykal** pots he had ordered. He had already paid the bill, so he threw the message down the garbage chute.

MORWENNA

The moment Morwenna discovered that she had been double-crossed and Jenna and her **Transformer** had fled marked the beginning of a feud between the Wendron Witch Coven and the Castle. Or, rather, it was the end of the truce that had existed since Silas, as a young Wizard, had rescued Morwenna from a pack of wolverines.

Morwenna considered she had paid her debt to Silas by taking him to his father. The flight of Ephaniah Grebe also angered her. After all she had done for him, he had reneged on his agreement to **Promise** and, she assumed, had taken Jenna with him.

Camp Heap was placed out of bounds for all the young witches, much to great their consternation, and the Heap boys suddenly found their lives much less comfortable, Jo-Jo especially. Marissa was forced to choose between Morwenna and Jo-Jo. Marissa was a true witch at heart and she chose Morwenna.

THE TOLL-MAN

The Toll-Man was never a pleasant character. It is doubtful that those who had known him before the Thing suddenly appeared in his tree house would have noticed any difference—apart from the licorice ring. The ring would have puzzled them because it was the Toll-Man's considered opinion that men who wore rings should be "shoved off the top of a cliff—that'll show 'em." Whether this showed the Toll-Man himself, no one will ever know.

But to be InHabited is not something to be wished upon anyone, however unpleasant. The Toll-Man was up in his tree house, keeping clear of the Foryx as he did regularly twice a day, when the Thing pushed its way in and made its intentions clear. Then, like Hildegarde and Ephaniah before him, the Toll-Man experienced a moment of pure terror—just as some reluctant toll-payers had when they refused him a gold tooth and suddenly found themselves plunging down through the mists of the abyss.

EPHANIAH GREBE

Ephaniah nearly died in the tree house beside the bridge. Even though Jenna, Septimus and Beetle left him as comfortable as they could beneath their wolverine skins, Ephaniah, like Hildegarde before him, was overtaken by a raging fever and became delirious. If he had not been so weak it is likely he would, in his confusion, have fallen from the tree house and died in the snow—or been eaten by the phalanx of Foryx. But luckily Ephaniah could do no more than lie on the cold wooden floor, shivering as waves of hot and cold ran through him and enduring the most frightening nightmares—even worse than those that followed the early days of his rat Hex.

It was on the midmorning of his second day in the tree house—although for all Ephaniah knew it could have been his second month—that his nightmares took on a frighteningly real turn. Overnight his fever had abated a little and he had regained a little strength. That morning he had rolled over to the door flap and poked his head outside. Luckily he was sensible enough not to tumble to the ground; instead he lay on his back gazing up into the snowy branches, his sensitive rat nose gratefully sniffing the fresh air and his tiny pink tongue licking the occasional snowflake that came his way. Ephaniah had lain there for some time and was feeling almost content when a terrible thud shook the tree and a great load of snow from the upper branches landed on his face. Shocked, he shook his head, rolled over and found himself face to face with the most realistic hallucination so far. A huge dragon stood below the tree house, its long scaly neck reaching up into the branches, its red-rimmed emerald green eye staring right into Ephaniah's.

A voice from somewhere—a voice that even in his befuddled state Ephaniah thought he recognized but could not quite place—said, "Can you see him, Septimus?"

Another voice replied, "It's all right, Marcia, he's here. He's okay. You are okay, aren't you, Ephaniah?" It was then that, almost hidden in a dip between the dragon's huge shoulders and the rise of his neck, Ephaniah noticed a small figure with a big smile, and a little farther back, sitting uncomfortably between the dragon's spines, a purple-robed woman squinting up at him with glittering green eyes that almost outshone those of the dragon itself.

"He looks very heavy," said the purple woman.

"He *is* very heavy," replied the boy. "I don't know how we're going to do it."

"I'll Transport him down onto the snow. Then Spit Fyre will have to carry him in his talons. Do you think he can do that?"

Ephaniah began to realize they were talking about *him*. It was a horrible nightmare. He wished it would go away.

"Easy. Spit Fyre carried Jen like that once, didn't you, Spit Fyre?"

"You never told me that," said the woman sharply.

"Um. No, I think I forgot."

"A dragon carries the Princess in its talons and you *forget?*"

The nightmare got worse. In fact it got so bad that Ephaniah lost consciousness once more and when he awoke a week later in the Wizard Tower sick bay he remembered nothing about a dragon at all. But Spit Fyre remembered him and from that day on the dragon never stamped on another rat.

BENJAMIN HEAP

Benjamin Heap had no wish to end up as a ghost floating around the Castle getting confused and retreating to the Hole in the Wall Tavern. He wished to end his days in the Forest, a place he had always loved, and this is what he did. Benjamin Heap, Shape-Shifter, became Tree. He became one of his favorites, a western red cedar, and stood tall and proud—and slowly growing ever taller.

When Benjamin Heap became Tree, his thoughts became Tree also. But there was always a small part in the core of that western red cedar that was Ben Heap, Ordinary Wizard, or Grandpa Benji as he was known to his numerous grandchildren. Ben Heap had married Jenna Crackle (sister of Betty Crackle, a white witch) one winter's day in the Great Hall of the Wizard Tower. They had seven sons, and all bar two, Alfred and Edmond, had had an assortment of children.

The Forest trees were always listening. People meeting beneath a tree exchanging whispered secrets, travelers talking, voices carried on the wind—the Forest trees heard it all. The rustling of leaves in the Forest was not always because of the breeze—it was often the trees talking.

This is how Benjamin Heap knew about the fortunes of his huge family. It was his youngest son—Silas, his seventh—who he followed the most closely. Silas was born late into the family, and when his last baby boy arrived Benjamin already felt old. He waited to become Tree for as long as he could, but when Silas turned twenty-one he could wait no longer. Benjamin Heap knew he had to go while he still had the strength to Shape-Shift into a healthy tree.

Silas had missed his father terribly. He had spent many long weeks in the Forest looking for him, but he never found him. And when at last, on one of his fruitless searches, he met the young and very pretty Sarah Willow gathering herbs in the Forest, Silas decided he had looked for his father long enough. He and Sarah got married, and Silas settled down to look after his rapidly growing family.

Benjamin Heap listened to the Forest gossip so he knew that Silas had had seven sons. For a long ten years he had also known that the youngest grandson was lost, and was in the Young Army. He had longed to tell Silas where Septimus was, but Silas never came to see him and there was nothing he could do except make sure that all the Forest trees knew to keep Septimus safe on the notoriously dangerous Young Army exercises. And so, when Morwenna took Silas to see his father, both were overjoyed—although there were serious things to discuss.

Silas told his father the dream about Nicko in a frozen forest. Benjamin told Silas that the frozen forest had once been warm and friendly, teeming with animals and small, happy settlements. But now it was under a **Darkenesse** and it was not a safe place to be. When Silas insisted that he *must* go, his father very reluctantly told him how to find the Forest Way.

Early the next afternoon as Silas and Maxie were leaving the Ancient Glades to start their journey, they met a large, shambling figure in white wearing a small licorice ring on the little finger of its left hand—although Silas was too surprised at bumping into someone in the middle of the Forest to notice the ring. When Silas looked at the figure's bottle-glass spectacles he felt very odd indeed—so odd that he babbled his father's instructions on how to find the Forest Way without even being asked. Silas was unaware that he had very nearly been **InHabited**—but Maxie's long growls and the sight of the hackles going up on the wolfhound's neck—not to mention his teeth—had persuaded the **Thing** not to bother.

Silas never did remember what had happened after he had left Morwenna. He put the lost day down to a witchy hex and worried about what he had done to offend the Witch Mother. He forgot that he had ever met his father.

Maxie led Silas back to the Castle. When at last, with tired feet and weary paws, they reached the Palace, Silas could not find Sarah anywhere. Billy Pot told him that Sarah had gone off with Marcia on Spit Fyre, but Silas would not believe him. Why on earth would she want to do *that*?

Billy Pot had shrugged. He didn't know either, but one thing he did know: there was no stopping Marcia when she wanted to fly a dragon.

SPIT FYRE

Spit Fyre liked his new field and he liked Billy Pot too. The only thing he missed about the Wizard Tower was his break-fasts. No one made his breakfast quite like Septimus. Naturally Spit Fyre wondered where Septimus was, but now that he was nearly fully grown, the dragon did not feel the need to see so much of his Imprintor.

Neither did Spit Fyre feel the need to see the person who he suspected was his dragon mother in disguise—as some dragon mothers are. But this person, who wore purple and shouted a lot, suddenly seemed to feel the need to see *him*.

But when Spit Fyre realized that the purple-dragon-mother had brought with her four buckets of sausages and bananas—one of Spit Fyre's all-time favorites—he changed his mind. And he didn't even mind when the purple-dragon-mother told him that she was taking the place of his Imprintor and he was *to do as he was told*. Spit Fyre would do anything for four buckets of sausages and bananas.

And that is how Spit Fyre set off on the longest flight he had ever made.

His new pilot did a good job, although her navigator—a thin woman in green—screamed a lot. Spit Fyre enjoyed the flight; he had needed to stretch his wings, and meeting his Imprintor at the other end was good too. It was nice of the purple-dragon-mother to arrange that for him. But it was a strange place she brought him to—cold, creepy and suffering from a distinct lack of sausages and bananas. And suddenly there seemed to be a lot of people expecting a ride. They wouldn't all fit on, and there was no point in the purple-dragon-mother shouting either—shouting something didn't make it any more possible. They would have to figure something else out. And where was his dinner?

SEPTIMUS HEAP

✠ BOOK FIVE ✠

Syren

morning I was up early getting some ghastly potion from Zelda for Ephaniah and Hildegarde—both of whom are still very sick. I need to keep an eye on Ephaniah tonight, but I shall set off on Spit Fyre first thing tomorrow morning to collect them all. They'll be back very soon, I promise."

Septimus looked at his purple ribbons, which had a beautiful **Magykal** sheen, like oil on water. He remembered Marcia's words: *"As Senior Apprentice, you may come and go without asking my permission, although it is considered courteous to inform me where you are going and at what time you intend to return."*

"I shall get them," he said, swiftly getting into Senior Apprentice mode.

"No, Septimus," Marcia replied, already forgetting that she was now talking to a *Senior* Apprentice. "It is far too risky, and you are tired after the **Queste**. You need to rest. *I* shall go."

"Thank you for your offer, Marcia," Septimus said, a trifle formally, in the way he thought Senior Apprentices probably should speak. "However, I do intend to go myself. I shall be setting off on Spit Fyre in just over an hour's time. I shall return the day after tomorrow evening by midnight, as this can reasonably be classified, I think, as a special occasion."

"Oh." Marcia wished she hadn't informed Septimus quite

so fully on the rights of a Senior Apprentice. She sat down and regarded Septimus with a thoughtful look. Her new Senior Apprentice seemed to have grown up suddenly. His bright green eyes had a newly confident air as they steadily returned her gaze, and—yes, she had known something was different the moment he had walked in—he had *combed his hair.*

"Shall I come and see you off?" Marcia asked quietly.

"Yes, please," Septimus replied. "That would be very nice. I'll be down at the dragon field in just under an hour." At the study door he stopped and turned. "Thank you, Marcia," he said with a broad grin. "Thank you very much indeed."

Marcia returned his smile and watched her Senior Apprentice walk out of her study with a new spring in his step.

╬ I ╬

PROMOTION

Septimus Heap, ExtraOrdinary Apprentice, was woken up by his House Mouse leaving a note on his pillow. Blearily he opened his eyes, and with a sense of relief, remembered where he was—back in his bedroom at the top of the Wizard Tower, **Queste** completed. And then he remembered that Jenna, Nicko, Snorri and Beetle were still not home. Septimus sat up, suddenly awake. Today, no matter what Marcia said, he was going to go and bring them back.

Septimus sat up, picked up the note and brushed a couple of mouse droppings off his pillow. He carefully unfolded the tiny note and read:

From the desk of Marcia Overstrand,
ExtraOrdinary Wizard.

Septimus, I would very much like to see you at

midday in my study.
I hope that is convenient for you.
Marcia

Septimus let out a low whistle. Even though he had been
Marcia's Apprentice for nearly three years, he had never had
an appointment with her before. If Marcia wished to speak to
Septimus, she would interrupt whatever he was doing and
speak to him. Septimus would have to stop what he was doing
right away and listen.

But today, his second day back from the **Queste**, it seemed
that something had changed. As Septimus read the note again,
just to make sure, the distant chimes of the Drapers Yard
clock drifted through his window. He counted them—
eleven—and breathed a sigh of relief. It would not be good to
be late for his first-ever appointment with Marcia. Septimus
had slept late, but that was on Marcia's instructions; she had
also told him that he did not have to clean the Library that
morning. Septimus looked at the beam of sunlight filtering
through the purple glass in his window and shook his head
with a smile—he could get used to this.

An hour later, dressed in a new set of green Apprentice

robes that had been left out in his room for him, Septimus knocked politely on Marcia's door.

"Come in, Septimus." Marcia's voice drifted through the thick oak door. Septimus pushed open the creaky door and stepped inside. Marcia's study was a small wood-paneled room with a large desk set under the window and a fuzz of **Magyk** in the air that set Septimus's skin tingling. It was lined with shelves on which were crammed moth-eaten leather-bound books, stacks of yellowing papers tied with purple ribbons and a myriad of brown and black glass pots that contained ancient things even Marcia was not sure what to do with. Among the pots Septimus saw his brother Simon's pride and joy—a wooden box with *Sleuth* written on it in Simon's loopy Heap handwriting. Septimus could not help but glance out of the tall, narrow window. He loved the view from Marcia's study—a breathtaking vista across the rooftops of the Castle to the river and beyond that to the green slopes of the Farmlands. Far, far in the distance he could see the misty blue line of the foothills of the Badlands.

Marcia was sitting behind her desk in her much-worn—but very comfortable—tall purple chair. She looked fondly at her Apprentice, who was unusually well turned out, and smiled.

"Good afternoon, Septimus," she said. "Do sit down." Marcia indicated the smaller but equally comfortable green chair on the other side of the desk. "I hope you slept well?"

Septimus took his seat. "Yes, thank you," he replied a little warily. Why was Marcia being so *nice*?

"You've had a difficult week, Septimus," Marcia began. "Well, we all have. It is very good to have you back. I have something for you." She opened a small drawer, took out two purple silk ribbons and laid them on the desk.

Septimus knew what the ribbons were—the purple stripes of a Senior Apprentice, which, if his Apprenticeship went well, he would get to wear in his final year. It was nice of Marcia to let him know that she would make him a Senior Apprentice when the time came, he thought, but his final year was a long way off and Septimus knew only too well that a lot could go wrong before then.

"Do you know what these are?" Marcia asked, mistaking Septimus's puzzled expression.

He nodded.

"Good. They are yours. I am making you Senior Apprentice."

"What, *now*?"

Marcia smiled broadly. "Yes, now."

"Now? Like, *today*?"

"Yes, Septimus, today. I trust the ends of your sleeves are still clean. You didn't get any egg on them at breakfast, did you?"

Septimus inspected his sleeves. "No, they're fine."

Marcia stood up and so did Septimus—an Apprentice must never sit when his tutor is standing. Marcia picked up the ribbons and placed them on the hems of Septimus's bright green sleeves. In a puff of **Magykal** purple mist, the ribbons curled themselves around the hems of the sleeves and became part of his tunic. Septimus stared at them, amazed. He didn't know what to say. But Marcia did.

"Now, Septimus, you need to know a little about the rights and duties of a Senior Apprentice. You may determine fifty percent of your own projects and also your main timetable— within reason, of course. You may be asked to deputize for me at the basic level Wizard Tower meetings—for which, incidentally, I would be very grateful. As Senior Apprentice, you may come and go without asking my permission, although it is considered courteous to inform me where you are going and at what time you intend to return. But as you are still so young, I would add that I do require you to be back in the

Wizard Tower by nine P.M. on weekdays—midnight at the *latest* on special occasions—understood?"

Still gazing at the **Magykal** purple stripes shimmering on the ends of his sleeves, Septimus nodded. "Understood . . . I think . . . but why . . . ?"

"Because," Marcia said, "you are the only Apprentice *ever* to return from the **Queste**. Not only did you return *alive*, but you returned having successfully completed it. And—even more incredible—you were sent on this . . . this terrible thing before you had even gotten halfway through your Apprenticeship— and you *still* did it. You used your **Magykal** skills to better effect than many Wizards in this Tower could ever hope to do. This is why you are now Senior Apprentice. Okay?"

"Okay." Septimus smiled. "But . . ."

"But what?"

"I couldn't have done the **Queste** without Jenna and Beetle. And they aren't back yet. Neither are Nicko and Snorri. They're still stuck in that smelly little net loft in the Trading Post. We *promised* to go right back for them."

"And we will," Marcia replied. "I am sure they did not expect us to turn around and fly back immediately, Septimus. Besides, I haven't had a moment since we returned. This

ANGIE SAGE was born in London and grew up in the Thames Valley, London and Kent. She now lives in Somerset in a very old house that has a secret tunnel below it. She is the author-illustrator of many picture books, and is also the author of the Araminta Spookie series. You can visit her online at www.septimusheap.com.

MARK ZUG has loved fantasy novels since he was a teenager. He has illustrated many collectible card games, including Magic: The Gathering and Dune, as well as books and magazines. He lives in Pennsylvania.

JOIN THE
Queste!

Visit www.septimusheap.com to discover the Magyk and experience interactive elements! Come back often for updates!

READ THE FIRST THREE BOOKS IN THE SEPTIMUS HEAP SERIES AND LOOK FOR BOOK FIVE, *SYREN*.

KATHERINE TEGEN BOOKS
An Imprint of HarperCollins Publishers

www.septimusheap.com